Natasha Boyd is an author with a background in marketing
and   relations. She holds a Bachelor of Science in
Ps   ST   from Royal Holloway, University of London and
li   e coastal Carolina Lowcountry, complete with
S   oss, alligators and mosquitoes the size of tiny birds.
Sh   husband, two sons and a host of internationally
sc   nd scared relatives who worry the next book will
be   hem. She is a member of Georgia Romance Writers,
R   Writers of America and Island Writers Network,
w   has been a featured speaker.
           t more about Natasha at www.natashaboyd.com,
ar   t with her online on Twitter @lovefrmlowcntry and
at   ebook.com/authornatashaboyd.

B   way by Natasha's powerful stories . . .

'T   books and characters out there that take a piece
of   rt and THIS is one of them . . . A beautiful story
of   eak, revelations, struggles, deceptions and
di   *A Bookish Escape*

'C   swept me away, heart and soul. I fell hard for
th   ry and its alluring characters. It encapsulated
th   e magic I hope to find every time I begin a new
bc   *Vilma's Book Blog*

'Y   lost in the characters and their stories'
                           Bookish Treasure Blog

'I   ntense pull . . . This book just made me feel
E'   NG'   *Star-Crossed Book Blog*

'A   story about love against the odds'
                           A Dream of Books

'An absolutel   lf and
discovering lc   k Blog*

By Natasha Boyd

Eversea Series
Eversea
Forever, Jack

Deep Blue Eternity

NATASHA BOYD
deep blue eternity

headline
ETERNAL

'The Steadfast Tin Soldier' by Hans Christian Andersen
is adapted from Jean Hersholt's translation.
Translation used with permission from www.andersen.sdu.dk.

First published in Great Britain in 2015
by HEADLINE ETERNAL
An imprint of HEADLINE PUBLISHING GROUP

1

Cataloguing in Publication Data is available from the British Library

ISBN 978 1 4722 1968 8

Typeset in Sabon by Palimpsest Book Production Ltd, Falkirk, Stirlingshire

Printed and bound in Great Britain by CPI Group (UK) Ltd, Croydon CR0 4YY

Headline's policy is to use papers that are natural, renewable and recyclable
products and made from wood grown in sustainable forests. The logging and
manufacturing processes are expected to conform to the environmental regulations
of the country of origin.

HEADLINE PUBLISHING GROUP
An Hachette UK Company
338 Euston Road
London NW1 3BH

www.headlineeternal.com
www.headline.co.uk
www.hachette.co.uk

For S., J., and W.

The tin soldier stood there dressed in flames. He felt a terrible heat, but whether it came from the flames or from his love he didn't know. He'd lost his splendid colors, maybe from his hard journey, maybe from grief, nobody can say.

He looked at the little maiden, and she looked at him; and he felt himself melting. But still he stood steadfast, shouldering his gun bravely.

A door was suddenly opened, and a puff of wind caught the little dancer. She flew like a sylph, straight into the fire with the soldier, blazed up in a flash, and was gone!

The soldier melted.

He was reduced to a mere lump. When the maid came for the ashes next morning she found him, in the shape of a small tin heart.

All that was left of the dancer was her spangle, and that was burnt as black as a coal.

Hans Christian Andersen, "The Steadfast Tin Soldier"

OLIVIA

OLIVIA

CHAPTER ONE

$\mathcal{I}$ wondered what would piss off my parents the most, the fact I ran away or that I stole their money to do it. Either way, I assumed they'd be relieved to see the back of me.

The train jerked and vibrated. What had felt like an interesting sensation against my cheek when I first pressed my face against the grimy window now made my skin numb and my teeth jar. Yet still I didn't move away from the cold glass where I watched the outskirts of our nation's capital roll and shudder past me.

I'd made the connection in Washington, D.C. without too much trouble, switching from my northeast-bound train from Atlanta in order to head south down the coast, and hadn't had to show my identification again.

It was a gamble, but I knew if my parents looked for me they were likely to follow the trail where I'd purchased the train tickets online from Atlanta to New Orleans with their credit card. I'd confirmed and printed the tickets. Online, I didn't have to show my identification. But when I'd bought the ticket to Savannah with my own cash and in person, I'd had to. I looked like the blonde girl in the picture. Too much like her, in fact. So no one questioned it. Oddly, the only way to head south toward Savannah had been to go north first. I reasoned it put me one step ahead of them if they decided to report me missing. I'd had to ditch my phone too. The idea made me jittery, as now I had no music to get lost in.

Upon entering the final train, I'd immediately located the restroom and pulled the wig off before finding my seat.

We rolled through a tunnel, and everything was pitch black, my stark pale face surrounded by jet-black hair and punctuated with black-rimmed eyes flashing back at me. I sat back abruptly, just as the daylight appeared again. It was going to be an uncomfortable thirteen hours. Rifling through my Indian fabric drawstring bag, my hand closed around the small cylinder. I pulled out the orange plastic and checked the label was what I needed. Amy Orr, whoever she was, shouldn't have left her prescriptions lying around. But I was grateful she had. I shook a small white pill that had cost me far too much into my hand and washed it down with my soda.

I still felt groggy when I woke up as the train pulled into Savannah around half past four in the morning. Pulling my cardigan closer around me, I wound my gray scarf around my neck and stood up on wobbly legs, my back stiff and sore. It was dark and would be for a while yet. I had no idea what time the sun came up in February, but I assumed it was probably after seven. The urge to just find a bench and get horizontal was overwhelming, but I could sleep when I got to the cottage.

I wondered what kind of shape the cottage was in. Grams had died almost ten years ago, and since she left it to Abby and me, and had barely spoken a word to my parents for as long as I could remember, the chances were high that the place had completely caved in. Still, it had to be better than where I was coming from.

And it was mine.

All mine, now that Abby was gone. My parents didn't know I knew about it, which made it the perfect hiding place. Abby had given me a key for it and asked me to keep the secret. I was so grateful I had. Would they even bother to look for me? Uncle Mike probably would, but he didn't know I knew either. The chance he'd find me would always be at the back of my mind, but it was a chance I had to take.

I'd left a note that was as bitingly sterile as the rare words either of my parents uttered in my direction, but hopefully ensured I wouldn't be considered a missing person.

> I'll get out of your way now.
> Don't look for me.
> Olivia.

Looking down at my trembling fingers, I tried to ignore my tight chest. I was scared about what I was doing. But more scared to stay. I'd waited as long as I could stand. A job to feed myself and maybe fix the place up was a necessity. The meager amount of money I had on me would barely get me by. But the idea that I could start over and be someone with no past and no expectations was a heady rush. A complete reinvention of who I was.

And I'd be safe.

I squared my shoulders, squinting my tired eyes at the signs to find the exit. Taking a taxi would dent my cash further. But according to the map I'd printed, the marina I needed to hitch a boat ride from was way too far out of downtown Savannah for me to make it on foot. I was almost free.

The marina was a hive of activity, with men yelling and nets being pulled out and rolled and items of indeterminate origin being loaded and unloaded.

After paying my fare, I opened the door of the cab. The stench of dead fish and brine slicked down my nose and throat, causing my empty stomach to heave. I swallowed thickly and moved my scarf up over my nose and mouth. Shifting my heavy pack on to my back with my free hand, I contemplated the scene in front of me. There were passenger ferries, I knew, but they weren't running yet and would cost a small fortune. I needed to find a fishing boat and see if they could give me a free ride over to Bloody Point.

The early morning wind was frigid off the river, the air slicing through my layers. I hadn't expected it to be as cold as it had been in Atlanta. I didn't know the next time I'd get a hot shower, and hadn't even thought about how to buy food out there, although I seemed to remember there was a small general store for basics. The logistical challenges of what I was doing started to crowd my head. It wasn't that they hadn't occurred to me, but I had deliberately pushed them aside, knowing I'd talk myself out of this crazy idea if I thought about it too much.

The familiar ribbons of panic wove their corset around my chest. *Shit*. I let go of the scarf at my mouth to press my shaking hand hard against my chest. An instinct. As if it could possibly stop the tightening. The shortness of breath. *One hundred, breathe out, ninety-nine, ninety-eight, breathe in, gross, fish, ninety-seven, ninety-six, breathe out, breathe in, breathe out, ninety-five, breathe in, breathe in, breathe in, shit, shit, shit.*

I stepped back, I needed to turn around. *Shit, shit.* Not here, not now. Something strong took my arm, and I jerked around and yanked myself free.

"Whoa, hey. Are you all right?" a gravelly male voice asked.

My vision swam with black dots as my oxygen lowered. I tried to focus so I could see the person. But the panic was hitting way too hard. The large form in front of me stepped closer, and I stumbled back, only to be pulled forward straight into the solid wall in front of me.

"Damn, careful," the voice boomed from inside the body that held me. "Pete, I need some help over here!"

I fixed my attention on the rough material under my cheek, trying to hook on to something, anything to bring me back. I mentally grabbed on to the knots and ridges of the fabric. Denim? Cord? Anything to anchor me.

The smell. His smell. I hauled in a lungful through my nose and picked out the soapy-fresh laundry detergent smell over the fishy smell of the air. Something spicy and male. And maybe perfume. Women's perfume, but faint. And a hint of alcohol.

It was the large, warm hand on my back running up and down my spine that finally did it. My mind tracked the downward stroke, the pause at the base of my spine, and the slow migration up to my shoulder blades. Again it slid down, and again back up. I imagined the hand was catching all the tight bindings around my chest and unraveling them a few at a time on each pass. God, it felt good. Soothing. Soothing when I normally didn't like people touching me. Down went the hand again, and then back up.

"Call 911," I vaguely heard.

No, no. "No." *Don't call 911.*

I became aware I was choking on large lungfuls of air and that I was now sitting down. God, did I pass out? I thought I was standing in someone's arms a few moments ago. The fog cleared, and I went into action mode. I needed the meds. I tried to fumble at my backpack, but it wasn't on my back. Had I put my drawstring bag inside my pack? I couldn't remember.

"My bag," I gasped and opened my eyes, blinking heavily. Trying to see through the blur.

"Here," a voice rumbled. "Do you have medication you need?"

I nodded, or tried to. My vision cleared enough to see the bag at my feet, with large strong hands working the zipper. I lurched down to help.

The hands grabbed mine firmly. Mine looked pale and sickly with their chipped black polish next to the tanned, rough ones.

"I've got it," he said. Then to another pair of legs standing close. "Grab a bottle of water, Pete, would ya?"

I relaxed my hands and pulled them reluctantly from under the warmth.

Sucking in a slower lungful of air, I sat up.

A man crouched in front of me, strong thighs in worn brown denim holding him steady. His shaggy brown-haired head leaned over my bag as his hands re-emerged with three pill bottles.

"Amy?" he asked, squinting at a bottle. His face, what I could see of it, beneath copious amounts of facial hair—*gross*—was as sun-beaten as his hands. Then he flicked beautiful golden-brown and startlingly familiar eyes up at me.

I momentarily stopped inhaling my much-needed air as confusion swirled in me. How did I know this person? Expecting to get the same reaction from him, I was startled when his gaze dropped back to the bottles and he said, "Or is it . . . Melodie?"

That's when he stopped. And looked back up at me, narrowing his eyes. Then just as quickly he shook his head as if to clear an unpleasant memory. I used the reprieve to grab the latest bottle from his hand.

"The Klonopin, thank you." I shook one into my hand and threw it in my mouth, swallowing before he could even hand me the water bottle that had just been delivered.

I was exhausted. I needed to get to the island. My crash was coming.

Taking the plastic water bottle from the man I presumed was Pete, I mumbled my thanks up to him. Pete was gray and portly, where the brown-haired guy seemed more lean and muscular. It was hard to tell under his heavy black coat.

Pete nodded. "Can we, uh, call someone fer ya?" he said, his voice gruff, like I imagined a pirate to sound. He looked agitated, though, like he had a million other things to be getting on with. Of course he probably did, this being a busy spot in the blue pre-dawn light.

Shaking my head, I forged ahead with my plan. "It was . . . just a panic attack. I'm so sorry, not sure why. I need to get over to Daufuskie, actually. I'm going to my grandmother's . . ." I dropped the white lie in there, hoping to hell they didn't ask me about her. There were only about two hundred and fifty residents on the island as far as my Internet research had shown. And almost as many pieces of property for sale. Go figure. If they knew the island, they'd know of her or know she was no longer there. I needed to prevail upon their chivalry just a little bit more. "I, uh, underestimated how much the train ride down would be to . . . visit . . ."

The men in front of me exchanged a small concerned look.

I clasped my hands together, twisting my fingers nervously. "Are you, I mean, is anyone going out in that direction this morning? To fish, or whatever? Do you think they'd mind dropping me off?"

Brown-haired guy stood up, unfolding to a six-foot, if not more, tower in front of me. "Pete's taking me over to Bloody Point. That work for you?"

Relief was surely evident on my face. That was exactly where I needed to go. Seriously, he must have similar color eyes to someone I'd met before. They were so unique. And as he watched me from out of that hair-covered face, I had the oddest sensation I was looking at a lion. A lion and a pirate. "Thank you. And thank you for the water." The small smile I attempted was quickly thwarted when lion guy turned abruptly on his heel. I almost missed the look of disgust on his face. Almost.

I followed the two men down the jetty, my heartbeat and breathing still slightly erratic. I needed to try and stay awake as long as possible. The boat was small but sturdy and piled high with fishing equipment and what looked like grocery bags.

Pete offered me his cold and callused hand as I gingerly clambered aboard in my heavy boots, then he motioned me toward a small bench he had cleared off. "An' stay put, or your foot will get caught in a net or rope or somethin'."

I hesitated. Lion guy scowled. There was only one place for us both to sit, and I suddenly became uncomfortable that I would be practically plastered against my savior, who clearly regretted helping someone he now assumed to be a dishonest druggie looking for a free ride. It was my least favorite part of what I'd been reduced to as well, so I didn't blame him.

"Pete, I'll give you a hand." A man of few but certainly effective words.

I sat where indicated on the hard and cold white seat and pulled my hoodie up, securing it with my scarf and tucking some wayward strands of black hair away so I could see better in the wind. Then I pulled my backpack off my shoulders and tucked my disconnected ear buds into my ears in an attempt to shut out the mistrust I could feel directed at me. I hugged the pack to my chest. I missed my phone, needed my music so badly right now.

Turning my head, I took in the lightening sky and the silver hue of the water. The marsh reeds of the Bull River that I always remembered as vivid green were brown and beige, casting a gloomy lens over my romantic memories of visiting down here. But then I'd never been in winter.

My blood felt thick and heavy in my veins. It was a large dose for my body weight. "How long does it usually take to get to the island?" I asked Pete as he caught a final rope from his other passenger. Lion guy pushed the boat away from the jetty and leapt in the back with hardly a sound. Just like a cat.

"About twenty minutes normally, but around to Bloody Point, more like thirty."

Shit. I hoped I made it. But already I felt my eyelids getting heavy and my arms slipped slowly from around my pack. I gripped with my hands, looping the straps in my fingers. I could just lay my forehead down on my bag. Just rest for a bit. The motion of the boat was so soothing.

I dreamed of my sister. I dreamed of Abby.

CHAPTER TWO

Six years earlier

$\mathcal{J}$ could see Abby through the crack in the door. I'd heard the argument Mom and Dad had with her. Well, odd disjointed words actually.

"This boy . . ." My father.

My mother's voice. ". . . financial sacrifices."

". . . slap in the face after what we've done for you." Again my mother.

"Fuck you both." My sister.

Her words had stopped the fast rhythmic strokes of my brown pencil where I'd been sitting in my room shading in the tail of the Little Mermaid. The real one. Or at least, my sketch of the bronze statue of her in the water off the coast of Copenhagen, Denmark. I'd see it one day, I swore it.

Now my parents were downstairs, their raised voices muffled enough for the words to be indistinct. I moved to stand quietly in the hallway outside Abby's room and watched through the tiny gap in the doorway as she rummaged in her bedside drawer before moving her thin, willowy body around the bed to the window. Her shoulder-length wavy blonde hair was mussed and careless; her pajama shorts made her look even taller. She would turn eighteen in a few days.

She pushed the white sash window up as high as it would go and slung a long, bare limb over the sill so she could sit half in, half out. Then, sticking a misshapen cigarette in her mouth, she fumbled with the box in her hands and after a few tries struck a match, bringing it to the end of the white cylinder. After a deep inhale, a pause, and an even longer exhale that pushed swirls of white clouds around her body, she rocked her head back against the window frame and spoke.

"Come in here, Livvy."

I jumped.

"Come on in," she said more softly and looked over to me as if she knew exactly how long I'd been there. "And let me tell you about the fucked-up but so-called perfect life we lead here in the Baines family." Her hand held her cigarette out the window.

I glanced over my shoulder, my heart lurching, but I could still hear my parents downstairs. Inching open the door, I eased inside my older sister's room that I'd hardly set foot in during the past year, and closed the door behind me. I was elated I'd finally been invited back in and terrified of who this sister was, who seemed so changed, yet still so eerily familiar.

The room was bigger than I remembered, or something seemed different, but I kept my gaze on my sister.

Abby watched me with her blue eyes. They were a shade darker than mine. Daddy always said she got the deep end of the pool while I got the shallow end. I used to love it before I knew that might not be such a good thing.

"You don't question anything, do you, Livvy?" Abby took another deep inhalation of her cigarette, holding it between her thumb and forefinger, her eyes slitting up as she assessed me.

I stood still, wondering what she meant, afraid to say anything in case she changed her mind about talking to me.

She removed the home-made cigarette from her mouth and held it toward me in offering.

Swallowing hard, I shook my head. Worse than the idea of sucking hot, dry smoke into my throat, the idea that I might not be able to do it without choking held me firm. I'd seen enough in the movies of people's first try with a cigarette to know that when I did it, I wanted to be on my own. Worse than this Abby who looked annoyed at me would be an Abby laughing at me.

"Well," she continued slowly, letting out the fragrant smoke she held in her lungs, "I don't think I questioned why Uncle Mike was so involved in our lives when I was eleven years old either."

Uncle Mike. Who cared about Uncle Mike? He was such a bore—trying too hard to be fun and funny with me and my friends. Asking us what music we liked and singing along in the car from swim practice. So embarrassing.

Abby beckoned me closer, her mouth a hard line, but I stayed put. The look on her face, the eerie distance in her eyes as if some other person inhabited her body, was giving me the willies.

When we'd been little, she'd treated me like a doll, dressing me up and playing with me, even when I got up to about five or six and didn't want to be ordered about so much. I still loved her attention. But after her thirteenth birthday— "Teenage-hood," my mother had trilled and rolled her eyes—

Abby's time for me plummeted exponentially with each year. As far as I could tell, teenagers were boring and it only got worse. Abby had pretty much ignored me for the last year. Not that she'd paid that much attention to me before that. But at least, even with her vastly reduced attention, she'd been sweet, always quick with a hug or ruffling my hair. Indulging my adulation.

I glanced warily about the room, noticing for the first time that she'd ripped all her posters down, leaving pockmarks and torn paper corners all over the walls. It looked bare and cold. No wonder it had seemed bigger when I first came in.

My eyes finally found their way back to Abby, and hers softened, her pupils darker. She gestured me closer again, and when I didn't respond she leaned out the window and banged her cigarette to stub it out before bringing it back inside, wrapping it up carefully and sliding it into a baggie. Getting up, and folding her long limb back in through the window, she moved to the bed and sank to her knees on the rose-colored carpet. Her hands reached under the bed and pulled out the monogrammed black duffle Mom bought her for her swim tournament in ninth grade. It was packed full, and she slid the clear plastic bag into the side pocket.

When she turned back to me, her eyes were shiny dark pools. "I know you won't understand yet, Livvy, but I'm leaving tonight."

"W-what?" Confusion moved through me. I felt the swell of fear in my chest. I didn't understand what was happening.

"I'm leaving. For good—"

"No!" I burst out, the fear exploding into full-blown panic in my chest. Lurching forward, I fell toward her, my arms out to grasp her. I knew, *I knew*, in a way I'd never be able to explain, that I was losing her. Perhaps forever.

"Not you, Livvy." I heard her voice as I pressed my face into her neck, inhaling the scent of our youth that came from the bottle of pineapple shampoo currently sitting upside down on the edge of our shared tub. "I don't want to leave you. But I can't take you, and I have to leave." She grabbed my upper arms, squeezing tight and shaking me. "I have to leave."

I winced with the pressure of her hands as they held me away from her body.

Her face was grim. "I'm sorry. But I have to go."

"But where are you going? I don't understand."

She shook me again.

And shook me.

And shook me.

"Wake up, we're here." A deep voice. Not Abby.

I snapped my eyes open, disoriented. Lion eyes stared back at me.

I pulled away and blinked, looking around. The island ahead was a wild tangle of gray-green, making it look as primitive and isolated as I remembered. It was so familiar, and so strange all at once. "I'm sorry. I'm really tired." I'd missed the ride in. I'd missed the dolphins in the marshes around Turtle Island. My favorite part.

Pete the pirate was looping a rope on to a metal cleat on the dock. He looked over at me as he finished. "Are you sure you're all right?"

I nodded, pulling my coat tighter around me. The dock was newer-looking than I remembered it.

"Who did you say you were visiting?"

I hadn't, and he knew it. If I said my grandmother's name, he might ask too many questions, seeing as her house had most likely been abandoned for years. I wasn't sure how much Pete knew about the goings-on of the island. "Actually, I'm just visiting a house. It belongs to my family. Thank you for the ride."

"I'll make sure she gets there, Pete."

I swung my head up.

"All right. Tommy here'll get you safely to where you're goin'."

Tommy? No, Tommy didn't fit. Not at all.

Pete went on, "Just give me a holler should you be needin' a ride back. I'll be fishing up the cuts most o' the mornin's this week." He held out a grimy card with even grimier fingers, black under the fingernails.

Captain "Fishy Pete" White.

I nodded and slid it into my bag, knowing these gestures were less about helping me out and more about what my business was here. Small waves rocked against the boat, and I grabbed Pete's outstretched hand and stepped up on to the steady dock. "Thank you."

Tommy stepped out after me, and I didn't wait for him. I didn't need him making sure I got to the cottage. Or knowing where I was headed. I strode forward.

The landing we'd come in at was on the New River side, where the island curved away from the Atlantic. It wasn't technically Bloody Point, although it was referred to as such, being the closest you could bring a boat. As the crow flew, the house was less than half a mile away. But of course, with the dense foliage and the marshes cutting inland, I had further to travel.

Heading over the sandy pine-needle-strewn ground, I could see through the saw palmettos, and I made for the dirt road that wound through the trees, not even stopping to appreciate the surroundings I'd missed over the years. The wind was still cold off the Atlantic, and I inhaled the fresh salty gust, hoping its chill would permeate all my senses and keep me alert and awake until I got to the cottage.

A few minutes along the cleared earth track that passed for a road, the whir and buzz of an electric cart closed in behind me, crunching over the coarse ground. I glanced back to see my fellow boat passenger riding a golf cart that had seen better days, and I remembered that no one used cars here. The expense of having them ferried over probably wasn't worth it to most locals. Especially if this was what the roads still looked like, and I suspected it was.

He pulled up in front of me, effectively cutting me off.

I stopped short. Annoyance had to be etched all over my face.

"We're headed the same direction," he said, leaning forward, one arm slung over the wheel. I expected his eyes to be assessing me, but instead they slid away uneasily. "May as well give you a ride."

"No. Thank you," I muttered and stepped sideways so I could continue. I seriously hoped this guy was on the up and up.

"Suit yourself." He sighed. "See you in a bit."

What the hell did that mean? *See you in a bit?* He took off, the cart shuddering along the track.

It was eerily quiet as I walked through the trees. Just once I heard the thwack of a golf ball and some low voices and realized I must be passing close by one of the tees of the Bloody Point Golf Club. It had been abandoned and in disrepair the last time I'd been here. Abby taught me to ride my bike on the fourteenth fairway, the grass all patchy and brown in spots.

Sure enough, as I rounded the corner, the fully restored clubhouse rose up to my right, painted white, with a fancy-looking porch and a dark red roof. It didn't seem to have much activity—not surprising in winter on an island with so few residents—but it was clearly operational. Maybe I could see about getting a job tomorrow. The thought lightened my mood, hatching a small kernel of hope.

After veering inland, and then heading right on another dirt track through the dark and eerily silent vegetation that towered above me so the sky was only periodically visible, I finally got to the turn-off for our road. My relief at the lack of development on this part of Daufuskie was acute. It meant I could be here in relative peace, and my grandmother's cottage, while it was probably overgrown, would be largely un-messed-with.

I could almost make the house out through the trees as I got closer. Forcing myself to slow down in my excitement and relief, I breathed deep and turned into the driveway. Okay, driveway was an overstatement. There was a gap in the vegetation and the cottage sat nestled in a clearing, embraced by a massive live oak to one side that was for sure several hundred years old. I remembered Gran saying it could even be a thousand years old. Thick with leaves, dripping moss and iced with green revival plants, the branches reached out majestically before snaking toward the ground and up again, as if they were arguing about whether to grow out toward the surrounding forest or reach for the sky.

The two-room-wide cottage was smaller and older than in my memory, but in that moment it was the most beautiful thing I had ever seen. And not as overgrown as I'd imagined. *Sanctuary.* The word rocked through me. A place to heal.

The white paint could no longer be called that, though

from what I could see, the metal roof looked good. It jutted out over the porch that spanned the front. There were two missing spindles in the railing to the left and the porch sagged there a little, but . . . wait. I swept my eyes from left to right. There was fresh white paint on the opposite end. New, *unpainted* wooden spindles every so often.

No.

I turned my head all the way to the left and confirmed what my brain had already processed in the periphery. Golf cart. The same golf cart, if I wasn't mistaken. The screen door squeaked open and *he* stepped out, the door banging shut behind him.

"What are you d-doing here?" I swallowed. There must be some mistake. There was no way my parents could have sold this. They couldn't! It was mine. Anguish and exhaustion closed around my throat. My eyes stung.

"I live here," he said matter-of-factly. I couldn't see his expression beneath all that facial hair.

This was not happening. I locked my knees and clung tightly to the straps of my bag to stop the shaking.

And then I was angry. So angry. This was mine. Mine. Mine. And I was so tired.

"Who the fuck are you?" I spat, because it was all I could do to speak through the indescribable helplessness that was threatening to do me in. Oh my God. I had nowhere. I had nothing.

"You must be Olivia," he said, his voice gruff and oddly flat. "I was wondering when you'd show up."

CHAPTER THREE

"*H*ow do you know my name?" I asked. Was he some kind of caretaker?

"You're Abby's little sister."

The shock of hearing my sister's name on this stranger's lips jolted me.

He stood, strong legs braced apart, arms crossed over his checked-shirted chest. He looked imposing. Almost savage.

"If you knew who I was, why didn't you say something on the road? Or on the boat for that matter?"

He cocked his shaggy head to the side, a lock of light brown hair falling across his face, and let out a breath I could hear from where I stood uncertainly looking up at him on the porch. "Why don't you come in."

It wasn't a question.

It sounded more like resignation.

He turned around and went through the door into the dim interior.

Questions and vague memories whirred in kaleidoscopic fragments through my mind, too disjointed for me to grab on to. For a moment, I stood in place before the one-story cottage that now held such mystery. This person knew Abby? Or did he just know *of* her? He was vaguely familiar and I guess maybe I'd seen him on the island when I was a child.

He could be a creepy serial-killer recluse. The recluse part was right. But I could hardly pass judgment on that since I was here to be the same.

A cold gust of wind made me shiver, and my stomach growled loudly. I climbed up the steps, my eyes sweeping side to side. My grandmother's white wicker love seat was still there, the chintz faded, the paint peeling and dulled to a shade of gray.

"Are you going to stand out there like the angel of death all day? What's with all the black?"

I gritted my teeth in annoyance and pulled open the screen, stepping into a chamber of memories. I slid my backpack to my feet on the warm wood floor. It smelled the same, but different. Cedar, but also something lemony. Whitewashed wood walls surrounded the one-room living room/kitchen, the huge scarred farm table that doubled as a kitchen island dwarfing the space. A string of seashells I'd collected with Abby one summer was still hanging at the kitchen window. Missing was the clutter and the floral touches that had made it the place I associated with everything good, but it was close enough. Waves of conflicting emotions tumbled through me, bringing the sting back to my eyes and the thud to my chest. My breath caught as I tried to breathe. I couldn't cry, I wouldn't cry, but I couldn't hold it in. The relief of being here, coupled with the stark reminder of everything I'd lost since the last time I'd visited, hit me deep in my gut. And I was tired. So tired. I tried to control it, but my breath released in a sob.

Strong arms took mine and steered me toward a chair. I

shrugged him off. All I wanted to do was be alone here, and I couldn't be. "I need to lie down, and you . . . you need to go," I said, not looking up. I stood and headed toward the bedroom on the right where Abby and I had slept.

"I can't," I thought I heard him say.

I didn't care if the beds had no sheets. I needed to be horizontal. Stumbling into the twin room I'd once shared with my sister, I realized vaguely this must be the room he used. The beds were pushed together, the closest one mussed, a navy blanket pulled back from rumpled white sheets. The sight was too much, too inviting, too needed, and my weighted body, boots and all, crawled into the spicy-scented cocoon of bedding. And everything went dark.

My eyelids kept turning bright red as light fluttered over them every few seconds. Irregular. A shadow, then. Sunlight, perhaps. Sunlight. I hadn't seen sunlight in so long. Not in the way I liked, anyway. In the way it cascaded through deep leafy shadows and dappled you in the bright hope of spring.

I'd come to in the night, several hours earlier, disoriented, trying to find familiarity with the sheets that smelled so foreign in a place I couldn't see in the dark. Remembering my escape, the exhausting train ride, my panic attack and the stranger in my house, I pieced together my surroundings from memory. But soon exhaustion slid over me again, and I sank deeper into the musky male scent of the sheets.

Now, even though my mind was awake, my eyes stayed closed. But it was day. And I smelled food. Toast maybe. My stomach was too empty even to growl. But the hollow ache was there, and I knew I needed to eat. And drink. God, I was so thirsty. But all I wanted to do was stay. Stay exactly like this and not deal with who *Tommy* was. The caretaker scenario seemed the most likely. And completely explained his familiarity, explained how a speck of memory teased me. He was older than I was, maybe late twenties. If he was a long-time island resident, it also explained how he knew me too, remembered me more clearly than I did him.

I peeled my eyes open incrementally. The wood walls were unpainted still, sunlight sliding across them from the window, where a breeze stirred the tall longleaf pines and the large oak I'd climbed since I was a child. The dresser stood against the wall next to a small antique campaign desk and lamp. The desk held stacks and stacks of haphazard papers and the old typewriter I remembered. But now, a white laptop cord snaked across the chaos, its small silver head hanging impotently over the side, a touch of modern incongruity in the vignette.

I sat up, curious, swung my legs over the edge of the bed and stretched my aching back and arms. I crossed the creaky wood floor to the desk and the papers. It looked to be a manuscript of some sort. Looking down, it suddenly occurred to me that while I was in my tights, I wasn't wearing boots. I had no recollection of taking them off. Had I? I couldn't remember.

A short, sharp knock sounded. I swung around to the door just as it opened.

He stood there, tall and imposing, wearing worn jeans and a dark sweater. Of course, he didn't do the normal thing and say anything like "Sorry to barge in" or "Good morning."

Only his eyes and his hands were visible, what with his facial hair and long sleeves. I had the fleeting thought that he was hiding himself. But it was gone in an instant, replaced only with my questions. Of course, I didn't ask them.

His brown eyes assessed me, then dropped to the desk. They were narrowed and back on mine a moment later. The implication was he didn't want me nosing through his stuff.

I tore my eyes from his before it became too uncomfortable and noticed my black boots sat neatly against the wall by the door. Oh no, he didn't!

I expected him to finally say something. I folded my arms, but all he did was flex his large hand on the door handle.

"I'd appreciate it if you didn't come into my room when I'm sleeping," I finally managed, my voice rough with first use.

His eyes narrowed. "Actually this is my room, and you're awake. Clearly."

"I meant removing my boots," I snapped.

He shrugged, turning away. "I thought you'd be more comfortable. See you in the kitchen."

Well, that was a good start.

Locating my backpack on the floor near the bed, I rummaged for my toothbrush and headed to the small shared bathroom at the end of the hallway. Sue me, but I wanted to have clean teeth before trying to convince someone to get the fuck out of my house.

I stepped inside on to the black and white mosaic tiles, and, closing the door behind me, breathed in a smell similar to the sheets. The shower beckoned; the lure of hot water and cleanliness was too much. The conversation could wait just a few minutes. Stripping, I turned the rickety shower head on and stepped into the claw-foot tub. I scrubbed myself from head to toe with a small cake of white soap, wanting desperately to steal some of his shampoo, but resisting.

I caved when it came time to brush my teeth, peeking out of the shower and seeing the mashed-up tube of toothpaste sitting on the edge of the pedestal sink. I brought it into the shower with me and brushed my teeth for over five minutes because it felt so good to run my tongue over slick teeth.

And suddenly I didn't care about using his stuff. I grabbed the shampoo and lathered up, even glancing back around the curtain to see if there was a razor. Of course there wasn't. I rolled my eyes, remembering his caveman face. What was that about anyway? Who did that these days? It wasn't "Movember." And he wasn't some crusty old fisherman like Pete. He seemed young enough that he shouldn't have a beard, though what did I know? He looked about ten years older than me, and I guessed when you were a recluse on an island, you stopped giving a shit what you looked like. Or you didn't want people seeing your face.

Or you didn't want to see your *own* face.

I paused at that thought, and then shook my head. Finishing up and turning the now chilly water off, I grabbed a familiar old blue towel off the railing. There were two, and this one seemed drier. It was thin and rough with age, but it felt good abrading my skin. I didn't want to put my dirty clothes back on, but I hadn't brought much, and my jeans were stuffed in my backpack in the room. Clever. I'd need to sort out some clothes. I grabbed my underwear and bra and washed them in the sink with soap. Wondering where I could hang them to dry, I settled for the handle of the shower since it probably wouldn't be used until tomorrow. I'd fetch them later tonight.

Securing the small towel around me and clutching my bundle of clothes like a shield, I gingerly eased open the bathroom door. My line of sight to the front door was clear, not a strange caretaker in the vicinity. I scampered toward my open bedroom door and yelped as I came face to face with him clutching the large sheaf of papers from the desk.

We both froze for a moment, and then in typical male fashion his eyes strayed down to my towel before he obviously realized what he was doing and snapped them back up to my face.

A chill went through me. I was so tired of how predictable men were. And here I was, alone on a sparsely populated island with a strange man in my house. Swallowing the bubble of nerves in my chest, I tried to sound calm. "Excuse me, do you think you could get out of my room?"

He stepped aside, still inside the door frame, not answering.

If he expected me to head in there while he occupied every free molecule of air, he was mistaken. I moved back instead and he rolled his eyes, brushing past me and heading down the hall to the kitchen. Jeez, the guy hardly said a word, but his non-verbal communication was certainly verbose. Him: too old for this shit. Me: stupid young female.

I darted inside and slammed the door, wishing it had a lock. Dumping my pile of clothes in the corner, I hurriedly yanked my jeans out of my pack, pulling them on along with a black T-shirt. Since my bra was wet and hanging in the bathroom with my thong, I shrugged my hoodie back on to hide my body. I yanked my brush through my wet hair, wincing at the lack of conditioner, and after squeezing as much water as I could out of it, tied it in a loose pony.

Then I headed to the kitchen in my bare feet.

FOUR

𝒥 came around the corner and stopped at the edge of the farm table, watching his broad back as he busied himself at the counter. His muscled shoulders moved under the soft fabric of his dark gray sweater, his brown hair curling over the collar.

I wasn't sure what to say, or how to start the conversation about Abby or the house, so I said nothing and settled for studying his frame. He was well built from what I could see. Strong-looking. Athletic. Again I wondered at his age.

"It's almost lunchtime, I'm making a sandwich. Do you want one?" He spoke without turning around, so he must have heard me come in.

My stomach finally let out a long, low growl. I cleared my throat quickly. "Uh, yes. Yes, please." I shouldn't accept a meal from someone I was about to kick out, but I'd be dumb to say no. Especially since I had no food. I'd also just enjoyed sleeping in a made-up bed and having a hot shower, neither of which I would have found had he not been in residence. "Thank you," I added and pulled a chair out and sat down. He turned with two plates, clearly having already anticipated

my answer, and placed one in front of me. I looked up at him.
Maybe it would be good to let him stay. To have a caretaker.
For the house, of course, not me. Perhaps my grandmother's
estate was covering this, and I shouldn't mess with it. We could
just pretend I wasn't really here. He could go on as normal.

With this fresh perspective on the situation, I felt uncomfortable with how rude I'd been since I met him. Especially
when the first thing he'd done was help me back at the docks
when I had the panic attack.

He nodded and turned back to grab two glasses of water,
and then sat down opposite me, folding his tall frame into
one of my grandmother's dinky farm chairs. It struck me as
funny for a moment, and I tried to stop my lips from curling
by sucking my cheeks in.

He idly tapped a long finger on the scratched wood. "So—"

"About the—" I tried at the same time. I blew out a breath
and took a bite of sandwich, letting him have the next word.

I was too hungry anyway.

I sank my teeth into the soft-grain bread and groaned.
"Thank you again."

"Why are you suddenly so polite, and not the viper who
arrived on the island yesterday?"

I swallowed my bite. "I was tired and, as you witnessed,
had just had a panic attack. I'm sorry."

"Does that happen often?" he asked, his tone casual but
laced with curiosity.

This was literally the best sandwich ever. "What kind of
cheese is this?"

"Manchego."

"Manchego's good." His eyebrows rose. Probably due to
my purposeful subject change. "You're the one who hardly
says anything," I added, acknowledging his look.

"It's not like you have the gift of the gab."

Gift of the gab? Who *says* that?

Then a more concerning thought occurred to me. What if he was a tenant paying rent to my parents? Oh my God, why hadn't I thought of that?

"About that . . . about you being here . . ." I paused expectantly, waiting for him to fill the gap. He knew who I was; it was time for him to explain what *he* was doing here.

He cleared his throat but didn't say anything.

"Well," I forged on, "*Tommy.*" His name didn't sound any better when I actually used it. It was like repeatedly referring to a dog as a cat. It just . . . wasn't. I decided to try another tack on why he was here. "Thank you for being the caretaker."

His brow creased, but he didn't refute me. Thank God.

I released a long breath. "I really appreciate you being here. Obviously, since I just turned up out of the blue, it would have been awful to arrive to a cold, empty house with no electricity and water—"

"Why *did* you turn up out of the blue, by the way? Where are your parents? Aren't you still in school?"

I scowled. It was actually hard to be civil to him. He was just so . . . under my skin with his disapproval. The tone of his questions. "None of your business, none of your business and, uh, none of your business."

"Well, that was certainly mature," he said lazily, finishing the last bite of his sandwich. "How about these for answers." He raised a finger. "Ran away." He raised a second finger. "At home worried sick, and . . ." he raised a third, "should still be in school. Did I cover it? Truancy is against the law, by the way."

Was he for real? "Are you a Boy Scout?" I asked sarcastically, looking at his three still-raised fingers.

"Do I need to make a phone call?"

"What? No!" My tongue felt thick. "No," I said again. Shit, here I was thinking I had the upper hand, it being my house and all. "Please," I added, realizing I needed him on my side, and unable to avoid the hint of desperation in my tone. I mentally cringed. "Please don't tell anyone I'm here."

He assessed me, leaning back, one arm slung along the empty chair back next to him, and his eyes narrowed. There was a gemstone that exact color. What was it called?

"Fine," he said finally, with a stiff nod.

"Fine?"

"Yes, fine."

"What are *you* hiding from?" I asked suddenly, not sure where the question came from.

I almost missed the flicker of shock in his gaze, before he shrugged nonchalantly. "And we won't ask each other questions."

"Okay," I agreed, with abundant relief, despite the weirdness of our situation.

Well, well, well. Wasn't that an interesting puzzle? Why would a guy who was obviously well-spoken and educated, from what I could tell, take on the lonely job of looking after an isolated cottage in the middle of nowhere?

The silence was extremely uncomfortable as we both regrouped.

Eventually he sighed. "You look better without the black shit all over your face."

Obviously he was referring to the black eyeliner and lipstick I'd taken to wearing. It matched my nails, my usual clothes and my mood. And it hid me. People's eyes glided away from me when I started dressing like that, so I kept it up. It made things easier for me out in the world. All I had to do was also block out the whispers in the hallways of my preppy school. It had the added benefit that my parents hated it.

"Well, you'd probably look better without that hairy shit all over *your* face." I bit my lip as soon as the words were uttered.

Seriously, sometimes I had no filter.

There was movement in his beard.

Was he actually going to smile? His caramel eyes crinkled up and suddenly his beard split open in a wide smile filled with perfect white teeth, and a snort of laughter came out. He was almost beautiful, not that I was into older guys. I didn't know where to look, but his wheeze of laughter was infectious and I found myself fighting my own smile.

Then he took a deep breath. "I . . . I was in love with your sister. That's how you know me," he said.

The words were out there so suddenly, and he looked so shocked that he'd uttered them, that neither of us spoke for interminable minutes.

No questions.

Abruptly, he got up, scraping the chair across the old wooden floor, and walked to the front door. He paused a moment, his shoulders rigid, then yanked the door and smacked the screen open. In a moment, he was gone, both doors slamming shut behind him, leaving a vast emptiness in his wake.

I stood in the time warp that was Gran's bedroom. She was a strong woman to have lived out here by herself for so long. Never seemed old. I realized now she must have dyed the gray in her hair for years, and I just never saw the lines on her face. Or could see past them. Her eyes were my legacy. Pale blue. It was our Slavic and Scandinavian ancestry, she told me.

Now I used those eyes as I took in every detail. It was all familiar and yet different, the way you've seen something for your whole life and just accepted it without really noticing its composition. Her faded patchwork quilt on the white wicker queen-sized bed. The picture of her and my grand-father on their wedding day next to the bed. On the wall, the framed picture of her with her parents and her two sisters, both also deceased, standing in front of an old white clap-board church.

Stepping toward the dressing table, I deliberately ignored the picture of two blonde girls. It was a photo of Abby and me taken on the live oak rope swing outside. I held my breath, willing my eyes not to stray toward it. I wasn't ready yet.

On closer inspection, time and neglect had left their covering of dust and cobwebs all over the room. The back of a once silver hairbrush was tarnished to dark brown. I wondered why my grandmother hadn't taken these things when she'd been moved to the home. Not that she'd been there more than a few months. I guess she'd known it would be a short stay, and there was no point moving her keepsakes and risk them not being given to Abby and me during the logistics of death.

I felt uncomfortable being in this room, but since this caretaker dude was already staying in the other room, I'd have to sleep in here for now. I wasn't sure I wanted him to leave. I'd been planning on being totally alone, but somehow I felt relieved at finding my plan had changed.

Approaching the bed, I thought of last night and felt disappointed that he'd been forced to stay in here. Disappointed at the invasion of my grandmother's domain and disappointed that I'd been so wrapped up in my own head and my own exhaustion that I hadn't even stopped to consider it would have been better for *me* to be in this room. He must have been so uncomfortable. It was so like me to go crashing into everything, upsetting the apple cart again, as my mother liked to say about me. I had no grace, no poise. No social intelligence.

Not like Abby.

I actually felt closer to her here. Walking to the bed, I peeled back the quilt. I would have taken it outside and beaten it to get the dust out, but it looked like the beating had already been taken care of. The sheets were slightly rumpled. I leaned down and inhaled the scent of detergent and a faint whiff of the mint and herb—rosemary?—smell I now associated with my male housemate. His shampoo, at any rate. I'd sleep in here tonight. I went across the hall and pulled the twin bed straight, then grabbed all my belongings and relocated myself.

He still wasn't back.

In the kitchen, I wiped the crumbs from the scarred butcher-block counters while humming in lieu of listening to my music. Seeing the small kitchen trash can under the sink was full, I pulled the bag out.

Might as well make myself useful.

I hauled on my boots, laced them up tightly, and wound my scarf around my neck. Picking up the small bag, I headed out of the house into the bracingly cold afternoon. I went around the side of the house to the fenced-off trash area and pulled open the large trash can lid to throw my bag in. And stopped.

I stared into the can at the box of bottles, all neatly capped. Reaching in, I pulled one out. Vodka. It was empty. They were all empty. They were all exactly the same. A case of empty vodka bottles. No other types of liquor. I wondered how long they'd been there, and why. Surely, if you drank vodka, you just threw them away one by one as you went through them. And how quickly had they been gone through? In one go? I shook my head. Did I even want to ask him? For him to know I was nosing into his business, snooping in the trash? I certainly didn't want him asking *me* anything. I'd seen the questions in his eyes when he saw the prescriptions in my bag.

I slammed the lid closed and wrapped my hoodie tighter around my body. Folding my hands under my arms to keep them warm, I aimed for the path that wound through the thick vegetation to the beach. You wouldn't even know the ocean was so close to the cottage if you didn't know of the path.

Drawn by the distant sound of crashing waves and hungry gulls, I ignored the swing hanging from the oak branch to my left, satisfied that it was still there at least.

Passing out of the shade of pines and gnarled live oaks on to the grassy dunes, I paused at the arresting sight of the dark gray ocean against the moody sky and breathed the frigid air that flew deep into my lungs.

Squinting against the wind, eyes already watering, I looked to my left, where a dark figure sat hunched over, rocking on his heels. His elbows were resting on his knees, his arms cradling his head, hands clutching tufts of unruly thick hair. His bare feet were sunk into the sand, his boots discarded several feet behind him.

It was a picture of desolation and grief, and it made no sense.

I stared.

He said he'd loved my sister, but she died six years ago. There was no way he was still grieving her, was he? I mean, I missed her every day, but she was my sister. What was going on with this man? I'd come here to escape my demons and suddenly it seemed like someone else was battling even bigger ones than mine.

Part of me wanted to go and ask him what was wrong, and part of me didn't want to know.

He'd come down here to get away. Now that I'd stumbled on his private sanctuary, I couldn't invade his space again. I backed up slowly, then turned back toward the path, hurrying away before he saw me.

He still wasn't home when dusk set in. I thought about walking back to the beach, but the darkness that blanketed this island at night was absolute and made me nervous. I made myself another sandwich, more Manchego and a sliced tomato. After a slight pause, I made one for him too and put the plate in the fridge. It was deathly quiet in the house, except for the ticking of the clock made from an old tin plate on the wall next to the refrigerator.

As it got darker, I went and found the small bookshelf in the corner of the sitting area. Running my fingers over the old spines, I came to a hardbacked illustrated version of Hans Christian Andersen's fairy tales. Gran had read these to us as children. Abby adored the Little Match Girl story, although it always made us cry so hard, I'd hated to hear it. I certainly wouldn't be able to read it now.

Should I wait up for him? Was he okay? He was probably fine, just didn't want to come home to a place where he could no longer be on his own. Close to midnight, I nodded

off on the couch, my last thought being that I should probably find a flashlight and go check if he was still on the
beach.

The crash of lightning, like an explosion going off behind
my eyelids, had me sitting bolt upright in the pitch darkness.
I fumbled next to me for the light I swore I'd left on, my
chest constricting. Coasting my fingers up the rough rattan
lamp base until I felt the neck and the switch, I put two feet
on the floor and tried slow breaths. God, storms. I hated
storms. What if the house got struck by lightning and caught
fire? What if . . . I pressed the switch with my thumb.

Click.

Click click.

Clickclickclick.

Shit. What if a serial killer timed his attack for a storm
so no one heard me scream? What was I thinking? No one
would hear me scream out here.

Breathe. Breathe.

Another sharp crack of lightning lit the room. And then
I was in blinding darkness again. No serial killers in the
room with me. I was alone, thank God.

But not thank God.

I was alone out here. I couldn't even lock the front door
in case Tommy came back. I laid my head down on my
knees, hooking my arms underneath them, curling myself
into a small ball. Were my eyes even open? It was so dark,
it was hard to tell unless I blinked. My grandmother's room.
My room. I could lock myself in my room. If I could get
there.

I stood up and took a tentative step forward, my arms
outstretched in front of me. My breathing got irregular and
shallow again. Calm, calm. Somehow, I got to the hall,

planting my palms on either side of me, relieved I was somewhat anchored and knew where I was, and then felt my way along the wall.

I stood for a moment in the open doorway, mentally visualizing the path to the bed.

Count my heartbeats.

Slow my breathing.

One hundred, ninety-nine . . . My pills were on the bedside table, so that was good. *Ninety-eight, ninety-seven, ninety-six* . . .

In retrospect, the slow rumblings of thunder were a buildup. I should have taken them as a warning. But when the crescendo came, so loud and so bright that the house literally shook, and illuminated Abby standing in the corner by my grandmother's dresser, the scream that tore from my throat felt like it ripped my chest clear open.

CHAPTER FIVE

Before

"Where is she?" my mother screamed, her eyes wild.

I tried to stand my ground, but she was terrifying me. "I d-don't know. I promise!" I sobbed.

In the next room, through the closed glass door, my father paced back and forth, the cordless phone to his ear. He was dressed in his striped pajama pants and a gray T-shirt, his hand raking through his salt-and-pepper hair. He wasn't paying any attention to my mother, who had now grabbed my upper arm and was digging her fingernails into my skin so hard I hissed through my tears.

"You know something. I can see you do, Olivia. Do you understand how serious this is? She's been missing for three weeks. And now you're telling me she's with this Whitfield boy. What else did she tell you?"

"Ow. You're hurting me." I tried yanking my arm free. "Let me go!" I screamed as loudly as I could, hoping my father would hear me. He looked up briefly, his eyes glazed, and then continued his pacing.

The front door banged open and Uncle Mike came in. I shuddered as dread coursed through me. Uncle Mike had been in almost a worse state than anyone. You'd think it was his own daughter he'd lost. "What does she know, Susan?"

The call had come in earlier that night. It was dumb luck I'd been walking to the bathroom and picked up the hallway phone. I hadn't even managed to say hello before a male voice said he needed to speak to Olivia.

"This is me. I mean, this is Olivia."

There'd been a shuffle, a sound of breathing, and then my sister's voice. "Liv, it's me."

Excitement coursed through my veins. Relief at hearing Abby's voice. I listened for the sounds in the kitchen that meant Mom and Dad were still down there. "Abby," I whispered, squeaking by accident in my joy at hearing her voice. I took a breath. "Abby, are you coming home? Mom and Dad, they're . . . worried sick."

"Did you tell them anything?"

"No! No, of course not," I assured her.

"Good, good. You've done good, Livvy. Listen, this is important. You can't ever tell them anything. There are some things that happened, bad things, and I'm worried they wouldn't understand. That you wouldn't understand. And I'm worried for you. Whit says I should be worried for you." Her voice sounded funny. Slurry and tired.

I could hear footsteps at the base of the stairs. "I miss you," I said quickly while I had the chance. My whispered voice broke over the last word.

"I miss you too. I left you something in your room. Under your soccer gear, bottom drawer. I wish I could explain it. I have to tell you so much, Livvy, but you're so young. God, you're so young. I—"

"I'm not," I denied emphatically. My father's head came up the stairs. I wanted to warn her I couldn't talk, but I didn't want to let her go.

My father looked at me with the phone in my hand, and I froze.

Abby's voice in my ear continued as he approached, but I couldn't focus on her words. Something about Whit and Uncle Mike and . . . I wanted to hang up but didn't want her to go, and then my father was right there taking the phone out of my hand.

He must have heard only two words of her voice before, "Abby?" His eyes scrunched in disbelief. "Abby? Is that you? Abby? Abby? *Abby!*" he yelled.

She'd hung up.

He looked at me in stupefaction as tears welled in my eyes. I missed my sister and I was scared. Scared that I knew something. But I didn't. I didn't know anything.

Now my parents and Uncle Mike were scaring me further.

"Where is she?" Uncle Mike asked me.

This was some bizarre nightmare where all the adults were screaming at me. "I don't know!" All I wanted was to be comforted, and be told my sister was okay, and that they loved me. I wanted my mother's arms around me, not hurting me.

I yanked my arm again, panic giving me another surge of strength, sharp, stinging pain over the dull, bruising ache as I tore free. I clutched my arm with my other hand, my fingers coming away smeared with a line of blood from her nail.

My mother's face transformed from anger to horror in an instant. She took a step toward me, but I jerked back, tripping over the sofa arm, and then scrambling clumsily to the wall, to the corner, where I sank down to the floor, hugging my knees to my chest.

"I'm sorry, Olivia, obviously I didn't mean to hurt you. I was panicked. You have to talk to us and tell us what you know."

Uncle Mike immediately came over and crouched down, running a large hand up and down my wounded arm.

I cringed.

"Your mother didn't mean to hurt you, but it's extremely important to let us know where your sister is."

"Whit," I whispered the name again, my voice hoarse from crying. "I told you already, she mentioned someone called Whit. That's *all* I know. I didn't even see him."

Abby had asked me not to tell. I had to keep part of the secret for her. Something was going on here that I didn't understand.

Uncle Mike swung his face up to my mother's.

"Whitfield Cavanaugh, I assume," she responded. "Senator Cavanaugh's son. She knows him from the country club."

I racked my brain for an image, anything, and came up blank. They were all the same, with their khaki pants, striped ties and blazers. Anyway, I only knew the kids my age.

"Christ," hissed Mike, a strange look crossing his face. It looked like fear for a moment. I blinked, and it was gone.

He stood up. "That's all we need. He's a complete wastrel. And his father's got half the squad on the payroll."

My mother pursed her lips at me, then addressed Mike. "Andrew is calling Senator Cavanaugh right now, or trying to. His number is unlisted. I think he's going through the country club directory."

"He'll get nowhere. Let me use my credentials, I know

someone to call." Mike headed through the door to where my father was. My mother followed.

He took the phone with a nod to my dad. "This is Michael Williams. I'm a consultant with the Atlanta PD." *He was?* "Yes. Yes, that's right. Listen, we have an emergency and I need a phone number. A missing teenage girl, and there's a chance Senator Cavanaugh's son is . . . also in danger." He paused, listening to the other end of the line. "Uh-huh." He snapped his fingers at my dad, motioning for a pen. "Uh-huh, yes, I very much appreciate that, thank you."

I listened over my irregular and choked breath. My arm ached. Was Abby in danger? She seemed so sure and so calm, and so grown-up. I couldn't imagine she was hurt.

But this was all bad. Really bad. Everyone was acting crazy and scary. I shouldn't have told them about Whit, or maybe I should have told them sooner. Abby would be so disappointed in me. But what if they really were in danger and needed help?

After another twenty or so minutes, Uncle Mike went rushing out of the house. I heard his voice speaking quietly outside the window I was closest to, then his car revved up and peeled away.

I sat there in the corner, my body aching with numbness, watching until the clock in the hall ticked past midnight and I turned twelve. Happy birthday to me. Then I quietly got up and slipped unnoticed past my parents, who were still sitting in the kitchen, and went to my room. I closed my bedroom door with a soft click, then looped my bathrobe belt from the door handle to the hook that held my book bag just inside the door and tied it tight.

Pulling open my bottom drawer, I rummaged through my clothes until I felt plastic wrapped round something hard. It was a clear Ziploc over a wooden box with an envelope taped to the outside. The envelope was addressed to me.

There was no sound from downstairs and I hurriedly took the package to my bed. I extracted the contents from the bag, hefting the weight of the simple wooden box with its small lock holding it closed.

Opening the envelope, I took out a folded letter.

The sound of footsteps on the stairs had me hurriedly stuffing everything back in the bag. I slid it under my bed and turned off the light just as a knock sounded at my door.

I lay still in the dark.

"Olivia?" my mother called softly, regret in her voice.

I closed my eyes as I heard the door handle turn, and the soft sound as the door reached as far as it could open with the bathrobe cord attached. A sliver of light crossed my eyelids. There was a small intake of breath, my mother's surprise at finding her way blocked. I knew it wouldn't take much to just force it open. After a few moments and a deep sigh, the door closed again with a soft click and it was dark once more.

When I woke up in the morning, Abby was dead.

As details emerged throughout the day, I became certain of three things: I'd never celebrate another birthday, I would never again trust my parents, and the name Whitfield Cavanaugh, belonging to the man who had stolen and killed my sister, would be the most hated name in Baines family history. On that last point, my parents and I would always agree.

There was still no sign of Tommy when I awoke the next morning. *Tom*, I decided. Way better. He was a single-syllable guy. One strong, short word was all he needed as a name.

His golf cart was still parked between a saw palm and an oak sapling, where he'd left it the day I arrived.

I was exhausted from my panic of the night before and my vision of Abby. Still jumpy, I took my daily medication, shaking the pills out on to the worn wooden table and counting. I had twenty days' worth. Forty if I could stretch to every other day. I hoped being here would help get me over the panic attacks at least; I didn't know about the rest.

There were two storage bins of old clothes in a closet in the hall. I feared anything that could fit me had probably been Abby's, and I tried not to let that bother me. Most things were small, but there were a few items that could work. Pulling on a pair of denim cutoffs that were definitely Abby's, and a faded floral blouse of my grandmother's, I took anything that looked wearable and tossed them into the stackable washer to get the musty smell out. For now, I too smelled like I'd been in a box for over six years, but it would have to do until I did the next load. Maybe I could head over to the golf club once I figured out decent clothes to wear.

I unpacked the few items in my bag, including my wooden box from Abby, laying it carefully on the dresser next to my grandmother's silver-backed hairbrush. Digging further into my bag, I came across the card Fishy Pete had given me. I wondered if I should call him and see if he knew where Tom was. And say what? *Tommy's missing*? How did I even know he *was* missing; maybe he had a girlfriend he stayed over with. I tried to picture the kind of woman Tom would be with and came up blank.

Anyway, he was a grown man capable of taking care of himself.

Walking out to the hall, I grabbed the wall-mounted telephone handset that had been there as long as I could remember, expecting to find it dead. To my surprise, a dial tone sounded. So the phone was maintained too. I put it back on its cradle for now and dropped back against the wall with a long exhale.

Day one of my new safe life, and I was bored out of my mind. I didn't even have music to listen to. At some point I knew I wanted to sort all of my grandmother's things. To my knowledge it had never been done after she passed.

Before I gave myself a chance to talk myself out of snooping, I walked quickly to the twin room I'd first woken up in, Tom's room, and eased open the door on a faint whine.

Pausing, my ear cocked to set a baseline for the lack of noise in case he returned, I looked toward the desk against the wall. No laptop. Damn. But it had to be here somewhere. He hadn't left with it. And his piles and piles of paper were still there. Satisfied I'd be able to detect the sound of his return, I sidled in.

TOM

"I'm cutting you off, Tommy." Marjoe's tobacco-saturated voice hammered out in unison with the palm she slapped down on the scarred bar top. The sound echoed around the large, dimly lit tin-roofed room and the concrete floors dusted with tracked-in sand from outside. "I know the beginning of a bender when I see one. You're out of here at three."

Named for both her mother and father, Marjoe had blonde hair over streaks of gray, and her lined face was out of focus for a moment as I pulled myself from my reverie. She was right. I'd had enough. Thing was, I still didn't feel like I'd consumed enough to obliterate the reality of my past catching up to me. My ass was numb from being on the bar stool since the place opened at noon.

"Fine. Give me a water. Rocks, lime and a teensy-weensy straw so it at least looks like I'm having a vodka." I winked at her.

"And you stink," she added. "You been helpin' Pete out this morning?"

I nodded. Normally, I'd head straight home to shower and change, but knowing what waited for me there, I'd decided Mama's famous shrimp 'n' grits sounded like a better option. And I could have a fucking drink.

It had been almost two weeks since Olivia arrived and I wasn't handling it well. After my first slip of mentioning that I'd been in love with Abby, I'd gotten the hell out of there.

I'd ended up calling Pete from the Bloody Point Golf Club to come get me in the boat, and after the storm hit and churned up the water so bad, I hadn't gone back to the cottage for two days.

Pete, bless his seawater-logged heart, hadn't asked a thing, and I crashed on the harbormaster's couch at the marina.

When I'd finally returned, Olivia didn't say a word. She looked up from where she was kneeling on the floor with the contents of a box from the attic spread all around her—papers, books, old kids' toys.

I'd never been up in the attic. I was too afraid of finding more of Abby. It was hard enough having the vision of her at eighteen branded in my skull. The last thing I needed was to learn about her as an innocent child.

Olivia slowly catalogued me from head to toe in a way that left me feeling like I'd just slithered in under the door, then, humming quietly, shifted her attention back to her project.

I'd pulled out a chair, sat down, and watched her for a few minutes, refusing to let her assessment bother me. I knew what she was doing. Her words, her scowl, her clothes were all barbed armor she used to keep everyone away from her. That way they wouldn't be close enough to disappoint her.

Her dark hair was tied away from her face, her blonde roots coming in, a tiny narrow white halo at her crown. From this angle her jawline reminded me so much of Abby, I wanted to reach out and run my finger along her cheek.

I struggled to form an idea of who this girl was. She was

young and confused, defensive and wary. She should be bright and beautiful and excited about life. Instead she was here, hiding. Running away from God knew what.

I shuddered as the possibilities crossed my mind, and I shut them down quickly.

The guilt I'd been carrying around for six years had nothing on what I was wading through with the broken product of my actions, or lack of actions, kneeling in front of me. And she *was* broken. I could tell by her wariness, her distrust, her attitude, her fear and anxiety. The way she hid her obvious beauty behind the flat, dull hair dye and black makeup. Thank God she'd stopped wearing all her black clothes at once.

Olivia Baines needed something and seemed unilaterally unaware of it. Her need was tangible and almost vampiric, like a vast, aching vacuum of loneliness that pulled me forward every time I was around her. It had from the first moment I saw her on the dock, before I even knew who she was. Comfort? Love? Parenting? My blood? Fuck, I didn't know. But I was the last person equipped to give it to her. She needed to be with family or something. But God, I didn't want to send her away. This was Abby's little sister.

As if she'd go anyway. And as far as I knew, her family wasn't worth shit. There was also no escaping my part in who she'd become.

She had as much right to be here as I did.

And so here we were.

Co-existing in this painful kind of hell.

On day five after arrival, when Olivia began going through the boxes all over again, I got the impression she was looking for something.

That night, I awoke to the sound of screaming. I leapt out of bed and stopped outside her door. My instinct was to go right in, but then I heard a soft whimper and the rattle of a pill bottle. Pausing, I took a breath, my heart hammering from reacting so swiftly. I knocked softly. "Are you okay?"

"I'm fine. Go away." Her tone was measured, with a wobble that told me she was moderating it carefully.

Clenching my fist to avoid reaching for the doorknob, I leaned my forehead against the door, letting the adrenalin ebb away. "Are you sure? Can I get you anything?"

"I'm fine. Good night."

"Night," I echoed, but didn't move. It was the most conversation we'd had in days, and it was through an inch of wood. What would Abby do if her little sister were having nightmares? Maybe if Abby were here, there wouldn't be any.

Olivia's pills wouldn't last forever. I wondered whether they were just for anxiety.

Minutes ticked by.

Suddenly the door creaked open in the darkness and Olivia gasped upon seeing me, hand to her white T-shirt clad chest. Light from the cracked door of the bathroom illuminated her small frame in the long shirt, her legs bare. Despite her shocked expression, exhaustion was etched into her features, like she'd been fighting all night.

I stepped back, unfolding from where I'd been hunched forward, hand braced on the door frame. "Sorry, I didn't mean to scare you."

Her eyes morphed from widened surprise to narrowed irritation, then slid down from my face. Too late, I realized I was standing there in the darkness, only in boxers.

She visibly swallowed, fear back on her face, her breath hitching.

I turned and headed back inside my room, closing the door firmly, and let out a long, slow breath. Having Olivia in the house wasn't like having another person around. It was like playing host to a whole horde of demons just waiting to let loose.

Marjoe placed the water disguised as vodka in front of me. I took a small sip and winced. "Why are you such a hard-ass, Marge?" I grumbled, but it was a half-hearted jab.

I was extremely fond of the woman who had basically been my bar-top therapist for the last five years. Marjoe, or Marge for short, had seen me at my happiest and at my worst. She'd seen me as a scared and haunted kid who was drinking underage and trying desperately to become an alcoholic, and as the quiet, reclusive, older and slightly wiser young man.

And as the one who was now drinking again in the middle of the day. "I need you to be sweet to me, offer me some down-home comfort," I added, for the benefit of Pete, who was next to me, watching the golf tournament down in Florida on the TV behind the bar. No reaction.

"Ah, Tommy, my beautiful boy. You let me know when you're ready to tell me what's got you picklin' the eggs while the sun is high. In the mean time, no more drinky for you."

"Oh Marge. Let me stay and drink," I whined, winking. "I'll tell you all about it. You can comfort me against your ample bosom." I earned a glance and a raised eyebrow from Pete.

Marjoe let out a booming cackle. "As much as I'd love you to drink me young and pretty, it would only end in tears. I'm far too much woman for you, Thomas. You'd never survive me."

"C'mon. Pete wouldn't have to know." I grinned and placed my arms on the bar, inhaling a deep whiff of hush-puppies and French fries as the door to the kitchen swung open. I attempted to lean forward and give her a good smoldering furrowed brow. It was our standard banter and helped divert her from questions about what was on my mind today.

"I'm sure *I* could handle you, honey," Pete cut in, winking at Marjoe. "You wanna give me a whirl? You'll be wonderin' *Pete who* by mornin'."

Pete's loud guffaw at his own joke almost drowned out the sound of the wooden door to outside screeching open. But it let in a white slice of winter light, and I glanced to my left. The silhouette of a woman came in, along with a cool gust of fresh, salty marsh air. She had slim and smooth bare legs. It was too cold to show that much skin. My eyes recovered from the light assault she'd brought in, and I was left staring at Olivia, her ugly dyed black hair pulled away from the porcelain skin of her face that held those accusing and cold pale blue eyes. Eyes that had probably seen far too much for their age.

My brief good mood popped and fizzled.

The door closed behind her and she stood, shifting slightly from foot to foot, looking around. It would take a moment for her eyes to adjust to the interior. I was not ready for this—for questions from the people I'd come to know here on this island. I had a fast decision to make. Pete and Olivia would recognize each other. But as of right now, Pete didn't know anything about how we were linked.

The exact moment I decided to get the hell out of there was the same moment she caught sight of me. Her eyes widened in recognition and I looked away, scraping back my stool. "I gotta hit the head," I said to Marjoe and slapped

Pete on the shoulder. I hoped my dismissal and lack of acknowledgment would let Olivia know I didn't want to be bothered.

Winding my way through the sparsely occupied restaurant, it was hard to miss Tyler Graham sitting at a back table staring at Olivia's legs. I hadn't even known he was in here.

I stopped. "Hey, man," I said in an effort to draw his gaze away. "I didn't see you there." I was never this civil to Tyler, or friendly at all for that matter. About my age, he was a douche of epic proportions. He thought of himself as insanely attractive to women, half of whom couldn't see the flicker of crazy in his eyes. I glanced back at Olivia, seeing her shift her confused eyes from me to Tyler. *Shit.*

Tyler slid his gaze away from Olivia, but not before winking lazily, then looked at me. "You know her?" he asked, motioning his chin back toward her and flicking a long black lock of hair from his forehead.

Hmmm. A conversation with Tyler. How did that go? "Not well," I hedged, trying hard not to look back at her. "And she's too young for you. So what are you doing here? Shouldn't you be over on Hilton Head Island selling pot to the school kids?"

Tyler's father had a plantation here on Daufuskie Island, ostensibly growing organic vegetables to sell to the resort kitchens. But I knew for a fact that a large part of their crop was weed, and probably a few more serious things.

Tyler grinned, unfazed by my public mention of his less than savory business practices. "Taking a day off. And those high-school girls don't think they're too young for me." He licked his lips.

Douche, cornhole, asswipe, dickhead. I came up with as many synonyms as I could to avoid reacting.

He went on, "Still hopin' to do some business with you and Pete. You know I'd make it worth your while." Savannah had the customers, he had the supply. All he was missing was a reliable boat, with legitimate business, to get it over there.

"Well. Keep hoping," I said, dismissing him and heading into the men's bathroom. God, he was a prick. But he was also desperate to break into the Savannah market. And in my experience, desperate men did unforgivable things. That made Tyler Graham dangerous to me. And as I looked briefly back at Olivia saying something to Pete, I realized it made Tyler dangerous to her too.

I exited the bathroom and saw that Tyler had relocated and was now leaning against the bar chatting up Olivia. Shit. And that wasn't the surprising part. I could have seen that one coming. The surprising part was watching the unrecognizable and confident woman smile and laugh, tuck her dark hair behind her ear and look up under half-lidded eyes. Olivia was in full-force flirt. I'd never seen a transformation like it. *Jesus Christ.*

I swallowed hard and headed over to them.

And then, *goddammit*, she reached out and ran a hand down Tyler's arm. If I told her we needed to leave, I'd give everyone the idea we were more than acquainted in one fell swoop. Opinions would be made, questions asked, and judgments cast. And Tyler would double his interest.

I walked up and slapped a hand down hard on the bar at my spot, making everyone jump. "Sorry," I said, unapologetically.

"Let's go sit somewhere we can talk," Tyler murmured to Olivia.

I grit my teeth and looked over to her.

Olivia cast her pale eyes over me, then shrugged and smiled back at Tyler. "Sure."

I waited until they were out of earshot, focusing on relaxing my tense shoulders. "I need help," I said quietly to Pete and Marjoe. "Keeping her away from Tyler."

"That boy's trouble all right, but why your interest?" Marge asked, never one to beat around the bush.

"I know—" My throat seized up.

I'd only told Pete and Marjoe about Abby and my situation with the house once, many years ago, and we'd never spoken of it again.

Marjoe laid a hand over mine.

I cleared my throat and started again, my face hot and my chest tight. "That's Abby's sister, Olivia." *Livvy* she called her. I closed my eyes at the memory.

Pete started in surprise and glanced over his shoulder. "Did you recognize her on the boat, son? Why didn't you say somethin'?"

"I didn't recognize her. Well, not at first. God, she was only eleven or twelve or something when I last saw her. I think. And her hair color . . . well, I was in total shock, and I didn't know what to say . . ." It was her eyes that I'd never forgotten.

Marge squeezed my hand briefly then let go before I became uncomfortable. "Pete told me she seems a bit lost. She's staying with you, then." It wasn't a question. "Does she know who you are?" Marjoe's brow pinched together.

I shook my head. "I thought she did, but no . . . I think she thinks I'm a caretaker for the cottage."

Pete raised his eyebrows.

"I know," I said. "I'll tell her."

CHAPTER SEVEN

$\mathcal{I}$ endured twenty-five more excruciating minutes at the bar, straining to hear over the music, the clink of restaurant activities, and the low lunchtime conversations for any clue as to what Olivia and Tyler were chatting about.

Eventually I couldn't take it anymore. Marjoe agreed to get Olivia to go outside while I went to the john again, then I would meet them there. I passed their table in time to see Olivia finishing off Tyler's pint.

After zipping my fly and washing my hands, I ran my wet fingers through my hair by habit. Stopping midway, I grabbed two fistfuls and looked up, staring myself straight in the eyes. They were bloodshot from lack of sleep and my early morning, and also glossy from my boozy lunch. And Marjoe was right—I stank like a fishery. Running my hand over my facial hair, I realized I'd kind of forgotten what I looked like under there. I hadn't shaved clean in almost six years.

I needed to come clean with Olivia and tell her everything. The extreme scenario was she left. *Good, right?* Not good. But why? And why had she come here? That's what I needed to focus on.

Every day she was here, I noticed her relaxing incrementally more. She no longer hugged her arms around herself
so defensively. But she still cried out at night. I needed to
do for Olivia what I'd failed to do for Abby. Be there for
her, keep her safe, get her back on track if she'd dropped
out of school, see if I could help her avoid the Tyler Grahams
of this world who preyed on human weakness. I needed to
be her father-figure or her older brother.

I headed outside.

Marge and Olivia were chatting in the cool afternoon sun,
trailing off as I approached.

"Let's go," I said to Olivia, harsher than I intended to,
and hopped in my golf cart that she'd driven here.

She scowled at me and turned back toward the restaurant.
Marge stepped in front of her. "Sorry, honey. You're too
young to be drinking in my bar."

Olivia swung back to face me. "Are you kidding me?" I
could tell she knew full well that if that had been the reason,
Marge would have stopped her when she first started drinking
Tyler's beer. No, she knew a set-up when she saw one.

"Nope. No joke. You're leaving. Now." I reached forward
and took her arm.

She jerked away with a hiss. "Don't fucking touch me."

"Get in the *fucking* cart," I growled, mimicking her exple-
tive. Why was I handling this so badly?

Marge looked from one to the other of us, her brow furrowed.

A gull screeched overhead, and a cold gust of wind rustled
through the trees at the water's edge. Olivia shuddered in
the cold and then sighed. "Fine. I'm freezing anyway." She
stalked past me and hopped into the passenger side of the
cart, staring straight ahead.

I let my shoulders down from where they'd been bunched up and smiled thinly at Marjoe. "Thanks. See you later."

Marjoe nodded and headed inside.

I started the cart, and we pulled off, crunching over the pine needles and crushed shells.

Olivia crossed her arms over her chest.

In a perverse moment, I swerved to avoid a small rock so she had to unwrap her arms and hold on to the side of the cart.

She glared at me, and I pressed my lips together.

"I don't understand you," she tossed out, looking away. "You hardly say a word to me but don't want me talking to anyone else?"

That's not what this was about. At all. "You don't need to be talking to Tyler Graham."

"Why? You can't tell me not to see him."

I clenched my jaw. Only when I saw her staring at my hands on the wheel did I realize my knuckles were white. I consciously tried to relax and breathe deep.

"You planning on seeing him again?"

"And? If I was?"

"I would object." Vehemently.

"In vain."

"He's a drug dealer, and a fucking oxygen thief," I snapped.

She laughed, unexpectedly. "What the hell is an oxygen thief?"

I looked sideways to see her raised eyebrows, then went back to watching the road ahead. "Some parasite who breathes valuable oxygen on this earth, oxygen that could be better used by someone of more worth. An animal has more worth," I added.

"You say that like animals are less than people. In my

experience, animals are usually worth more." She turned her head toward the trees and vegetation lining the road that cut across the interior of the island.

It was really cold in the shade, especially with the air whipping by us. The normally smooth skin on her pale bare legs was covered in raised goose bumps, the skin getting mottled. But I wasn't looking.

"Did it occur to you the reason I wanted to speak to Tyler was *because* he's a dealer?" she asked quietly.

I swallowed. "You want to start getting high now in addition to all the other shit you've got going on?"

"The other shit I've got going on?" she repeated. "You mean like the fact that I need *prescriptions* to deal with my shit. And those prescriptions are running out? Did you ever wonder what the hell I'm going to do when they run out?"

"Of course I did. You wake me up almost every night."

Her sharp inhale made me feel bad for throwing it out there so casually. "Well if Tyler deals, then he can probably get access to what I need."

I stopped the cart, dumbfounded. "The street value of that shit you're taking must be astro-fucking-nominal. How the hell would you even pay him?"

She folded her arms back across her body, her jaw tight, back rigid.

I waited, fury and panic coiled inside me so tight I could barely breathe. Please God, no.

She looked away.

My breath left me in a rush, my chest caving in. "You mean you'd fuck him," I rasped, barely able to find my voice. Anguish and regret and too many emotions I couldn't process were squeezing my body so tight I thought my head would explode. A vein throbbed in my temple. I couldn't decide if

I wanted to roar, cry, vomit or let it happen all at the same time.

"I just do what I have to." But her voice was small.

My stomach heaved and bile crawled up my throat. "You just . . ." I couldn't even articulate it. Swallowing the acrid taste, I grabbed on to the one emotion that could help me steer through this. Anger. *Jesus Christ.*

"I don't have to sleep with them. There's other stuff I could do. I get to be in control of it."

Said like the young, naïve little girl she was. Was she fucking kidding me? *Them?* She'd done this before? And by *other stuff . . .*

Hell, no. "You'd put someone's filthy cock in your *mouth*, and you think that gives you *control*?" I asked, injecting as much disgust into my voice as possible. "Well, that just makes you fucking stupid."

She flinched. "It's the guys who are stupid. So fucking easy."

I don't know how, because I remembered nothing about the rest of the drive except the ice in my veins, but finally we pulled up in front of the cottage. The last thing I wanted to do was be in there with her. It would be like putting a pressurized canister in a hot oven. I wanted to shake her until her teeth rattled.

"If Abby weren't already dead," I ground out, knowing my next words were the cruelest thing I could come up with, "meeting the person you've become would kill her."

Launching myself out of the cart, I went to the side of the house, wanting to hit the shit out of something. I paced, my hands in my hair, my insides raging. There were too many things to process. Vaguely, the sound of the front door told me Olivia had gone inside.

Oh God, Abby.

Abby, I'm so sorry.

We already had a shit ton of wood for the fireplace, and winter would be fading soon, but I headed for the ax. Heaving it out of the stump where I'd buried it, I set it aside and, groaning, hefted a huge log off the adjacent pile into position. *I should have stayed afterward, Abby.*

I grabbed the wooden shaft and adjusted my grip under its weight. Swinging the ax up and letting my arms loosen, I let go on the downward swing with a grunt, my teeth clenched, basking in the satisfying sharp crack and splitting of the wood. *I should have stayed and made sure Liv was okay. I'm sorry.* I hauled the heavy ax up again.

God, Abby. I'm so sorry.

Thwack. A new log.

I should have stayed there and made sure.

Made sure she was safe.

Thwack.

I shouldn't have even made you go back.

More wood. Thwack.

I hauled my thick heavy shirt and undershirt off as sweat formed. The wind was ice on my damp skin.

Another log. Crack.

I'm sorry, Abby.

God, I'm so sorry.

The wood blurred in front of me, the icy feeling from the wind on my body now stinging my eyes too, and I realized I was crying. Wiping my arm across my face, I blinked and tossed the ax down. My chest heaved. God, I couldn't stop it: the anguish came up in a tidal surge. I grimaced and choked with the force of it, trying to hold back the sob. It came through with a broken howl, and the relief of letting it go weakened my knees. I sank to the grass, wrapping my arms around my middle.

I grieved for Abby and I grieved for Olivia. I sobbed and I drowned in the crashing tsunami of guilt until all my breath was gone. My body was left with racking spasms and shuddering breaths. And there was nothing left inside me but the one question that burned constantly. The question I buried over and over, never asking, never dealing with . . . until Olivia came here and forced me to face my cowardice. There was nothing left to bury it with. I would have to ask her.

Had Mike Williams, Abby's uncle, raped Olivia like he had Abby?

CHAPTER EIGHT

I'm not sure how long I sat on the grass in the biting wind, the wood chopping forgotten, but when I opened my eyes, Olivia was in front of me.

She'd pulled on jeans and wrapped herself up in a large gray sweater and was knee to knee with me on the grass. She held out my stinking shirt.

The questions were swimming in her pale blue eyes, but I didn't see what I'd expected. Knowing that she'd witnessed my epic meltdown, I'd anticipated pity or even uncomfortable embarrassment along with her curiosity.

"You'll get sick," she said, her voice strangely hoarse. "Put this back on."

I nodded and took it, shrugging the fabric over my head.

She looked over to the trash can at the side of the house. "Are you an alcoholic?"

My chest released and I laughed in a short burst. It felt odd after the class-five emotional rapids I'd just run. She wasn't going to ask me what the last twenty minutes were about, but she'd ask me if I was an alcoholic?

"No. I keep those there to remind me it's not an option."

"So you *were* one?"

"No. Once an alcoholic, always an alcoholic, even when you're sober. I tried, trust me. But it didn't stick. It would, though, if I tried hard enough. I never want to get that far."

"Why?"

"Because after trying for a long time to forget the things I wanted to forget, I suddenly got scared I'd never be able to remember."

Her brows pinched together as she contemplated my words. "I wish . . . I wish I could forget everything," she murmured. "I wish it every day. The only thing I want to remember is Abby, but when I do, it comes with everything else."

Everything else.

The words screamed in my head.

Her eyes cast about and landed on the swing that hung from the oak branch. The wind picked up and slapped her escaped hair like evil black whips across her cheekbones. God, she was beautiful. Or would be one day.

My question, *the* question, burned like acid in my throat, and I swallowed it, forcing it back down into my guilt.

"You were drinking today," she stated.

"Yeah, I was."

"It's the anniversary today. Of her death."

I schooled my features and nodded simply.

"It's also my birthday." *Shit.* What a memory to have of a birthday. I'd ruined those for her too.

She looked back at me, one eyebrow cocked. "You basically called me a whore on my birthday."

Because you basically told me you were. "Happy birthday. Eighteen?"

"Yeah. And it's not being a whore if you're dating them."

"That's debatable. And you seem smarter than that."

She sighed. "Look. I don't expect you to understand. In fact it would be better if you kept your judgy opinions to yourself, but in the interest of *facts,* I don't 'date' anyone I'm not attracted to."

"*Judgy?*" I snorted. "I never thought I would be one to judge, but you're right. I feel weirdly protective of you because you're Abby's little sister."

Olivia blinked, then looked away.

"You find Tyler Graham attractive?" I asked.

"He has the bad boy thing going on." She shrugged. "I'm sure I'm not the first girl to find that hot."

I barked out a humorless laugh. "You have that right." I saw her flinch and cushioned the blow. "At least you're self-aware enough to know it."

"Why are you such a dick?"

"Are you kidding me?"

"Yeah. You act like you give a shit, or *think* you give a shit because of Abby or whatever, but honestly? You don't know the first thing about me or where I've been and what my life has been like. The shit that's happened."

"I know you ran away. From what, I *don't* know." I prayed I didn't know. "I *do* know I'd like to help you. I don't have an idea how, but I will if I can." The sincerity in my voice surprised even me. I didn't know where the offer came from, but I meant every word of it. "I *do* give a shit." If there was some way I could make amends for letting Olivia—*Livvy*—become like this, I'd do it.

She snorted and looked away from me.

"I mean it, Olivia. I know you don't know me and have even less reason to trust me—"

"So you see me as something broken that needs to be fixed. Maybe you think I'll bring you closer to Abby. I won't.

You're bored out here all alone on your island, and you need a project." She got up, her eyes going cold and hard. "Excuse me, but I don't feel like being one."

"You're right. I do need a project." I climbed to my feet too, bringing the ax up with me and burying it back in the stump. "I need a project, not to bring Abby back, or fix you, but because I need to try and fix *me*."

OLIVIA

OLIVIA

CHAPTER NINE

A few days after arriving on the island, the day after Tom returned the first time, I had gone by the golf club to see about a job. I'd been eating Tom's food and had no way to repay him.

I couldn't believe I'd thought I would be able to survive here on my own. Even with the small general store, most people took a ferry across to Hilton Head Island or Savannah to buy stuff. I'm not sure how I'd blocked that old memory.

The golf club had been a bust. Especially since it was off-season. I thought about the two island restaurants and tried the one that had the general store attached, with no luck. I didn't even bother with the other, knowing already what the answer was. I'd have more luck in a few months, closer to summer, as tourism picked up.

Tom had said early on it was no big deal, and I could eat what I wanted. He looked at me like I was crazy when I'd mentioned it. "You think I'd starve you? You eat like a bird anyway. It's no big deal." I'd thanked him. But I hated feeling more and more like a guest in the house that was supposed

to be mine. And at times I felt like a charity case. Or worse—
like he was my parent.

So almost two weeks after I arrived, I'd decided to give
it one last shot and headed over to the last option for a job
on the island, the restaurant I hadn't tried. Mama's. And
that's where I'd found Tom.

And where we'd had the golf cart ride from hell.

After we'd arrived back to the cottage from our mini
showdown in front of Marjoe, and he'd effectively made me
feel like less than shit, I'd gone inside, heaving out angry
breaths, my teeth clenched.

He made me feel like such a stupid little girl. He had no
idea what it was like for me. None. I wanted to yell at him
and slap him, but more than anything, I wanted him not to
disapprove of me, and I couldn't understand why. I'd never
cared what anyone thought of me before. In fact, I'd gone
out of my way to inspire less than comfortable thoughts in
people. It was the way I operated. It was the way I'd survived
the last few years in high school.

I realized with a start that I'd begun feeling comforted by
his presence. We were building some form of quiet friendship. And the thought that he was disgusted by me caused
shame to burn through my gut. But with that came anger.
How dare he make me feel this way? Who was he to pass
judgment on me? And pulling out what Abby would think
had been such a low blow.

I was pacing back and forth, coming up with the words
I would hurl at him to get even, when I'd caught sight of
him through the small kitchen window and stopped dead.

Tom was ripping his shirt off over his head. He flung it
angrily, his bare chest heaving. Jesus, he was ripped. Picking
the ax back up, ribs arching, he swung it over his head,

bringing it down with such force that every muscle and sinew bulged and flexed with the power of it.

I sucked in air, realizing I'd been holding my breath. Emotion rolled off him, the air electrified. Wind I couldn't feel tossed his hair. It was raw and almost painful to watch. He was part wild animal and part insanely beautiful human.

His body was a blur of motion, and he seemed oblivious to the icy air. A strong working body. A man's body, not a boy's. So much man. No muscle unused.

I'd been living with this huge, larger-than-life, virile male for almost two weeks.

Old fears skittered down my spine.

And then his chest wasn't just heaving with breath, his whole body was shuddering and curling in on itself. His knees folded, hitting the ground so hard, I winced. His arms wrapped around his middle as if he was trying to hold his body together. It was at once both shockingly strange and also familiar. I knew the kind of feeling that made one's body do that.

Pain.

The kind of pain that threatened to tear your soul in two.

Instantly, I was uncomfortable, like I'd seen something I shouldn't have. I couldn't move. I couldn't think, and yet I wanted to know everything all at once. My eyes wanted to drop, and at the same time I couldn't tear them off him.

I finally turned away, telling myself to take deep breaths. The clock to my right ticked loudly as I stood gripping the counter top, contemplating what to do.

Looking down and seeing my chilled flesh, I mechanically went to my room and changed into jeans. Wrapping my dark gray oversized cardigan around me, I headed outside with the idea that if nothing else, I could encourage him to get warm. It was too cold to be outside bare-chested.

He was oblivious to me as I knelt in front of him and picked up his fishy-smelling shirt from the ground, pulling the sleeves right side out. Eventually he looked up, his eyes clearing. Beautiful and bleak caramel-colored eyes with flecks of emerald, swimming in bloodshot pink.

I desperately wanted to ask him about Abby. How did people love that intensely, in a way that never died, even after six years? Because surely that was what his meltdown was about. I couldn't imagine loving someone like that—if it was even possible and not some fantasy conjured up by authors, poets, and screenwriters, each word building on and perpetuating the lie.

And did he know about Whit? That she'd been with another guy when she died? Were she and Tom having a long-distance relationship, or was it one-sided on his part. The idea that he was in the grip of some unrequited and long-lost love should make him seem pathetic and deluded.

But nothing about Tom was pathetic. The very opposite. His quiet strength had somehow managed to creep under my guard over the last two weeks.

And I didn't want to be a silly child he had to look after.

I headed back to Mama's first thing the next morning. Marjoe was hard to win around. "I can't afford any additional help off season," she'd explained gruffly as I trailed her outside so she could have a smoke.

"Please, Marjoe."

"But this'll give me a chance to sort out the store room and my office. Been putting it off forever."

Finally she agreed to give me two lunchtime shifts but no serving of alcohol under any circumstances.

"Yes!" I pumped my fist in the air.

She humphed and took a long drag on a slim cigarette, her lips pleating around the end. "'Sides, I'd do just about anything for that boy."

"Thank you, Marjoe." I surprised us both by giving her a brief hug. Clearing my throat, I stepped away. "So which days do you want me?"

"Let's do weekdays, say Tuesday and Wednesday, and I'll move you toward the weekend as you learn the ropes and as it gets busier closer to summer. You gonna be here that long, right?"

I hadn't thought very far ahead, but I couldn't foresee leaving. To go where? I nodded.

The next day was Wednesday, so I had my first day of work.

Everyone was really friendly, and after Marjoe introduced me as a "family friend" of Tommy's, no one even asked too much about me. There was another waitress called Bethany, who was very sweet but wore way too much perfume, and a huge, tall, dark-skinned man aptly named Big Jake who was the main cook. He had a deep rumbling voice, and a little girl's laugh so incongruous and infectious it made everyone smile. And he laughed about everything. There were two other younger guys who helped him out, prepped, bussed tables, and basically did whatever needed to be done. One, who never said a word, was apparently his son, Jake Junior, or JJ, and the other, his nephew, Ray.

"You be ol' Miz Williams' gran'babe?" Big Jake asked me on my second day.

Surprised he'd put it together, I nodded.

"She dun' lef' you any her struc'shuns for buckruhbittle?"

"Uh . . ." *What?* I looked around helplessly.

He whooped his high-pitched laugh. "Buckruhbittle be the

Gullah word fer white man's food. I jus' be messin witch ya. But she be makin' cakes. 'Mazin' cakes. Our customers be missin' her cakes."

"And you, Big Jake," came Marjoe's sandpaper voice from behind me as she bustled into the kitchen. "You gone lost forty pounds since Mrs. Williams passed."

Jake let out another laugh and nodded his agreement, then started humming as he went about his work.

I shook my head, a bemused smile on my face. This lot was an odd crew. I actually had found my grandmother's hand-written recipe book but hadn't even opened it. I'd never baked a thing in my life.

"Oh, Thomas is out there asking for you," said Marjoe, nodding to the door.

My stomach dipped.

I spun on my heel and headed out of the fluorescent light of the kitchen and into the dim restaurant area. Tom was sitting by himself near the platform apparently used as a stage when they had live music during the busier months. Seeing him made my pulse skitter with nerves.

He was already looking at me as if he'd been waiting for me to come through the door, his leg bouncing rapidly. Wearing his worn jeans and a soft faded flannel shirt that molded to his muscled frame, he sat up when he saw me and gave a small smile. I think. His hair was wildly mussed, I assumed from the wind outside.

I immediately smiled back at him without thinking, and then felt self-conscious about it, although I didn't know why, and dropped it. Tucking my hair behind my ear, I stopped in front of him. "Hi."

"How's it going?" His voice pitched low. "Marge working you to the bone?"

"Hardly," I murmured, casting my eyes around the mostly empty interior. "You checking to make sure I'm not hanging with Tyler?" The second the words left my mouth I regretted them. Tom's eyes shifted, and I realized how warm they'd been before.

Something uncomfortable squeezed inside me, and I folded my arms. When he didn't say anything, simply watched me with those leonine eyes of his, I asked, "Can I get you anything?"

He shook his head slowly. "I just came to ask you the same thing, actually. I'm heading over to Savannah, I'll be gone overnight. Will you be all right?"

He'd never asked me before, having disappeared without a word several times since my arrival. But over the last few days, small gestures—making me something to eat before I even knew I was hungry, pouring my coffee as soon as I entered the kitchen—all added up to someone who was taking care of me.

I hated the dread that immediately formed, knowing he wouldn't be in the house when I got home. "There are some things I need. Maybe I can go with you next time?" I was due for my period in the next few days, and while I'd brought tampons with me, I needed to stock up. The general store only had pads, and I hated pads.

"You can tell me, I'll get whatever it is."

My cheeks heated, and if I could have seen his face properly, I'd bet I'd have seen him blushing too as he realized I probably needed personal items. Instead, I saw his throat bob, his leg continuing that endless fast-paced rhythm. Well, if he wanted to be all parenty with me, this is what he'd get, right? "Bring me the receipt so I can pay you back," I started. "A box of tampons for medium flow, a box for heavy flow, and," I have no idea why I did it, but somehow I wanted to rattle him further, "a box of condoms in case I do decide to date Tyler."

His eyes betrayed nothing but his leg went still. Then he got up abruptly, chair scraping on the concrete in a sharp whine.

"Better safe than sorry," I added as he towered over me. What was wrong with me?

His nostrils flared, his eyes were flinty as he leaned down to my ear. "I'll be sure to find extra-small ones then, so they don't fall off him. That would be embarrassingly awkward," he growled.

My skin broke out in goose bumps, my hairs standing on end.

He turned and strode out, briefly blinding me with a slice of sunlight, and then leaving me in chilled darkness.

I headed back to the kitchen and finished out my shift.

When I stepped outside Mama's later, I had to take a deep, fortifying breath before beginning the journey back on foot through the heavily wooded interior of the island. The sky was clear blue above me, but it was winter in the shade and dark amongst the trees.

After walking forlornly home to the empty cottage, I ate a bag of carrots and a piece of chocolate and read a book of fairy tales, ending with "The Little Mermaid".

That night when I awoke screaming it was because Abby was sitting on my chest pressing down with all her might.

CHAPTER TEN

$\mathcal{I}$t was impossible to fall back asleep after waking up because your dead sister was trying to suffocate you.

And then, of course, my thoughts immediately went to the way I'd acted toward Tom, trying to goad him. Trying to piss him off. The memory caused a heavy brick to form in my gut. I thought back to his topaz eyes frosting over and the pulse ticking with tension in his temple. I'd been prodding at a sleeping lion. I was lucky he'd only growled.

By the time I peeled myself out of bed the next morning, I felt wretched, tired and annoyed at myself. With no job to go to that morning and every single inch of the cottage having been inspected for hidden secrets and memories, I decided to wrap up warm and go find the stray cat I'd seen outside Mama's when I was leaving. She was heavily pregnant, and I didn't know where she'd find somewhere warm to give birth. She had to be ready to have kittens within days, if not sooner. I couldn't imagine Marjoe being okay with letting her settle down in her storage room. It had to be violating all kinds of health codes. But I'd seen Big Jake leaving out a small bowl of water and some leftover shrimp, and I knew I'd have a sympathetic ear if I needed one.

It was windy again. I couldn't wait for some warmer weather, although, if memory served, I'd be dripping with sweat and desperate for winter in just a few months. The air conditioning at the cottage consisted of a living room fan, and a window unit in each bedroom. Goodness knows if they were still operational.

At least the morning sun was trying to stream through the trees and foliage. That gave me hope spring was around the corner. When I stepped out of the trees to the waterside vista ahead of me, I had to pause and appreciate the view.

Far in the distance, over the marshes and open water, I could see the smoke stack of a Savannah factory along what were probably the banks of the Savannah River. The Intracoastal Waterway was still gray and churning, the marsh grasses brown and ready for new spring growth. I wondered if the tides would wash away all the old stuff when it was time, and where it would end up.

Only Big Jake was there when I arrived at Mama's. Marjoe had told me she was headed over to the beer distributor in Beaufort his morning. Jake was carrying three large red plastic stackable glass racks.

"Mornin', Miz Baines."

"Hey, Big Jake. Please, call me Liv."

He nodded, once. "You be workin' today, Miz Liv?"

I trotted forward to hold the back door to the kitchen open, and then wedged in the cement block that was there for the purpose.

"Nah." I looked around. "You seen that cat?"

"She done ready to have her babes." He dropped his load on a stainless-steel trolley cart and headed back toward me.

"I know. I was worried she didn't have a spot, you know? And it's been cold."

Big Jake stepped out. "You don' mind me sayin', but yous look like you been up makin' fine with the devil hisself."

Well, I knew I looked tired, but I didn't realize it was that obvious to someone I barely knew. I thought of my sleepless night, and the fact that Abby was basically haunting me. "Not the devil, but my sister," I said truthfully, expecting Jake to take it to mean I'd been up partying.

He paused halfway toward the storage shed for his next trip and turned. "Yo' dead sista?"

Shocked that he knew, I nodded.

"You done got you a boo hag?" he asked incredulously, shaking his head. His dark brown eyes were large; the creases from years of laughter were now smoothed out and serious.

"A . . . what?" I asked with half a laugh.

He touched two fingers to his lips, then his chest, and aimed his face to the sky through the canopy of live oaks and pines, his long lashes resting on his cheeks as he closed his eyes.

"Big Jake?"

"A boo hag," he whispered, and then glanced around into the trees. Almost as if he was scared of uttering the word.

A chill went down my spine.

"A boo hag," I repeated, just to make sure I got it right. "As in *boo, I scared you*, and *hag*—an ugly old witch?"

He nodded gravely. "Yes'm. A boo hag be a spirit who don' want ta go. They be tricky, makin' all kinds o' fuss."

I smiled. "Big Jake, my sister was anything but a hag, I promise. Anyway, I know it's all in my head. I've had trouble sleeping for years. This is nothing new."

Well, I corrected myself, seeing her was definitely new.

But it was all still in my head, not that that was more comforting.

"I know. I done met yo' sista." He stepped up close, eyes wide. "But lemme ax ya, she be stealin' yo' breath?"

Surprise lodged in my throat.

Even as I was attempting to form an answer, Big Jake nodded, his forehead creased. "Yep," he murmured, more to himself than me.

"What on earth are you talking about?" I folded my arms, finally finding my voice.

He shrugged and went back toward the shed, his hand flicking out in a casual gesture. "Always happen in these parts. Too many spirits roun' here, don't none get no peace."

"Well, thanks a lot," I huffed, staring at his broad back as he disappeared inside the shed. Now I had real live ghosts to get creeped out about. As if panic attacks and my overactive imagination weren't enough.

"But what do you mean? How did you kn . . . I mean, what makes you ask about me losing my breath?"

"'Cuz that's what they do." His voice emanated out the shaded interior as he hefted boxes around. "They done sit on ya, ride, do whatever they hafta. Legen' says the bad ones will even steal yo' skin."

"What? Steal my . . ." I shook my head. "Whatever, Big Jake, now you're bullshitting me."

"Whoo!" Big Jake's voice went up to his falsetto as he laughed. "Come, look see here." His request was followed by a string of unintelligible cooing and clucking.

I spurred forward. It had to be the cat. As I entered the shaded interior of the shed, my eyes took a moment to adjust.

Big Jake was crouched over a spot in the corner where

the cat lay on a pink towel, tiny bundles of fur all blindly wobbling and falling over each other.

"Did you put the towel out for her?" I asked quietly.

He shook his head. "JJ done it. He be helping out Miz Laura, what have the cat land down near Haig Point."

"Cat land?"

"She be rescuin' cats all over. But JJ, he want one o' these here kitties so he din' bring her Miz Geechee. I 'spect he'll do it in a few weeks. After they been weaned."

Miss Geechee was clearly the momma cat's name.

"Do you think he'd mind if I had one too?" I hadn't given a thought to taking on one of the kittens, but somehow it felt right.

Big Jake gave a nod. "Course." And we turned back to watching Miz Geechee.

The cat blinked sleepily, then stretched her calico neck forward to lick one of her babies, a small white and brown kitten that had been left out of the liberal doses of black splotches the other ones had. Except . . . I peered closer and saw a small heart-shaped black smudge above its wet pink nose.

"So, if I get a choice, will you tell JJ I want that one?"

"Sure 'nuf," Big Jake said and shifted back. "I best git her some water."

I followed him out into the bright sun that finally topped the leafy trees and hit the clearing. It was odd that there were so many leaves in winter. I guess they didn't really get fall in this part of the country. "So, Jake, I'm not sure I believe the boo hag thing. But if one was to have a . . . boo hag problem . . ." I cringed internally. "If there was one. What does one do, exactly? I mean, can you make them go away?" Not that I wanted Abby to go away. If she was even around. *God.* I was sounding nuttier by the minute.

"Well now, you could keep the broom by yo' bed, or—"

"What on earth can a broom do?" I laughed lightly.

"Well, she gon' be distracted, see?"

I shook my head slowly. I really didn't see.

"The straws. She get busy countin' the straws and leave you to yo' sleepin'."

Okay, Big Jake was certifiably nuts, and I couldn't believe I had even indulged in the conversation.

"Or put burned matches in yo' hair. They done hate the smell."

"Okay, Jake. Thanks for the advice."

"Or salt 'em," he added.

"Salt them? Oh, never mind. Hey, I gotta go. Don't forget to tell JJ about the kitten." I smiled and waved, walking backwards.

"Will do."

I told myself it was all silly Gullah superstition, but the walk back through the trees with all the rustling of unseen creatures through the underbrush was creepy as hell. Even in the middle of the day.

A boo hag. Seriously? Then again, this part of the world was known for its spirits and legends. There were slave burial grounds all over the place, especially near the water so their souls could swim back to Africa.

After a short walk on the beach to kill more time, I headed back to the cottage.

The swing that hung from the branch of the live oak by the cottage called my name as I approached. The branch, twenty feet or more above the ground, was sturdy. The ropes were tied about two feet apart, half a foot wider than the mossy, aged wooden plank they held.

I paused a moment, hand on the coarse rope, and tried

in vain to remember the last time I'd swung. All I could think of was the picture inside of Abby and me on the swing, without any recollection of actually being in the moment the camera captured.

I wasn't ready to sit on it yet, so I headed inside.

There was no sign of Tom, but sitting on the kitchen table were two boxes of tampons and a box of condoms. Heart thudding, I picked up the tampons and then, after a pause, the box of condoms, turning them over in my hand. A twelve-pack of lubricated condoms for maximum pleasure. Hearing a sound behind me, I dropped them like a hot coal and realized my heart had pumped all my blood to my cheeks.

I swung around to confirm that Tom was indeed standing behind me, hands shoved halfway into the front pockets of his jeans, hard shoulders hunched and tensed under the heather gray of his thin T-shirt. His chin-length hair swung forward on one side. His beard was shorter, clipped closer, so I had a better impression of his face. His lips. Eyes that dropped to the two boxes in my hands.

"Thank you," I croaked and cleared my throat before hurrying past him. My arm accidentally brushed the bare skin of his, causing him to flinch away as I angled for the hall.

When I left my room later, after hearing the front door slam and the cart start up, the box of condoms was still there.

They sat there all afternoon and into the evening. I wasn't going to touch them.

A simple black and purple box that held the potential for choices, pleasure, decisions, messy feelings, and regrets. I didn't want that box. It seemed Tom didn't either. And so no one touched it.

Our conversation over the next few days consisted of "Good morning," "Good night," "I'm making spaghetti, would you like some?" "Can I turn the coffee off?" And those were the highlights.

And every day the damn box grew bigger until it seemed the only thing I saw. Why the hell didn't he take them away? Clearly, at this point he must have realized I didn't want them and had simply been trying to irritate him by asking.

He would disappear some evenings but come back late after I was already in bed. I started to stay up by the fire reading, seeing if I could outlast him. Unfortunately, I usually fell asleep on the couch when I did that.

One night, I woke up from a particularly odd dream and was tiredly heading to my room just as he came home. He stopped when he saw me, then immediately his eyes darted to the right in the direction of the table and the box that still sat there. As if he couldn't help it. Just like I couldn't.

It irritated me beyond comprehension.

Then he frowned and stalked past me down the hall to the bathroom, where he flicked on the light and shut the door.

"Well hello to you too," I muttered. The displaced air from his abrupt move wafted the scent of him over me, bringing with it the faint hint of liquor and a woman's perfume. Something light and floral that made me faintly nauseous.

Jeez, how all over someone did you have to be to be wearing her scent so strongly that you polluted the air wherever you went?

I walked up to the bathroom door and pounded on it. "You seem like you could use them more than me. Take that damn box away. I'm tired of looking at it."

The door flung open and Tom stood there shirtless, jeans slung low, toothbrush in hand. Dammit. The man should be gracing magazines and Tumblr accounts.

I held my breath without meaning to.

His eyes narrowed. They were glassy, and I wondered just how buzzed he was. I fought to keep looking at them and not stray down his naked torso.

"Th-the condoms," I managed.

"What about them?"

"You should have them. I don't want them."

His eyes dropped to my mouth and lingered. "Okay."

I swallowed, taking a step back. "Okay."

Back in my room I leaned against the door, belly swirling.

My gaze landed on the broom I'd taken to keeping nearby. Shaking my head, I picked it up and laid it at the foot of the bed before crawling between the sheets. I fell asleep listening to him shower, and then later the sound of him typing. My last thought was that I couldn't wait for his next trip away so I could sneak into his room and see what he was writing.

$\mathcal{J}$ looked forward to my work days and went above and beyond everything that was asked of me. I desperately hoped Marjoe would give me more hours.

Miz Geechee was up and about, stalking Big Jake for food, before scurrying back to pick up her rambunctious kittens who were now boldly trying to escape and explore their surroundings. It was a familiar sight to see her trotting across the sandy clearing back toward the shed, a small furry body dangling from her mouth. I checked regularly that my little guy was still there.

The chilly weather dragged on. Every day that felt a bit warmer and closer to spring would be stamped out by an arctic breeze the following day until it felt as though we would only make it there in fits and starts and by a strong will of the mind.

I got to know a few more of the island residents. They were an interesting cast of characters made up of retirees, artists, writers, and the odd fishermen who stopped in. I learned at one time there'd been a thriving oyster business on Daufuskie Island, but the arrival of a paper factory on the Savannah River had poisoned the water, and within a matter of days the industry had folded. Now the only local oysters were harvested further north on the May River. Which was apparently more of a tidal estuary supplemented by a few small creeks than a river. What a difference a mile could make.

Tyler came in each day I was working. My meds were dwindling, and I agonized over whether to ask him if he could get me some.

Back in Atlanta, it had been an easy choice. I knew I was going to leave and needed to stock up beyond what my doctor had written out for me. Call me motivated, but I'd engaged in some activities I'd rather forget.

I knew a guy from school, Jamie Riggs. He was on the football team, played center, and had a girlfriend in my social studies class, Lindsay Kearns, with light brown hair and plump lips. They were a good-looking couple, but I was sure all the guys on his team could only think of blowjobs when they looked at her. It didn't stop him asking me for one too, though. He drove a gray pickup with dark-tinted windows, and rumor had it he was the go-to guy for people who needed help. Steroids for training, Ritalin during midterms, whatever. He rarely dealt in weed. When I slipped him a note asking him to meet me behind the Brookhaven McDonald's, I didn't have one ounce of concern he'd show up. He looked at me the way most of the guys at school did, with disdain that barely concealed the lust, and I wasn't exactly revolted by him.

The McDonald's was close to my house, so I could walk. It was the start of a beautiful friendship that included a lot of compliments like "You're sexy as fuck" and "I won't tell anyone, just keep doing that." And best of all, "No one needs to know." It was revolting, but it was the only way I could stock up on my medication. And at the time part of me enjoyed seeing him weak; it made me feel strong. Was that really so bad?

Now, I was starting to weigh cost. As Tyler and I became better acquainted, and I knew he was days away, or less, from asking me out, I had a choice to make. I didn't want to date him, even if he was good-looking. But it was beginning to look like I might have to.

The following morning, Tyler was back for his third visit since I'd started working. After another sleepless night, I broke down and told him I needed some pills, citing some vague references to a sleep thing I had, and then named two of the meds I wanted. To his credit, he didn't even blink, immediately telling me about his contacts in resort housekeeping who regularly had access to the prescriptions tourists left out while vacationing.

Before I left work that day, Big Jake pulled me aside and handed me a bucket of paint. "This here's for yo' shutters," he said. "Don't right know why there ain't no haint paint on yo' house, but Tommy tol' me I could make ya'll some."

Confused, I took the paint can from him. "Not sure I understand, but thank you."

"You jus' give that to Tommy. He'll know what to do. And I tol' him, me and JJ can come hep. Don't let de hag get you."

I gave Big Jake a bland smile and lugged the paint all the way to the cottage, my fingers screaming with the weight of the can. I left it out on the porch.

There was a note on the table. Tom's handwriting was painstakingly neat.

Gone to Savannah.

I sighed.

The box of condoms was gone too.

At about five the next morning, having given up on sleep, I got up and made coffee, pouring myself a large cup. Humming

'The Funeral' by Band of Horses, I pulled out my grand-mother's recipe book, followed the directions for brownie brittle and popped it in the oven.

Then I stepped quietly into Tom's room, as if I didn't want the cottage to know I was there, lest it should tell on me later.

Since the first time I'd snuck into his room a few days after I'd arrived, I almost yearned for the moments when Tom would leave the house. It was the only positive aspect to his absence. I'd sneak in and read his latest pages. Sometimes when I was awake in the night I could hear him typing away and printing things out. If I woke before the nightmares but still had the irrational bands of anxiety around my chest, I'd listen hard, the soft clacking calming my racing heart. I'd hear the printer burping out pages, then hear him curse softly, scrunch up the paper, and ping it into the trash can.

I didn't know why he didn't just delete the pages, why he needed to print them out first and then throw them away, but I wondered if the things he threw away were the things that were the most true.

He wrote beautifully.

He wrote of loss and of grief. He wrote of a golden-haired girl who desperately wanted to get into heaven, who went through all the things in her life she felt she'd done wrong that could be preventing her from getting there.

I wished I had access to the Internet so I could search and see if he'd published anything. Apart from that first time when I'd thought he'd left his laptop, even though I never found it, he'd always taken it when he went to the mainland with Pete. Even if he'd left it, I knew now I wouldn't touch it. I was too nervous of being found out. It was enough that I snooped in his bedroom.

I'd asked him what he did and where he went when he wasn't helping Pete, and he'd shrugged and said, "Around."

Placing my cup of coffee down on the edge of his desk, I saw there was some new trash. I mentally brushed aside the niggling feeling of how much I was invading his privacy and how I'd feel if he did the same to me. Smoothing the papers out, I learned that the girl, Aislyn, had exhausted all her explaining and reasoning and had teased out all her memories. She was emotionally exhausted, scared, and still not able to work out why she was being denied access.

She had just met another being. I suspected he was a fallen angel though I wasn't sure. She was so drawn to him, and I wondered if it was something about him that made her confide in him or the fact that she had no one else to trust. Zaek his name was. A mangled form of Ezekiel?

"It's not about heaven, sweet Aislyn. Heaven is a mirage, a simplistic ideal, a yearning, a carrot dangled above all souls to make them strive for more. It's simply about belonging somewhere, anywhere. You haven't found a place you belong."

"Are you telling me heaven doesn't exist?"

"Oh, of course it exists," said Zaek. "In the same way that an exclusive country club exists on earth, and those who are members must extol its virtues and exclusivity endlessly, becoming blind to its restrictions and prejudices, simply to justify the expense."

"But what expense is there to heaven?"

"So many, so many," he mused. "But for one, the inability to fully explore all aspects of your humanity. And you have so many facets—some good, some . . .

not so good. But tell me, why did God give you such complexity if you are not allowed to fully experience it?"

What an ass, I huffed. I'd never been particularly religious, but I found myself growing angry that Aislyn was buying this crap. I knew Zaek was going to try and turn her against heaven. I'd been enjoying her purity, her naïveté, her hopeful romanticism. Zaek was going to crush her spirit. I knew it. I reached the end of the pages. *Damn.* Sighing, I crumpled them back up and tossed them in the trash. Keeping them would give me away.

Looking around, I drained the last of my coffee. Apart from these pages I furtively read, there was nothing in this room to give me a clue about my mysterious housemate. No pictures, no keepsakes, not even a speck of mail. God, I'd take junk mail at this point just to know something more about him. Getting up, I went to the armoire. Inside were haphazardly folded jeans and shirts, but with some fairly high-end labels. Interesting.

At least he folded like a normal person. I realized I would have been nervous if everything in here had been perfectly neat and tidy. Perfectionists freaked the hell out of me. I closed the door and leaned against it.

A soft trilling sounded. The phone. I stood abruptly, my cheeks burning, my belly feeling faintly nauseous, and bolted guiltily out of Tom's room.

I grabbed the handset and pressed it to my ear. "Hello?"

There was silence, and for a split second I wondered what the hell I was thinking answering the phone. It never rang. What if it was my parents?

"Olivia?" Tom's voice. Hearing it made my throat close with the surge of guilt over my snooping. But damn, I was relieved.

The acrid smell of burning chocolate reached my nose.

Shit! The brownie brittle. "Hang on," I gasped and dropped the phone. I grabbed the dishcloth and yanked open the oven door. Smoke poured out, hitting my eyeballs and the back of my throat. Coughing and waving it away from my stinging eyes, I managed to get the pan out. No! I'd been really looking forward to that. Disappointment flared and I scraped the burned crispy flakes into the sink. What an annoying waste. What had I even been thinking? I hated baking. Hated it.

"I hate baking!" I yelled at the top of my lungs and wedged the front door open to get the smoke out. The kitchen was a disaster and I was worse. I started laughing at myself, and it was so damn funny it took me a while to remember to get back to the phone.

Putting the receiver to my ear, I sniffed and gasped out the tail end of a hysterical laugh. "Sorry."

"What the hell is going on there?" he asked, his tone amused.

"I was trying to cook. Turns out I can't bake worth shit. And I've used up everything in the kitchen, so you need to get more eggs and stuff." I looked behind me at the mess I'd made, and the smoky haze. "Sorry," I added.

"No problem. It's . . . good to hear you laugh."

I waited a beat. "Soooo, this is weird. You calling."

"I know." There were a few moments of excruciating silence. Phones were the absolute worst. They should be fucking outlawed. Texting only, please. I missed my cell phone something vicious.

"I'm bored," I huffed, more to fill the silence than anything else. "God, what do you do out here day in day out for years on end?"

The silence hung again. I twisted the cord around my finger and heard him exhale in a long sigh.

"There's not even any music to listen to," I went on,

further lamenting giving up my phone. My music. "And I've read those fairy tales, like, fourteen times. Ugh," I said into the awkwardness, conscious I was the only one talking. "Never mind. What did you call for?"

"Oh." He cleared his throat. "I, uh, was thinking of staying here another night."

I frowned. Disappointment dropped like a stone in my gut. And dread. I dreaded waking up in the night without him here. Like last night. And where did he spend the night when he was gone? Images of him bare-chested and with a woman flitted through my mind. Using the condoms lubricated for maximum pleasure. Twelve of them.

"But then I wanted to see if you were okay. If you needed me to come back."

"I'm fine," I clipped out. "Why would I care if you stayed away?"

There was another long pause. "Okay. I got the impression you slept better when I was there," he said, seemingly unfazed by my childish tone.

I swallowed at the truth of that. How did he even know?

"I know your meds are running low. But if you're fine . . ."

"I'm fine."

"No worries then. See you tomorrow."

"Wait—"

A dial tone hummed in my ear. I smacked my head against the wall and put the phone back on its cradle.

Why did I do this? Why was I like this with him? Just when he was trying to be thoughtful, I acted like the most juvenile form of myself possible. God, he'd done nothing but be caring, even if he sometimes hardly uttered a word, and I was such a stupid little bitch every time. I couldn't even call him back to apologize because I didn't have his number.

Shit. I didn't have his number. What if something went wrong? I'd burned the brownies. I could actually start a fire. My chest tightened.

The phone trilled again.

"I'm so sorry," I said breathlessly as I picked it up, meaning the apology with every fiber of my being.

"Olivia?"

"Who is this?" My mind scrambled to identify the male voice.

"Oh, hey. It's Tyler. You okay? You sound out of breath."

My shoulders sagged. "Tyler. Hi."

"Don't sound so excited, babe." He laughed.

Babe?

"Sorry, I just burned something in the kitchen. It's fine now. What's up?" I asked, injecting as much enthusiasm as I could into my voice to mask the disappointment that it wasn't Tom. Wait. "How'd you get my number?"

"Tommy's number is listed."

"But how'd you know I live here?" He'd never asked me once in all of our interactions at Mama's.

He laughed. "You do know you live on a small island, right? So listen, some friends and I are heading over to Hilton Head to hang out tonight. You want to come party with us?"

Did I want to party? On the one hand, partying was my comfort zone. Staying out past my curfew, taking a few illegal substances but nothing too crazy, and enduring my parents' shocked and disgusted looks when yet another random guy dropped me home. No matter how they tried to threaten, ground or control me, I wouldn't be stopped. But that was part of the joy, wasn't it? That and the moments when the guy I was with made me feel something besides the cloying numbness that was otherwise only broken by panic and anxiety. Here, I had no parents waiting up for me, no shocked or even resigned faces to look forward to. Where was the joy in that? Why bother?

Not even Tom would be awaiting my return tonight. No, because Tom was off doing whatever the hell it was he did when he left this godforsaken island prison. The kitchen clock ticked loudly. I wondered what his reaction would be to me going out with Tyler.

"Sooo?"

"Yes." I jolted back to the present. "Sorry, yes. Would love to. What time and where should I meet you?"

He laughed. "Phew. Totally thought you were gonna say no."

You probably should have, a nagging voice told me.

"You know the dock at Mama's restaurant? We're leaving from there around six. It takes about an hour. Wear a jacket or something, it's colder than a witch's tit on the water."

"Okay," I responded. "See you then."

"Wait. You got a fake ID, right?"

"Yeah."

"Cool. See you later then. Oh, and I got a few of those things you were looking for."

Meds. Thank goodness. "Oh, thank you," I said casually.

"You can thank me later, babe."

Yep. And that's how it went. I could *thank him* later.

I rummaged around for my skinny jeans and my push-up bra and headed to the bathroom armed with my makeup bag and a cheap plastic razor.

I knew Tyler was the worst choice possible, but I had to get out of this cottage.

And frankly, I felt like kissing a boy.

CHAPTER TWELVE

$\mathcal{J}$ walked to the dock by Mama's and waved to Marjoe, who was carrying a box around the side of the restaurant.

She nodded and then scowled when she saw Tyler leaning up against the piling on the jetty, fingers of one hand stuffed into the front of his jeans, the other hand holding a cigarette to his lips. His dark hair flicked down across his forehead.

Tyler's mouth curled up into a grin as he exhaled a plume of smoke, the scar on his lip making it a little cruel and a little sexy. He perfected it in the mirror, I'd bet. He was exactly the type of guy I went for. Had gone for. Whatever. He was good-looking, slightly seedy, and perfect for my needs. Although I wasn't all that clear on my needs anymore.

"I can't wait to see what you've got on under that jacket, babe, but those jeans are smokin'," he called out as I neared him.

He flicked his cigarette away and pushed from the piling. Walking up to me, he grabbed my head, his mouth coming down on mine hard. His taste was smoky with a slightly sour undertone, and I flinched and then froze under his wet tongue as it pushed into my mouth.

"Damn, you taste like sugar," he said, pulling away, thankfully making the onslaught brief.

I felt like rinsing.

"Did I say you could kiss me?" I struggled not to let my disgust show. I really hoped Marjoe hadn't seen that.

Tyler's eyes widened a fraction, then he grinned. "Feisty," he hissed. "I like it. Well, babe, just letting my buds over there know not to mess with ya." He motioned behind his shoulder with a flick of his head.

I looked over and saw two rather sketchy-looking guys in the boat, both looking at us.

We walked over to them and climbed on to the small skiff. "This here's Twitch," Tyler said, motioning to a huge guy with a shaved head who was pulling a beanie on. Twitch nodded at me, and then busied himself with untying the ropes. "And this is Cal. This, boys, is Olivia."

Cal, tall and skinny, definitely had a few years on us all. With pockmarked skin, he had a crucifix tattooed in faded green ink on his right cheek. He gave me a slow and appraising smile, revealing a yellowed set of teeth, a front one chipped. His eyes travelled down the length of me then back up to my face.

I shuddered, wanting to climb out of my skin, leave my clothes standing there, and take my soul away. I knew that look. I'd seen that look. I'd borne the brunt of a nightmare that started with a look like that. I shuddered, the ice inside me having nothing to do with the weather, and stepped a little closer to the devil I knew. Tyler. So that's why he'd made a show of kissing me. He knew the type of guy Cal was. How chivalrous, I thought sarcastically.

Tyler drew me down to sit beside him and we cast off. What the hell was I doing? Heading out to who knew where with three men I didn't know? One had staked a claim on me, and not just for chivalry's sake; one, I felt certain, was capable of rape, and the other was strong enough to hold me down or take out anyone who came to my aid.

The light had almost completely faded. "So is it safe to go across in the dark?" I asked, suddenly thinking about how I was going to get home. *Home.*

Tyler chuckled. "Well, those markers out there are lit at night so you don't wreck on the oyster beds. Don't worry, babe. We drive at night all the time." I just bet they did. "Let's get you warmed up with a shot." He passed me a small flask. I wiped the spout with my jacket and took a hit, letting the whiskey scorch a path to the pit of my belly before handing it back. Hopefully it would dull the edge of my jumped-up nerves. Tyler nodded approvingly.

He hadn't been joking when he said it was cold on the water. I huddled into my jacket and unwillingly into his embrace, still shivering. The ice-cold wind slapped my cheeks, making my eyes water. Thank God for waterproof mascara.

We headed around the inland side of the island until we hit the open water of Calibogue Sound. There was a red-and-white-striped lighthouse lit up in the distance across the black water, although we seemed to be headed for a different marina. A dark duffel sat at Tyler's feet, and he reached in and handed me a wool hat, which I gratefully pulled on, covering my wind-bitten ears.

When we finally arrived at a small marina, Tyler handed me the duffel to carry as he helped get the boat secured.

The place we'd pulled into was sheltered in a horseshoe shape with some dated stucco condos rising on each side. There seemed to be a couple of restaurants that were fairly quiet, and in the middle, an outdoor bar aptly named the Hurricane Bar was blaring Jimmy Buffet.

We made our way to a free table near one of the heat lamps. Twitch and Cal took one side and I sat opposite Twitch, suddenly understanding his nickname as I noted the repeated tic in his right eye. Weird.

Tyler slid into the chair next to me, immediately placing his hand on my thigh beneath the table. I pretended not to notice and looked around at the clientele as the guys chatted about the game on TV and something about a meeting, although their coded language was hard to follow. It was still early, so there were a few tables of families, and the rest were an odd assortment of men and women in varying levels of dress from casual to more businessy, presumably depending on the job they'd just come from.

The waitress came to take our order, and Cal "accidentally" knocked a coaster to the floor, watching as she had to wind her blonde hair over one shoulder and then lean down to pick it up.

I ordered a Coke and the guys ordered beer. They kept chatting and I was relieved to not be included.

After reading a text on his phone, Tyler abruptly said, "Let's go," and tossed money on to the table.

I frowned but got up to follow, grabbing the bag that held our hats and stuff. What a gentleman.

We piled into a gray sedan they kept parked on the island that stank of old burned things, herbal and otherwise, and drove for about ten minutes.

The next bar we went to was more of a nightclub. It was busy for so early in the evening. Back home the clubs I frequented didn't really get going until close to midnight.

I missed music so much, it felt great to stand in the middle of the dark, crowded room and feel the beats drum through my body. I didn't want to dance with Tyler, but I felt the urge to lose myself in the music. I resisted though, even when Nine Inch Nails came on.

The soundtrack traded between rough rock and gangsta rap, with an assortment of radio hits seasoned in.

We had found a table near a dark corner. Tyler ordered us four tequilas from a waitress who looked like she was wearing boy shorts underwear with her tight T-shirt. Cal was in his element. I used the diversion to shrug off my jacket, already regretting my choice of bra and low-cut black shirt.

"Don't suppose you'd let me slam my shot off *you*, would you?" Tyler quirked his eyebrow at me.

I rolled my eyes. The thought of Tyler licking salt off my skin was repellent. "Uh, no."

His eyes flashed in warning, and I quickly smiled to take the sting out of my rebuff. He leaned in close to my ear. "Watch it, sweetheart," he whispered, squeezing my leg. Then he smiled back blandly, eyes cold. Blinking again, his eyes cleared and he laughed. "Kidding."

His attention reverted back to the other two, but his hand never left my leg. What the hell was I doing here? Oh yes, I needed some pills. I just had to get through this evening.

The waitress delivered our drinks, and we all slammed them down. I was the only one to grab my lemon, my eyes watering at the tartness while the alcohol burned my head and chest from the inside out, the fumes scorching my nasal passages. I was nervous as hell and needed the edge off, but I wouldn't be able to have too many more.

Cal headed to the bar when our waitress failed to come back soon enough and brought back a round of drinks, a rum and Coke for me. There was no way I was drinking if he was providing. God knows what he'd put in it. He and Tyler seemed to be having a bet of some sort, or an argument, I couldn't figure out which over the music. I just wished Cal would take his eyes off my chest.

Eventually Tyler tugged on my hand and motioned to the dance floor. He gave me a friendly smile when I was expecting a lecherous one. The temptation to dance was too strong, and I was getting pretty relaxed. And for me, relaxed equaled as close to happy as I got.

As we hit the dance area, Tyler pulled me through to the middle so we were surrounded. I had this odd flash, that back in my old life, before coming here, this, right now, was exactly the kind of night I'd sought. Tyler was attracting the perfect amount of attention with his good-looking bad-boy persona, and I was the object of his desire. So apart from the fact that this evening was scaring me a little, why wasn't I feeling the usual buzz? The usual need and desire to get him aroused, to feel that power over a guy?

"Jesus, you're gorgeous. You know that, right?" Tyler growled in my ear over the music.

I gave him a shy, practiced smile.

He pulled in close to me, fitting a leg between mine, his body almost flush against me as we moved to the rhythm. "I just don't get you. Maybe you're playing hard to get, but this hot and cold crap is pissing me off," he said in my ear. "Or maybe it's making me want you more."

Then he said all the things I expected to hear—my body was incredible, my lips sexy as hell, how we should find a corner somewhere. Not that a corner seemed to be a concern as his hands didn't seem to mind kneading my ass in full view of the entire club. I'd never expected anything else.

I'd never felt so numb.

"Hey, so where are my pills?" I asked and ground against him more firmly, earning a groan.

"Not yet, babe. God, you feel good. Imagine if I was inside you right now."

Ugh.

Unfortunately I could, and the thought made me nauseous.

"I'm thirsty after all this dancing. Can we go back and sit for a bit?"

He nodded and winked, like we were in on some secret together. "Yeah, I need to get back there anyway. A guy could forget his whole life with you around." Taking my hand, he led me back through the throng to our table.

I hated that I'd left my drink unattended, although Cal had bought it, so I imagined anything he'd intended to do to it was already done. "I'm just going to get some water," I told Tyler as he sat down.

He pulled my hand. "Sit, I'll get you some in a minute."

I frowned.

"Sit," he said and pulled harder. I sat, not wanting to make a scene, and he planted his hand back firmly on my thigh.

"So you in high school, baby?" asked Cal, earning a swift kick from Tyler under the table, although I was unclear whether it was for the "baby" or the high-school implication.

"I'm done with high school," I said evasively.

"Tyler here likes 'em young too. Don't you, Ty?"

"Knock it off," Tyler said, although half his attention was now focused over Cal's shoulder as he scanned the club.

"How old are you, Tyler?" I asked, trying to change the subject and get his attention back.

"Twenty-six," he replied absently.

"You eighteen yet?" Cal continued, leering at me.

I nodded.

He smiled in the dark. "Shame. I like 'em before they're legal."

I glanced toward Tyler, unease building in my belly, but there was no reaction.

"But in your case, I could probably make an exception if Ty was up for sharin'. We like that, don't we, Ty?"

"Cal," Tyler snapped.

Cal shrugged and downed whatever brown liquid was in the bottom of his glass.

I took a tentative swallow of my drink to quench my dry throat. It tasted fine, but I wouldn't allow myself more than a few sips. I wanted out of here. I was done now, I shouldn't have come. My head was starting to ache, probably a leftover from the ice-cold wind on the water, and being dehydrated, rather than my drink. But the stupidity of my situation was finally penetrating my mind. I was playing just a bit too close to the fire tonight.

Suddenly Tyler leaned over to me. "That duffel you've been carrying, under the table by your feet . . . a nice chatty guy will be over here in a moment with a black bag just like it. He'll set it down while we all catch up. You'll trade it out."

My jaw dropped. "Are you kidding me?" I hissed, earning hostile stares from Twitch and Cal. I didn't care. I reached under the table, knocking Tyler's hand off my leg.

He latched back on and dug his fingers in hard, getting up in my face. His other arm came around my neck, drawing me in really close so I couldn't lean away. To anyone looking, we'd be having a quiet, intimate moment.

I gritted my teeth to keep my face stoic.

"No, I'm not kidding. You'll be a good girl and do as I say."

I shook my head, my heart pounding. "I didn't sign up for this, Tyler. I don't deal, okay." God, the last thing I needed was to get caught: they'd probably call my parents. God, or Mike. I shuddered.

"Keep your fucking voice down," he growled, wafting his stale breath over me, even though there was no way anyone would hear me over the music. "And give me your hand." He took my hand under the table, closing it over a baggy that felt like it had pills in it. "I got what you asked me for."

And just like that, I was officially in debt.

I was too stupid to live right now, and I knew it.

CHAPTER THIRTEEN

A guy with a backwards cap and a gray Seahawks T-shirt came over to our table, a big goofy grin on his face, a backpack on one shoulder. It wasn't a duffle, but it was still black. He stood at my end of the table. "Hey, guys," he said, all smiles. Then he slid the bag off his shoulder to the ground, ostensibly to shake hands with everyone.

I ignored him as he came around to me.

Tyler nudged me with his elbow and I looked away. What if I just refused to do it? "How are you, Rob?" Tyler greeted our new guest.

"Good, man. Good."

"This here is Olivia." *Dammit.* He bumped the side of his foot against mine. "Olivia's new to the area. Which one of us do you think would be better suited to show her a good time? You think it should be Cal?"

What the hell?

Icy tendrils of terror snaked through me, making my stomach heave, and I looked up to see Tyler's smirk as he raised the stakes on my coercion. God, he wouldn't seriously toss me into the alligator den, would he? I felt like Cal was his weapon of persuasion rather than to be actually deployed, but I couldn't be sure.

"I think Cal has the lead at the moment," Tyler continued, making sure I understood his implication. "You think she'd have a good time, Rob?"

How did I get out of here? Even if I did, where did I go? I only had a few dollars on me, and I was an island away from safety. My heart rate ramped up to a flat-out gallop. I hauled in air. *Oh God.*

Safety.

The cottage was safety.

Tom was safety.

And I couldn't even call him. Why had I done this to myself? If I could just get back to the cottage, I'd never go anywhere ever again. I'd stay there where I'd finally found safety. And acceptance. Tom accepted me. No matter what I did or said to him, he was simply *there*. If I could just get back there in one piece, I'd never gamble like this again.

My chest went painfully tight, and I grabbed at it with my hand.

I vaguely heard Rob clearing his throat nervously. This obviously wasn't going the way he'd planned either. "Can we, uh—"

"I think, actually, I'll be taking Olivia home now."

Tom's gravelly voice, dripping with ice, came from behind me. God, I had to be dreaming. Maybe I'd conjured him up somehow.

I sucked in an agonizing breath and whipped my head around as Tyler started in surprise but stayed seated. I'd never seen a more welcome sight. How had he found me? What was he doing here? I didn't care. I wanted to sob in relief.

"Get up, Olivia." Tom flicked his eyes over me and back to Tyler.

I didn't hesitate.

Tyler grabbed my wrist, holding me in place. "We are *not* done, babe," he hissed, then let me go, raising his palms and shrugging to Tom, as if he'd just reassessed Tom's look.

I slid out from the table, careful not to trip over the two bags now at my feet.

Tom picked up my jacket from the back of my chair and held it for me to put my arms into. It was a strange and slow courtesy in a situation we both clearly wanted to get away from as fast as possible. I guess we were making sure everything looked normal in case anyone was watching. Or perhaps he was giving me a chance to calm myself? As I put my second arm in, he turned me around to face him. Oh my God, I wanted to stare into his beautiful caramel eyes forever.

"Do you have anything you need to return?" he asked for my ears only, his eyes searching mine.

The pills. I swallowed and nodded.

He let me go, and I wondered how to give them back to Tyler without being obvious. The concern about what to do must have been evident on my face because Tom leaned in. "Do what you have to, right?" he said, throwing my careless remark back at me. "I'm sure it works the same in reverse."

His words cut me.

I swallowed the hurt down and steeled myself to get this over with. Turning back to Tyler, I leaned over him. He looked up, his expression smug as I zeroed in. My left hand slid around his neck into his hair, and I lowered my head, touching my mouth to his beer-soaked lips.

Someone whistled softly.

My right hand skated over his chest to his breast pocket where it left behind the little baggie of pills. I finished off the kiss, trying not to gag, and stood. "Thanks for a great evening, guys. And Tyler? You and me are squared up."

I turned quickly, before the glazed look faded from Tyler's face. I didn't want to be around when he realized I'd returned his merchandise.

Tom's face was completely devoid of expression as he swiveled abruptly and strode out of the club.

I hurried to keep up, hugging my coat tightly around me as I hit the cool night air. He slid into a waiting taxi, leaving the door open. I followed into the lighted interior and closed the door, plunging us into darkness.

"Back to the marina, please." Tom's voice was flat as he spoke to the cabbie. We rode in tense silence. As my eyes adjusted to the darkness, I stared at Tom's shadowed profile, his strong, straight nose, his forehead. His closely clipped beard, even. It was shorter than I'd ever seen it. I wondered if it was coarse or soft.

He looked and smelled like home.

"Thank you," I whispered. My head was aching, and I felt weak and sick with relief.

I thought his jaw clenched, but I wasn't sure. In any case, anger radiated off him. "I don't want to act like your parent, but what the fuck?" He left the question hanging.

"How did you find me?"

"Marjoe called me when she saw you leave. I made a lucky guess as far as the club was concerned. There aren't that many choices for assholes with his agenda."

"So Marjoe called, and you came to get me. That sure *seems* like a parent thing to do, for someone who doesn't want to act like one." What was wrong with me? I couldn't understand the way he pressed all my buttons and made me speak to him like this.

Tom turned his head to look in my direction. Then his entire body shifted toward me, moving my breath from my lungs, and his face came close to mine. "Then stop acting so fucking childish. What do you think might have happened tonight if I hadn't showed up? Because from where I was sitting, it looked like you were about to take part in a drug deal."

And probably not just that. The unsaid words dropped like a heavy stone between us.

I shut out the thought of Cal, Twitch, and Tyler and swallowed at Tom's nearness. I wished there were at least street lights so I could see his eyes again. Instead I had to feel his contempt as strongly as I felt his breath wash over my lips. It smelled like expensive wine and dark chocolate.

He sat back abruptly.

I shook my head. We were at the marina I'd arrived at earlier. He opened the door, dousing us in light. His strong hands had a slight tremor as he pulled out a wad of cash and peeled off several bills to hand to the driver.

Pete was there with his boat, bundled up. Oh God, this night got better and better.

"I'm sorry, Pete," I mumbled as I climbed on board.

He nodded.

I sat huddled in my useless jacket, with no embrace to snuggle into no matter how unwelcome, and no hat to keep the biting wind from stabbing deep into my ears. My headache got worse.

Tom stood holding a floodlight over the water ahead, legs braced apart, other hand holding on to the back of Pete's seat. It was the longest fifty minutes of my life.

Pete dropped us at Mama's dock, it being too far around to Bloody Point. He handed Tom a flashlight, which Tom promised to return, and the two off us set off down the roadway across the island.

Walking along Prospect Road in the middle of the day was eerie. The sounds of the island at night were scary as hell. Screeching, croaking, and the beating of wings so large they had to belong to something man-sized. At one point, I jumped clear off the ground at the sound of something crashing through the underbrush to my left. "What the hell was that?" I gasped.

"Possum, probably," Tom said dismissively.

My nerves helped me ignore the bone-numbing cold. "Not an alligator?"

"Alligators are sleepy and lethargic at this time of the year. It's too cold for them."

I hurried to keep up with his long stride. My jaw clenched tight against the shattering cold. "Tom!"

He stopped. "What?"

"I'm s-s-sorry, okay? But can you s-slow down?"

He barked out a humorless laugh and strode on.

We finally got to the cottage and he marched up the steps, flicking the lights on and tossing the flashlight on to the kitchen table with a clatter as I followed him in. I closed the door behind me, reveling in being back inside my safe haven. He headed for the bathroom and returned with a bottle of mouthwash.

"Rinse that fucker out of your mouth," he said, holding it out to me.

I stopped in front of him, out of breath and stuttering from the cold.

We stood in a staring stand-off. It was ridiculous and could have ended in a laugh if the unspoken words, accusations, and questions weren't weighing us down. That and something alive and pulsing, pulling down through my body.

CHAPTER FOURTEEN

$\mathcal{J}$ felt woozy. Perhaps there'd been something in my drink after all. I wet my lips at the thought, and Tom's eyes dropped to my mouth before he closed them. He exhaled and turned away, placing the mouthwash I hadn't taken on the table next to the flashlight.

He peeled his large fleece jacket off. In designer-looking jeans, a pressed blue button-down shirt, and black blazer, he was dressed up. Wow. His old boots were the only sign of his normal wardrobe. "Were you on a date?" I asked before I could edit myself.

"That's none of your business," he said, heading for the fireplace. He squatted down, his jeans stretching across his muscled thighs, and lit a match to the kindling. "You should sit by the fire. Get warm."

I watched as the fire caught the bone-dry wood, and Tom stoked the flames.

"You know how I spent *my* evening," I said, taking the bottle after all and gargling with it over the kitchen sink. The thought of Tyler still being in my mouth was pretty gross now that I thought about it. And to think I *wanted* to make out with him earlier. "Why can't I know how you spent yours?"

"Well, I didn't spend it the way I planned, did I? So what does it matter?"

I came back around to the fire.

"So is it blue balls contributing to this mood of yours?"

Why? Why? I winced.

"Christ," he exploded, tossing the log he'd been holding into the fire. It let out a shower of sparks.

I jumped.

Maybe I just liked to see him react. Because he didn't react often, or show emotion at all except for when I provoked it, or the day with the ax.

"Watch that damn mouth of yours," he growled and raked a hand through his hair. "And I don't need a reason to be pissed off that I just had to freeze my ass off to come and get you from being a stupid fucking headline!"

He threw a few more logs on, then stood up. Folding his arms across his chest, he gazed at the fire. "God, you act like a child, a teenager, and a jaded whore all at the same time. After everyone at that club saw you grind yourself all over that piece of shit, I doubt many people would be surprised to hear you cry rape tomorrow."

I inhaled sharply. Rage came so fast, I couldn't hold it back. My hand lashing out caught him on the side of the head. I connected with him hard, immediately following with my other.

He pulled back, eyes storming, and my hands hit air. "You bastard," I screamed, but it came out half sunk as I drowned in anguish at his words, my chest heaving. I was crying, dammit.

Vibrating with tension, he stood still as stone, his hands

clenching and unclenching as he watched a tear roll down my face.

I wanted to swipe it away but thought better of it. Let him watch how he upset me.

Then he shrugged and headed past me to the kitchen and pulled a beer from the fridge. "You seem to be the only one too naïve to understand how the men you associate with work. You're making the wrong choices." The nonchalance of his words didn't reach his eyes, as if he knew what a complete asshole he was being right now. Grabbing a chair from the table, he pulled it out to face the direction of the fire. "Go to bed, Olivia."

I stood for a moment, pulling myself together. Control. I needed control. "How old are *you* anyway, Mr. Know-it-all? Twenty-eight? Thirty?"

"Old enough not to be taking shit from an infantile goth chick."

"You don't find this look attractive, huh?" I let my jacket slip from my shoulders to the floor.

He saw my outfit, and, taking a swig of beer, looked away toward the fire.

"You think I'm young and don't know anything about boys?" I went on and stalked over to where he sat rigid, legs slightly splayed and firm on the hard ground in his worn work boots.

His eyes came back and watched me warily. He had no idea what was coming.

But I knew men. I *did*. I knew how to get what I needed by giving them what *they* needed. And what I needed was for Tom to stop looking at me like a child. I kept my face carefully blank at first so I could get close. Then I ran my tongue over my lip and smiled at him slowly.

His eyes flickered in a moment of confusion, but they tracked the movement of my tongue.

I definitely did not imagine *that*.

"You're a *guy*," I said softly. I dropped to my knees between his legs and grasped the top button of his jeans, popping it open. I moved quickly, suddenly wanting very much to touch him, suddenly caring very much who it was I was touching. "You'll never turn down a good cock-su— Aaah!"

Pain lanced as his fingers squeezed my jaw, yanking my face up and away from his groin. My knees skidded an inch forward on the splintered floor.

His eyes were murderous and inches from mine. "What . . . the . . . *fuck* . . . do you think you're doing?" His mouth was so close, I could smell the beer on his heaving breath and feel the droplets of spit.

My neck strained as he pulled my face closer to his. I couldn't swallow in shock or even take a breath through the agony.

He squeezed tighter, mashing the soft skin of my inside cheek into my teeth, bruising my gums and the thin flesh over my jawbone.

Whimpering, I tried to speak, to plead with him to let me go, but only a strangled sound came out. The rapid and reflexive rage of his reaction dawned on me with horrific clarity. He was completely disgusted. Disdain and contemptuous fire rained down from his eyes.

It gutted me.

If I could just brace myself on his legs so I could find purchase to get up, to get away from his grip . . . but the moment my hands found his thighs, he pushed me forcefully away.

I lost my balance and fell back. My hand went up to my face, my jaw, tears spilling down my cheeks on to my fingers. I curled up on my side, cradling the pain in my face. In my head and my chest. I heard him pause, hesitate, and kept waiting to feel his hands pull me up . . . and then he stalked across the floor toward the front door.

It slammed behind him and my body jerked.

What have I done?

What have I done?

What have I done?

Exhaling a choked-up breath, I finally stood up and walked to the bathroom. Turning the shower on as hot as I could stand, I stood in it crying and scrubbing all my shitty makeup off.

It was late, and I was reading by the fire Tom had laid, when I heard him come from the bedrooms. I would be able to apologize, but what would he think of me? How much more awkward would we be around each other now?

I wished myself luck and looked up.

Instead of Tom, I saw the one face I'd hoped never to see again. Uncle Mike.

Feeling like someone had just crushed my lungs, I froze and the book slipped from my grasp.

He smiled, revealing his perfect bright white capped teeth. "Hi, Abby."

Abby?

"How did you find me?" My voice was strange and tinny, like it was trying to project around a large obstruction in my throat.

"I've been looking for you," he purred, stalking toward me. "I can't believe I got so lucky and found *him* too. What luck!"

"Found who? Tom?"

He laughed, his balding head bobbing back in glee. He was dressed in his faded green Hawaiian shirt tucked into pleated khakis, his belly protruding over his belt line. I remembered that shirt all too well. My stomach heaved and rolled, fighting to get its contents past my heart, which was currently ballooned in my throat. "Oh, he hasn't told you. That's good. That's good. So much less complicated that way." He came closer, and I scrambled back toward the wall, knocking the floor lamp as I went, the book skidding across the floor.

"Don't run, honey. We have a little time before he comes back. I won't tell and you won't tell. It will feel good, okay? I'll make it feel good, like I always do."

"No," I begged as he advanced slowly. "No, please. I don't like it. Please, no!"

"Shh, it's okay. I know you like it, and you feel guilty that you do. But it's okay, I won't tell. It's our secret, okay?"

"No! I hate it, I hate it, I hate you!" *God, no. Please, no.* Where was Tom? I needed Tom. "Tom!" I yelled, my voice hoarse with terror and panic.

TOM

CHAPTER FIFTEEN

*H*oly fucking Christ.

I got out of that cottage so fast, I physically shuddered at how hard I slammed the door. Disgust and rage clawed at me. I couldn't believe that my body, my own fucking traitorous body, had actually reacted to that little display of hers.

I'd told her she played the part of child, teenager, and jaded whore all at once. But what I'd wanted to say was she was beautiful and sexy and didn't need to play games to prove it.

But how the hell did I articulate that without making it sound like *I* found her beautiful and sexy? I couldn't. The very idea of it revolted against everything inside me that saw her as a victim with a mangled childhood, a girl who needed to be left alone to heal and not be objectified. She needed to find *her*. Without all that other shit.

And not forgetting I'd done the absolute classic and told her it would have been *her* fault if she'd been assaulted or raped tonight. Nice. Really fucking nice. Like it was her fault that assholes like Tyler and his friends existed. I was a real piece of work. She'd clocked me in the side of the head. And frankly, I was grateful. I needed it. I couldn't *believe* I said that. To *her* of all people.

But hearing she was with Tyler tonight had twisted my gut inside out. Telling myself it was for her safety, I'd launched into action to get there and get her back to the cottage. And it *was* about her safety.

Ninety-nine percent about her safety.

It was the other one percent I was having a hard time with.

And if I was honest, which I was really trying to avoid being right now, it was more eighty–twenty.

My fists clenched and unclenched as I stood in the frigid cold.

Seeing her intimate with Tyler, sliding her small pink tongue into his disgusting mouth, had sliced me open somewhere. I'd sprung a leak and I couldn't fucking find it.

I wanted to show her what a real kiss was, from someone who would hold her face reverently in his hands, like he was afraid she would disappear or never again give him the honor. And once I thought about it, I couldn't stop. Couldn't take my eyes off her lips. Her perfect lips, stained with faded lipstick.

It had been all I could do to shrug and act like I just didn't give a shit, when I hated what she'd gone through, the situation she'd put herself in, the way she looked at me like I was some fucking hero when I was anything but. I hated it all.

And then she was suddenly on her knees in front of me. How the hell had I let that happen? She was right. I was a *guy*. My body had reacted and I'd flipped out.

It had to be because she was a version of Abby, right? Except she wasn't, not really. Not at all.

I pulled my cell phone out my back pocket. I only had three bars, but it was usually enough to make a call, so I punched in the numbers.

It was answered right away, a soft, sleep-filled voice.

"Bethany? Sorry to call so late."

"Tommy?" she asked. "Hey, babe."

"Hey." I swallowed. "Sorry to wake you."

"That's okay. Was everything all right?"

"Yeah." I expelled the balloon of air in my chest. "Yeah, it was fine. Had to get her home. Sorry to cut our evening short."

"Mmmmm, you wanna pick up where we left off?" she purred.

Fuck it, I should say yes. I needed to say yes. I had an ill-gotten hard-on, and a stranded date. One and one should make two, right? I tilted my head back and covered my eyes with my free hand as if it could somehow make me do the right thing. But there was no right thing here.

"No. Thanks." *No thanks?* I grimaced into what I knew was surprised silence emanating from the other end. "I can't right now. Speak to you tomorrow." I ended the call before she could say anything, even though I knew I'd been rude, and then flung my phone down on the ground. Hard.

I put Bethany out of my mind. I had no bandwidth for that right now. I'd hurt Livvy, and not just with my words. What was wrong with me? I'd never physically hurt a woman in my life, and I'd done it reflexively and with my bare hands.

My fists bunched as I remembered.

My only defense was that she'd shocked me; that, coupled with my rage at the way my body reacted to the sight of her kneeling between my legs, and anger that she would possibly think I'd let her do that, made me do whatever I could to get her mouth, and those damn beautiful haunting eyes, away from my body.

God, and I'd left her on the floor. Hurting. The mental image I had of her curled up holding her face from pain I'd inflicted made my stomach roll and burn with bile.

What kind of a monster was I? But I physically couldn't walk back through that door. I kicked at a pebble and grabbed my hair. Walk, I could walk and get myself calmed down. Figure out how to apologize. Was that even possible after the way I'd reacted?

I should have gathered her up and held her. In a big brother kind of way. In a non-threatening way. To show her that she didn't have to seduce me to get me to *see* her.

I saw her.

Clear as cut glass.

I saw the way she interacted with the people she worked with, the customers she served. She was too tough to crack on the outside and dying for a connection on the inside. I saw it in the way her eyes lingered on a friendly interaction or a hug two people shared. She watched it all like she was curious about it. Like she'd never had anyone just . . . hug her. And a look of yearning would flicker over her face.

She was going to bring one of those damn kittens home, I was sure of it.

She was graceful. She was likeable. She was kind. She had a great laugh, all the more potent for its rarity. And she sang. I'm not sure she knew she did it, but she had a fucking unbelievable voice. All smoky and bluesy. As messed up as she was, Livvy was stunning. In the way that when she smiled, one was literally . . . stunned.

But my self-assigned job, my only damn job, was to give her a safe place to grow into that person I was starting to see. I took my eye off the ball one fucking time to go get my rocks off with Bethany and I blew it all to shit. Because I was horny. Jesus, what was wrong with rubbing one out in the shower? It wasn't like I hadn't done it for years during dry spells. And there were a lot of those out here on the island.

The problem was the shower often had, or was about to have, Livvy in it. Or had her underwear hanging in it. It felt wrong.

After walking all the way to the beach, and then almost killing myself coming back in the dark, I went quietly up the porch steps. I stopped outside the door, making sure my head was clear, and stepped into the cottage.

The fire had died to a low glow, and the warm, damp smell of a fresh hot shower wafted down the hallway. Her door was closed.

I got the rest of the six-pack of beer out the refrigerator and proceeded to sit on the couch and power-drink them one by one, wishing for something stronger.

I'd never hated the male species I was a part of as much as I did at this moment.

I was no psychologist, but it was pretty clear that the only way she believed she had any worth with men was through sex. And I'd rejected her so brutally. I'd thrown the only currency she thought she had back in her face.

Not with gentleness, not with understanding, not with compassion. But with disgust.

If only I could explain that it was disgust with myself, because for the tiniest fraction of a split second, I'd been buying what she was selling.

Completely.

I came to on the couch in front of the dead fire. Was someone crying or shouting? Maybe both? I strained into the silence and heard a choked sound and then a rasp.

Shit. I sat up.

"Tom!" Livvy's voice sounded broken, desperate. She'd never called my name before. Visions of an intruder, or her having fallen or something, ripped through my head. I leapt up, tripping over the edge of the coffee table, and slipped on the book of fairy tales she was always reading. Finding my feet, I skidded to her bedroom door and crashed it open, just as she screamed my name again.

She sat up at my entry, the light from the hall ghosting over her pale features, her eyes wild and not quite lucid, as if she didn't see me. A dream. She was in the grip of a dream. Relief flowed through me at the same time as I felt utter helplessness that she was fighting some unknown thing every night that I couldn't protect her from.

Not even stopping to think, I went for her. To hold her like I should have done when I'd left her on the floor. The way I should have done when I'd known how scared she'd been of Tyler earlier. The way someone should every night she woke up.

Hearing my name on her lips with such desperation sent chills down my spine.

The moment I had her in my arms, she tried to push me away, still half dreaming, but then she was crying. I'd never seen her really cry until tonight. Until *I'd* made her cry.

Every sob seemed to suck the strength from me, leaving me weaker and more lost as to how I could help her. And so I held her. And soothed her. "Shh, it's okay. I've got you."

I don't know why I said that last part. But I realized in that moment, I would do whatever I could to keep her safe. Even against a specter in the dreams I couldn't see. If it helped her to hold her, hold her I would.

"I was so s-scared." Her voice was weak. "God, I was so scared tonight. I'm sorry. I'm sorry. I'm sorry I was so stupid. Th-that I went there. So s-stupid."

"Shh, I know. I've got you. You're okay. You're going to be okay," I assured her. The craziness of the situation she'd been in earlier hit me full force. If something had happened to her tonight . . . fuck. How would I even survive it? Having abandoned her twice? I needed to come clean, tell her everything, seek punishment or forgiveness, and I wanted to echo her words . . . *I was so stupid. I'm so sorry. I'm sorry I was so stupid.* "God, we're a pair," I muttered.

The way I was sitting, having climbed across the queen-sized bed and pulled her up into my arms, meant I was at the most awkward angle. My liver, which was busy processing my evening, was folded in on itself, my spine bent. Prone and strained. My leg was cramped.

"Do you want to tell me about your dream?" I asked.

"I dreamed of my uncle Mike." She inhaled deeply, her face buried in my shirt.

God.

I'd suspected, but hearing her say his name . . .

"I think I was Abby in my dream," she added.

I concentrated on not reacting. My cramped leg screamed, but I didn't want to end this moment where she was actually talking to me. Where I actually felt useful to her. She was so light in my arms. If I just stretched out, head against the headboard, she could lie down easily, without having to be shifted too much. I eased my leg to the side and lay back and tried not to think about the fact that we'd gone from barely exchanging three words a day to her lying in my arms. Maybe if I didn't think about it too hard, it would be okay.

For a moment I couldn't feel her breathing, and I worried I'd gone too far by lying back. "When you wake up in the night, is it always because you dream of him?" I asked, desperate for her to keep talking, to keep letting me in.

Her body quaked. "Sometimes I just wake because I feel like I can't breathe, or I have a nightmare but I can't see who it's about."

I didn't know where to go from there, and I felt like she hadn't really answered my question. So I stayed quiet, settling for the fact that she seemed to be calmer.

"My head hurts," she whispered. "Do you think they drugged me?"

God, I'd kill those motherfuckers. My arm tensed around her and I squeezed as I swallowed thickly. "Did you drink much?"

"No, and I drank a ton of water after . . ."

After a while, her breathing evened out.

"I'm sorry I hurt you tonight," I whispered in case she was already asleep. There was no response, and before I questioned myself, I ran my fingers over her jaw, the skin smooth over her delicate bones, wishing I could take back the bruises that would be sure to come. Her skin was hot and feverish under my fingers. The scent that was pure *her* was hard to detect under the smell of the shampoo we both used, but I inhaled deeply, not allowing myself to question what the hell I was doing. I didn't know my violets from my patchouli, but I could safely say her scent described her. Dark subtlety, mysterious and fragile, but also full of imprisoned light.

I snatched my hand away. *God.* What the hell was I doing? It was one thing to comfort her and . . . Well, that was it. Comforting her. Like an older brother.

Brother. It was literally the only role I could play here. Friend too. She sure as shit needed one of those. Had she ever had anyone? A best friend? Just a female friend of any kind? The loneliness that pulsed around her said no. Then again, I wasn't exactly the most gregarious person I knew.

I didn't know what I was feeling. It wasn't brotherly, and it wasn't friendly, it simply felt dangerous being this close to her.

$\mathcal{L}$ivvy slept in. I guess. She wasn't up when I finally woke late. Her door remained stubbornly closed. The door *I'd* closed after leaving her room last night.

I wasn't sure what today would bring between us. And I had shit I needed to take care of. I showered and threw on some jeans. I needed a damn haircut, or I was going to have to start borrowing ponytail things from Liv. And I needed to track Bethany down and apologize.

Pete was already at Mama's dock when I arrived, having presumably stayed with Marjoe after our little late-night escapade. Sitting in a foldup chair, a fishing line in the water, he held a steaming cup of something in his large callused hand and was chewing on the end of an unlit cheroot.

"Are you ever not trying to get a fish on to land?" I asked him, walking down the jetty.

He smiled and removed the brown tobacco from his mouth. "Mornin', y'all get home all right?"

"Yeah." I set down the flashlight by his feet clad in hiking boots that had seen better days. "Thank you for last night. I'm sorry."

"Needed to be done." He waved his hand. "That Cal Richter ain't good news. I been hearing he may have a record somewhere near the Okefenokee. Ran into a spot o' trouble over in Folkton, Georgia. I reckon he stays on the Carolina side o' the state line for a reason."

"I guess that's why Tyler needs a legit way to deliver to Savannah."

Pete took a sip of his coffee and squinted up at me, the low morning sun having just crested the trees behind us. "He still askin'?"

"Yep." I nodded out to the waterway that reflected the ice-blue sky. "You're awfully late getting out on that smooth-as-glass water today, Pete."

"Yeah, well, it's hard to get outta that woman's bed. And the ol' ticker ain't what it used to be." He winked at me. "'Bout time I took a day off."

Pete taking a day off. Unheard of. I stayed quiet. He knew I understood his unspoken words. He wasn't feeling good. He'd had a lung cancer diagnosis last year, and it didn't look promising. I only knew because I'd taken him to the doc in Savannah, having foiled his plans to sneak off and do everything by himself. "Have you told Marge yet?"

Pete let out a long sigh.

"She deserves to know, Pete. She deserves to have time to come to grips with it." *To say goodbye.*

"Look, son, I don't want to waste my last God-given times livin' in a puddle o' woman tears. Her fussin'. Lookin' at me like I'm gonna keel over at any moment," he groused, shaking his shaggy gray head.

We disagreed on this almost weekly.

I stuck my hands in my pockets and leaned against the piling.

Pete shifted in his chair. "On the subject o' talkin'—"

"Don't even." I cut him off.

"Just sayin'."

"Well, don't."

Pete's eyes crinkled up, and he stuck the cheroot back in the corner of his mouth and bit down. "You find out why she came down here at least?"

"I have a fair idea, and I don't think I'll like the story."

"Things are never as bad as you make them seem in your head."

"This will be, trust me."

"Whatever happened to her wasn't your fault, you know."

Pushing off and walking a few steps to the end of the jetty, I looked out across the mirrored water that lapped gently beneath my feet and inhaled the sticky, organic smell of pluff mud and salt marsh. "It is, Pete. There are no two ways around it. I'm as much to blame as if I did it to her myself."

Pete clicked his tongue. "That's bull. You were a bystander to something her parents should have been responsible for. But anyway, ain't nothin' to be done about the fish you missed yesterday. You can only mend your nets so you don't miss none tomorrow."

I snorted an unamused puff of air from my nose. Again the thought of something happening to her last night crawled under my skin. My immediate concern this morning was how to remove the threat of Tyler, and now Cal. Knowing Cal had a record made it worse.

"What are you cookin' up over there, son?"

I shrugged, not wanting Pete to know I might need to borrow his boat.

"I reckon we might see about luring that Cal fella over the state line."

Swinging around, I sized Pete up.

He pursed his lips. "Maybe shut down Tyler at the same time."

He was *serious*.

"What are you looking at, boy? There's life in me yet. An' if you think I'm leaving this mortal coil without makin' this world a slightly better place, then you're gravely mistaken."

I raised my hands and grinned. "No offense, Pete. I was just surprised you and I were on the same wavelength, that's all."

After we hammered out a vague and amateur plan that would make a vice squad shudder, I placed the call to Tyler from my cell.

"Sorry to bust up your party last night," I said to him when he answered.

"No you're not. What do you want?"

"I want you to leave Olivia the hell alone. She's off limits. To *all* of you."

There was silence while I imagined him grappling with his pride. The idea brought me a small measure of satisfaction.

"Becaaaause?" he drew out. If he thought I was going to lay a romantic claim on her, he'd be waiting a while.

"I don't suppose you'd do it because I asked you to, would you?"

Tyler snorted. "She came willingly. Anyway, I don't see why I should. You know what I want from you, so let's figure something out."

I pretended to mull it over and hesitate. "Look," I said finally. "Some things have changed. I might, uh, need some cash. So if you'll promise me Olivia is no longer in the game, we can probably work something out."

"Well, well, she sure is a talented girl. That mouth . . ." He sucked in a lascivious-sounding breath through his teeth. "Guess she got to you too, huh? Is it as good as I think?"

Squeezing my eyes shut, I focused on the vein throbbing in my temple, thankful he couldn't see my face right now. "Whatever." I sounded perfectly calm. Bored even.

"What about Pete?" he asked, back to business when I didn't rise to his bait. This was where it could all fall down.

I took a deep breath. "I don't know if you're aware, but Pete has some health issues. Been seeing a specialist in Savannah. They don't come cheap, and he's in a bind. He and I discussed it this morning. He'll do it one time, and one time only. So you best get your contacts lined up to get your shit off the boat as quick as possible, and make it an amount that counts, because we're not doing it again."

"How much does Pete need to pay his bills?"

"How much are you paying to get the job done?"

We discussed the amount; all the while I acted like I was pissed I'd been reduced to doing this for him.

"Expect my call in the next few weeks," Tyler said. "You'll only get one hour notice, and one hour to get to the drop point." He hung up.

"Fuck you," I said into the dead air.

I figured the time frame was to lessen the chances of us being followed or set up. I didn't give a shit. If all went to plan, we didn't need any notice at all. They were going down, one way or another.

Pete was inside handling the other part of the plan, in case Tyler checked out the legitimacy of his need for cash. Which he would.

I cringed and hung my head as I heard Marjoe crying

softly. But in the end, it was the only way. And that conversation was long overdue.

Big Jake and JJ arrived for work and I pulled them aside, explaining that Marjoe probably needed them to run the place without her today.

"It's Pete?" Big Jake asked. How this guy always knew everything was beyond me.

I nodded.

Big Jake shook his massive dark head and went inside.

"Hey, JJ," I said, glancing at the smaller version of Big Jake. JJ stopped and nodded, his eyes looking over my shoulder. It was disconcerting to talk to someone who never looked at you, but he'd always been this way and never uttered a word. He understood everything, though. I'd venture to guess he probably saw and understood more than anyone.

"You still work packing up the vegetables for old man Graham's delivery to Hilton Head?"

JJ nodded again, and I told him what I needed. I had no idea if he'd do as I asked, but the plan hinged on it, so I would hope for the best.

When I finally got back to the cottage later that afternoon, Liv's door was still closed. Her coat was in the living room, so she was definitely here. I'd been hoping last night wouldn't make it awkward between us, but the closed door said otherwise.

I knocked softly and got no answer. "Liv?"

Knocking more firmly, I pressed my ear to the wood. A small black kernel of fear uncoiled inside my chest. "Liv," I said against the door. It was silent. Too silent.

I turned the knob. "I'm coming in." The last thing I wanted to do was disturb her if she was napping, but I needed to make sure she was all right.

She was lying on the bed on top of the bedclothes in the long white T-shirt she slept in, deathly still, her skin a waxy sheen. "Shit!" I rushed to her and touched her face. I'd almost expected it to be ice cold, and I was relieved even as I winced at how hot she was. Christ, what the hell should I do? I fumbled for her wrist to feel her pulse. Not finding it at first, I tried her neck. Her skin almost burned under my fingers. Her body was trembling inside. Wait, that wasn't trembling, that was her heart. Fuck. Her heart rate was insane. I laid my hand on her chest to confirm, feeling her delicate breastbone through the thin T-shirt. Tyler—that bastard.

I snatched my phone out of my pocket.

"Tyler, you motherfucker," I said as soon as he answered. "What did you give her?"

"Well, hello to you too."

"Shit, Tyler, Olivia's taken something, or this is left over from last night. Just tell me. I have to hang up and get an EMT."

"Jeez, calm down. I didn't give her anything."

"What about the pills?"

"She gave those back."

"All of them?"

"Yes. I counted."

"What about in her drink?"

"Fuck you, Tommy."

"Would Cal do it?"

There was silence for two agonizingly long beats. "He might."

I growled. "Did he?"

"I don't know. I'll ask him and get back to you. Call the EMT."

I dialed the Haig Point fire number, my other hand resting on her chest. Most of the volunteers were at least first-aid-trained if the main crew were off duty. I waited for the call to be answered. *Shit*. I knelt on the floor by her side, hating myself for being gone all day.

Would there be any end to the ways I could let her down?

OLIVIA

𝒥 floated through a deep mist. A gray heavy-metal mist, ice cold where it blanketed my skin, making me shudder. And the heaviness. I struggled under it, its weight making me ache deep in my bones. Even my skin felt stretched to bruising.

Someone was saying my name. I strained to hear, but even that hurt. Trying to see through the fog meant peeling back my eyelids to allow painful spears of the whitest light to sear my eyeballs. I groaned in pain.

"Liv?" I finally heard a voice. A deep voice. Panic ripped through my chest, adding to my pain. *God, no.* I struggled harder. I needed to get out of this fog. Oh God, my body hurt so much. I forced my eyelids unstuck and felt like screaming at the needles that sank through my eyeballs into my skull.

"Livvy? It's me."

Wait. I liked this voice. This voice was different.

"Livvy?"

Turning my head was too hard. Thankfully the light faded, and I made out a tall figure leaning over me. "Sorry," it said. "I've closed the curtains now."

My body spasmed, my bones rattling. Why did I hurt so much?

"Livvy? It's Tom." *Tom?* I liked this person, whoever he was.

"There's a doctor coming, okay? Luckily he's on the island at the moment. Did you take something, Livvy?"

"I hurt," I whispered. At least, I think I whispered. I imagined the words and tried to force them out of my mouth, but I couldn't be sure I'd managed. Something cold and wet touched my forehead and then my lips. Despite how cold I was already, I welcomed it.

When I woke again, the shuddering had gone away. Perhaps under the weight of my bones I was simply forced to stillness.

I had the feeling someone was lying next to me. When I was little and had a bad dream, sometimes Abby would lie next to me, her hand on my back, until I went to sleep again. Sometimes she'd stay there all night, the two of us thrashing our limbs in wild and abandoned sleep until we woke, hot, sweaty, and tangled in blankets. I felt like that now. My body was clammy and warm, desperate for cold air.

The bone-jarring shivering had stopped, thank goodness, but I still hurt. Especially when I tried to move my eyes, which seemed to be immobile and bolted securely into the back of my skull.

Wincing, I eased a leg out from under the covers into the blessedly cool air and tried to shift on to my side so I might make out the figure I was sure was next to me.

God, I was so weak. And thirsty, wow. How long had I been in bed? Mid-shift, I became aware that a heavy arm was draped across me. I froze and swallowed, my parched throat sticking closed. Jerking, I heaved the arm away, and the body moved in the shadows.

"Sorry," it mumbled, and my chest relaxed.

"Tom?" I rasped.

"Mmmm."

He was still here? I peeled my sticky throat open through another swallow and forced out a whisper. "I . . . I need water."

His shadow sat up, dragging a hand down his face. He inhaled noisily like he'd been in a deep sleep. His body swung to the side of the bed. "I gotta turn on the lights, okay?" he said quietly. "They're on dim, but you might want to close your eyes."

I did. My head still ached, but now it felt more to do with being thirsty than the kind of rusty-spoon-gouging-into-brain-matter feeling I'd awoken to before. I listened to the rustle of him moving about the room and coming to my side of the bed.

"Okay," he said. "Do you think you can lift your head?"

Keeping my eyes closed, I pulled the covers from my face.

"Never mind. I've got it." A rough hand slid under my neck and eased my head up. Cool glass touched my lips, and I let the sweet water soothe my dry mouth and throat. I wrapped a hand around the thick wrist that held the glass and greedily swallowed more, protesting as he eased it away.

"You'll choke. Take it slow."

I lay my head back down and blinked my eyes open.

Tom blurred in and out of focus before stabilizing. What I could see of his face was drawn and tired. His caramel eyes were bloodshot. His hair was in wild disarray, looking more like a lion's mane than ever. I smiled, or tried to, wincing as my lips cracked. "Ow," I whispered, squeezing his strong wrist where I still held him, his pulse thrumming beneath my fingers.

He pulled back gently, and I closed my eyes and held on

to him. "Let go," he said, his voice soft. Amused. "I'll be right back."

Reluctantly I relaxed my hand and he pulled away. A few minutes later, he pressed a rough, warm palm to my face, cupping my cheek. I opened my eyes in alarm.

"It's just lip balm, okay?" His thumb slid along my lower lip, back and forth. I nodded once, my heart thudding, and he moved to my top lip, massaging the ointment into the cracked skin until it was smooth and soft, pliant beneath his strokes. I watched his eyes as they tracked the movement of his finger. Then he blinked and pulled his hand away, as if he only suddenly realized he was touching my lips.

My throat felt dry again. "Thank you," I whispered. "For being here."

He looked up briefly and nodded before busying himself with the tube of lip balm and clearing his throat. "How are you feeling?"

"Better after some water, thank you."

"Good. You've been out of it for a while. A few days. If you hadn't woken and asked for water by morning, we were going to have to get a drip."

"We?"

"The doctor. Dr. Butler. He was on the island for a wedding, thank God."

"I don't remember."

"I don't doubt it, you were pretty delirious. You have the flu."

The flu? I'd been out of it for days?

He laid the lip balm next to the water. Seeing me eye the glass, he brought it back to me for another sip. Water had never tasted so good.

"I should let you rest now that your fever has broken," he said and moved toward the door.

"Tom?" My voice cracked.

"Yeah? Oh, sorry, I need to turn off the light." He headed toward the bedside light he'd turned on when I'd first woken him.

"Will you stay in here? Like you were?"

He stopped mid-stride.

I looked away, lest he see how much I needed him to say yes. I focused on the patterns of faded florals decorating the comforter.

"Uh, sure," he said finally.

"Thanks," I mumbled and sank into my pillow, squeezing my eyes shut.

The red behind my lids went black as the light clicked off and the bed shifted under Tom's weight. I inhaled his smell of salt and weathered wood.

"No problem."

"You were right. I do sleep better when you're around," I admitted quietly. The darkness made it easier to speak.

"It's fine . . . good night."

We lay in the dark, and I listened to his breathing, waiting for it to even out. I'm not sure if I thought he'd leave as soon as I was sleeping, but I wanted him to sleep first. I thought about what I might be really afraid of. Why did I feel so comforted having this man, who'd been a relative stranger to me just a few weeks ago, close to me?

I should feel threatened by him, shouldn't I? I mean . . . he was a man. Men had urges. Needs. Needs that made them act like animals. Needs that controlled them.

For me, the things I did had only ever been a mechanical

necessity. A curiosity. A way to control someone or something. A situation.

Did Abby enjoy sex? Had she had it with Tom? With Whit?

I slept most of the next day, and Tom checked on me frequently, giving me water and some chicken broth when I finally felt hungry.

He walked me to the bathroom, his arm wrapped almost completely around my waist, and I got the feeling he just wanted to pick me up and carry me there. It made me feel tiny and protected. My mind was too groggy and tired to think on it much. But I knew I'd look back and be embarrassed.

When the light beyond the thin curtains began to fade, I wondered how to ask him to stay again. When I woke late in the night in the dark, I felt him next to me.

"Tom?" I whispered.

"Yeah?"

"Do you see her sometimes? Do you see Abby?" I desperately wanted to know if it was all in my mind, or if somehow Abby was imprinted here in this cottage, and that's why I kept seeing her. Her ghost? I'd never believed in stuff like that, but I couldn't deny that it felt like Abby was with me all the time, trying to tell me something. Or my subconscious was. Or my meds were making me crazy. Speaking of meds, I hadn't had mine for days.

"See her?" He let out a long, slow breath.

I waited.

"You remind me of her sometimes, despite your hair. But no. No, I don't see her in you. I just see *you*."

God, that wasn't what I'd meant at all. But I stayed silent, absorbing his words. Somehow he'd answered a question I hadn't even realized I needed answered. And the *way* he'd answered it made my stomach clench. He'd just offered me something I'd been craving in the deepest parts of me . . . I wanted to be *seen*. I didn't want to just be Abby's little sister to anyone. And especially not to Tom. But who did I want to be? And what did I want to be to Tom?

CHAPTER EIGHTEEN

As we lay there in the dark, the silence wasn't remotely relaxing or conducive to sleep. It seemed heavy. Laden. Pregnant. Tense. A weird energy pulsed between us. Pulsed deep inside *me*. Like a low-grade buzz in my belly, making me restless.

Shifting on to my side away from him, I closed my eyes. As I lay there, I suddenly realized something monumentally confusing, that filled me with utter shock. Something I knew but had refused to acknowledge.

I was attracted to Tom.

Completely.

On a visceral and bone-deep level.

This was no longer a curiosity or me reacting to him just because he was a male. This wasn't about the way I admired him, depended on him, felt safe with him. And I had no idea what he even looked like really, if he was good-looking or nerdy. He was strong, his body was beautiful. I'd basically ogled it out the kitchen window the other day. Etched, defined and tanned, the kind of body I'd cut out of magazines and Abercrombie & Fitch catalogs once upon a time and pasted into my journal.

But had I been attracted to him back then? I didn't think I had. Maybe it was his gentleness with me, or the way I saw him struggle to be even-keeled even though I was a bitch on a daily basis. Maybe it was his writing. The way I felt like I'd had a sneak peek into his soul. Perhaps it was his shock and disappointment at hearing me talk so casually about sex and act like some fucked-up Lolita, which for the first time in my life actually made me feel ashamed.

It had hurt him for some reason. And, I realized, that hurt me.

But seeing him crack the other day and go apeshit with the ax had done something to me that I couldn't explain. I'd never known a man capable of that kind of raw emotion. I was realizing now that it may have cracked something in *me*.

I just didn't know what to do with this new information. I'd felt defensive and antagonistic toward him, and now I was feeling weirdly tender. No, it wasn't tenderness alone. Perhaps after everything, it turned out I could actually feel something sexual for someone. Unfortunately, that someone turned out to be older. Way older. Someone who was sort of looking after my sorry ass.

Christ, did I have daddy issues or what?

And shit. Now I needed to pee, again.

I already knew I was still too weak to get there on my own. And the thought of his hands wrapped around my waist made my breath stop. The humiliations just kept coming.

I gained strength over the next few days, and Tom left one morning for Savannah but was back before that night. Unfortunately, I missed my Tuesday work day, and again on Wednesday.

"It's a bad idea. You're not up to it yet," Tom had informed me on that Tuesday morning.

I disagreed. And felt like I should walk to get some exercise.

I made it about three minutes down the road before I sat on a fallen pine, exhausted. Tom rode up thirty seconds later, having predicted my demise. "Well, you certainly are consistent in your stubbornness," he laughed.

I gave him the finger and rolled my eyes as I climbed into the cart, which just made him laugh more.

Something had shifted in me since my realization. I wasn't sure how to act around him anymore. I'd started off switching between barely speaking to him and trying to goad him. Now, I agonized over every word I said. Though my childishness seeped out every now and again, I strived to sound smart, intelligent . . . older. Which resulted in me clamming up. If he noticed I'd suddenly become wooden around him, he didn't say anything.

"I have something for you," he said when we got back to the cottage. He shut off the engine and came around to my side, offering me a hand to help me out. I took it, reveling in the sensation of my hand feeling tiny in his large, rough one. He didn't let go until we got to the front door, and I ached when he did.

"Call Marjoe first and let her know." He nodded to the phone in the hall.

Marjoe knew about the flu and hadn't been expecting me anyway. I hung up with a promise to come in as soon as I could. The thing was, I was desperate to work and do something. More desperate than ever to get myself together. Not be a burden to Tom.

I walked back out to the kitchen area. Tom was sitting on the other side of the table, arms folded. Sitting in front of him, in the middle of the table, was a smartphone. With a tilt of his head, he indicated I should sit down.

I sat. "You got me a phone?" I wasn't sure what to think. It was an extravagant gift, first of all. But I was also confused as to his motives. "Thank you."

"It's not just a phone."

"Yeah, I know. It's a smartphone, access to the Internet, et cetera, et cetera." The idea that I could have a link to the outside world terrified me all of a sudden. I didn't want anyone piercing this bubble I'd built out here on the island with my lonely lion guy. I'd almost broken it the other night with the stupid Tyler stunt. Not only did I not want to break the bubble, but I didn't want to even peek out of it. I realized that made me borderline agoraphobic in a way, but I didn't care.

"Actually, there's fairly limited data access out here, so no. That's not what it's for." He brought his hands up to his face, rubbing them over his eyes.

I frowned. "I don't understand."

He exhaled and sat up straighter. "Okay. Just hear me out."

"This is sounding less and less like a gift, you know," I mused.

"I know. Sorry. Look, the thing is, when you were sick and Dr. Butler was here, I asked him about your anxiety and your panic attacks."

My heart hammered in a weird dance of betrayal. He'd been discussing me? While I was incapable of being a part of the conversation? I was so shocked, I couldn't react right away.

"Well, I told him which medications you were taking, and obviously I didn't know the history of why or when you started taking them and how often. I didn't want to tell him some of them might not have been prescribed—"

"You had no right," I finally choked out. How dare he? I pushed back from the table, my anger leaking out of my eyes in the form of tears.

"I'm sorry, Liv, but—"

"Don't call me that! That's Abby's name for me, not yours. Only people I trust can call me that."

He flinched and sat back, but I barely gave it a thought.

"I can't *believe* you'd speak to a doctor about me, it's not your right. You have no right," I repeated. Part of me knew he'd done it out of care and concern, but it didn't make up for the fact that this was *my* problem. Mine. It was *my* battle to fight.

"Please, Olivia." Ugh, I hated that. *No, please keep calling me Liv.* "If I thought you'd take the suggestion, I would have asked *you* to do it and not done it without your permission. But I also didn't plan on it, okay?" He raked his fingers through his hair. "First of all, I thought you'd been fucking drugged. And I'll never be completely convinced that wasn't part of it. Plus, you went days without taking any of your meds, and I needed to know what to do. He was here, and I was scared shitless I was doing something wrong or not doing something I should be. For all I knew, you were slipping into a coma, which was not outside the realm of possibility given how out of it you were," he finished, chest heaving.

I stared at him and saw in a clear and unguarded moment deep in his eyes, now locked to mine, how legitimately scared he'd been. I hadn't truly thought about it from his perspective. Come to think of it, I hadn't taken much medication in the days leading up to getting ill either. I'd been trying to space them out and make them last longer, and it occurred to me that perhaps my attacks were lessening. Not my night-time ones, but my everyday anxiety that could sometimes be tripped by a simple feeling of nervousness or unease. A prime example was the night I'd been with Tyler. Everything about that situation should have set me off, and perhaps it would have manifested later, but Tom had showed up, and I'd thankfully never know.

"So what did Dr. Butler say?" I asked, surprising him with my abrupt change of attitude.

Tom sat back. "Well, like I said, without knowing your medical history, he did happen to mention that in some people, use of psychiatric medication to relieve a certain symptom can sometimes have the effect of worsening it. Especially with anxiety and depression medication, doses can be very important, as well as the age and chemical makeup of the person taking it. So, I'm just throwing this out there because I am in *no way* telling you your anxiety isn't real and based on real stuff—"

"It sure does sound like it," I snapped, my initial forgiving mood eclipsed by the need to defend my condition. "You sound like my damn parents. You are *not* responsible for me, Tom."

"You're the one who showed up on my fucking doorstep and made me responsible. And if your parents knew this was a problem, why didn't they try to get it altered?"

I barked out a laugh. "Because getting me medicated was the primary objective. Once that had been accomplished, why on earth would they spend time and money asking a shrink to tinker with the doses? If I freaked out, I got more meds. That was it. My parents were happy because they got to feel like they'd done something about their problem, the shrink was happy to write another scrip, and I was happy to have an arsenal of medications to drown out the world around me."

He stayed quiet as my outburst ricocheted around the small cottage. I'd never really articulated my feelings about what my parents had done, but I realized this was exactly how I felt.

God, the kitchen clock with its ticking was driving me crazy. How did he stand it? I got up and walked over to the bookshelf, pulling out the book of fairy tales absently, then sliding it back in with my index finger. "And by the way, it's *my* doorstep."

"How old were you when you first starting taking medication?" he asked quietly, ignoring my childishness.

"Fourteen."

"Why?"

I knew the questions were coming, and I felt too weak to put up my defenses. "Because I started having panic attacks and night terrors."

He exhaled slowly. "Do you know *why* you started having panic attacks and night terrors?"

He was asking the wrong questions. I suddenly, desperately wanted to talk to him, to tell him, but I didn't know how. Not unless he asked me the right questions.

"Stop trying to be my therapist." My tone was biting. I paused and looked over to where he sat hunched over the table, so weary, so . . . concerned. "And stop making me feel like your pity project."

"I'm not. You're not," he said, blithely spinning the phone around on the table with a finger. "I'm just facing our obvious predicament that, firstly, we aren't sure you're taking the right stuff in the right amounts, and secondly, you're going to run out of it soon if you haven't already."

"No shit. So what's the phone got to do with anything?"

He cleared his throat. "I know that having the medication is . . . comforting. That sometimes just having it nearby affords you some kind of lifeline, if you will, a means of rescue, should you need it. And that alone can be calming. Right?"

I nodded. "I guess."

"So I was wondering, hoping actually, that you'd let me be that for you."

CHAPTER NINETEEN

$\mathcal{I}$ looked at Tom in shock. He wanted to be my . . . *what*?

His shoulders were tense, his shirt sleeves rolled up to reveal his strong, tanned forearms. "I want you to be able to pick up the phone whenever you want—whether you're at work or I'm at work helping Pete, or if I'm in Savannah—and know that I will always be there. You don't even have to call; you can just text me, send me a code or something, and I will *always* come. As soon as I can."

I wasn't sure what to make of what he was saying. My head slowly shook from side to side.

"No, listen, Li— Olivia—"

"Liv," I whispered.

He gave a single slow nod. "Liv."

I shook my head again, not really able to articulate a response yet. Part of me felt completely humbled that he would put this albatross around his own neck. I was also insanely mad at him that he would do this to me, make me feel so indebted and guilty, and intensely terrified of giving up my control to him. Because that's what it would be. When I had medication, it helped me feel in control of handling my attacks. He was asking me to give that up and trust *him* to be the one to talk me down. What was even more unsettling was that he seemed to *know* how much he helped me, or he never would have seen this as a viable option. It was almost too much to process.

"Liv," he said gently. "I can see all the reasons why you'll tell me no whirring through your head, but here's a good reason why you should let me do this. I'm not saying I'm magic and that you don't need your medication; I'm saying until we can figure out what to do about it, please help *me* not to worry. When I'm not home, I think about whether you are having a panic attack, and how scared you must be on your own out here, or that you might fall and hurt yourself, or leave the stove on and burn the place down while you sleep because you were too panicked to think of turning it off."

"Careful, you'll be the one sounding like an anxiety case soon." I gave a small smile to cover just how precisely he'd hit on my own fears.

"I know. Trust me, it crossed my mind."

If only he knew how much I depended on him already, he would know that asking me to do this, to depend on him like this, would make my enslavement complete. But for some reason I didn't care. He already made up the largest part of my universe; why not make him the center? The magnitude of the thought went off like a sonic boom in my chest.

"There's more," he added, an eyebrow raised, oblivious to the fact that I'd realized he was my sun.

"God, what?" I croaked.

"There's a bonus in it for you, if you agree."

"You mean in addition to getting to hear your sexy voice down the line whenever I feel like it?" I meant to sound joking, but I'd accidentally tripped over my own elephant. My cheeks instantly heated and I looked away, not wanting him to see my weirded-out reaction to what I'd said. "What? What is it?" I asked.

"I know you miss having music. I have a ton on my laptop, so I'll try and be better about playing it, though you can just ask if I forget. But anyway, I loaded some of it on to the phone too."

Uh, okay. Cool, but we probably had vastly different tastes. "How do you know what music I like?"

"Because you hum and sing a lot."

"I do?"

"Yeah, you do." He smiled, revealing his beautiful straight white teeth.

"But only happy people hum, don't they?" I asked sarcastically and couldn't help my small grin.

He laughed. "Except you. You hum when you're tired, when you're in the shower, when you're going through all the boxes stored in the attic looking for whatever it is you're looking for, when you're making a sandwich. Even when you're reading those happy little fairy tales. You actually may hum in your sleep. You hum all the freaking time."

"God, really? I had no idea. I'm sorry." I was mortified.

"Don't be. I figured it was a calming thing. You've actually got a great voice. I like it."

I flushed again, remembering my comment about his sexy voice. Gah.

"Anyway, I recognized some of what you sing, so I used that as a starting point." He slid the phone across to me.

I took it gingerly, swiping the screen. "By the way," I said, looking down at the phone, "those fairy tales are definitely not happy."

"I thought all fairy tales had happy endings."

"Not these." I scrolled down through the music and with every entry felt my incredulity grow. Man, this guy paid attention. A lot of my favorite bands were there, and a few singer-songwriters, some of whom I'd never heard of but, based on Tom's perception, was eager to try. Obviously I hadn't hummed any of my heavy-metal choices. Or I had and he hadn't recognized them.

I'd been a weird, freaky bitch to him from the moment I'd arrived and he'd just kept on paying attention and figuring me out. It was humbling. I opened my mouth to thank him but words and feelings scrambled over each other and clogged my throat. Before I knew it, a tear escaped, which I swiped at frantically. "Thank you," I finally managed.

"So you'll do this for me?" he asked, staring at my cheek where I'd wiped away the tear.

I was under no illusions that he was doing this for me and not himself, but he was right: *I needed* to believe I was doing it partially for his sake rather than mine.

"Thank you for the music," I said, hedging. "It was a nice sweetener. And I'll use the phone. For *you*," I emphasized. "At some point, though, I'd like you to tell me about Abby."

He seemed to consider my words. "Only if you tell me what your bad dreams are about."

"Checkmate. I'm not ready."

"That's not a no."

"Yours wasn't either."

He tilted his head in acknowledgment.

"Wannna play chess?" I asked, and he burst out laughing, his head dropping back and exposing his tanned throat where his beard stopped.

I smiled too, unable to stop myself. "Chess it is then."

And I got up to dust off the game board that obviously hadn't been played since the last summer I'd been here with Abby. "And let's get some tunes on, yeah?"

"Sure. But winner gets a question."

I tensed. "Not one of the ones we've mentioned tonight."

"Fair enough."

Setting the board between us, I decided to clear the air a bit more. "I'm sorry I've been a burden—"

"You're not."

"A pain in the ass, then. I get bitchy. I'm sorry. I just . . . sometimes I feel . . ." I fingered a chess piece, trying to find a way to explain something even I didn't understand.

"You feel?" Tom prodded when the silence continued.

"Like you see through me. Into me or something. Exposed. I feel vulnerable and exposed. I guess I respond by being . . . difficult, doing things that make it difficult to like me. That way it doesn't hurt me as much when you don't, because I know I made it happen."

My cheeks throbbed. I couldn't believe I was being so honest, but it was an apology that needed to happen. I snuck a quick look up to see Tom still watching me thoughtfully.

"What would you say . . ." He shifted, his brow furrowing as if wrangling the right words into submission. He looked away, around the comfortable cottage with its simple rustic decor, around our safe place, *my* safe place. "What would you say if I said I felt the same way?" His dark eyes flicked back to mine. "You make me feel the same. Threatened, kind of, even though I'm not sure quite what I mean by that."

I swallowed against the strange butterfly sensation beating tiny wings up my throat from my chest. The clock ticked through a full revolution as I tried to formulate a response.

If he didn't know what he meant, then how the hell was *I* supposed to? "I'd say . . . I don't believe I'm a threat to you."

I wasn't sure if I expected him to say the same, that he didn't believe he was a threat to me either. But he didn't, and the silence that followed spoke louder than anything.

It was a tough game of chess. Each one of us advanced and retreated. But he'd opened with the Sicilian Defense, and so I got to anticipate most of his moves. We both suffered some severe casualties, and he threw me for some loops. But mostly I could see him sizing me up and looking at me with renewed respect.

We paused for soup and rolls.

When I finally slid my queen to G7 and whispered, "Check," it was to see those golden eyes look up at me in stunned disbelief.

"Holy shit," he said in awe. "How'd you do that?"

I shrugged. "It's called the Stonewall Attack. You can look it up. Although I almost couldn't make it work," I added, throwing him a bone.

"But, I mean, how did you learn?"

"There's an app for that." I grinned, totally loving his surprise. At his skeptical look, I rolled my eyes. "Seriously, I was advanced placement. I'd basically finished high school and didn't feel like doing anything additional, so I killed time doing other approved activities."

"I thought you dropped out. Isn't it mid-year?"

"I did drop out, but I'm done with all of my requirements to graduate. Except the state test."

"Which you'll go back to take."

"Wasn't planning on it."

"But you want to graduate, right?"

"What does it matter to you? In the meantime, it's time for my question."

He sighed and sat back, looking at me warily, linking his fingers behind his head.

I needed to get as much as I could into my one question. I already knew I couldn't ask him about Abby. Yet. Anyway, I'd lied earlier, I wasn't ready to hear it. In fact, the more I got to know Tom, the less I wanted to know about his past with my sister.

I thought of the thing I wondered most on a daily basis. "What do you do when you go to Savannah?"

CHAPTER TWENTY

Tom sat across the kitchen table observing me.

"What?" I asked as he rocked back on the hind legs of the chair. "It's a simple question. Where do you go when you're in Savannah?"

"It's not that; I just didn't expect that to be your first question. And also, there are many answers to it, and surely I only owe you one. But which one? I ask myself."

"You owe me them all," I countered. I wasn't sure what real flirting was, where I actually cared about the outcome, but I felt sure it had to be close to this.

"How so?"

"Well, a lie of omission is still a lie, is it not?"

"Oh, we have to be truthful?"

My eyes widened.

"Kidding." He raised his palms. "I'm kidding."

I scowled, and he laughed.

"What's the point in lying?" I asked. It only complicated things. People didn't believe the truth anyway.

"General lying or right now?"

Hmmm. "Good question. Generally."

"Generally. Let's see. There is no point because it's exhausting. I don't do it."

"Ever?"

"I have. I try not to. You'd probably have to make up twenty more lies to keep it going."

"Ayn Rand says lying is an act of making yourself a slave to whom you lie." I nervously played with one of his captured white chess pieces. A pawn. "You become imprisoned in your own falsehood that *they* control. I can't remember the quote, but it's something like that."

He looked away a moment. "Wow, you beat me at chess and now you're quoting Ayn Rand. Who are you, and where have you been since you arrived?"

He didn't mean anything by it, but I still took a small measure of offense. In fact, I started to feel acutely embarrassed. "Well, I'm paraphrasing, not quoting." I dropped the chess piece and drew my hand away from the table, and his flashed out and grabbed it. His hand was warm and rough. I stared at it. Tanned where mine was pale. Large where mine seemed tiny. A surge of something warm rolled through me, and I shifted in my seat.

"Don't go," he said.

I looked up, my eyebrows pinching together. "I'm not."

"I mean don't go away mentally, like you do." He cleared his throat and released my hand, dropping my insides off a ledge. "You go off somewhere sometimes. I didn't mean you acted dumb before."

I pulled my hand off the table to my lap. "I didn't think that. I just . . . this is new, weird, for me."

"What is?"

"Bantering, I guess. Using my skills, things I know, to interact with someone. I . . . I suddenly felt relaxed and it didn't even occur to me . . . " I trailed off, not really knowing what I was trying to say.

"Didn't occur to you what?"

Occur to me that I was trying to impress you, and that I really, really cared if it worked.

"Meh." I shrugged, then raised my eyes in surprise. "That you were trying to distract me from answering the question. I almost fell for it, too. Now come on, what do you do in Savannah?"

He steepled his fingers. "Well, I shop."

"Mmmmm. Aaaand?"

"For shampoo and other stuff."

"For food."

"For tampons." He shuddered good-naturedly.

I grinned at his reaction. I was so thankful my period had waited until after I was strong enough to walk to the bathroom on my own. Then I remembered the condom incident and moved on. "And apart from shopping?"

"Help Pete get contracts with the local restaurants and distributors for his fish."

"Oh. Cool."

A silence ensued. His steepled fingers began to twitch and fidget and his eyes still watched me.

I waited.

"And I go somewhere I can hop on to Wi-Fi and read the news, send emails, et cetera."

"Somewhere liiike . . ." I slowly moved my head from one side to the other.

"Depends. Sometimes the library, a coffee shop, the university."

"University?"

"Yes. This really does seem like more than one question."

"You were the one who had to complicate it by doing all these things there. Why the university?"

He cleared his throat. "I'm studying there, and that really did count as another question."

"You're studying there?" Why did that not even occur to me? "How old are you? What are you studying?"

"That is *definitely* additional and unsanctioned questioning."

I frowned. "They're sub-questions."

"Whatever. I recently started doing a BS in criminal justice, studying in a part-time program. Sometimes I have night school, some courses are available during the work week, but most of the course load is online. And that is all I am answering for you." He got up and moved our soup dishes to the sink.

I'd just learned more about Tom in the last ten minutes than I had in the last three weeks. Criminal justice. Interesting.

"What's your last name?" I asked.

Tom paused in his rinsing. "*That* is definitely for another game," he tossed over his shoulder. "But now that I've seen you play chess, we have to play something else."

I got up, perused the bottom shelf that held the board games. There were a ton of puzzles, all of which Abby and I had completed at one time or another.

Why do people keep puzzles? The joy is finally realizing that a piece that's been sitting in front of your nose, that you keep passing over because the shape seems a bit off, or the smidge of red isn't quite the same shade as the robin's wing, is the one you've been looking for the last three hours. Abby would call a side switch, and lo and behold it would be the first piece she'd snap cleanly into place. Granted, I did the same to her. But once we *knew* all the puzzle's secrets, we didn't ever do the same one again.

"Scrabble?" I asked.

"What was your favorite subject in school?"

"Uh, I think you have to play and win first."

"Well, you read Ayn Rand, and if your favorite subject was English lit, then I could have a problem."

"Chicken."

"Fine. Bring it."

I spent most of the game in the lead until he played JAUNTY for sixty-one points on a triple word score. Which included an extra seven points because he put the Y right under the B from my stunning play . . . BAT.

"Jaunty?" I said, my voice laced with mock disgust.

He looked ridiculously pleased and smug. "Yep. Jaunty."

"That's an abomination of a word."

"It very well may be, but it's a word."

I huffed and proceeded to chase his score for the rest of the game, until we'd boxed ourselves into one corner of the board. "That's annoying," I said as he managed to slide DRIP down the side with the D making SHAPED. Who the hell had whole words left at this stage of a Scrabble game? Tom, that's who.

"Now, now, don't be a sore loser." He cracked his knuckles and looked around. "What should I ask, what should I ask?" he mused to himself.

"We're not done yet."

"You have the Q, I presume. I really don't think you have a chance. We should call it."

I doubled my focus.

Then smiled a massive smile I really couldn't hold back.

I placed my second to last tile, my Q that Tom said I couldn't play, right next to the I on DRIP. It wouldn't win me the game, but damn, I was pleased with myself. I vibrated with giggles.

"That's not a word," Tom frowned. When he looked up and saw me, he seemed momentarily frozen.

"Yeah, it is," I snorted, my eyes watering as I lost it. It felt so good to laugh.

Tom stared, his mouth twitching. Because seriously, how could you stay straight-faced while someone in front of you lost their mind? Eventually he chuckled along with me, shaking his head.

We sobered and counted up our points, as neither of us could play our last tile. I lost by seven. And of course, he went to the bookshelf and pulled the official Scrabble dictionary down. "Well, fuck me," he muttered.

"I thought we covered lying." I winked.

I *winked*? Who the hell was I?

"I was just checking. You may have been . . . mistaken. Anyway," he said, heading back to the table. "I said *I* don't lie. I don't think you made a claim either way."

I rolled my eyes.

As he came past me, he patted my head. That was it, two short, light, *friendly* taps on the crown of my head where my hair was pulled back into a pony. And my bubble burst. I sank my face down to the table and thunked my forehead on the scarred wood. *Ah fuck.*

"What's the matter?" he asked as he scooped up the Scrabble pieces.

"Nothing. I'm tired, I guess," I mumbled into the wood. "I'm going to bed."

"It's only five p.m. and you've slept for five days."

I shrugged. Then, getting up and leaving him to put away the game, I headed to my room.

Five minutes later, I opened to his knock, eyeing him warily. He stood holding my new phone out to me, one eyebrow cocked up over a caramel eye.

I took it, careful not to touch the skin of his fingers. "Thank you."

"You're welcome," he said, turning away. Then he swung back. "Are you sure you're okay?"

I nodded and closed the door. I felt like my face might betray me at any second. I didn't know how, but I was sure of it.

That night marked the first night since I'd gotten sick that he didn't sleep next to me. He must be relieved not to be babysitting me anymore and sleeping fully clothed.

Right before I fell asleep, earbuds in my ears, listening to songs on my phone, it chirped. I looked at the glowing screen.

Don't think I've forgotten I get to ask you a question. Sleep well.

A few days later, Tom headed to Savannah. I was sitting on the porch with a coffee when he left. The air was cool and bright and laced with a hint of early-blooming magnolia.

"You gonna be okay till tomorrow?" he asked, pulling his backpack over one shoulder.

I nodded, clutching the warm mug between my hands, my knees drawn up to my chin.

Tucking his hair behind his ears, he pulled a black baseball cap on. Then he trotted down the steps and headed out to the tree-lined road, leaving me the cart.

"Hey," I called. "When can I come with you?"

He stopped, seeming to think on something. "You feel up to coming today?"

"I don't think so. Besides, I haven't got my paycheck yet. Next week?"

"Uh, sure." He turned and headed on down the road.

Don't sound so enthusiastic, buddy.

It was strange knowing now why he went to Savannah. I couldn't work out if it was better or worse.

I brought out my grandmother's recipe book again. Despite my previous failure, I realized I'd like to do something nice for Big Jake.

And, when I thought about it, for Marjoe. If she hadn't called Tom when I went with Tyler . . .

And for Pete.

And well, for Tom too. Definitely Tom.

For the first time in my life, I felt like there were people who cared about what happened to me. It was a strange and sobering thought. I'd never realized the lack as keenly as I did now that I'd met this interesting cast of characters. They didn't need anything from me, they'd just absorbed me into their daily lives as if I'd always been there.

I closed my eyes, with a sort of happiness in my chest, a simple contentment, in contrast to the unwelcome ache caused by Tom's absence.

Before

"Can I taste the icing, Gran?" My arm was tired from beating the butter so hard. All the powdered sugar was smoothed in, with a dash of vanilla and lemon zest. It smelled delicious. My tongue tingled and my mouth watered.

"Hold your horses, dear." Gran bustled over. Her blonde hair, shot through with icy tones just like the frosting, was pulled back, braided and wound into a tight bun to keep it out of the way. "You'll get your chance. Let's just get these cakes iced first. Then you can lick the bowl clean."

"Promise?" I swung my legs back and forth under the table.

Gran ran her rough palm over my head and then bent and kissed my forehead. "Promise. You are such a help, thank you."

Abby was out riding her bike with two kids she'd met who were renting a house near the golf club for the week. I'd tried to keep up with them, but couldn't, and Abby kept leaving me behind. I had a scraped knee and bruised elbow for my efforts. Gran decided I needed to help her instead.

"You're welcome." I grinned, proud of my work and pleased to get to do this with Gran on my own for once.

"Well, if it's a nice sunset tonight, I think we'll bathe and eat early and put you both in those new little summer dresses I bought you. I must take a picture of you clean at least once this summer, and not like the little beach-bum hooligans you are." She shook her head, smiling, and moved the spreader back and forth in waves as she smoothed the frosting on to a stacked cake.

The clock on the wall ticked loudly. A curious thought popped into my head, one I kept forgetting to ask Gran about. No time like right now. "Gran?"

"Yes, honey?"

"Why don't you like Mom and Dad?"

Her hand stilled. "What do you mean? I love your mother. She's my daughter. And I like your father just fine too."

"Oh." But that didn't make sense.

Gran resumed spreading frosting, careful not to stop watching what she was doing.

"Well," I tried again, "it's just we never all come here, and I thought I heard . . ."

Gran looked up.

"Um, I heard Mom and Abby talking once . . ." I trailed off again.

"About what, honey?"

"Just that Mom wanted us to see you, but that Mom and you had a fight about something and you weren't ever going to forgive her. Like ever. Forever, ever." My nose prickled, and I felt my chin wobble as I tried to speak steady.

Gran put the spreader down and came around to my side.

"What did she do, Gran, that you can't ever forgive her?"

Her arms went around me. "Oh Livvy . . ."

"Wh-what if Abby or I do something real bad one day . . ." I couldn't hold back the tears or my cracking voice, "like by accident, and you, you stop loving us?" I finished on a cry that snuck out of my heart and hurtled past my last word. And now I couldn't hold anything back.

Gran pulled me to her. "Oh baby girl."

My heart was bursting and painful with worry, and squeezing it all up into my head so all I could do was let tears out. "Wh-what if you don't want us to come here anymore?"

She mashed my wet face against her soft shirt that smelled of sugar and fresh-baked cakes. "Livvy, Olivia, listen to me . . ."

"What if no one loves us, no one wants us anymore?"

Gran squeezed me tighter, almost stopping my air, then pulled me away, taking my face in hers. "Listen to me, Olivia. You are good. You are pure," she said fiercely. "You and Abby are the most wonderful gift from heaven. And you will always be able to come here. No matter what. Here will be your safe place. Forever. Okay?"

I stared at her through my blurry tears. Her eyes were filled with tears of her own, but her mouth was set in a determined line.

"Do you understand?" Her hands dropped to my shoulders and shook me. "You can always come here. This is a place of love, Livvy. Always."

I snapped out of my memories and focused on the task at hand. After a massively failed attempt at a lemon cake, and dwindling supplies, I decided on cupcakes. At least if I got it right, I'd be able to share them out. I took my new phone out of my back pocket with the idea of seeing if I could pull up a webpage out here, and typed, *Why did my cake flop?* into the search bar. After watching the wheel spin for what felt like an eternity, I texted Tom.

Can you do an Internet search for why my cake flopped?

I got a text back immediately.

Not even going to mess with that one. Is this an emergency?

Yes.

Riiight. Hang on.

I waited.

And waited.

You know how to do an Internet search, right? You're not looking it up in the library or something.

God, you're a smartass. And I think this counts as an abuse of privilege.

What? The privilege of having a phone?

Yes. Stop bothering me so I can go through the thousands of things you've probably done that made your cake flop.

Thousands? Shit.

Baking powder expired?

I went to check. The cottage phone started ringing, so I veered off course to answer it. "Hello?"

"It's me." Tom's voice had a smoky flavor to it that really did a number on my stomach.

"What are you calling me for?"

"I was tired of typing. Did you check the baking soda?"

"Ugh. I was going to check when I had to come answer the phone, nimwit." I was smiling.

"Nimwit? What kind of a word is nimwit?"

"A *jaunty*-sounding one?"

Tom broke into a bellow of laughter that made me feel like I'd just won first prize at a swim meet. I could start to like talking on the phone if I got to hear this all the time.

"Hang on, okay?" I let the phone dangle on its cord and headed back to the pantry. My phone chirped.

Hurry up.

I rolled my eyes, my cheeks hurting from grinning, and checked the expiration. All good. I headed back to the phone to let him know.

"The eggs," he said next. "Did you let them reach room temperature?"

"The eggs!" I yelled jubilantly. "That's it. I took them straight out of the fridge."

"Damn," said Tom.

"Why?"

"I was hoping to make you run around a bit more."

"Funny. Okay, thanks for your help. I better get baking."

"Have fun."

"I will."

"I'm glad you're doing something."

"Well, it makes me feel closer to my grandmother. To Abby. We baked together when we were here. And thank you."

There was a pause. "You're welcome."

I hung up and got mixing and measuring. A few minutes later I got another text.

You better make an extra batch.

Don't worry. I'm making cupcakes for you.

Thanks, but make extra for you. You're far too skinny. I'm going to shove cupcakes in your mouth when I get home. Put lots of frosting on them.

The images my mind conjured up of Tom feeding me made my heart beat erratically, so I clung on to the one word that had calmed me down. *Home.*

CHAPTER TWENTY-ONE

$\mathcal{I}$t was late afternoon by the time I made it to Mama's, arms full of passable baked goods. I backed through the door carrying the large plastic containers packed full of cupcakes, and one full-sized lemon cake for Big Jake. I didn't know which one of my grandmother's cakes was his favorite, but I supposed I'd find out soon enough.

The place was empty, lunch over and dinner not yet begun.

"Hey, hun," a female voice called behind me. "Let me help you."

I smelled her floral scent before I turned and Bethany reached out to relieve me of my containers. Her long auburn hair was in a loose braid over her shoulder. Everything suddenly clicked into place, and all my fragile confidence and security, the bubble of friendship and trust I'd built with Tom, popped and fizzed in a gooey mess down through my body, leaving me light-headed.

"Are you all right?" she asked, her luminous eyes full of concern. She laid the containers on a nearby table and came toward me.

I stepped back. "F-fine. Just, uh, felt woozy for a minute."

"Oh, honey, you've been so sick. Poor Tommy was out of his mind with worry. I can't believe you are up and about so quickly. Here, come sit down for a few minutes."

I couldn't help cataloguing everything about her. Long hair, slim body, tight pink T-shirt over boobs twice the size of mine. Her teeth were slightly crooked, and her skin bore a few small acne scars that simply made her prettiness more real. I'd just never noticed it before. Why hadn't it ever occurred to me that Tommy was seeing someone on the island, someone who worked at a place he frequented fairly regularly?

"I'm fine, really."

"Come and have something to drink and eat while you're here." With a friendly smile, she closed her hand over mine. "Tommy'd be upset if I sent you back down the road feeling so out of sorts."

How much talking about me to Bethany did Tommy do? A lot, it seemed. My empty belly that held nothing but taste tests wasn't feeling so great. Was this what jealousy felt like?

Bethany chattered on as she sat me on a bar stool and poured me a large glass of water.

"So what did you make?"

I frowned. "What?"

She nodded at the plastic containers.

"Oh. Uh, I found my grandmother's recipe book, so I *attempted* to do some baking. I wanted to make something for Big Jake. Not sure how it turned out."

"I'm sure it's great. I wasn't here when your grandmother was alive, but Big Jake never shuts up about her cakes."

I swallowed. "So, um, you . . ." The words had a hard time getting out of my throat. "You and Tom are, uh, you know . . ."

She flushed and shrugged, a small grin playing around her lips. "Yeah, I guess."

She guessed? Having the man who drowned every room he entered with his mere presence *in her bed* wasn't definitive enough?

"Oh," I managed. "Sorry about ruining your date the other night."

"That's all right. He had good reason to be freaked out when he heard you were with Tyler." She rolled her eyes and shuddered, her mouth screwing up with distaste. "You're lucky. What I wouldn't have given for a big brother like Tom to save me from some of *my* past mistakes."

Big brother.

I swallowed. "Yep."

She sighed, a dreamy smile on her face. "Anyway, it was so honorable and dashing, it just made him a thousand times more attractive in my eyes." Then, presumably at the scowl I couldn't control, "Not that you see him like that, I know, sorry. Ewww. But damn, the man is hot and so very . . ." She fanned herself dramatically.

I slid off the stool. "So is Big Jake in?" I hated my terse and dismissive cut-off, but I couldn't stand another second. This girlie bonding was just . . . ugh. And she was sooo . . . nice.

"Uh, sure. Sorry, you must be wanting to get home, not feeling so good and all. And here I am yammering on."

She went through the swinging door into the kitchen.

I covered my face with my hands and took a breath. Then I straightened up, pulled myself together, and followed her.

The cake was a success. Or they were just being really, really nice. Honestly, until Bethany wrote *Lemon cake—only 3 left* on the chalkboard outside that passed for a menu, I thought they were kidding. And maybe they still were.

I left a container of cupcakes for Marjoe and went to check on the kittens.

They were nowhere to be found.

"Big Jake," I called breathlessly, flying back into the back door of the kitchen. "Where's Miss Geechee and the babies?"

"Oh, Miss Liv. They done got inta trouble with a possum over a set o' ribs. That possum was rabid. It done kill two kittens."

"What?" My hand flew up to my chest, my voice wobbling.

"JJ done shoot 'im dead," Jake said, his big head shaking from side to side in his usual manner whenever he encountered something that didn't bear laughing about. Which was thankfully only about ten percent of life. Maybe less.

"What about my little guy?" I whispered, my eyes stinging.

"JJ took 'em back to the house. I jus' don' remember which ones he got." At the look on my face, he threw his handful of salt into the lobster pot full of grits and went on, "Don' choo worry, Miz Liv. I'll check on it and have JJ bring you your little fella. It's gone be awright."

I nodded and swallowed a watery gulp. Then nodded again, emphatically, as if I could gain strength from simply agreeing.

"Okay," I said, finally. "Okay." And I ran a finger under each eye.

It occurred to me I hadn't seen Marjoe, so instead of going back out the kitchen door, I waved goodbye to Jake and walked through the restaurant to find Bethany. "Hey, do you know where Marjoe is? She in her office?"

Bethany, capably holding three water jugs in each hand, nodded over to the back wall. "Tommy here this evening?"

"No." I shook my head. "He's in Savannah."

"Oh." She stopped and looked up from setting the jugs down on the cart. Then she resumed, moving them all into two rows. "He said we'd go together next time he went. To make up for . . . Never mind."

For me breaking up your sexy rendezvous with the condoms lubricated for maximum pleasure? Twelve of them?

"Uh, I . . . I think he said he had class or something," I said instead.

"Yeah, I know." Her sweet eyes pinched together for one second, then relaxed. "Oh well, he's probably fallen behind in the last week."

What with me being sick and all . . .

I liked that he'd been taking care of me instead of being with Bethany. Did that make me a bad person?

"Yeah," I said like a good little sister to the girl who likes her older brother. Then a thought occurred to me. "Where does he stay when he's in Savannah overnight?"

"Oh, his boat finally came back from the shop. Far as I know, that's where he stays now."

"A boat?"

"He didn't tell you?" she asked with zero guile, but still I hated her for the knowledge she possessed. "He has a little sailboat. Keeps it up on Bull River. Finally bought it last fall, but the motor was having trouble, so instead of winterizing, he put it in the shop to get it fixed up."

"Oh," I said. "Oh. Okay."

Marjoe took that moment to head out of her office. She looked like hell.

"She had some bad news about Pete," Bethany whispered under her breath, her lips barely moving.

I stepped forward. "Hi, Marjoe."

She swiped at her face and fluffed her hair. "Oh hi, hon. God, I must look like a skinned squirrel."

I grimaced. "Well, you've looked better, but I wouldn't go that far."

Bethany glared at me, but Marjoe barked a laugh. "You're a breath of fresh air. Just ain't no guessin' with you, is there?"

I shrugged. "Well, are you okay?"

"Nope, I'm not. Pete has lung cancer. Lung cancer! Can you believe that big old shit didn't tell me?" She flicked a hand out. "And damned if I can stop being a sniveling idiot about it. Not sure if I'm more pissed at myself or him. What are you doing here anyway? Thought you were still recovering?"

"I brought some cake for Big Jake and made some cupcakes for you." I bit my lip. "To say . . . thanks."

"That was sweet of you, honey. But thanks for what?"

"Just . . . giving me a chance, I guess. And also . . ." I glanced at Bethany, who'd moved back to get the condiment baskets, and dropped my voice. "Uh, could I speak with you privately?"

Marjoe didn't miss a beat. She turned and headed back to her office and motioned with her chin for me to follow. I scuttled up and followed her into the fluorescent room. It had white walls and an acoustic-style ceiling with water marks, and a chipped wood-veneer desk that was basically swimming in haphazard paperwork. It reeked of fresh and old smoke.

Marjoe motioned to the office chair on the other side of her desk and went around to her side, rummaging in the breast pocket of her denim shirt for something. A lighter. Then she flipped open a packet of menthol cigarettes and pulled one out, offering me the pack. I shook my head.

"Good. That's good. I gotta . . ." Her voice collapsed into a squeak, then she cleared her throat, her eyes tearing up. "I gotta give up." She stuffed the cigarette back in the box and threw the whole lot into the metal trash can in the corner. It dinged, loudly. "For Pete, you know. Least I can do. So, what can I do you for? How you feelin'?"

"Good, I'm good. Tired, but getting there."

"Well, we had a few customers down with it, but let's hope it doesn't continue its rounds. All this almost-hot-then-cold-again weather ain't helpin'." She shook her head, then pulled out a small compact from her drawer and wiped under her eyes. "I hope Tommy doesn't get it. Dang, I look terrible."

"I'm really sorry to hear about Pete. I had no idea. Tommy didn't mention it to me."

"You think Tommy knew?" Her eyes grew round and pinned me.

"No, no. I have no idea. He barely talks to me anyway."

Marjoe studied me while she snapped her compact closed and slid it into the drawer. "Y'all haven't talked much since you been here?"

"No." I shook my head. "I mean, more lately. We're becoming friends, I guess. Not that we weren't," I hastened to add. "It . . . it was just I'm not used to, uh, I'm not good at just being . . ." I trailed off, not really knowing how to explain myself.

"You haven't had many friendships, is what you're saying?"

"I guess." I gave a nervous laugh and wiped my damp palms on my jeans. "That sounds weird. I mean, I'm used to being on my own. Counting on myself. It's been strange to have someone else there who . . ."

"Cares about you?"

"No. Well, yes, someone I should be accountable to."

"Only if they earn it."

"What?"

"You should only be accountable to people who you care to be accountable to. And to earn that, you'd have to hold them in high regard, and they'd have to hold you likewise. I'd say Tommy's a good person to be accountable to."

"Well," I said, flushing as my memory decided to serve up my ridiculous seduction attempt. "I'm not sure he holds me in high regard. But he has been caring."

Marjoe played with the lighter, then pulled open her desk drawer absently before glancing at the trash can. She did it all without really leaving our conversation. "How much has Tommy told you about why he came to the island?"

"Nothing." I sat back. "Well, I guess I never asked." How self-absorbed did I have to be to never ask him where he grew up, why he came here?

"Hmm, well. First lesson in friendship is it goes two ways. Not that it did me any good. Did Pete see fit to tell me he was fixin' to die?" She growled the last word. "Nope. No way. Not me. I mean, why would he? I only just adore the man and been keepin' his bed warm the last eleven years. Wouldn't even make an honest woman out of me." She slapped her hand on the desk. "But anyway, Pete and me's a different relationship, but it's the same with friendship and family: you gotta just ask sometimes. Ain't nobody a mind-reader." Her eyes grew watery again. "I shoulda asked him. I knew he wasn't feeling good. I had a feelin'. Just shoulda asked him point blank, 'Are you sick?'" She shook her head.

"I'm so sorry, Marjoe."

She sniffed and waved her hand. "Men. So, honey, how can I help you?"

"I'm sorry I got the flu, and I'll make up my hours if I

need to, but actually I was going to ask you about how you pay us."

"Oh, by check."

"Even Big Jake and the boys?" Surely they didn't leave the island to visit a bank.

"Well, Big Jake was in the Marine Corps, Vietnam, so he's a member of the credit union. Only bank on the island."

"So that's what I wanted to ask you." I clasped my fingers together to keep them from fidgeting. "I don't have a bank account."

"Well that's no problem. You can set one up easily in Savannah or over on Hilton Head Island."

"I can't. I, uh, need a social security number to do that. And I . . ."

"You're not an illegal, are you?" Her eyes grew wide with amusement. "You look and sound American to me."

I gave a small answering smile. "It's not that." I'd agonized since I started about whether to just say I didn't have my social with me and couldn't prove it, or to tell the truth and hope she understood. In fact, I even had Abby's driver's license, so I could totally fake it, but that would require Marjoe paying Abigail Baines—deceased. *Definitely not.*

"I have one. It's mine," I clarified and swallowed what felt like a lump of leather. "I . . . I just can't use it."

"Oh." Her eyebrows pinched together, forming a vertical canyon in her already wrinkled forehead. "I see." And I could tell she did.

$\mathcal{I}$ dropped my eyes to my lap. I shouldn't have come to speak to Marjoe. This was ludicrous. "Maybe you could just pay Tom?" I asked quietly, in a last-ditch attempt to keep the job. I mean, since I'd started, I'd technically missed a third of my shifts and was now an Internal Revenue Service headache for her. Not to mention she'd already told me she didn't really need me and was just doing it as a favor to Tom.

"What? No way. Would never do such a thing." She shook her head. There went my last hope. "A girl needs her own income." Her eyes got fierce. "Don't you ever let me hear you think a man's gonna take care of you, okay? I won't hear it. I don't care how good you think the guy is. If you don't have a way to leave, then you'll always be trapped. Doin' things you don't wanna do. You got that? I learned that bitch of a lesson way too early." She huffed. "I'm droppin' pearls here, you catchin' 'em?"

"Yes . . . yes, ma'am." I suddenly felt compelled to address her with utmost respect.

"I ain't givin' Tommy your paycheck, and just looking at you, I can tell you ain't gonna tell me why you're hidin'.

But you've been fairly upfront, and honey, that's good enough for me. We look after our own here on this island. I'll pay you cash. And if you ever need to tell me anything, I've heard just about everything."

I nodded, too moved to speak.

"Did Jake like your cake?" she asked.

I nodded again. "They put the last three slices up for sale, though."

"Then they love it. You want to practice a bit more, then sell me some for the tourists come summer?"

"Yes," I burst out before I could think it over.

Marjoe chuckled her husky laugh, then wound her bleached-blonde hair up into a knot at the back of her head and stuck a pencil in it.

"I mean, yes. That would be awesome. Thank you."

"Great. I gotta get back to work. See you for your Tuesday shift?"

"Yes, ma'am."

"Marge is fine."

"Yes, Marge. Thank you."

"You too skittish for hugs?"

"Uh . . . um."

"Come here." She smiled and pulled me into her soft, pillowy chest for an embrace.

I stood in it stiffly, and before I could even begin to convince myself this was all right and I could probably hug her back, she let go. "See you later, sweetie," she said and swept out the door.

At least I'd made her forget her tears for a moment.

I headed out. "Bye, Bethany," I called magnanimously.

"Bye, see you tomorrow. I'm going to come by and make y'all dinner. Just spoke with Tommy."

"Oh. Oh good." I smiled with a massive effort and gave her a *jaunty* wave.

As I headed back across the interior of the island in the twilight, I was struck by the eerie stillness of the forest around me. Usually alive at night with the kind of sounds that could run as a soundtrack to a horror movie, it was bizarrely still.

Perhaps I couldn't hear the forest waking up for the night over the whine and buzz of the cart, or the sound of the cart made all the creatures freeze until I passed.

The trees faded in and out of high density, sometimes letting you see past their trunks to the black, still, swampy grounds within that waited, dark and oozing, ready to let out the horde of reptiles come spring. Ugly frogs, hungry alligators, and some of the most poisonous snakes known to man.

I shuddered.

Parking the cart in its sanctioned spot, I was filled with relief when I saw that the bucket of haint paint had been moved out to the middle of the porch and the door behind the screen stood slightly ajar. Tom must have decided to come back tonight. Hopefully we could finally get the paint on the shutters. I knew it was silly superstition, but honestly, even just the idea of it made me feel better, and that had to be worth something.

Tom was probably inside eating the rest of the cupcakes already. "Hey," I called and trotted up the steps. I couldn't help the grin stretching across my face. "You better save some for me."

The kitchen was empty and still. Everything exactly the same as how I left it, mixing bowls in the sink and the container of cupcakes on the table. "Tom?" I called out and got no response. "Tom?"

I went back out to the porch and called outside. Maybe he'd headed back in the Bloody Point direction, where Pete usually dropped him. Shit, I should probably clean up the kitchen. I'd been hoping to do that before he got back anyway.

I hung up my jacket and rolled up the sleeves on my black T-shirt, then scrubbed the kitchen top to bottom and put everything away. While I was at it, I reorganized the pantry.

I flicked the lamps on and pulled out my phone. It was almost fully dark outside. Maybe he needed a ride.

Hey, where are you?

It was chilly. Especially since he'd left the door ajar earlier. I thought about laying a fire, but Tom was way better at it, so I'd wait. I never made a fire when he was gone: I was too scared of falling asleep with it still going.

My phone beeped.

Walking into the Pirates' House to meet a friend from class.

There's a Pirates' House here? How cool! Why?

Why what?

Why are you going to a Pirates' House at night-time?

You're funny. Asking myself the same. It's an overpriced tourist trap. I'll show it to you when you come here.

Come here? I halted midway across the room where I was heading to my bedroom to get a sweater. A jolt of uneasiness flipped my stomach. Why was I suddenly feeling so off?

Um, are you in Savannah?

Yes???

Oh. Shit. My hands trembled as I suddenly warred with my overactive imagination. Someone had been in the cottage. My eyes and my nose stung as my chest constricted, forcing my body to acknowledge my fear.

No, there had to be a rational explanation. Had *I* left

the door open? It was entirely feasible since I was carrying all those containers. Maybe it didn't latch properly. But dread continued snaking through my body. I just couldn't be sure.

I took a deep breath, conscious of my spiking pulse, and then mashed my lips tight between my teeth. I looked around me, the comforting cottage in the fading light now starting to show its shadowy corners.

Liv?

With one hand gripping the phone so tight it was in danger of shattering, and the other shaking badly, I tried to think of a non-alarmist response.

Thought you had come back, sorry.

No, am here, but why? Are you okay?

My breathing was coming too fast as I kept glancing around me, now turning around in a continuous circle.

I don't know.

I winced as I gave in to the need for his help. I'd just tell him and he'd tell me I was crazy. It would all be fine.

I think I'm imagining things. Door was open when I got back from Mama's and Jake's paint was out. But maybe I did it and don't remember.

I'm going to call you, hang on.

The phone rang in my hand and I answered immediately.

"Hi," I said, my voice breathy with restrained panic. I attempted to swallow it down, but could feel it oozing up my insides.

"Okay. God, okay," he said like he could hear everything in my single greeting.

I latched on to his voice like a lifeline.

"Just stay on the phone with me," he said, when he got no response.

I closed my eyes at the smooth rumble of his voice in my ear and nodded. "Okay."

"Let's go through this step by step."

"Uh-huh."

"Walk back to the front door and turn the porch light on."

Clenching my fist, I willed myself to focus on his instructions. "It is, I did that already." Though we usually didn't do it because it attracted so many insects.

"Okay, good, now lock the door. Don't ever worry about locking me out, I have a key. No one else does. Okay?"

I nodded as if he could see me, weak with relief at having him in my ear.

"No one else has a key, got it?" he assured me again. "Say okay, Tom."

"Okay, Tom."

"The only other one is hanging on a hook in the pantry cupboard."

"Okay," I whispered.

"Now, I want you to start at the kitchen and check each window. And tell me when you are done. I'm just going to cover the phone for a second to speak to someone, then I'll be right back."

"Okay." I cringed as I realized he was probably making apologies to whoever he was meeting for having to talk down his psychotic charge.

Starting at the kitchen window, I worked my way around. My heart pounded and my fingers shook as I fumbled to check each one. It also took a supreme mental effort to try not to look out into the darkness beyond my reflection and imagine something was out there watching me move past each pane of glass.

I closed the drapes at every single one as soon as I was done checking the locks. The lock in the living room was broken.

"Tom?" My breath hitched.

"Yeah, I'm here."

"The lock on the window in the living room is broken."

"Okay. I forgot about that one, but it's one of the older windows and it's painted shut. I've never been able to get it open, no one can. It needs to be replaced. Just haven't done it yet."

Nodding even though he couldn't see me, I tried to tell myself it was true. "I've checked all these then."

"Now my bedroom."

I headed down the hall, flicking on the lights, and entered his bedroom. "Say something," I said.

"You in my room?" he asked, sounding breathy, like he was walking.

Pausing, I inhaled deeply. I could just about smell him if I closed my eyes. I listened to his voice and breathed the faint scent of him that lingered.

"Yes," I said after a moment and walked to his window, checking the locks and pulling the dark denim across the panes. I was standing by his desk. "What do you write about?" I asked.

"How do you know I write?" Shit, he could be writing term papers, not fiction.

"I hear you typing sometimes. I just assumed. That was before I knew you were studying."

"I'm also doing a creative writing minor."

"Will you read me some of your stuff sometime?"

"Read it to you, or let you read it?"

"Read it *to* me. I . . . I like your voice." There was no

response. I scrambled to fill the void. "Okay, your window is secure."

"Now the bathroom. You'll have to reciprocate if I do that. And it's a big if. I'm not sure I'm ready to share it yet."

I pursed my lips with guilt at having already invaded that privacy. "Reciprocate?"

"If you read me one of those so-called depressing fairy tales out loud, I'll consider it. I like your voice too."

There was a heavy silence as my chest swelled, and I worked out how to respond. Our banter had calmed me down enormously. Incredible.

I opened the shower curtain and climbed over the tub to the small frosted window high on the wall. A black shape appeared in my peripheral vision. I shrieked and dropped the phone as a huge spider landed in the bathtub and went scuttling toward my foot.

"Fuck," I yelled and leapt out of the bath, stumbling backward. I yanked off my shoe with shaking hands and then slammed it down on the grotesque thick body, once, twice, feeling the give and pop as it squashed. And did it *hiss*? I think it fucking hissed. The sound of my shoe against the cast-iron tub boomed in the small tiled room. My stomach heaved. "Die, motherfucker!" I screamed with all the pent-up tension from the last ten minutes of panic. I lifted the shoe. Lumpy black and brown remains were smeared all over the white tub. I dropped the shoe and retched into the sink, tears finally springing from my eyes.

The faint sound of yelling brought me back. I ran the cold water, splashing it over my face, then dried myself and grabbed the phone off the floor.

"Liv?" Tom shouted.

"I'm here." I sniffed, breathing hard. God, I was a wreck. "I'm here."

"Jesus H. Christ." It sounded like he was running. "Are you okay? What the hell was that?"

I let out a hysterical laugh, my heart pounding in my throat again. "I'm okay."

"Fuck, do I need to come and help you hide a body?"

"Yes, a big-ass spider. I hope he wasn't a friend of yours. Shit, he was huge. Ugh." I shuddered again, my stomach still not feeling great.

The sound of Tom running had slowed. "Oh, you mean Bert? Aw, man, poor guy. Wow, you killed him."

"You knew there was a massive spider in here and you didn't tell me?"

"Well, I only saw him once, and I didn't want to freak you out when I couldn't find him again."

"So waiting for me to come face to face with him was a better option?" I snorted. "I just literally died a thousand deaths. I think my heart actually flatlined. And I threw up the meager amount of food I ate today. In fact, maybe it was Bert out for a stroll who left the door open and moved the paint. He was certainly capable."

"Sorry," Tom said, still out of breath, but I could hear the relieved laughter in his words that I was joking around, and that I was okay.

"Yeah, right. You better bring a litter box and supplies when you come back. I'm going to see a man about a spider-killing feline tomorrow. I need a henchman." I hoped my little guy was still alive, and that he was fierce and loyal.

"I'm proud of you for killing Bert. Just goes to show you have some fight in you."

"Survival instinct," I muttered. "It was him or me."

Tom laughed. Damn, that was a good sound. Warm, but with bite. Like a shot of whiskey in my chest.

"But I'm never touching those shoes again. Were you running?" I asked, suddenly remembering.

"I'm on my way home."

A surge of guilt. "You don't need to, I'm okay. Maybe . . . maybe you can just stay on the phone for a bit while I get ready for bed? You should go back to your, uh, meeting or whatever."

"Are you sure?"

I nodded and shook my head at the same time. "Yep," I said cheerily.

He let out a long breath. "Go get ready for bed and then call me one more time before you fall asleep so I know you're okay."

"I will, and thank you," I said and hung up.

I brushed my teeth, then stepped into the hall. Instead of going to my room, I veered into Tom's. Stripping down to my T-shirt and underwear, and leaving just the desk lamp on, I slid into the cocoon of his woodsy, spicy scent with my phone, wrapping him around me, and dialed his number.

TOM

CHAPTER TWENTY-THREE

J paced back and forth along Bay Street. Having already ditched my let's-grab-a-drink-after-class meetup, I was now questioning the point in staying overnight here when Liv would probably be better served having someone in the house with her. She'd sounded so freaked out when she'd first picked up the phone after I'd texted that I was in Savannah. I didn't blame her: it must have been scary to come home and see things out of place.

Jesus, and the spider-killing episode? My heart was still pounding from the adrenalin pumping through my veins. I thought a wild animal had gotten in the cottage or something.

Should I jump in a cab to the marina? It was still early enough that I was pretty sure I could get a ride with someone.

My sailboat was ready to be out there, the engine having been completely overhauled, but did I want to risk testing it out in fading light through the marsh creeks? There were lighted markers in the waterway, but not the creeks: I could easily run aground on a sandbar or, worse, the oyster beds. Just because the oysters around here were too poisonous to eat didn't mean they weren't prolific and lying in wait to gouge the bottom of a boat or rip anyone to shreds who thought to get out and push their boat free.

There was no harm in going down to the marina and seeing if someone was around. I hailed a passing cab and climbed in just as my phone buzzed.

"Hi," I answered, then covered the phone with my hand as I directed the driver.

"Hi." Her voice was muffled.

"You in bed?"

She hesitated. "Yes."

"Are you doing okay?"

"Yeah, I'm good. I still feel a bit freaked, but better since talking to you. I . . . I don't know how to thank you."

"Glad I could help. And you can call me anytime, okay?"

"I got so used to you being next to me when I was sick, it's weird not to have you home at all."

Neither of us had spoken much about us sharing a room, and then she'd put an end to it herself after our board games. Responses suddenly jumped over each other in my head, trying to get out, trying to be the right one. There was no guile in her tone, no trace of the vixen trying to be flirty; she was simply stating a fact.

I breathed out. "I'm sorry I have to be gone so much. It's not that easy to get back to the island after an evening class," I said neutrally, even as the cab zoomed along the Islands Expressway toward the marina so I could try and do exactly that. And why was I doing it exactly? I wasn't sure.

"It's okay. I shouldn't have to be babysat."

"It's not babysitting, it's—"

"Yeah," she cut me off. "It is. I'm just sick of not being in control of my body and my mind. When stuff like this happens I feel like I'm . . . like I'm going crazy. Imagining stuff, you know?"

"I don't think you're going crazy. Maybe forgetful. And maybe I did move the paint this morning, and *I* don't remember."

"You didn't. I was sitting outside on the porch when you left, remember?"

Of course I remembered. I remembered the way my gut clenched when I walked out, and she was sitting all curled up on the wicker love seat, face completely devoid of makeup, pale eyes telling me not to go. But she didn't say a word, except to ask me if she could go with me next time.

For the first time in a long while, I dreaded going across to Savannah. I'd rather be there with her. Which was the weirdest feeling.

"Yeah, I remember. So how did the baking go today?"

"Great." I heard the smile in her voice. "Thanks for your help. I made a lemon cake for Big Jake and they may put it on the menu at Mama's permanently. And I made cupcakes for you."

"Us."

"Us." She laughed, then yawned.

My cab was nearing the marina. I hated to hang up when it seemed that chatting with me was helping her relax. "You sound tired. Why don't you try and get some sleep."

"Okay." She yawned again, and I couldn't help smiling at the sound.

"Sleep well, good night."

"Night. Wait . . . Tom?"

"Yeah?"

"I, uh, I hope it's okay but I'm sleeping in your bed. I . . . I like the way you smell."

Just like that, the blood left my head and went straight to my groin. My gut cinched tight. I gritted my teeth in horror at my reaction.

"I hope you don't mind," she whispered at my silence. "I . . . It's just, if I can smell you, I can pretend you're here. God, I'm sorry. I really do sound nuts. And creepy. I'm sorry, I'll go to my own room."

"No," I barked out. "I mean . . ." I cleared my throat, "it's fine. Stay. Stay where you are."

"Are you sure?"

"Yes." I swallowed. "Yeah, I'm sure. If it helps, you should stay there."

But there was no way in hell I was going back to that cottage tonight. Not until I got my head in the game and my priorities straight. What the fuck was wrong with me?

I paid the cab driver and stepped out into the bracing salt wind that blew in off the water. A perfect substitute for a cold shower. The harbormaster's light was still on, but there were no other boats that looked to even have occupants who might be up to making the trip. That solved that.

I walked down the long pier, past the marina office, then turned right along the weathered floating dock to my little Catalina sailboat. My indulgence. One of the few good things that came out of who I'd been once upon a time.

"Tommy, that you?"

"Hey, Gator," I called back up to the marina office balcony, squinting under the outdoor floodlight. The harbormaster's large frame was a shadow.

"You sleeping out here tonight?"

"Thought I would."

"Glad you got your boat back. I'll bring you some joe in the mornin'."

I thanked him and climbed on board. Lifting the berth, I pulled the waterproof bag out of the storage compartment that held the pillows and sheets. They smelled musty, but were otherwise clean.

As soon as I got settled in my cramped space, I lay there wide awake. I didn't want to waste the battery on my cell, but it was too early to sleep. Besides, it was too cold to be sleeping out here unless you had a warm body next to you. I was nuts to even be trying.

I'd told Bethany we could come over to Savannah and stay on the boat, which we'd been planning to do the night I'd had to go rescue Livvy from Tyler's clutches. Now I was relieved. The idea of Bethany sharing this private space with me just seemed wrong somehow.

I dozed to the gentle rocking motion, never fully going to sleep. There were only so many times I could check my phone still had charge without feeling like a tool. I should have stayed out and gotten a few drinks.

Having finally dozed off sometime in the night, I woke a little before five a.m. I was painfully hard—some classic morning wood—but with an ache deep inside me I couldn't ever remember feeling. It had been a while since Bethany and I had slept together. Deciding that the best way forward was to quickly deal with it rather than try to will it away, I slid my hand down my stomach and pulled myself free of my boxers. I tried to remember the last time I'd been with Bethany, her ample breasts bouncing in my face as she sat astride me, and gritted my teeth in frustration as the image failed to set off the necessary reaction.

The image of Olivia kneeling between my legs slid into my head, her pale eyes looking up at me. I swallowed. Just between me and my sick and twisted conscience, *just this once*, I imagined smoothing my fingers over her jawline and sliding into her hair, where I'd take a fistful of it. She would open her mouth and take me in . . . *Fuck.*

The buzz raced down my spine and up my legs, pulled from the top of my skull and the blackest parts of my soul. I erupted quickly and violently, in a collision that had me hissing in agony at my weakness.

I rolled over and punched the pillow next to me.

Fuck.

Fuck.

Fuck.

The marina was waking up as I stowed my bedding and changed. I pulled my big fleece jacket on and opened up the cabin to the chilly morning air. The sky was gray, the water choppy. Gator was heading down the stairs from the marina office with two coffee cups.

"Hold up, Gator, I'll come to you," I called.

"How d'ya know this one's yours?" he groused and turned around. I grinned and jogged up the jetty.

"Got my first dolphin tour of the season today," he said as soon as I entered. "Group staying on Tybee."

"Thanks," I said as I grabbed the cup he held out. "The sky says otherwise."

"P'shaw. It'll hold off till late afternoon."

And based on Gator's prior predictions, he was probably right.

"It's gonna be a good summer. You give any thought to doing some sailing classes for me?"

"Not yet. It's not that I don't want to, but with school, and helping out Pete, I'm not sure I'd have much time," I evaded.

The truth was, I didn't want to be in the public eye. The chances of running into someone I knew would go up exponentially. Not that my old blue-blood crowd who grew up spending summers at the country club, or learning to sail at Camp Seagull, would be taking lessons on a ropy-looking Catalina moored at Bull River. They'd probably be further up the creek at the Savannah Yacht Club if they weren't summering in Nantucket.

But they *might* come this way. And that was reason enough.

Gator studied me from under his duck-bill cap as he brought his mug to his mouth, nestled in a long, shaggy gray beard. The fisherman's version of Santa Claus. "How about we put you on a schedule two afternoons a week—"

I shook my head.

"Now, now, I'm not done. And, *and,* I take their names and call you first before you decide whether to take the job." He took a long, noisy slurp of coffee.

Pursing my lips, I shook my head again, this time with resignation, as I watched him put his coffee down, a smug grin on his face. "You're not called Gator for nothing. You're a tenacious old fart, aren't you?"

He swung his feet down to the floor with a thud and grabbed a rolled-up paper. "Who you callin' old, boy?" he boomed and swatted at me.

I raised my hands to cover my head. "Get off," I groused, laughing. "*Old* you object to, but *fart's* fine?"

"Now, now," Pete's gruff voice cut in.

We both straightened ourselves up.

I saluted Pete as he walked in, then headed to the small bathroom to wash up and brush my teeth. I tried not to look myself in the eye. When I stepped out, I caught the tail end of something Gator was saying about the Department of Natural Resources patrol in the marshes having been stepped up. "Fisheries are joining up with the coast guard to cover more area. That means there'll be less competition for y'all who do it by the book. Be a good season for you."

Illegal fish being brought ashore in Georgia was a common problem, either because the fish weren't reported in trip tickets to the Department of Natural Resources or because they were being fished by people without valid licenses. Add the fact you had to be a legal US resident to even get a commercial vessel license, and it meant you tended to run into people on the wrong side of the law fairly frequently.

It was great for us that they were cracking down, and it was *not* great for us that they were cracking down. I caught Pete's eye and wondered if we should let Gator in on what we were planning with Tyler in case we needed someone to vouch for us. But Gary "Gator" Hill would want us to call law enforcement right away and have them handle it. They'd miss Cal Richter that way.

No, the fewer people who knew, the better. For now.

"You're over early, Pete," I said, changing the subject.

"Weather service issued an advisory for this afternoon. Not sure how long this front will last. Figured if I didn't get those crab traps dropped this morning, it would be a few days before I could do it."

Gator took my empty cup and walked it over to the small kitchenette along the back wall that had seen more fish gutting than cooking. "Hopefully it'll bring some warmer weather on its tail."

Pete and I bid him farewell and headed down to Pete's boat.

"Well, that's gonna make it trickier," he said when we were safely out of earshot.

"Or easier to get the job done if the authorities are closer," I said.

Pete scratched at his beard. "I guess so. You ready for a ride back? Mind if we stop for an hour or so in Wright River for a nibble?"

I nodded. I could spend all day out here on the boat rather than go back and look Liv in the eye. And my bed would probably smell of her tonight.

CHAPTER TWENTY-FOUR

The cottage was quiet and still when I got back at nine a.m. Considering I'd been up since five, with barely a wink of sleep, it felt like mid-afternoon. Liv was right, the paint can was literally right in the middle of the porch in front of the door. Weird.

Her door was cracked, but mine was closed so I figured she was still in my bed. I started the coffee and took off my boots, then padded past the bedrooms to the bathroom.

Her spider-killing shoe was the first thing I saw, abandoned on the floor. Grinning, I took care of the mess, then tossed her shoe out on the porch to deal with later.

The smell of much-needed coffee finally hit me, and I poured a cup while I eyed the container of cupcakes on the table. Taking the lid off, I picked one of them up and inhaled the smell. Wow, that was good.

"Drop. That. Cupcake." Liv's voice morphed from dramatic to laughing as I jerked and literally dropped the cupcake face down on the table. I looked up and found her watching me in her skinny jeans and a tight long-sleeve white T-shirt, hands on hips and one foot turned in. Her rare smile was infectious and I tried not to smile back. Her dyed hair was fading into a dull dark blonde and growing out, and on anyone else it would be ugly as hell.

"Shit," I said dumbly and scowled. "I was really looking forward to that."

"Five-second rule," she said and lunged forward to save my cupcake. She picked it up carefully and smoothed out the icing with her finger. A finger she proceeded to suck clean in her mouth with a pop.

Then she shoved the entire cake into her mouth.

I stood there in complete shock, my own cupcake-sized mouth hanging open and empty.

Catching sight of my expression, she and her stuffed chipmunk cheeks burst out laughing, snorting cupcake all over the place. Holy shit, this girl was certifiable. And she was laughing. I loved seeing her laugh.

"That was mine," I said, nonplussed.

She made unintelligible sounds around her mouthful of cake, her eyes watering with mirth. She tried to swallow quickly, but realizing she couldn't communicate, she picked up another cupcake and held it in front of my mouth.

She clearly meant for me to eat out of her hand, since she hadn't held it lower. I hesitated, then leaned forward warily and took a small bite.

She watched my mouth, the laughter in her eyes dying down.

The cupcake melted into soft buttery caramel flavor. Really, really good. "Mmmm," I sounded, wanting to tell her she'd done a great job and trying to ignore all the weird undercurrents. There were no undercurrents; it was only my fucked-up mind playing tricks.

I opened wide for another bite and she mashed the entirety

into the general vicinity of my mouth and laughed her head off. I totally fell for that one.

"These are really good," I finally said when I could talk.

"Thank you. They're actually pretty mediocre." Her nose twitched in a small show of distaste. She cleared her throat and swiped the back of her hand over her mouth. "When was the last time you had a cupcake?"

"It's been forever."

"When you were little?" she asked. "How little?"

"I mean like, I was a kid, at a birthday party, and probably slept in Spider-Man pajamas, forever ago little."

"More. Say more." Her eyes were wide and hungry.

"Back when my childhood consisted of cheese whirls and powdered punch. When the most difficult challenge was fending off the teasing about how early my mom called me in for dinner versus the other neighborhood kids. Back before my father's political career took off and we moved to our mansion, set in lush acreage, with nine-foot-high fences and wonderful climbing trees."

I stopped. Shit, what was wrong with me? I saw her sifting over my words, teasing out the throwaways and keeping the stuff that mattered.

"A child's paradise."

"For an only child." Lonely as hell. "What about you, cupcake memories?"

She blinked.

I could actually see her going back, over the hurdle of Abby dying, to a time way before. "Pink, sprinkles," she whispered and looked past me into a distance only she could see. "Pink butter frosting and multicolored sprinkles. I ate fifteen before my friends arrived and threw up so bad I had to miss the party. I've hated pink ever since."

"But not cupcakes in general, just pink ones? That's beneficially selective."

"Not just pink frosting, pink the color."

"The whole color? Wow, poor pink."

She pulled out a chair. "I know. It's a shame, though. It's such a jaunty color."

"Way too jaunty for you with all your black," I agreed gravely and poured her a cup of coffee, adding sugar and milk.

"Thanks."

"You're welcome. So about us getting a cat—"

"Us? He'll be mine."

"All yours?"

She nodded. "I can't send him on missions if he has another owner. He'll feel conflicted."

"So it's a *he*? I'm not sure how I feel about that."

She laughed. A light, cascading sound. It was mesmerizing. Like when we'd played board games and she got the giggles, and I couldn't tear my eyes off her.

"Why would you feel weird about it being a he?"

I shrugged. "He'll want to sleep on your bed. And keep you company. And then where will that leave me? You won't need me anymore." I quirked an eyebrow in a teasing manner to show I was joking. I was, of course. "But you know what? It might be okay. You know why?"

"Why?" she asked, her expression neutral.

"Because he probably won't smell as good as me."

The flush of red crossed her smooth chest and swept up her neck and into her cheeks. Her eyes dropped.

I'd embarrassed her. And not in a good way. I felt like the worst kind of heel. I'd taken her admission offered in the quiet of her post-panicked state last night and turned it into some sport or something. And why?

Was I actually flirting? The realization hit me.

What the fuck? I was flirting.

Sending signals.

The last thing I should be doing. God, what was wrong with me? Was there a way to be friendly and not do that?

Shit. This girl needed just *one* guy not to abuse her trust, *just one*, and I couldn't even manage that. "I'm sorry." The words grated out of my mouth. "I didn't mean to embarrass you. It was kind of cool actually," I played off, "that I could comfort you from afar."

Please let her not think I was hitting on her.

Please.

"Right. No worries. It was still idiotic of me to say that to you and totally inappropriate to sleep in your bed."

"It's fine."

"Fine." She stood up. "Anyway, I best go get showered and changed so I can see about the kitten." Her eyes glanced toward the bathroom, and I saw her shudder.

"I cleaned Bert up."

"You did? Thank you," she said with a long exhale.

"I didn't bring supplies for a cat like you asked, though, sorry. Maybe we can rig something up with a plastic box and sand, and we'll get real stuff next time. Do you know where JJ lives?"

She shook her head.

"Okay, go get ready. I'll drive you there in the cart. I think they sell pet food at the general store."

She headed to the bedroom, and I had to tear my eyes away from her tight jeans. Turning my back to put our mugs in the sink, I heard her stumble.

I spun to see her fall back against the wall outside her bedroom, then look to me, her face completely drained of color.

"What?" I scrambled around the table.

She gasped in a breath, her hand clutching her chest. And gasped again.

"God, what?" I reached her and took her arms. "Liv? Liv? Calm down. Talk to me." Simultaneously I kicked a leg out to her bedroom door, slamming it open to reveal the empty, perfectly neat room. No intruder, no nothing.

"Liv? Is there another spider? Shit, speak to me."

Her breathing seemed to have completely stopped; her face was frozen. I shook her. "Liv!"

Her eyes finally seemed to focus on mine.

"Livvy, what is it?"

"B—" She sucked in a shuddering breath, her entire body quaking under my hands.

I willed her to keep talking before I had to shake her harder.

"B—box."

"Box? Did you say box?" What the fuck did a box have to do with anything?

She nodded, her face crumpling as life came back to it in the form of crying. Great.

I turned my head to look but didn't understand what she was talking about. Then I saw it, placed squarely in the middle of the perfectly straightened queen-sized bed. A small wooden box. I made to let go and she clung, shaking her head. "Livvy, is it your box?"

She nodded, then shook her head, then nodded.

"I don't understand," I said gently. "Is it yours?"

"Y—yes, but Abby gave it to me."

"Okay. What's in it?"

She shook her head. "I . . . I don't know."

I frowned, trying to make sense of what the hell was going on. "You don't know what's in the box?"

She shook her head again.

Why the hell not? "Did you put it there?"

Her body shuddered badly. Like she was in shock. "No," she whispered.

Either someone was messing with her, or Liv was doing things and not remembering. Neither scenario was comforting in the slightest. I tried to ignore the chill that was creeping over me. Maybe she did need medication. Stronger medication.

"Was it there last night?" I continued asking questions in a soothing tone as my mind examined and tossed aside every possible scenario rather than the one I was facing. That she could legitimately need psychological help.

"I don't know. I never went in my room."

"Wait, I thought you checked all the windows?"

"I only got as far as the bathroom, and then the spider . . . and then I just wanted to . . . I went straight to your room."

I pulled her small frame against my chest and tucked her head under my chin, wrapping her up in my arms. We stood like that for a long minute. Then I gently released her and steered her back to the kitchen. "Sit here, I'm going into your room, okay?" She was still shivering violently, so I grabbed my fleece and draped it around her shoulders. She shrank down into it, pulling it more firmly around her frame.

Apart from the perfectly made bed—as far as I knew, she didn't normally make it up apart from pulling it straight in the mornings—and the box sitting on the comforter, there seemed to be nothing else out of the ordinary. Her window was closed but unlocked, which didn't say anything.

I looked around, but everything seemed normal, so on impulse I crossed to the picture of her and Abby on the swing outside that had been taken when they were young girls. Their smiles were incredible. Abby sat on the wooden plank while Liv stood on it behind her, one dirty foot peeking out from Abby's light blue dress, her little hands curled tightly around the rope. Two white-blonde angels giggling with joy.

When did it all go so fucking wrong?

I sensed Liv at the door. She was calmer. "How old were you both in this picture?" I asked, drawing her attention away from the bed.

"I was six, I think." Her brow furrowed. "So that makes Abby twelve."

"Who took it?"

"My grandmother. It was only ever the three of us out here; my parents never came."

"Never?" I frowned.

"They didn't speak to her except to organize our trips out here for the summer. Or she didn't speak to them, I'm not sure."

That was strange, to send your kids off to spend time with a person you never spoke to. But I guessed her parents simply wanted them to have a relationship with their grandmother, even if they didn't.

"Your mother's mother or your father's?"

"Mother's"

"Do you know why they never spoke?"

"I'm not completely sure," she whispered.

I turned to face her. She was staring at the bed. The box.

"Why don't you know what's in it?"

"Because I never opened it, okay?" she snapped. "It's locked. I don't have a key and Abby told me not to."

"She told you not to?"

"In the letter she left me."

"But she's dead."

Olivia flinched, but I couldn't help my raised voice. "You don't think after she died perhaps you should have just broken it open? Surely at that stage it was pretty imperative. She can't have meant *forever*. Why the hell did she give it to you otherwise?" What if it held information that could have helped? Could have helped Olivia? Or me? *God*. The idea was almost too much to process.

Olivia was staring at me like I'd grown two heads. "What do you care?"

Shit. I swallowed. "I care because . . . I care about you. And if it has something in it that could have helped you . . ."

I trailed off.

"What?" She folded her arms across her chest, her eyes questioning.

"Helped . . ." My throat was blocked. Lying about who I was had only condemned me to faking reality from then on. It hadn't been an act of survival or of selflessness to protect Liv in her fragile state; it had been an act of utter self-abdication. I'd made myself a slave to my lie, and I would never be able to get free without breaking Olivia in the process, once and for all.

"Helped how?"

The quote from Ayn Rand I'd looked up after Liv brought it up the other day rolled around in my head as I stood mutely in front of her. About how there were no such things as white lies. All lies were black and destructive. A white lie was truly the blackest of all.

$\mathcal{I}$ turned away, my mind reeling, and stared at the picture again.

Liv crossed to stand next to me. "I don't remember Abby ever smiling like that in the years before she died. When I first got here, I couldn't even look at it. It seemed wrong to see all that joy."

"I don't see you smiling like that either," I said.

She was letting me off the hook.

But I didn't want to be let off. I gritted my teeth and took a deep breath. "Your uncle Mike molested her."

The statement was a gunshot at close range.

Liv's eyes closed and she pulled her lips between her teeth. Minutes passed.

"How do you know that?" she asked, her voice barely audible. I'd expected some kind of accusing tone, but there was none. How was Liv not drawing the conclusion that I could have helped her?

"Abby told me."

She didn't open her eyes, but her knuckles got whiter as she gripped the chair.

I questioned the sanity of what I was doing right now when her mental state seemed so fragile, but I couldn't take it back. I had to move forward. I had to know. "Did he molest you too?"

I don't know what I expected her reaction to be, but the way she went utterly still was even more terrifying. It was almost like she'd left her body. That she was no longer next to me. I didn't even want to imagine the mental gymnastics of what was going on right now. Was she shutting down or about to talk? I didn't know. Dread was a revolting feeling. I wished I could vomit it up.

Finally her head moved.

A small, slight nod.

And the world stopped.

Even though I knew it was coming, I could have sliced my own body open neck to navel and pulled my insides out piece by piece, and it would have hurt less than seeing that nod.

She took a deep breath and turned away from the picture.

"Did *you* do it?" she asked, her tone biting. Okay, here it came.

"Do what?"

"Put the box there to make me talk?"

"No." I was shocked. "God, no."

Olivia stood silently with so many emotional walls up I could almost see them shimmering in front of her. Her eyes were hard, back the way they'd been when she first arrived. But they weren't accusing like I'd expected.

"Please," I started. "Talk to me. Don't shut me out."

She laughed hollowly, looking away. "Shut you out? How can I when you know every sordid thing about me? You know I've been molested. Touched and caressed by a man old enough to be my father. I touched him too. I bet you didn't know that?" She cut her eyes to me. "Does that revolt you? It should. Most girls who've been molested hate sex, don't they? That's what I've read. Not me, though, right? What does that make me?"

I couldn't answer. She didn't avoid sex, that much was clear. That didn't mean she didn't also hate it. How could she not?

She moved away and then faced me. "He was gentle in the beginning."

My stomach rolled.

"He felt guilty. He told me all the time he didn't mean to. But he couldn't stop because . . . *you remind me so much of her,* he would say. *You hold all the power. Take pity on me and touch me,* he would say, *see how weak you make me.*"

It was like watching a hologram talk. She was there, I could see and hear everything, but I felt like the Liv I knew was gone. And my body was gone too. I was achingly hollow inside, her words dropping like copper pennies down an empty well.

"Did you tell anyone? Your parents? Your therapist?" I flinched at my lame questions.

Liv seemed to come back to me for a moment and her eyes narrowed. "Did I tell anyone?" she asked sarcastically. "I tried. But it seems he'd gotten there first." She laughed. An ugly, jarring sound. "Uncle Mike was a respected man, an ex-cop. Apparently he'd had a confidential talk with my parents when I was twelve, before he ever even laid a hand on me. He told them he was worried about me making inappropriate and precocious advances to him. *When I was twelve fucking years old.* A reaction to the grief, they thought. I don't know why they chose to believe him over me, and I didn't know he'd even said that about me until my therapist told me years later. He waited patiently for two years before he started."

And *I* could have stopped it all. Every word she said ripped me further open. I wanted to kneel down and ask her to end it. End me. Take her pain and revenge out on me.

She glanced at me. "You're thinking that since you knew about Abby, you could have done something to protect me."

God, she was so close to the truth, how could she not see?

"Well you couldn't," she went on. "They would never have believed you. No, the only way it might not have happened is if Abby were still alive. Maybe she could have stopped it. Maybe they would have believed *her*. If she hadn't run away with that fucking—what was your word?—oxygen thief, and ended up dying because he was a drunken idiot who shouldn't have been behind the wheel."

I pulled out the dressing table chair before my knees buckled.

Liv was so deep in her memory with her story, she didn't even notice. "Uncle Mike robbed her of the ability to make good choices, I guess, just like he did me. Isn't that what you said the other night? I'm making the wrong choices? Well, Abby *chose* to run away and die with some idiot guy she knew from high school and leave me at the mercy of that disgusting man. And I hate her for it. I hate Abby." She looked around, her eyes searching the room wildly.

A chill went down my spine.

"I hate you, Abby!" she screamed loudly. "Is that what you wanted to know? Why you won't leave me alone? Well, now you do. I *hate* you."

My hair stood on end.

Then she looked at me dead on. "I hope they are *both* rotting in their graves."

OLIVIA

CHAPTER TWENTY-SIX

After my emotional morning, Tom made me take a hot shower. To his credit, he didn't push me anymore after my confession and outburst. He didn't try and comfort me or pity me; he simply got up from where he was sitting, picked up the box from the bed, and put it on the dresser. "Go take a long hot shower. We have to go and see about getting a cat before JJ leaves for work," he said, and walked out.

It was like the last half-hour hadn't even happened. Perplexed, I did as he said.

It was a long ride through the interior of the island, past the old wooden schoolhouse that novelist Pat Conroy had once taught at. Tom broke our tense silence by telling me about it. "Conroy didn't call it Daufuskie Island in his book, he called it Yamacraw Island. Everyone here knew it was about Daufuskie, though."

I simply turned my head, inviting him to continue.

"And it painted island life exactly the way he saw it, warts and all," he said as we passed the small building that had finally been refurbished as a community center. A regular tour guide he was.

"Hey, so someone told me Daufuskie was actually Gullah dialect for 'the first key.' Do you think that's true?" I asked.

Tom seemed relieved I was engaging in the conversation. "Well, there are two schools of thought. What most people don't realize is there were Indians here thousands of years before slaves and colonists ever populated the area. Daufuskie, in terms of anthropological finds, is actually considered ancient. Like ten thousand years ancient."

"Damn, that's pyramids old."

"Sure is. Anyway, some people will tell you that Daufuskie is an Indian term meaning 'sharp feather,' though whether that's because of the shape of the island, or a name for the oyster shells that surround it, we'll probably never know."

"You're kind of interesting, you know that?" I scrunched up my nose.

"Well." He pursed his lips. "I've got that going for me then."

We pulled down a dirt lane, even narrower than the road to our cottage, bordered by dense vegetation. It was dark down here amongst the trees. In a clearing ahead there were some small cinderblock and wooden houses clustered together, and a couple of trailers. A large rusted metal drum was full of soapy water, and a line with various items of clothing draped along it ran between the trees.

The bottoms of the whitewashed buildings were splashed brown from the red clay in the soil. Moss, both Spanish and green, seemed to coat everything. Two chickens flapped and squawked across our path as we slowed to a stop.

We peered at the houses, and I noticed a small child with dark skin who looked to be five or six standing half concealed in a doorway of one of the buildings. Barefoot and dressed in a dirty white T-shirt and blue pants, he watched us, eyes wide with curiosity. Someone behind him spoke, and he scampered back into the dim interior. A woman came out, eyes suspicious. When she saw Tom, she broke into a huge smile. "Jake," she yelled toward the woods.

"Is there still a school on the island?" I whispered to Tom, thinking of the building we had passed. Maybe I could do some tutoring again sometime.

"Daufuskie kids get ferried over to Hilton Head Island to go to school. Weather permitting. But some of the Gullah, well, they don't really feel like sending their kids. I'm sure they've got their reasons."

Big Jake suddenly loomed out of the forest to the left of us, three dead squirrels hanging from a string in his hand. Blood dripped down their silver fur. I couldn't tear my eyes away from the macabre sight.

"You ain't never eat squirrel?" Big Jake boomed and laughed his high-pitched giggle.

"You couldn't pay us to try," Tom responded, climbing out of the cart.

I shuddered dramatically and followed suit.

"She's come to see JJ about the kitten. Is he here?" Tom said.

Jake indicated a small wooden house set away from the others.

The forest was noisy here. Not the bone-chilling night-time sounds, but the normal gentle rustling and chirping of a place alive and at one with its human settlers.

Tom knocked on JJ's door and after some scuffling it swung open. JJ looked over our shoulders and seemed momentarily unsure. Tom pointed at me. "She came to ask you about a kitten."

"Hey, JJ," I greeted him. "I'm so sorry about the two that got hurt by the possum."

JJ crinkled his almost black eyes for a few beats, then nodded. He closed the door in our faces.

I stepped back in surprise, and we both stood staring at the peeling and cracked blue paint before exchanging perplexed looks.

"What happened to them?" Tom asked me. "The kittens you mentioned."

"Big Jake said a rabid possum killed them, and JJ had to shoot it."

Tom scratched his head. "I didn't even know JJ had a gun."

"Is it safe for him to have one?" I asked quietly, for Tom's ears only. "I mean, is he okay in the head?" I hated to ask, but it was a valid question, I thought.

"As far as I know, he's fine, he just doesn't talk. Never has."

Suddenly the door opened again, and JJ appeared holding a squirming ball of brown and white fur that was attempting to burrow inside his shirt. He pinched it by the scruff of the neck and held it out. The kitten, the small black heart still on its nose, mewled piteously. Relieved that my little guy had made the cut, I gingerly took him with both hands. His needle-like claws immediately grabbed on to my wrist, and I winced in surprise.

JJ took the kitten's front paw and squeezed it flat, so the claws spread, then made a scissor motion with his other hand.

"I think he wants to know if you want him to declaw it?" Tom told me.

"You can do that? What, just cut them?"

"No, they'll grow back. They need to be pulled out one by one at the root."

"What?" I gulped, immediately feeling sick. "No way, poor thing."

"Probably a good choice. I doubt there are any pain relievers or antiseptic, am I right, JJ?"

JJ shook his head and shrugged. Then he took the kitten back by the scruff and pressed a kiss to its nose before handing it back to me. It was such an unexpected gesture from this silent man who'd just offered to inflict ghastly pain on the poor creature. He shut the door again.

The kitten immediately squirmed and tried to climb up my arm to my shoulder and head. "Damn, you're a handful," I scolded it. "Settle down, would you?"

I turned and headed back the way we came, talking to the kitten, trying to convince it to keep still.

JJ opened his door again, and I glanced back in time to see Tom take a plastic grocery bag from him.

"You got what I asked for?"

JJ nodded.

"Thank you, JJ." Tom cast his head back to look at me, and I quickly turned away from their exchange.

"You get paint on them shutters yet?" Big Jake asked us as we climbed back into the cart.

"Not yet," I said. "Now that I'm well, we'll get on it."

Jake inclined his large head. "Jus' lemme know if I can hep. And don't forget to get those balls chopped off afore he starts sprayin' everywhere."

Tom blanched, and I laughed. "The cat, you idiot."

"I know," Tom said thickly. "It's just the idea makes me cringe." He started up the cart.

"You better take me home and go to the store for cat

food without me. I'm not sure how I'll manage to hang on to him much longer." As I spoke, the cat had burrowed into my jacket and was now making his escape out the back of my collar. Tom reached behind me and grabbed hold of him, causing him to hiss and scratch me.

"Ow. Motherfucker," I yelled in surprise.

Tom snorted with laughter. "You wanted a cat."

"What should we call him?"

"Oh, so it's *we* now? Earlier he was *your* cat, and now that we know he's gonna be a pain in the ass, he's *ours*?"

I shrugged innocently.

"Well, whatever you call him, you need to clip his nails."

"Ivan?"

"I'm not naming him. Pick what you want, he's your cat."

"Ivan the Terrible. Oh, wait, what about Terrance? Terror for short?"

"I told you, I'm not doing this."

"Fine. Lancelot it is then. Because he's got nails like little lances, and I hope he'll be my knight in shining armor if any of Bert's cousins show up."

Tom pressed his lips together.

"Hmmm. Perhaps not. What about something sweeter, like Buttercup?"

"You can't call him Buttercup," Tom objected, then grunted, clearly irritated at rising to the bait.

I grinned. "So you have an opinion at least. That's good." Leaning my face down, I cooed and tried to rub noses with the little feline demon, who promptly bit mine.

"Fuckhead!" I howled.

Tom shrugged. "That's a good one."

CHAPTER TWENTY-SEVEN

After peeling the Tasmanian devil off the curtains for the fourth time, I locked him in the bathroom while I rummaged in the kitchen cabinets for some antibiotic ointment. Little asshole. I was scratched all over.

His favorite game so far had been to wait on the ceiling beam until I walked underneath, then launch himself at my head.

I came across some old nail clippers at the same time the cottage phone rang. Bingo. Now I just had to keep his paws still.

"Hello?"

"Olivia, it's Bethany."

"Oh, hey, Bethany. How are you?" There was a crash from the bathroom. I winced.

"So I was wondering what time I should come over to make dinner?"

Oh. Of course. Was it just yesterday I'd discovered Tom had a girlfriend?

"Uh, Tom went to the general store. You can call him on his cell."

"Actually, I was hoping to ask you if I could, uh, well . . ."

Oh God. "What?"

"Well, I was thinking we could spend a little girl time, uh, bonding. In case you haven't noticed, there aren't many young folk on the island, and, well . . ." She trailed off. The unspoken aspect was that I lived with Tom, and she needed to assess me to see if I was a threat. I was fairly familiar with female jealousy.

I took pity on how obviously uncomfortable she felt, since I felt the same way. "I, uh, I'm not very good at girlie stuff, I mean I haven't really . . ." *had a lot of friends*, I finished in my head.

"Oh good, phew. Okay, we'll bond. Somehow we'll figure it out. I'll bring makeup." How did she get a yes out of that?

"No, you don't need to do that."

"I insist."

Awesome.

We hung up and I texted Tom.

Tommy, your girlfriend is coming over to cook for you and girlie-bond with me. And hurry up, Fuckhead is tearing up the bathroom.

You? Girlie bonding? Impossible. I'll see if they have anything pink here.

The brick in my belly was the only sign I'd noticed he didn't dispute the girlfriend label. And why would he? Even if they weren't boyfriend and girlfriend, he didn't owe me an explanation. Me and my stupid, stupid crush. The sooner I got used to the fact he was dating Bethany, the better. Bring on the girl time. But, oh God, what if she stayed the night?

I saw a movie once where this thirteen-year-old girl was invited out to a restaurant to meet her father's new girlfriend, her future stepmother. The girl was well brought up and was excruciatingly polite, all the while wanting to pounce across the table and stab the woman with a fork. That was a vague approximation of how I felt.

"So where do you live, Bethany?"

I was on one side, they were on the other, the table having been set by Bethany, of course. How it could have been arranged better, I wasn't sure. Maybe the two bonding girls could sit on one side, Tom on the other? Or maybe Tom should have fucking cancelled dinner.

I was seething and felt raw and exposed. Our quiet, safe, comfortable little life had been ripped open this morning, and before I'd even had a chance to assess the damage, Tom had allowed a stranger into our domain. He knew all the revolting, sordid things about me, and now he was sitting opposite me with his pretty little girlfriend, leaving me feeling like a smelly piece of shit on the other side.

The rubbery chicken and mushy noodles made their third circuit around my plate.

Bethany's left hand was on Tom's shoulder, fiddling with his hair where it curled over his collar. Was his hair soft? "I rent a guest house over a garage at one of those lovely big houses in Haig Point," she said.

I'd forgotten what I even asked her.

She looked at Tom. "It's nice there, isn't it, babe?"

Why didn't she just piss on him?

And the whole *let's have some girl bonding*?

Lie.

"Yeah, it's all right." Tom shrugged, his movement dislodging Bethany's hand.

"All right? We never stay here at the cottage, so I thought you preferred it." She never stayed here? Hallelujah!

Tom caught my eye. "You wouldn't want to stay here anyway. It's a bit isolated."

"Well *you'd* be here with me, silly."

"It's really drafty," he tried and looked at me. Was he asking for backup?

I cleared my throat. "Oh yeah, really drafty."

"And massive spiders."

"Oh God, yes." I shuddered. "You should have seen the size of the one I killed last night."

"Ugh, I hate spiders," Bethany said, eyes wide.

"Mmmm," both Tom and I agreed at the same time. On the same wavelength.

He winked.

And all of a sudden, the evening took on a whole new aspect. My Tom was still there.

"So about that girlie bonding, we should totally do that now before Tommy runs you home," I said.

Tom's eyes widened.

Bethany looked confused.

"Well, we already established that Tom prefers to stay at your place, right?" I assured her, warming up to my idea of making sure Bethany didn't stay here tonight. Eyeing her tight, low-cut pink T-shirt, I realized I still might have to contend with him staying at her place. "So let's talk girlie stuff. I'm dying to see what I look like in pink."

Tom made a small choking sound.

"Shall we go to my room? Tommy will clean up the kitchen. Won't you, Tommy?"

I dragged Bethany to my room and sat her at the dressing table. Peeling my shirt off, I unclasped my bra too. Her eyes flicked away, embarrassed. "I need my push-up to try on your shirt, don't you think?" I was deliberately trying to make her uncomfortable. I didn't know why, but I couldn't seem to help it.

Fishing the bra out of a basket of clean clothes, I put it on and fluffed my boobs, gratified with the effect.

"Yes, totally!" Bethany finally found her voice and joined in my enthusiasm. "So what is your plan for your hair?" she asked.

"Oh, I know, growing out dark color is the worst. Luckily I didn't choose a permanent dye, but the way it looks now, I feel I might never get back to my natural color." I studied myself in the mirror, turning my head this way and that, then glanced at her reflection. "Look at your gorgeous chestnut hair. I wouldn't have had to dye mine if I could have your color."

She smiled, pleased with my compliment. I was relieved I'd managed to get my weird cattiness under control. "Thanks. Come switch places with me," she said, hopping up.

I sat down and she rummaged around in her purse and pulled out a large black makeup bag. "Oh, yikes," I said.

"Trust me," she said. And I did, but only because I knew she'd never risk Tom being irritated with her. She pulled out tweezers and went for my eyebrows.

"Ow!" I yelped, eyes watering.

"Hold still. It'll get better."

She shaped my eyebrows, then carefully painted things on my face layer by layer. That's what it felt like anyway, but she wouldn't let me see.

It took a while.

Tom knocked at the door eventually. "Go away," we both yelled, and laughed. Bizarrely, I was actually having fun.

"What's going on in there?"

"A makeover," said Bethany. "Dang, girl, your cheekbones are insane. Like Keira Knightley insane."

"A what?" Tom said through the door. "Oh, never mind. I don't want to know. Liv?"

"Yeah?"

"Do you want Fuckhead to stay in the bathroom permanently?"

"Don't move," said Bethany to me. "She can't talk now. And please, for the love, give the poor cat a real name."

"I have to answer," I whispered, then raised my voice so Tom could hear me. "He needs to stay in a small room for his first few days in a new house. So leave him be."

"Do I get to see what you're doing in there?"

"When we're done," Bethany called. "Okay, let me fix your hair before you look," she said. "And here's my T-shirt. Careful you don't smudge anything pulling it on."

She took her T-shirt off, revealing her ample assets that put even my pushed-up pair to shame. I gingerly took it. I'd been kind of joking about trying it on. "It sure is very . . . pink," I said and held the neck hole open as I eased my head through. It wasn't as tight as on Bethany, but with the push-up, it was still form-fitting. No matter how racy my clothes got, they were usually black. Black seemed safer somehow. Pink was practically nude. I leaned over and pulled a largish shirt out the hamper for her to borrow. "They're clean, I just haven't folded. I'm sorry I don't have anything more stylish."

"No worries. Wait." She put the shirt on, then stepped behind me and fussed with my hair, pulling it back, loosening it and twisting it around itself. She stuck a clip in it to keep it up, and then artfully pulled a few strands free around my face. "There. Are you ready to see?"

"Sure," I said and turned to face the mirror to take stock of the garish look.

Except it didn't look garish. At all.

Holy shit.

"Holy shit," I whispered. "What did you do?"

"Looks great, right? And you could always cut your hair short and start from scratch," she suggested. "I used to work in a hair salon, I could give it a go. It would look spectacular short."

I stood up. I had to get out of here. Away from her do-gooding and bonding, from all this sticky sweetness.

"What's the matter? Do you hate it?"

I pushed past her and flung open the door. Tom was mid-stride outside my room and stopped dead.

We locked eyes.

I felt naked.

I backed up into my room and ripped the pink shirt off, not caring they were both staring at me. Grabbing my black sweater, I hauled it on with no regard for my hair or makeup. The clip tumbled out. "I hate pink," I choked out. "I'm sorry, Bethany."

Looking at her aghast expression and Tom's shocked one, I pushed past them both and grabbed my jacket to head outside. I should have gone to the bathroom and cleaned my face, but Fuckhead was in there. Walking to the beach was out; I'd kill myself if I attempted it in the dark. Bursting outside, I plopped down on the wicker seat on the porch, drawing my knees up to my chest and making myself as small as possible.

My phone buzzed in my back pocket. I pulled it out.

What the fuck was that?

I shuddered at his tone.

You saw it, what do you think?

You look beautiful. Stunning.

Like Abby, I know.

I felt the cold bite of the breeze stinging the wet lines down my cheeks.

No. Like YOU.

Right. I bit my lip.

You. Are. Beautiful.

I let out a half-sob. God, I couldn't do this. Was this what it felt like to fall for someone you couldn't have? Feeling every kind word they said pierce painfully into your heart? I thought of the Little Mermaid dancing on knives for her prince as he married another. How she would rather throw herself into the waves and become foam upon the sea than take his happiness away.

Amazing what some makeup can do. Why are you texting me?

Because I needed to tell you that immediately, and I have to take Bethany home so I won't be able to. We'll be out in a moment.

What was Bethany doing while he texted?

Where are you?

I'm in Fuckhead's kingdom.

I smiled thinly, in spite of myself.

Don't come back. It's late, you should stay with her.

There was no response for a few moments.

I don't want to leave you alone.

My heart thudded painfully in my chest.

That's exactly the reason you should stay with her. Please don't make me into more of a burden than I already am.

The front door and screen opened.

I stood. Here went nothing. Bethany stepped out, Tom leaning to hold the door.

"Bethany." I sniffed and wiped carefully under my eyes to compose myself. "I'm sorry I freaked out. I'm not sure if Tom told you, but my older sister Abby was . . . well, she was beautiful. Always perfect, wore makeup perfectly. She was gorgeous. Anyway, for a moment it was like you'd made me up to look like her."

At Bethany's horrified expression, I leaned forward and took her arm. "It's okay, I know you didn't plan to, how would you? No more than I could plan to flip out when I saw myself. It, it just . . . for a split second my reflection reminded me of Abby. To be honest, I couldn't believe how beautiful I looked. You have an amazing gift."

I stepped forward and hugged her stiff body, then let go, ignoring the way Tom watched me from the shadows behind her, the weight of his gaze heavy and uncomfortable.

"I'm sorry I ruined an otherwise fun night. Maybe, now that the shock has worn off, you could show me how to do this for myself one day." I tried a small smile. "Thank you for dinner."

Bethany nodded. "Uh, sure. And you're welcome." She turned and headed down the steps.

"I'll be right there, Beth, I just gotta send Pete a text before we go and before it gets too late." Tom pulled out his phone and stood typing under the porch light. When he was done, he canted his head toward me casually then headed down the steps. "Night, Olivia," he tossed over his shoulder.

"Night," echoed Bethany.

Well.

Didn't I just remind myself of my place on the food chain? I was a taker with nothing to offer. Superfluous. Edging toward extinction.

My phone buzzed as Tom revved up the cart. I hauled it out again.

Liv, go inside. Go back and stand in front of that mirror. Please. Do it for me. I wish I could make you see what I see. Look at yourself closely. Look past all your bitterness and your pain. Past the fear and the bad memories. Look past your sister. See the girl I see. You get to choose this. You get to choose to be the person I see. Choose her. Please. She is absolutely breathtaking.

The sound of the cart, of Tom and Bethany driving away, finally faded into the night, and I couldn't move.

CHAPTER TWENTY-EIGHT

𝒯our: the number of times Bethany came over during the following week.

Three: the number of pills I had left.

Two: the number of spiders Fuckhead killed.

One: the number of hearts beating painfully on a daily basis. Mine.

Zero: the amount of nights Tom and Bethany spent together.

It was my only joy.

Tom and I were back to tolerating each other's company, like when I'd first arrived, and I didn't know how to bridge the gap. But this time the tension was thick and cloying, and clearly he was using Bethany as a shield between us. He had come back that night after dropping her home, but the following week she was at the cottage often, presumably at Tom's invitation.

It was a violation. Like he'd allowed our delicate existence, the sanctity of our home, to be soiled.

I couldn't help but watch him when he wasn't looking. He had a funny habit of sliding both his hands into his thick hair and mashing it around. It seemed to be whenever he was thinking hard on something. And not that I ever saw him type at night, but I imagined he probably did that constantly as he mulled over word choices. So it wasn't always the wind that whipped his hair all over the place after all.

I sat at the kitchen table one morning as he did it, and my fingers suddenly itched to smooth it down, which filled me with so much irritation I slammed my coffee cup on to the table harder than I meant to. This earned me a perplexed scowl from Tom before he disappeared down the hall to the bathroom.

The clocks changed.

Winter finally peeled her frigid fingers off our island, leaving her cool chill to loiter in the shade of the leaves. And the extra evening hours lit by lingering sunsets brought more customers to Mama's, full of the frisky fever of spring.

Marjoe let me work into the dinner hours to accommodate the uptick in business.

Fuckhead was finally allowed out of the bathroom after Tom said he tried to bite his dick off. I couldn't even imagine the events that had led up to that scenario, but I laughed so hard when they both came crashing out, Tom wrapped in a towel, practically throwing the poor cat down the hall.

I set the litter box up next to the washer and dryer, and we were both extra careful not to let the cat outside the cottage lest he run away.

I brought the chess set back out one morning, set it up and made a move. Then I went for a run on the beach. I felt like all I'd done since I'd been here on the island—and for as long as I could remember, if I was honest with myself—was just survive. Running felt like I was moving forward, adding to my daily schedule, forcing myself to live again. I'd never really been into track or anything, but it felt good. Head-clearing.

The spring tides had washed massive clumps of dead marsh grasses on to the beach, along with their stench of decay, but in return for the inconvenient detritus, the actual marshes around Mama's were alive with fresh light green growth. Everything seemed brighter. Everything but the cottage.

Tyler came into Mama's one of the days I was working and Marjoe refused to serve him. I was embarrassed and humiliated that she knew about my stupid escapade, but at the same time speechless that she would take a stand to protect me.

"Don't you get produce from his father?" I asked.

"I'll just have to make other plans if he's that stupid," was all she said and waved me off as if it was no big deal.

Tom and I were now playing an estranged game of chess, each one of us taking a turn in our own time. Every day that went by, Tom seemed more agitated and tense until I wondered if it had anything to do with me at all.

One night he was gone again overnight, and I got a single text.

You okay?

Fine. Thank you.

I was grateful for the extra hours at work. Before long, I had three hundred dollars cash in my pocket from pay and tips and the occasional cake order. The crisp bills were the sweetest things I had ever held in my hands. I almost didn't want to spend them. Almost.

I wasn't sure when Tom was going to Savannah next, so I left the money on the kitchen table with the old receipt from the tampons and condoms, and also a shopping list. But what I really wanted was for him to take me with him.

Next time you go to Savannah, can I come with you?

I wasn't really sure why I wanted to go, I just did. Maybe I wanted to see *his* Savannah, how he spent his time, his boat. Something. I missed him.

He didn't respond for hours. I was making a salad for dinner and opening a can of tuna that Fuckhead was going nuts over when he finally walked in, windswept and disheveled, in jeans and a white T-shirt. I stopped what I was doing to stare, and the cat leapt over my feet and between my legs, meowing repeatedly.

"Well, can I?" I asked.

"I don't know. I have to do something for someone, but if I don't, you can." His eyes flicked to me briefly.

"Cryptic much?"

"Sorry, I just, uh, I just have some stuff going on right now."

"With Bethany."

"No. Yes. No, not to do with her." He raked his hands through his hair, taming it, then headed to the fridge.

"Who are you?" I asked.

"What? What do you mean?"

"I mean, I thought we had a, a friendship or something, and I don't understand what I've done wrong." Addressing it made a weird emotional bubble grow in my chest, and my eyes started to sting.

He stopped and turned around.

I blinked rapidly, trying to dissipate any water that was collecting. The cat let out a mournful moan.

"You haven't done anything wrong, Liv."

"Then why do I feel like I have? Are . . ." I swallowed. "Are you disgusted with me now?"

"What?" he whispered. His face creased like he was in

pain and his eyes did a slow blink. Then he took a step toward me and just kept coming. And suddenly I was wrapped up in his arms, my face pressed into his hard chest, breathing him in. Breathing in his unique scent of laundry and male exertion and the fresh outdoors. Salt and weathered wood.

I froze, stiff with surprise from the sudden contact, then endured the brazen heat that whipped through my belly. His head dropped on top of mine, and he breathed into my hair. "I know you don't mean that."

"Mean what?"

"How could I ever be disgusted with you? I . . ."

He lapsed into silence, just holding me. His chest was warm, his heart beating hard under my cheek.

Lifting my arms tentatively, I slid them around his waist. I thought I felt him shudder. His muscles were bunched tight, or he was tense. I didn't know. He was hugging me. I could hug him back, right?

The cat embarked on a continuous series of desperate meows and threaded his body between our legs in a figure eight. I willed him to shut the hell up and stop ruining this moment, but it was no use.

Tom chuckled and pulled away.

"Fuckhead," I growled vehemently at the cat, who proceeded to give me a nice view of his butt.

I looked up, and Tom was watching me, amused. He reached his hand up and slid it behind my head, and I stopped breathing. His gaze flicked to my mouth for a millisecond. My lips burned. My eyes fluttered closed as he drew me in and placed a soft kiss on my forehead. His beard, which he'd taken to wearing clipped closer to his skin these days, torturing me with glimpses of his beauty, grazed my brow.

I swallowed the painful lump in my throat, my heart hammering.

He drew away slowly.

I kept my eyes closed. I couldn't bear for him to see what mine must look like. Desperate. Yearning. Drowning in agony.

And the knowledge that I could never tell him how I felt, that I had to keep it locked in my heart where it couldn't ruin *this,* was almost a comfort. I would be safe and able to stay here with him as long as I didn't mess this up. God, and I'd come so close to doing that when I came on to him.

I hated the memory of myself, of who I'd been then. How could a person change so much in so short a time? It was both the beauty and the agony of my lot. Falling in love with him had forever altered me, but to let it out of my heart might lose him forever.

"You want some salad for dinner?" I asked thickly.

"Fuckhead does. Count us both in."

"He's in it for the tuna," I said. At the word, the cat let out another long yowl. "Dang, you're noisy," I grumbled.

"I'm not sure he needs tuna; have you smelled his breath recently?"

I laughed. "Yes, every morning when he bats my head, trying to wake me up to feed him."

Tom slapped a hand to his chest and scowled at the cat. "Dude, I thought *I* was your go-to guy in the mornings. I'm so hurt."

Fuckhead glanced at him, then came and sat down right in front of me, glaring and swishing his tail sulkily. "Wow, it didn't take you long to grow an attitude, did it?" Tom said to the cat. "Don't even think of trying your luck with me tomorrow morning. We need to keep you lean and mean to take care of the spiders, snakes, and rats."

"The what?" I dropped the salad tongs with a clatter.

Shrugging, and clearly trying not to smile, Tom pursed his lips and gave me a look that said, *Poor you, you thought spiders were your biggest threat . . .*

I shuddered and returned to salad-making. "Is this going to be enough for you?" I asked.

Tom grabbed a can of soup out of the pantry and tossed it in the air, catching it deftly.

We ate dinner and compared notes about the cat, whom I now adored for giving us a neutral topic of conversation. We both agreed he probably needed a new name. But as usual we disagreed on agreeing. "Will you read me some of your stuff tonight?" I asked as we cleared up dinner.

"Hmmm." Tom paused. "Yes, but you have to read to me first. It's non-negotiable," he added at my raised eyebrows.

"You're hoping I'll fall asleep while you drone on and not get to pass judgment on your writing skills."

"Nah, never. Anyway, I thought you liked my voice?"

"I do."

"Okay then, there'll be no droning."

I glanced wistfully at the fireplace. "I wish it was cold enough to lay a fire."

"That's what doors are made for." He grinned. "We let out a little of that spring warmth that's built up in here, so we can still enjoy a fire."

"Even though those evil no-see-ums seem to make it through the screen." I grimaced. "But let's do it."

Tom laid a fire, and I got comfy on one end of the couch with a quilt from the closet in my room. I hefted the large tome of fairy tales on to my lap and spent a long time pretending to find the right page as I watched him bend and stretch over the fire to get it going. His ass was . . . well, it was . . . He turned around, and I dropped my eyes to the page.

"*Far, far from land,*" I started.

"Wait." Tom came over and settled himself on his end of the couch. "Go on."

"*Far, far from land, where the waters are as blue as the petals of the cornflower and as clear as glass, there, where no anchor can reach the bottom, live the mer-people. So deep is this part of the sea that you would have to pile many church towers on top of each other before one of them emerged above the surface.*"

"A deep blue eternity," Tom interjected, his eyes on me.

"What?"

"Sorry, it's lame. When I was younger, in school, high school, I was asked to describe what I thought love was. And that's how I thought of love. Blue and infinite, clear but deep, where no man could truly reach. A deep blue eternity."

I stared, waiting for him to crack a joke or something.

"Whatever. Go on," he said, shrugging and taking a sip of the beer he'd gotten out of the fridge.

I cleared my throat. "*Now you must not think that at the bottom of the sea there is only white sand . . .*"

I went on, reading the beautiful and heartbreaking tale. "*. . . The youngest was the most beautiful. Her complexion as fine as the petals of a rose, her eyes as blue as the clearest lake . . .*"

Tom finished his beer and set it down, then laid his head back and closed his eyes. On I read, even though I knew he was sleeping. "*. . . The prince opened his eyes and looked up at those who stood around him. He did not look out to sea where the mermaid was hiding, for how could he know that it was she who had saved him . . .*"

Was he snoring? He looked so peaceful, I let him be. The cat jumped on to my lap and settled himself, finally getting comfortable by wedging his head right under the book. "... *Many a night she heard the fishermen talking about how good and kind the prince was ... more and more she grew to love human beings and wished she could leave the sea and live among them.*"

Tom let out a deep snore and woke himself up. "Shit, sorry."

"I was about to kick you, aren't you lucky. Anyway, I'll go on ... She's at the part where she wants to know how to win a soul, and her grandmother's telling her how."

"What? I don't remember that part of the story."

"You saw the Disney one?"

He nodded sheepishly. I rolled my eyes. "Anyway ... *And he cared so much for you that all his thoughts were of his love for you ... While he promised to be eternally true to you, then his soul would flow into your body and you would be able to partake of human happiness. He can give you a soul but yet keep his.*"

"Impossible."

"Peanut gallery, shut up."

I read on until I was sure he was asleep again. I read through the sea witch telling the mermaid how stupid she was, that her choice to be human would only bring misery. The mermaid traded her voice and accepted that every step she took would be like a sword to her soul; she became human and was cast up on the shore, where the prince took her in, his little foundling. "... *Day by day the prince grew fonder and fonder of her; but he loved her as he would have loved a good child, and had no thought of making her his queen.*"

Okay, I was depressing myself. Why did I read this one? Out of all of them? Stupid, stupid, stupid.

"Go on," Tom said.

I jerked in surprise that he was awake.

He had dropped his head sideways and was staring at me. "Please."

Clearing my throat, I cringed internally as I continued. ". . . '*I saw her only twice,*' *the prince said.* '*But she is the only one I can love in this world; and you look like her. You almost make her picture disappear from my soul.*'

". . . *Never had she danced so beautifully; the sharp knives cut her feet, but she did not feel it, for the pain in her heart was far greater.*"

They'd been read and heard a thousand times, but reading one of these fairy tales out loud was so much harder. Acutely aware of his eyes on me, I tried to remain stoic.

". . . *She cast herself upon the waves and felt her body changing into foam . . .*" I was near the end, thank God. "*Mermaids have no immortal soul and can never have one, unless they can win the love of a human being.*" I took a deep breath. "*She saw the prince and princess searching for her. They looked toward the ocean in sadness, as if they knew she had thrown herself into the sea . . . and the mermaid was borne into the pink sky of dawn to become a daughter of the air. There she could earn her soul to ascend to God's kingdom.*"

I knew I had tears on my cheeks. It was so humiliating.

"Fuck, that was depressing," Tom said, his head not moving from where it lay pitched back on the couch, tilted toward me. Laughing and sniffing through my tears, I set the book down. "I know. I told you they weren't happy. Whoever came up with the phrase *fairy-tale ending* was extremely misinformed."

"Right back," he suddenly announced, standing up. From the sound of it, he went to the bathroom and then his room. He stopped by the fridge and brought back two beers along with some tissues and some papers. He set everything down, then picked up a bottle and, after twisting off the cap, handed it to me.

"Underage drinking?" I asked.

He smirked and handed me the tissues too. "You look like you need it."

I proceeded to blow my nose and wipe my eyes, then take a long pull of beer. What the hell, right? I clearly was past trying to win his affection by hiding my human foibles. He'd already had to walk me to the bathroom to pee, for God's sake.

"Okay, you ready?" he asked.

"Hit me," I said. Drinking my beer, I listened to his tale about Aislyn. Some parts I'd already read and some I hadn't. I was mesmerized by the sound of his voice and the words he used, and knew I had to come clean about snooping in his room.

And then I fell asleep.

When I woke up, I was instantly afraid and piecing together my surroundings. Another dream. Someone had come into the cottage. It wasn't Mike, but it was. Abby was yelling at me, trying to tell me something. Wait, I was still on the couch, it was dark, but the fire had burned low, its glow still casting about the room. We'd started reading when it was light so we hadn't turned on lamps. Tom? It was my next thought as I frantically puzzled everything together. Where was he? Then I felt the slow, deep breath on my nape. I turned, shifting my body under his heavy arm and upsetting his position. "Hmmmm," he groaned as I faced him.

"Tom," I whispered quietly in case he was just dozing.

His eyes blinked open slowly. "Liv?"

"Yeah," I whispered, now regretting waking him up when I could have had him hold me all night.

His eyes focused on mine, then slid down my face to my mouth. "Are you okay?" he whispered.

"I had a dream. I'm sorry I woke you. I, I don't want you to move. This feels . . . this feels really good. Safe," I added for clarification. "Comforting."

Tom's eyes closed briefly and he dragged me closer, his arm tightening around me until his forehead was against mine and I could feel his breath on my mouth. "Good." His whispered words tickled my lips. "That's good."

My stomach tumbled over. I inhaled his air. Warmth from his body spread down throughout mine; a hot pulse liquefied deep inside my belly. The feel of his mouth only millimeters away, breathing with me, made my mouth water and my heart beat on the outside of my skin. I could close the distance by just twitching. My tongue instinctively wet my lips. If it had touched him, it was so light I didn't feel it, but he inhaled, and a small sound emanated from him. *Please*, my mind screamed.

"What time is it?" he whispered.

"I don't know."

I would never close the distance. I couldn't. It had to be him. And I wasn't even sure he was fully awake to know how close we were. I opened my eyes.

He was awake. Definitely awake. He was watching me, eyes glittering almost black in the dim glow. Our mouths practically touching. He never moved. Neither did I. And we breathed each other in.

I woke alone and chilly on the couch. Snuggling further beneath the quilt, I touched my fingers to my lips. There was something between us. I wasn't imagining it, was I? But I couldn't afford to be wrong. And even if I was right, and there was, he was fighting it. I didn't know why. Was it Bethany? Or was it that although he was attracted to me, he didn't want to be. Did he see me as too young for him? Too damaged? Too Abby's-little-sister-ish? Maybe it was just a weak moment and a warm body. Perhaps he didn't feel a thing.

The latter was confirmed when I got up twenty minutes later and found a note on the kitchen table with the money I'd left the evening before. *I'm sorry about how inappropriate I was last night. Tired and too many beers. T. PS You left too much money.*

"Fuckhead," I shouted. The cat came scampering into the kitchen. Huh. A cat that knows its name. How novel. "I didn't mean you," I told it grumpily.

I decided to be equally as thoughtless. See how he liked it. I pulled out my phone.

You definitely droned on last night, I fell fast asleep.

No. Why did I do that? The thought that I'd hurt his feelings, attacked something so personal to him, made me squirm. How did I take it back? Pretend I was joking maybe?

Sorry. I never claimed to be any good.

Dammit.

I was joking. I enjoyed it very much. I must have been super-tired too. Where are you?

I went to get my boat and bring it to the island so I can start using it more.

Oh, cool. By the way, I think Zaek is an ass.

What? Why?

Because he doesn't realize he loves Aislyn. He's going to

ruin her if he keeps her, or break his own heart when he realizes what he's done.

And what has he done?

He hasn't yet, but he'll make Aislyn fall in love with him and believe all the bad stuff about herself so that she can be in hell with him. When he realizes he loves her and could never condemn her to that, it'll be too late.

Are you psychic? And here I thought I had an original story.

You do have an original story. It's effing brilliant. And heartbreaking.

Yes, heartbreaking. Yes, it is. How did you get all that out of what I read last night? You slept through most of it.

Confession. I may have seen some pages in the trash and been curious. I'm sorry.

I mashed my lips together as I waited for a response to my admission.

Ha, had a feeling you might have. No worries.

My lips opened to release my held breath. I typed in: *I wanted you to kiss me last night.* My finger hovered over the send button. Three dots came up to show that Tom was typing, so I waited.

Again, I am so sorry about last night.

It really shouldn't hurt so bad, it wasn't like he hadn't just said the same thing in a note. But it did. His words slugged a punch to my chest.

"*I'm* not," I said out loud into the quiet cottage and put my phone down on the table.

It was stuffy today. There was a heavy and oppressive feeling in the atmosphere. A high-pressure front—I'd heard people talking about it—would be followed up by a spring rain storm. Although from some of the reports rolling in from Alabama and Georgia, it was quite a violent storm. Regardless, it was hot.

I rummaged around in the clothes left by Abby over the summers and finally found a simple sundress, white with faded pink flowers. Pink. But it would have to do. At least it looked like it would keep me cool as the humidity grew throughout the day, especially if I got really busy at work. I showered and put it on.

Trying not to think about Tom and what had almost happened last night was exhausting. What if I'd just leaned forward and made contact? Not kissed him exactly, just pressed my lips against his. Would he have kissed me then? Or would it have shocked him into pulling away completely? Perhaps I should just be happy with the moment of intimacy I'd gotten. But the more I thought about it, the more annoyed I became. He was right to apologize. How dare he do that to me? Surely he had to know I was attracted to him, otherwise why would I have stayed like that with us almost kissing?

He just didn't *want* to be attracted to me. Maybe if I started developing an interest in someone else, he would acknowledge it. Or that would make him move more comfortably into Bethany's arms. God, I was giving myself a headache thinking about it.

I finished getting ready and then headed to work.

It was busy for a weekday. Bethany and I were slammed, but she bounced around on cloud nine like . . . well, like she'd just been laid.

A few schools must have been on spring break because there were lots of boats in the Intracoastal Waterway and many of them pulled in for lunch and/or drinks. A preppy-looking group came in, and one of them, a cute, clean-cut guy with khaki shorts and a blue polo, kept trying to catch my eye. His friends were egging him on, and when I saw him flush red with embarrassment, my scared-o-meter seemed to die out and I relaxed. So much so that a few hours later, when he stopped me on their way back to their boat, I didn't avoid him like I knew I would have on any other day before this one. Perhaps I should start being more sociable.

"Hi, I'm Jason," he said and held out his hand. He had blue eyes and disheveled brown hair.

I switched my tray to my left side and shook his firm hand. "Olivia," I said.

"So, I know this is a long shot, as I can't imagine that you don't have a boyfriend, but uh, um . . ." His cheeks grew red as he spoke, and it was so cute, I had to smile. "Wow, uh, yeah, so can I get your number?"

His friends were in the background high-fiving and being goofballs.

"Is this for a dare?" I asked.

"No! No, I mean, they didn't think I'd do it. I, uh, well, normally I don't do this kind of thing, ask for a girl's number. Especially, uh, since I don't know you."

He was so red in the face, I had to put him out of his misery. "Well, I don't normally give mine out to boys I don't know. But sure," I added hastily as his face began to fall. I didn't know my own number so went to grab my phone from where I'd stashed it in the cart. I came back and scribbled the number down on my order pad and pulled off the sheet. He took it and folded it carefully, putting it in his shorts pocket. "Thanks."

"Sure."

"I'll call you." He backed up with an awkward wave and then joined his friends, who from the looks of it were going to give him hell. I wasn't sure I'd answer his call if he ever went through with it, but for some reason I felt like I'd just crossed some kind of threshold, a rite of passage. Something. It was hard to imagine, I would guess, that a girl my age had never been asked on a date before. Of course, if you compared me to other girls my age, there were a lot of things I'd done that they wouldn't dream of doing.

Bethany came out grinning. "I saw that." She waggled her eyebrows.

"Saw what?"

"You getting hit on by that cutie. And no wonder: you look great, by the way."

"Thanks," I mumbled, glancing down at my dress. "Have you seen Tom today?"

I don't know why I asked. I shouldn't have. She giggled. "Yep. This morning, before he left to go get his boat." She winked and headed inside.

Had he really almost kissed me last night and gotten out of bed this morning to go have sex with Bethany? Not that I knew for sure, but Bethany's perky attitude said so.

I grabbed my phone.

I'm thinking of dating.

A few minutes later, my phone dinged.

Okaaay?

I pursed my lips, wondering if I should tell him about the guy asking me out and see if he got jealous. No, juvenile.

Who?

Well, now I had to come up with something. I settled on a good old-fashioned prank.

I dunno. I'm getting bored. Tyler isn't sooo bad if I can make sure he's not with his friends.

Are you fucking kidding me right now?

I thought about a comeback, but felt bad for messing with him. I ended up typing: *Yes, of course I'm kidding! Sorry! Just seeing if you had an opinion, LOL,* and hitting "send" just as another message popped up.

If you want to fuck Tyler and be that stupid, go right ahead. I'm not your parent or your keeper and have no interest in being either.

My chest caved as my breath literally punched out of it.

I was stunned.

Gutted.

Immediately another text came up.

Sorry.

Fuck you.

The phone rang. I turned it off and walked it back over to the cart, tossing it into the cup holder, my hands shaking. Thunder rumbled in the distance, even though the sky was still blue.

Customers began to clear out after the first signs of the coming storm. I was relieved. My head was no longer in the game. I felt sick with hurt, like my one lifeline had been yanked away and I was drifting. It was nauseatingly close to how I'd felt before coming here. Before being on this island had changed everything. Before Tom changed everything. To feel it again after such peace and security was like being hit by a semi.

I barely held myself together to finish out the afternoon and hardly said a word to anyone. The clouds rolled in and the wind began tossing things around, some plastic chairs and an umbrella. We got everything inside and Marjoe and Big Jake pulled down the big hurricane shutters that rolled over the doors and windows.

Despite my hurt, and my anger, I hoped Tom wasn't out

on the water. Please let him have gotten back safely. I looked at my phone. Twenty-seven missed calls.

The first splash of rain arrived as I headed home in the cart. And then it came down in sheets. I could barely see as I drove, the tires hitting newly formed puddles and ruts. Luckily the top of the cart mostly protected me from hazards above, but the wind meant the rain was coming at me sideways, and in seconds I was drenched, the steering wheel slipping in my hand. A massive splintering crack sounded behind me, followed by a large boom. Glancing back, I saw that a huge limb had come down right where I'd been seconds ago.

Gripping the wheel with white knuckles, my body and shoulders rigid with tension and nerves, I finally approached the turn-off to our small lane. The mud was thick, and the tires spun for a moment then gave as they found purchase on the rocks and shells sprinkled in. I slid and lurched toward the cottage, the rain so heavy and the sky so dark it felt like it was almost night. The warm glow of lights was a welcome sight.

I leapt out into the storm and jogged toward the porch, the full impact of barely being missed by the huge branch finally penetrating my mind. I was shaking with shock rather than cold.

The front door opened and Tom, his hair and clothes soaked, appeared. He must have just beaten me here. I was so relieved to see he was safe, I didn't register that he was coming toward me.

CHAPTER TWENTY-NINE

"*W*hy do you do it? Why do you provoke me and make me act like this?" He roared the words, his voice fractured and desperate as he came toward me over the muddy ground.

He really wanted to do this? Really? "Because I want you to feel!" I screamed over the wind and the rain. I was tired of fighting and hiding behind jokes and provocations. "I want you to feel something for me. *God*, even if it's irritation, anger, disappointment. Just feel something, for God's sake! Stop just tolerating me, I can't bear it." I choked out the last part, my hot tears suffocating my words and colliding with the chilled rain streaking over me.

He lashed out, grabbing my arms and hauling me forward. I slammed against him. It punched the air out of me. His body was steel, vibrating with tension, and his face was a mask of agony as our bodies met.

"I do feel. Goddammit." His voice was hoarse. "I fucking feel *you*. I *feel* for you. I feel *everything* I shouldn't fucking feel."

Thunder boomed, rocking the earth. Underscoring his words. He looked stripped bare at his admission, his chest heaving against me. His eyes fell to my mouth.

And then his face came down. Or I pulled him. But our mouths crashed together, lips hard and bruising, and still it wasn't enough. I opened to him, but his hot tongue was already plunging inside, consuming me, burning me from within, scorching a path straight down through my center. I could have died with the pleasure of it, with the taste of him. Lustful hunger, sweet and sharp, deep and greedy, exploded inside me. God, his taste . . . rainwater, mint, a deep, dark smoky Scotch that I wanted to drown in.

His hair was a wet mess under my grasping fingers as I clutched his head to keep him from leaving me, from ever stopping. Days, weeks, months of needing coalesced as we drank from each other.

He pressed closer, his hands molding me to him, twisting in my hair, down my back, running over me desperately, pulling me closer, pressing his need and his want into me. *Hard*. The word reverberated in my head. So hard. For me. The answering ache between my legs made me shudder. I had never *wanted* like this. No, *needed*.

Our feet slid in the mud, and we were falling, hanging on to each other, our mouths fused. My legs came out from under me, his knees hit first, and our mouths were wrenched apart.

"I'm not allowed you. I'm not allowed this. Please," he rasped. "Please stop." And I didn't know if he spoke to me or himself, but his battle was clearly lost as his mouth found me again and slid down my neck, blazing over my icy wet skin.

Hands fumbled and grasped at my dress straps, pulling them down, and then I was bare to the rain as it sluiced over my breasts. Tom's eyes feasted greedily for a nanosecond before his hands were full, his mouth and his teeth closing over my nipple.

I cried out and grabbed his head. *God.*

It wasn't enough. Nothing was going to be enough.

Dress sodden and heavy, I climbed over his knees.

His warm hands slid over the cold bare flesh where my skirt had ridden up. Needing to get closer, I arched against him, gasping as my body found his straining erection under his coarse jeans.

He groaned. "God, Liv." He pushed against me again, making me whimper at the friction. The pressure. The ache that desperately needed to be eased. "You don't know what you're doing," he hissed through kisses that ate me alive, sucked my tongue, bruised my flesh and stoked my desperation. His hands roamed up my skirt until he was clutching and kneading me.

"Ah," the moan escaped through my breathy gasps. "I need you, please," I panted, completely unembarrassed at my plea.

His fingers moved behind me and stole between my legs, slid into the slick heat between my thighs that had soaked through my underwear.

Desperately I looked to him for help.

"Christ," he gasped, his eyes open and glassy, deep, dark pools of diluted pupils. Then they closed, and his mouth grew hungrier, sliding over my flesh.

I arched against his hand, pressing down as his fingers slid beneath the scrap of material. "Please," I sobbed, grinding against it. Something in my body coiled painfully tight.

The storm blew around us, thrashing the earth. It was relentless. And dangerous to be out here. It was right on top of us. We were right in the center of it and I didn't care. We didn't care.

Then his finger speared me, sinking deep. Frantic and

fumbling, I leaned away to grasp at his jeans, terrified that this would be over, that he would come out of this haze he was in. My hands shook as I freed his erection.

"God, Liv," he barked out as my hand closed around his perfect thickness.

My mouth went dry, despite the rain sliding down my face and over my lips.

And then he was helping me, lifting me, positioning me. My underwear was a torn scrap on the rainy ground next to us.

He tensed, paused, his hands either side of my face. Eyes sweeping inside mine, he raked my soul bare as his long fingers slid into the hair at my nape, his thumbs grazing reverently over my cheek.

And I held his eyes in mine as I lowered down on to him, my unpracticed body resisting his blunt thickness for just a moment before the exquisite ecstasy of it, and the way his face flushed and his lips parted, made me sink down and take all of him in one long, slow, deep roll of my hips.

We both released strangled sounds of relief and further agony. Before I could move, his arms swiftly wrapped around my frame, his face dropping into my neck, and pressed me down hard, not letting me move, like he could somehow get deeper inside me. Or like he never wanted to leave. And I felt him all the way up to my heart.

His body quaked beneath my hands. The air charged up around us, my skin sang and prickled. And I felt his head shaking side to side in my neck. "No," he muttered, brokenly. "No."

Panic danced around the edges of my all-consuming need for him, almost like my body could feel him withdrawing from me emotionally, even as we were locked together physically.

I pulsed and throbbed around him, brought to the very edge but held at bay. His arms loosened a fraction, and I rocked, needing him. Still desperately needing him. "Tom, please," I whispered.

He groaned, and grabbing my hips painfully, pulled out and thrust deeply inside me.

I cried out at the force.

"I'm sorry," he rasped and went dead still.

I tried to rock against him again, grabbed his face to look into his eyes. To understand what was going on. He held my hips firmly. "I'm sorry," he said again, his eyes shuttering, a look of dawning realization stealing over his face, like he was waking from a dream.

Tears welled. "Please," I pleaded.

"Oh God, I'm so sorry, Liv. I'm so sorry." He pushed me up, unlocking his body from mine. "Oh God," he said again, squeezing his eyes shut a moment, then shifting away so I was sitting on his thighs.

I stared at him, confusion and shock rendering me mute and frozen as I struggled to understand what was happening here. My mind and body still scrambling to catch up.

Protection. That's why he was stopping. That's all it was.

But I knew it wasn't.

He raked his hands down his sopping face, exhaling harshly. The rain had eased somewhat, it wasn't so loud. Yet it fell steadily. Spattering all around us, seeping into our skin, diluting our haze of lust. Washing Tom with reality while leaving me swimming in an ocean of unrealized want.

And all I could hear was his breathing, sawing in and out of his chest. And my own.

"Tom," I whispered.

He snapped his head up. His eyes swimming in despair and regret and a thousand other things I couldn't pin down that weren't supposed to be there. Emotions that had no business being in this moment.

He shook his head, and his hands went between us, putting us back to order, tugging on my dress like he hadn't just been buried inside me. Pulling my straps up.

"Tom," I pleaded. "Speak to me."

"I'm sorry. I'm so sorry."

"Stop saying that. What the hell just happened?"

He shook his head. "I can't . . . you can't . . . I can't believe I did that to you . . ."

"*You* didn't do it! *We* did it. We were doing it. And I want it, Tom. I want you." My voice broke.

"You don't want me. You don't know what you're doing." He kept shaking his head. Like he couldn't believe what had just happened.

"But I do know what I'm doing."

"You don't. *I* don't." His voice was harsh and mangled.

The wind had died down, but the rain was incessant. I pulled strength from the steady thrum of it, the certainty I felt in my bones. "I know what I'm doing," I said calmly. "I'm loving you."

His face went blank. With shock? I didn't know. I didn't care.

It was all so clear to me now. I grabbed his face and looked into his eyes. "Every look, every touch, every time I conceive of ways to get you to react, to talk to me, to think about me, every damn breath I take to keep living is me loving you. You saved me, Tom. You gave me strength when I didn't even know I needed it. You gave me an anchor. You gave me a deep blue eternity to look forward to, instead of running away, which was all I'd done until you. I love you. I'm loving you. I'm in love with you."

"You can't," he whispered brokenly.

"Don't tell me what I'm feeling, and if I'm *allowed* to love you." I ran my hand down his arm, and he shuddered under my touch.

"You can't," he said again. His voice sounded strangely hollow, like a man on the track staring down a train he knew he couldn't avoid. "You can't, Livvy . . . because you've been actively hating me since you were twelve years old."

His words hung, his tone, like a deep, dark abyss, a terrible gaping horror, dragging me forward.

"What?" I shook my head. "What do you mean?"

"You know what I mean, Liv. You know who I am. You've met me before. You've blocked it out, that's all. I kept waiting for you to remember. But then it went on, and you thought I was the caretaker or some stupid shit."

I swallowed.

"And then it became harder and harder to tell you because I felt like if you knew, really knew, you would run."

I shook my head faster, my skin getting tight and cold. This was not real.

"And you would've run. But I needed you to stay. I needed to right the wrong. To make sure you were okay. To . . ." his throat bobbed heavily, "to make up for not saving you."

What?

"Saving me? From what?" But the knowledge crept in around the dark recesses of my mind. Crowding me. Pressing in on me from all sides.

"From—"

"No," I whispered.

The world stilled. Everything around me slowed and quieted and disappeared except the light brown eyes in front of me.

Air expelled forcefully out of my chest like I'd been punched. "No," I gasped.

And I saw the truth in all its ugliness forming in the tears that were welling in Tom's eyes. His hateful, fake, deceiving eyes. The truth spilled out, raw and brutal, carving its way over his cheeks, rivulets that dripped off his chin to the ground. And now that the rain had ceased, there was nothing to hide it. Nothing to wash it all away.

"Say it," I said.

"My name is Thomas Whitfield Cavanaugh." His voice was strung out like barbed wire. "My family, and yours, knew me as Whit."

CHAPTER THIRTY

"But you're dead. You're supposed to be dead. You and Abby are supposed to be dead." My teeth tried to slam shut, even as my mouth hung open in shock. I scrambled backward in the mud.

He dropped his head and gripped it with his hands, now free of me, his knuckles white.

"Speak to me!" I roared, not even recognizing my own voice. My body was shaking. With anger? Shock? Cold? I didn't know.

"Yes," he rasped. "I was driving the car she died in. And I wish I'd died that day too. But I *didn't*. Not in the way I wish I had."

"But you did!"

"You were *told* I did," he responded tonelessly. "I think you'll find there's no actual record of me dying."

"I don't understand. Why would anyone lie about that?"

Tom's hollow laugh was his only answer. It would have sent chills through me if I wasn't already numb.

"I hated you," I said. "Hated you for taking her away. Letting her run away with you. Hated you for not letting her come back to get me, to say something that would have saved me. And I couldn't tell you that because you were dead too."

I was so confused, reactions and questions popping through me so fast I could only ramble. "You took her. She could have told them about Mike. She could have taken me away."

I looked around helplessly, as if I could find a way out of the nightmare. The cottage stood, quiet and warm, beckoning me back within its safety. Inside, where I'd been living the worst lie I could imagine. I remembered the day I'd found the box on my bed. Tom knew what Uncle Mike had done to Abby. "God, *you* could have told someone. You *knew* she had a sister. You knew about me. You knew *of* me." I heaved in air, trying to catch my breath, shock making it hard to even blink. "You said Abby told you about Mike and what he did, and I thought you must not have known back then that she had a sister. God, I just thought the best of you. You would *never* abdicate responsibility on something like that."

I paused, trying to gather my thoughts while Tom sat still like a statue. "You were *admitting* it," I said incredulously. "And I was so blinded by you that I didn't hear it." My empty and unamused laugh pinged the earth between us. "There I go again making those fucking bad choices about men, right?" I got to my feet. My legs felt like rubber. "I hate you," I rasped, my voice falling into a sob as my face crumpled, my hands coming up to hide it. "I *hate* you."

The rain continued its patter around us, and thunder rumbled. Another round was gearing up.

"I know," Tom whispered. "I know you do. And you should. That's the only thing you should feel for me. I fucked up the only chance I had to make it right."

"Make it *right*? How can you undo something so horrible. If I'd known from the beginning, *Whit*," I dragged out his name with disgust, "there would never have been this chance you think you had." I tried to gather my thoughts. "A liar once told me he wasn't a liar, and I believed him. But you believed your own lie too, didn't you?" My voice grew louder. "You thought you could be nice to me and make up for it, erase everything. Make up for a little girl being *petted*, being made to touch someone in return, being made to feel like she was special because of it, even though she knew it was wrong.

"But she was so fucking lonely because her parents were so wrapped up in grief. She was lonely from being made to keep the secret from her parents, even though all she wanted was for them to get closer and help her, not go further and further away."

I sucked in more air to keep going even though I wasn't sure I was making any sense. My voice grew and grew until I felt like I was raging along with the wind, and drawing my strength from the ocean and the trees and the rain and the air and the thousands of miles of earth beneath my feet. "And you can't *ever*," I spat, "make up for that girl trying to change herself to become invisible so he wouldn't want her anymore, so he'd leave her alone, and instead, he was so angry that he, that he, she was . . ."

My voice collapsed to a whisper, picking the only acceptable word, a word that had become an easy one to say, when the reality was so much worse. "Raped. Raped as punishment for not looking like he needed me to look."

I tried to draw another breath, but pain was trying to get out at the same time, and they wheezed and clashed in midair. "As if," I squeaked, "as if the years before hadn't been punishment enough. Oh no, he saved *that* for later. Until everyone thought I was certifiably crazy and delusional anyway. I kept thinking, maybe he wouldn't have done it if I'd just stayed the way I was, if I'd just looked like her for longer. He wouldn't have done that to *her*."

Tom looked like he was going to be sick. He got to his feet and started toward me. "No, Liv. He did."

Stumbling back, I held out a hand to ward him off.

"Please, no," I managed. The thought of anyone touching me right now was like asking me to exfoliate a third-degree burn. I'd never told anyone the things that had just come out of my mouth. Even though my voice didn't sound like mine, I still knew it was me. And to think I'd just spewed all that at Tom . . .

No, not Tom, *Whit*.

This was Whit.

Whitfield Cavanaugh—a player who lost his college football scholarship because he kept getting in trouble. Not even his influential father could save him. I racked my brain for the rest of the rap sheet everyone seemed to talk about in hushed tones back then. But all I could come up with was the way Abby talked about him. Like he was going to save her.

This wasn't my Tom, this was Abby's Whit. Thomas Whitfield Cavanaugh IV. *Deceased*.

I was mute, staring at the fire. Tom had finally convinced me to go inside out of the rain, so I'd parked myself on the couch, soaking through all the cushions. I didn't want to do anything he told me. In fact I wanted him to just . . . disappear. For the last hour not to have happened. For me to have never come here. For my heart to not have known him. *God*, and I'd had him inside my body. Abby's Whit. I winced.

"Did you and Abby have sex?" I asked suddenly.

Tom was sitting in the chair closest the fire, legs apart, his body propped up by his elbows and his hands and head hanging listlessly. He lifted his head wearily. His eyes were a shock. Their caramel color was drained to dry mud. Flat nothingness. "That's what you want to know?"

I shrugged. "The only guy I willingly chose to have sex with turns out to be my sister's boyfriend. It seems like a legitimate question."

His face was expressionless.

Perhaps he didn't hear the part where I was admitting I wasn't as sexually experienced as he thought, despite my bravado and my attitude. That none of the things I'd experienced were things I wanted. That he was the only person I'd ever really . . . chosen.

"Husband."

"What?"

"Husband." He swallowed, loudly. "Abby and I got married in Beaufort before coming to the cottage. I was trying to . . . trying to do it right. I guess I thought I could protect her better. I don't know."

And the kicks just kept coming. I pressed my lips together. "You're . . . you're my brother-in-law. Wow. At what point from the moment I arrived here did you think I didn't need to know that? I mean, did you look at me and think, *She looks dumb enough to buy this caretaker bullshit*?"

"I never called myself that, you did. I just didn't know how to correct you."

"Obviously it would have been hard to tell me. But don't you think it would have been better than this? Better than allowing me to, I don't know, to start to feel . . ." My voice gave out. I tried again. "To feel happy, to live again, to, to

. . . *want* things, only to pour gasoline on everything and strike a match. I get that you didn't care enough about some little girl you hardly knew . . ."

"Of course I cared, but I couldn't do anything back then."

I ignored him and continued. ". . . enough to save her from a monster, but then to start pretending you care about me and let me, let me . . ." I couldn't finish. We both remembered the words I'd said to him outside.

I'd fallen in love with him. I'd fallen in love with an honorable, strong, caring, funny guy, who lay with me when I was sick, who scared my monsters away, and whom I never believed could be capable of hurting me. But he wasn't that guy anymore. He'd *never* been that guy.

"I wanted to tell you, but I didn't know how. I was so shocked when I saw you. When I realized who you were. And it got harder and harder. Especially when every day you were here I saw the person you are inside finally coming out, and I didn't want to hurt you again." He blew out a rough breath and raked his hand over his head, gazing up to the wood-beamed ceiling as if it held answers. "Can you understand that?" he asked, looking back at me. "I know I should have told you, but I didn't want to inflict any more pain on you. It was wrong. But I didn't know we would get this far."

"*Get this far*," I echoed and choked out a laugh at the words.

"Answer me honestly, if you'd known who I was when you first got here, would you have stayed?"

I swallowed. "I don't know. I may have had to; I had nowhere else to go. What I know *now* is I don't want you here anymore. You can go live on your boat, move in with Bethany, or do whatever the fuck you like, but you need to get the hell out of my face."

"Liv—"

"Olivia. Or don't address me at all."

"So you don't want to know anything else? What happened when Abby died, or why—"

"It doesn't change anything, *Whit*."

His eyes flickered, in a vague approximation of a flinch, except he didn't move. Not a muscle. Nothing.

"It doesn't change that Abby died. That you were a part of it. It doesn't bring her back or stop what Mike Williams did, and it doesn't change the fact that you lied to me. As far as I'm concerned, it doesn't really matter anymore."

I stood up, scooped the kitten from where he'd curled into a round purring ball at my hip, and headed for my room. The storm thrashed for the rest of the evening as I lay in bed, covers over my head so I couldn't hear Tom moving around. Was he packing? I tried really hard not to think about what it would be like to wake up in the morning and find him gone, and never, ever coming back.

I'd had so many questions for so long. If I'd known Whit was alive, would I have asked him what I needed to know, or was it safer just to hate him? And he'd married Abby. God. They were in love, and I'd betrayed her utterly. My stomach twisted with renewed remorse. How could he have done that to Abby? Unless . . . unless I reminded him of her so much that he couldn't help it. Twisting into the pillow, I opened my mouth and screamed silently, soaking it with my tears of agony.

TOM

CHAPTER THIRTY-ONE

$\mathcal{L}$ooking around the room I'd called my own for six years felt oddly unemotional. Maybe because the time might as well never have happened. I'd had six years to turn myself from a lost and terrified nineteen-year-old kid into someone worth something. And failed spectacularly.

I couldn't believe I was even able to move with the pressure squeezing my chest and the raging in my skull.

Opening the armoire, I pulled all my clothes out and stuffed them into a duffel. It was sobering to realize how little I needed to pack. The bathroom was equally bare. I left the shampoo.

Had I always known deep down this day would come? I'd bought a sailboat and made sure it had the most powerful outboard engine on it I could afford. I hadn't done that so I could tool around the Intracoastal Waterway. No, subconsciously I'd been poised to leave when the time came. Was that what happened when everything you cared about was ripped away from you, and all your roots were crudely severed? You could never grow *any* back?

Marjoe and Pete had become like surrogate parents to me,

but how much would they really miss me when I was gone? If my own parents could let me go, this had to be way easier. The ocean would be perfect for me: definitely no roots growing there.

I could finish my degree online. And at least do something worthwhile with the rest of my sorry life. Maybe I'd work to expose corruption, or find abusers; wouldn't that be ironic? It might even get me killed all over again. This time for real.

There was so much I wanted to tell Livvy. Things she needed to know before I left that would allow her to finally live. And she *would* live, I had no doubt. She was hurting now because of me, but she'd grown in the time she'd been here. She'd grown strong. She thought she loved me, but she didn't. How could she? It was based on a lie about the kind of man she thought I was. She had so much love to give; I was just the closest target. The most important thing she'd done was develop the capacity for love. And that was worth more. So much more.

But to all intents and purposes she was a child. And that made me the worst kind of man. Was I any better than any of the men who'd taken advantage of her? Was I so intoxicated by the way she looked at me, like I was the center of the world, that I couldn't help but descend into wanting to make her mine?

I'd fought it.

God, I fought it.

I'd spent hours last night with her lips a hair's breadth away, and willed her to close the gap, because I refused to. With everything she'd been through, there was no way I was going to kiss her, even though I wanted to do it more than breathe.

So I waited for her to do it.

She saw herself as something broken and damaged, and I saw her as absolutely fucking perfect. She saw herself as spoiled and ruined, and while I'd seen a lost, abused girl when she first arrived, I now saw her as something so pure and so light that no amount of knowledge of what had happened to her could taint her for me. Except what *I* could do to her.

My restraint in not kissing her the night before had gone out the window the instant I'd gotten her text and had to think of her making a choice to be with anybody else but me. How had that happened? Her light, fun, flirty text telling me she was thinking of dating suddenly ripped a hole through every barrier I'd erected between us. I was blindsided by my reaction, and so I was gaping and raw when she mentioned Tyler a few seconds later.

In retrospect, *obviously* she was joking, trying to make light of what had been a horrible situation. And being able to look back on something stupid with wiser eyes was healthy, right?

In retrospect.

Everything made sense in retrospect. Like *in retrospect* I probably should have told her who I was before I completely violated her trust by not just finally kissing her—oh no, nothing that simple—but finding myself buried inside her within minutes. I mean, how many minutes was it? One? Ten? How did that even fucking happen?

But *in retrospect* I knew why I hadn't told her who I was, because that's where I *wanted* to be. And if I'd told her, it never would have happened. *We* never would have happened. So yeah, I grew a conscience as soon as the shock of feeling her pulsing around me broke through the haze of my lust-addled brain.

There were no answers for why I was in so deep with her. None that I liked. I almost felt as if . . .

No. I wasn't even going to go there.

I saw the way she watched me. I saw the way she looked at Bethany with mild confusion, trying to figure out what made Bethany a better choice for me than her. But what the hell had I ever done that made me worthy of her love?

Well, I hadn't done anything. I'd taken advantage of her. Plain and simple.

I finished getting all my shit together and stepped out of my room. As I passed her door, I grabbed the door frame on either side, rested my head against the wood, and simply breathed.

Finally I headed to the front of the cottage and dumped my bag by the door. My phone sat on the table; the fire was low. I wouldn't sleep tonight and there was nowhere to go until morning. I picked up the book of fairy tales and started reading. Christ, she wasn't kidding when she said these weren't your typical fairy stories. After a particularly depressing one about a tin soldier, I snapped the book shut. It was my turn at chess. I might as well make my last move.

I stared at the chess set for what felt like an eternity before sitting back in resignation. I wasn't going to win, so what was the point in trying?

"Aren't you going to make your move?"

I jerked around in surprise. "Shit, you scared me."

She'd changed into the long white T-shirt she slept in. Her slim legs were bare and one foot was pointed in. She always stood like that. I smiled inside, tucking it away as a keepsake. Looking at her was agony, knowing that this was the last night I'd see her, and wishing I'd stared at her every possible moment until now.

"When are you leaving?"

"You're beautiful," I said at the same time, hating myself for letting it come out.

Her jaw slammed shut and her eyes narrowed. She began to turn away.

"Wait. Please."

She swung back, but her eyes were vacant. Pale and cold. Like freaking arctic ice shelves where I'd gotten used to them being like the frolicking sandy waters of the Caribbean Sea.

"What?" she snapped.

I wanted her to stay but wasn't sure how to make her. Offer to talk? Play chess one last time? "Why did you come out here?"

"To see if you'd gone."

Ouch. Okay, chess then. "Let's finish this game." I motioned to the board.

"Then make your move." She walked to the kitchen and put the kettle on to boil. I'd gotten the chamomile tea that was on her list last time I went to Savannah. It helped her sleep. She looked at home, and in command of her domain. Suddenly I was the awkward visitor at the cottage, and she was the long-time resident. I didn't want to question why she was tolerating me right now, so I tried to concentrate on my next move, knowing I would fail. In the end I moved a pawn just to do something.

She walked over with her tea, blowing on the surface of it, then leaned down, exposing more of her incredible legs that I would never touch again, and captured my pawn with her knight immediately. "You can't just throw the game to get it over with," she said.

I wanted to howl with laughter, and not the funny kind. "Why not? Is there any point to my playing when I can't win?"

"Then why did you ask me to play?"

"Liv, sit down." We locked eyes for a long moment. "You've asked me to leave, and I will. But until then, neither of us is sleeping, because we're . . . we're not done."

At the sight of her head moving side to side in a gesture of rejection, I forged on. "I'm not saying it will change anything. It won't. But I know you must have questions. Ask them while you can. While I'm here. I know about regrets, Liv. You don't want any. And you need to move forward. Move on. So go ahead. Ask."

"Why did you do that earlier?"

"What?"

"Say 'You're beautiful,' just like that? After everything? After everything has turned ugly and disgusting."

Ugly and disgusting. The words mixed in nicely with the cesspool in my stomach. "Because you *are* beautiful."

"You have no right to think I'm beautiful," she snapped acidly. "Was it not enough to have one of us? I'm not her, you know; we may have gone through the same hell, but I'm not her. I'm not your second chance with her." She shuddered as if nauseated, as if her skin was crawling.

She thought . . . *what?* "You and I . . ." My voice sounded like it was scraping through a pit of rocks in my chest, and it hurt just as bad. "We were *never* about Abby."

Liv shrugged. "Whatever you say."

"Was Abby really so perfect, Liv?"

She nodded.

"Really?" I pressed. "Because I can hardly remember what she looked like." I wasn't trying to disparage Abby's memory; I honestly couldn't remember. I remembered I loved her, of course, as much as my immature younger self had been capable of. And I remember she was pretty. Really pretty.

And also a lot messed up. What I'd thought I felt for her was nothing compared to the crushing pain I was experiencing right now.

I tried a new tack, to break through. "She didn't want to go back, you know. After we left, she didn't want to go back." I stared hard at her, pressing myself with words into her comfort zone. There were things we needed to get out there.

"I know she didn't. She said so in a letter she left me. So why did you?"

"Because I convinced her to. She kept saying that telling your parents wouldn't help. It would only destroy everything. I didn't understand what she meant, but in the end I finally convinced her to go back. I mean, I guess it seemed cut and dried to me." I stood up and turned, stirring at the embers of the fire with the metal poker. They flared with new-found oxygen. "I thought I could get my father to help. We could get Mike Williams arrested. Or investigated or something."

"And did you? Did you tell your father?"

I laid the poker against the wall, then folded my arms. I realized I was bracing myself. I couldn't turn around. "Yes." My brows pinched together.

"Turn around." Her voice was curious.

I exhaled and turned, hating what she must see. I was haunted by my father's reaction. Blindsided, really. Still.

She stared at me carefully, hardly blinking. "So you told your father? And what did he say?" Why was she asking like it would change history?

"My father and mother," my lips twisted, "told Abby and me to shut our mouths about it."

I saw the shock as it hit her. "What?" she rasped. "Why?"

I picked my king off the chessboard, removing him from

play, staring at him as if he held some clue. But in the end, facts were just that. There was no spin to this. "My father was up for a potential vice-presidential nomination."

She heard my words, and her mouth opened in surprise. I saw her mind turning it over, piecing together things she must have heard. "The night she died . . . I heard him—Mike—saying something about your father having people on the payroll. Was that true?"

My parents had been in full-blown sanitize-the-family mode. "My father paid a lot of people for a lot of favors. Most of the time it was to get them to look the other way on certain issues. When he needed extra security, off-duty cops supplemented their salaries by helping him out, and if one of his cronies ever needed them to lose evidence, well, my father's money was too sweet for them not to comply. They—"

My cell phone rang. It was too late for anyone to be calling unless there was something wrong. We both looked at it. My first thought was Pete, and I leapt up to grab it before it rang off. I was too late, but it was Tyler's name on the screen.

Oh shit.

Not tonight of all nights. The house phone rang. "Leave it," I barked to Olivia, earning a scowl. "Sorry, just hang on," I said and dialed Tyler back from my cell.

"You sure picked a fine night for it," I said, my voice mangled from trying not to sound like my chest was caving.

"When things are lined up, things are lined up. Anyway, consider it a favor that I picked a time when you're least likely to run into anyone."

"Whatever. Like Pete and I have ever done a fish delivery at night. You're an idiot."

Tyler hissed.

I was being reckless. I knew it.

"Not now," he said. "First thing in the morning. Five a.m., it'll be waiting for you on the boat. Call Pete and let him know. Consider it a favor I'm giving you more time. Just get the job done and everyone will be happy. And don't fuck up. Cal's been talking non-stop about little Olivia, and there's only so much I can do to stop him sneaking around that cottage."

My heart slammed. "What are you saying?" *Christ*. Was it Cal who'd been in the house, messing with Olivia's head? Fuck. My eyes snapped up to see her staring at me hard, her bottom lip sucked between her teeth as she chewed the hell out of it. Her thinking face.

"Just that," Tyler's voice responded innocently in my ear. "There's only so much I can do."

My bunched fist slammed down on the table. Olivia flinched. "You tell that sniveling piece of shit that if I hear anything close to that again, I'll tie him up and saw his fucking nuts off."

"Calm down, calm down," Tyler said, his voice thick with satisfaction. "I can call him off any time. Anyway, I'm not so sure I'm ready to give her up to him. Maybe I'll keep her for myself. You just hold up your end of the deal, and I'll hold up mine."

I mashed the "end" button, breathing hard. This was what real panic felt like.

"What the hell was that about?" Olivia asked, her pale eyes wide.

"Nothing," I bit out. Shit. This better not fail. What the fuck was I even doing? I'd put her at risk even coming up with this damn scheme. But no, she was at risk anyway, and had been since the moment Tyler had seen her at Mama's.

I stared at her porcelain face and cerulean eyes. Why had fate, God, or who-the-fuck-ever seen fit to keep placing this girl in the firing line?

$\mathcal{S}$he was cursed. Olivia had to be cursed.

Some kids grew up without ever seeing the ugliness she'd seen. And she'd not only seen it, she'd lived and breathed it, and now it continued to pulse around her, just waiting in the shadows for a chance to take her again.

Was this why I'd met Abby? Not to save Abby, but to save Liv? I'd failed, of course. Something I would never forgive myself for. Nor would Liv. But for some reason I was being given this chance. Because horror was still thirsting for her, waiting to take her down.

"Stop staring at me like that." Liv stepped backward. "Who was on the phone?"

Did I tell her about the threat from Tyler and/or Cal, and risk her being in a full-blown panic without me here? Or was forewarning her actually fore*arming* her, in case I failed? I needed help. And I needed to tell her.

"Liv," I started.

"Olivia," she growled.

"Fine. Olivia. When I leave, I need you to lock the doors and windows. That was Tyler. I have to go do something for him, a favor, and he . . ." I blew out a breath as if it would help me lay it on her easier, "he threatened you if I don't do it."

Her eyes narrowed. "What kind of favor? Tell me you aren't going to try and pull one past Pete and put some of Tyler's shit on his boat?"

Pull one past Pete. Her words dinged in my skull. I didn't want to put Pete at risk. With our original plan of pretending Pete had changed his mind and was dumping the stuff in the marshes so Cal and Tyler had to come get it, he'd be a target.

Pete didn't need to do this.

I could do it without him, now I had my boat. Way less risk. I was only putting myself in danger, and who the fuck cared about that? Certainly not me.

And Liv was concerned about Pete before she even asked about herself.

Without thinking, I reached out to tuck a stray strand of hair behind her ear. She flinched and shrank away. It felt like someone had slid a knife under my breastbone.

"How did he threaten me?" Her voice was small.

When I didn't answer, she smashed her hand over her mouth.

"I know you don't want me here," I offered. "But I'll stay until morning and then go get this done for Tyler. The plan is for him to be no longer a problem. Cal too."

We locked eyes. She dropped her hand and nodded as if drawing strength from my plan.

And I couldn't help my gaze sliding to her mouth. Would I ever again feel anything close to what had happened to me a few hours ago in the storm outside? Or, for that matter, what had happened to me over the last few weeks.

"What are you going to do?" she asked, blinking and breaking the spell. My spell. My curse.

"The less you know, the better. But first thing in the morning, get yourself over to Mama's and stay with Marjoe, or even Bethany, until you know you're safe. Okay?"

"Are you—"

"I'm not coming back, Liv."

Her lips compressed, and her body trembled.

I mean, I could literally see it quake.

I had an immediate recollection of my hand pressing against her breastbone, desperate to feel her pulse when she was sick, her bones so delicate under her skin, it was like feeling the bones of a bird in my hand.

"Liv . . . I'm sorry I lied to you." I finally addressed it. "I can never change that, and even if you could find a way to forgive me, or to understand why I did it, I can't forgive *myself*. Not for being part of Abby's death, not for abandoning you afterwards, and *never* . . . for abusing your trust in me . . . or for what I just did to you." I took a breath. "So no. I'm not coming back."

Her eyes watered over, and I fucking had to watch a tear roll down her cheek and not wipe it away.

"But you're stronger now, Liv."

"I'm stronger because of you," she whispered.

I hated her words. I didn't want her needing me just because she was scared to stand on her own. I wanted her to need me because . . . "Dammit." I gritted my teeth. "You were always strong. Don't take that away from yourself. The shit that happened to you was just that, it was shit. Shit you didn't deserve. And you fucking *survived*. You found a way to survive, to get away. That took courage, Liv. You're stronger than anything life is gonna throw at you, okay?"

I shook my head. When I compared the girl in front of me now to the one who showed up on my doorstep, who was so terrified and so broken and hollow, I realized maybe for the first time just how much it had taken for her to get here, not even knowing what awaited her. An empty, run-down cottage, no food, no electricity, but paradise compared to where she'd been. What she'd endured.

I didn't call Pete. He'd be mad as a copperhead with a flat tail, but damned if I was going to send him on a suicide mission. He only had a finite amount of time left. I didn't need him wasting it on me.

It was after midnight and sleep was not on the agenda. I needed to be ready to roll in less than four hours.

"You need to go to bed, Liv."

"I fell asleep when you were packing earlier, and I dreamed someone chased me from here all the way to the beach. So excuse me, but I don't feel like seeing what else my subconscious has to offer." She settled on the couch, drawing the quilt she'd brought out yesterday over her legs. Was it just last night I'd lain there, breathing her in?

"What happened when you got to the beach?"

"What?"

"In your dream, what happened?" I sat in the chair closest the fire, putting us right back into the positions we'd been in earlier when we'd first come inside after I tore her world apart.

"Abby was there." She furrowed her brow. Her gaze seemed distant as she remembered. "She told me to go into the water to get away. But I knew if I did that I'd drown. Whatever was chasing me made it a really viable option, though." She shivered.

"God, it would be a psychologist's wet dream to extrapolate theories from that one," I mused.

Liv pressed her lips together as she sat opposite me, and her hand shook as she took another sip of tea. "I told you I hated her. I was angry with her. In my dream, I didn't trust her." She looked at me. "So what did you do when your parents told you they wouldn't help?"

We had a few hours left together: it seemed she was taking my advice and getting as much out of me as possible. I leaned back on the chair, folded my arms across my chest, and closed my eyes. Exhaustion settled over me. My mind slid back in time. "I wouldn't drop it. How could I? My fucking parents solved every single one of my problems growing up by throwing money at it, until the only thing left I could think of doing was snort it or drink it." I was too tired and emotionally spent to try and worry about how I sounded. It was the truth, anyway. "I finally got my head together, got on the straight and narrow and went to them for help with something real and terrifying, and they told me to drop it and asked how much we needed to stay out of the way for a few years."

I opened my eyes to find her listening to me, her lips slightly parted and her eyes filled up. There was pity there, maybe because it turned out my parents were as fucked up as hers were, but I also saw suspicion. She wanted to know if I took the money. "Ask me."

"Did you take the money?"

"Not that time."

Her hand pressed against her stomach. I knew the feeling. Mine was trying to rearrange itself into my hollow chest or my legs or anywhere but where it should be.

"So what did you do?" she pressed.

"That's when we made our mistake."

"What was the mistake?" she whispered.

"I decided we needed evidence. So I made Abby call him and ask to meet. We went to this bar. I should have known right then something wasn't right. We thought we could . . . record him or something. Record him admitting it, I thought. Fuck, we were dumb. *I* was," he corrected. "Abby didn't really want to, she didn't want to see him again, but I made her do it. I thought it was the only way."

The kitten padded out from the bedroom and jumped up on to her lap, settling into a round ball of brown and white. Her hand immediately settled on his fur.

"You should have seen it, two underage kids walking into a bar full of cops. What the hell were we thinking?" I shook my head. "Mike was all *hey, look who it is*, and smiling, introducing us around. Abby looked like she was going to faint. One of his buddies, another cop, gave us a drink each. Alcohol." I shook my head. "It was weird as shit. Of course we didn't drink them, and we got the hell out of there about ten minutes after we arrived. She was shaking so bad. We got in the car and sat there trying to figure out what the fuck to do. She kept saying we just needed to go back to the cottage." My eyes closed as I remembered, letting the night I'd blocked out for years slowly slither back into my head. "I asked about you, and she said it wasn't about you, and you were still too young, and we had time . . ." I trailed off.

"I don't want you to say anything else," she whispered. "I know what comes next."

But she didn't, not really. And it was probably better that way.

My phone alarm chimed, and I jerked awake. It was time to go. My neck was stiff from where I'd dozed on the chair.

Easing up, I ran a hand down my face, chasing away the sleep. It was still dark out and would be for a while with the time change. The fire had died out, and I could barely make out the small shape of Liv curled on the couch, the kitten snuggled against her belly.

I stared, waiting for my eyes to adjust so I could see her more clearly. Quietly, I got up and walked over to her, easing down to a crouch. My hand moved to her hair, and I hesitated for a moment before letting instinct take over and smoothing it back from her face.

She sighed and shifted. The kitten let out a barely audible squeak, then broke into rhythmic purring.

I tensed, hoping I hadn't just sparked some crazy nightmare by touching her. But her face surprised me by tilting toward my hand, as if it sought me out.

All I was planning to do was wake her enough to let her know I was leaving, but I couldn't make myself stop touching her face while she slept, seeing if her subconscious mind hated me as much as her conscious one did. Letting my hand descend to cup her delicate cheekbone, I reveled in the warmth of it, before my thumb brushed lightly over her lips.

Instantly her breathing changed, and I knew I'd woken her. *Just open your eyes, Liv*, I willed her. If she opened her eyes, I would kiss her. Say all the things I wanted to.

I waited.

After a few moments she turned her face away, and my heart sucker-punched me from inside my own body. I squeezed my eyes closed and forced myself to stand. I walked numbly to the kitchen, turning on the dimmest under-counter light, and made coffee. Then I went to the bathroom and took one last shower, throwing the same clothes back on since I'd packed everything else. Making my way quietly back to the kitchen, I saw Liv was awake, sitting on the couch, knees drawn up to her chest.

Unanswered questions flowed and pulsed around the cottage. But as if we both knew that addressing them now, at this late stage, would cause more harm than good, we stayed quiet. The time for answers and recriminations had passed. Liv was going to move on regardless. I poured a quick cup of coffee and drank it while it was still scalding; maybe it could cauterize my heart on the way down. I rinsed the cup and put it in the sink.

The weight of Livvy watching me slowed all my movements.

I grabbed my duffle, slung it over my shoulder, and headed to the front door.

"Please lock up after I'm gone." I spoke quietly, easing into the heavy silence. "And head to Mama's as soon as you can. Don't stay here today, okay? And . . ." I stared at the wooden door as if it was a mirror that could reflect her back to me from where she sat, "if you need something, if you are in trouble, or scared . . ." *Shit.* I exhaled roughly. "You can still call me or text me."

"Just leave. Please."

I nodded. Opening the door and the screen, I walked out into the cool, dark morning air, letting the screen slam behind me.

OLIVIA

$\mathcal{J}$ slept heavily, and dreamlessly. For once. When I awoke on the couch, it was still early morning. The kitten was sitting on my chest, staring at me. I jerked with surprise at being studied at such close range. The kitten yawned, baring his tiny white pointed teeth and barb-covered pink tongue, and then puffed fish breath all over me.

Daylight filtered into the interior of the cottage. It wasn't sunny but at least it wasn't raining anymore.

The cottage was threateningly and painfully quiet. I looked around, unsettled. The aching void left by Tom's departure wasn't just inside me.

I moved mechanically, feeding the cat, drinking burned coffee left on from the early hours, showering and getting dressed in shorts and a T-shirt. I needed to head to Mama's. Not just because Tom had made me promise, but because I wanted to see if I could help if anything had been damaged. I wasn't sure if the branch that came down behind me the night before had blocked the whole road, so I decided I would leave the cart and walk. I hurried to get ready. Searching for my phone, I remembered I'd left it in the cart when I'd arrived in the storm last night. *Shit*. It was probably ruined.

It was warm outside, but the rain had broken the mugginess, although the heat of the day would soon hit the leftover dampness, steaming the island. The air smelled of earthy mud and split wet wood.

The first thing I saw was my torn underwear, caked with mud and drying in the morning breeze. My skin flushed hot and prickly with embarrassment, and then my belly dipped at the erotic memory. I grabbed the material, my chest pounding with painful emotions I refused to acknowledge. My phone was dead and waterlogged. *Dammit*. Feeling the first stirrings of panic, I jogged back inside and stuffed it into a bag of rice. Let's see if that shit actually worked.

I picked up the cat and gave him a gentle squeeze. He meowed mournfully. "Don't think I don't know you can't wait for me to leave so you can climb the curtains again," I admonished.

Mama's looked worse than it actually was. Tables and chairs were strewn around but mostly undamaged. Pete's boat was gone. I wondered if he was on it with Tom—Whit, I corrected myself—and crossed my fingers reflexively, saying a quick prayer that whatever he was planning would be done fast and effectively.

The hurricane shutters were half removed. I got busy righting some chairs and tables and heard Marjoe talking inside. I decided to head in and let her know I was here. She was talking with Big Jake, saying something about Pete. "Hi," I greeted, approaching. I looked around to see if anyone else was inside. Bethany was coming through from the kitchen. When she saw me, she almost ran toward me.

I stopped, suddenly terrified for Tom. She grabbed my arm and hauled me back outside. "What's going on with you and Tommy?" she spat, and I realized it wasn't worry in her wide eyes.

"What?" I said, taking a step back in surprise.

"Is this some kind of sick joke or something?" Her eyes were full of tears now. "I thought you guys were like brother and sister or something, and to find out you've been . . . God!" she choked out. Her tone turned acid. "You're sick! No wonder he's barely touched me in weeks; he's been quite well taken care of."

"Bethany, what the hell are you talking about?"

My God, had Tom come here and told Bethany that something happened between us? I couldn't fathom he'd do that. Shock made my mind spin. Caught off guard, I decided to stick to current facts. "There's nothing going on between me and Tom."

"I'm so stupid, so damn stupid. I can't believe you both did that to me. And to think I felt sorry for you. Were you having a good laugh? Having me over for dinner and then laughing at me when I was gone?"

I grabbed her arm. "What the hell are you talking about?" I raised my voice, trying to break through to her. And she felt sorry for me? Fuck that. Now I was mad, in addition to confused.

Marjoe slammed outside. "What is going on out here?"

"Get off me," screeched Bethany, wrenching her arm out of my grip.

I dropped my hand quickly, hoping it didn't look bad to Marjoe.

Bethany pointed at me. "She's fucking Tommy, like the sick little slut she is."

Blood drained from my head. "I'm not," I whispered in agony.

"I saw you!" she shouted.

Staring at her in horror, I felt my heart ooze up to beat in my throat.

"I saw you! I was worried about Tommy being out in the storm so I raced over there. In. The. Storm." She emphasized every word. "To make sure he'd made it back safely, only to see you . . . you and him . . ." She sobbed and turned away.

"Is this true?" Marjoe's rough voice asked, surprise lacing her tone.

I swung my face in her direction, but could hardly focus. My mind was replaying everything from last night, trying to see it through someone else's eyes.

"Honey," she soothed, and I blinked with relief until I realized she was talking to Bethany. "I'm sure you must have misunderstood what you saw."

Bethany fell crying into Marjoe's arms. "I didn't."

"She didn't," I said quietly, barely finding my voice. Bethany had seen every ugly, dirty, and desperate moment.

Marjoe looked up, confused and . . . disappointed. My mother always looked disappointed. But disappointment had never skewered me so thoroughly.

They both looked at me. And I backed up, one foot stumbling behind the other.

Turning, I ran as fast as I could. I was almost glad I didn't bring the cart. Having to stop right now and start it up was beyond the simple commands I could give my body. *Get away* was all I could think. Go where I was alone, where I only had to worry about me, my feelings. My feet pounded along the dirt, my chest heaving, my head full only of the sound of my breathing. The warmth of the day and steam from the earth tried to sap what little energy I had left.

Halfway back, I stopped running. I was tired and emotionally spent. I paused, bending over to catch my breath.

I knew I had some explaining to do to Marjoe, and Bethany too, at some point, and I began to feel pissed that Tom had carried on with Bethany and used her so badly. Look at me grow, I thought in an abstract and lucid moment just as the sun filtered through the leafy canopy above.

God, what was I going to do? Would Marjoe ever have me back? And a waitress? Was that who I wanted to be forever? The "what next?" was too much to think about through the pain in my heart. I'd never felt so lost.

Even thinking beyond walking home to the empty cottage was crushing my head and my heart. I needed to do something, to just get through until my mind caught up, and I felt like I could breathe. Today, I was going to paint those damn shutters. I knew there was no boo hag to be worried about, but the haint paint was actually a lovely gray-blue color. White tinted with indigo. The shutters needed painting. The cottage was my responsibility now that Abby was no longer around to share it with me. Or Abby's widowed husband. The thought was still alien to me.

The kitten—I couldn't call him by his given name anymore—was ecstatic to see me. He leapt from the rafter, narrowly missing me, then started hissing and meowing and climbing up the curtains again. As soon as he put on an ounce more weight, they would shred under his efforts. "What the heck is wrong with you?" I muttered.

A sound came from the hall.

Time slowed as I looked at the cat and realized it wasn't

him making the noise. A step. Breathing. Then my pulse slowed to stillness and I turned.

Cal Richter stood silently watching me, in one hand a thin white rope that he was looping through his fingers absently, an odd grin quirked on one side of his face. The non-tattooed side.

"Helloooo, sweet Oliviaaaaa," he whispered. His eyes were jaundiced and dark around the dulled green irises, and his grin stretched wider to reveal his yellowed teeth. The scent of him assaulted me, making my stomach roll. Sour sweat or vomit, unwashed body and old ash, laced with a vague smell of feces. How had I not smelled him right away?

My thoughts immediately went to my phone sitting in a pile of rice five feet and seventy miles away from me, not even working. Oh my God, I didn't have a way to call Tom. Could he even answer? Was he okay? Agony and panic raced down my spine, and the air I gulped stuck in my throat, encouraging it to close. My chest and my brain pounded. So loud, so loud.

With my eyes pinned to Cal for any sign of movement, I counted backwards like my therapist taught me, trying to slow my breathing and my heart. I needed to be able to get this under control, so I could function and think. But what if I couldn't calm myself enough and I blacked out? What would he do to me then? That thought slung a lasso around my chest and yanked hard. What if I fainted and never woke up? Was that better than waking up and knowing what he'd done? Why would I want to wake up if Tom was dead?

I didn't.

The thought made me oddly calm. Not unafraid, but calm. Was I giving up? I didn't know. Maybe I was just paralyzed with fear. Tom would be so disappointed in me. I needed to fight. To survive. I looked at the phone on the wall.

"Tommy can't come and save you this time," Cal wheedled. "Tyler had to go take care of his mess, and him, and I get to . . . *take care* . . . of you." He sucked in a whistling breath and shook his head, pleased. "I always get the best damned jobs."

His hand moved to his dirty jeans and my eyes dropped to track the movement as he slipped a pocket knife out and released the blade. Then he leaned over to the phone cord next to him and severed it to drop into an impotent coiled mess on the ground.

A hot, wet streak of liquid snaked down my leg and pooled into my shoes and on to the floor.

Had I always known I would end like this? It was pre-written. If it wasn't Uncle Mike, it was going to be this way anyway. What had Tom said? It was just shit that happened to me? Well, yes. It was just shit that happened to me. To my body. I just had to survive it. But did I even want to?

Cal Richter looked at the pooling mess on the floor and took an exaggerated inhale, sniffing the air with his eyes half lidded. "Aaaah," he rasped. "The smell of fear. Always my favorite way to begin."

My eyes leaked as well, blurring my vision as my body completely betrayed me, and I stepped back.

He took a step forward and his smile got wider.

Was I dreaming? This was not happening to me. This couldn't really be happening.

Stumbling as I tried to move back further, my ankle hit the low table by the fireplace. I frantically cast my eyes around for something. Anything. There was nothing. I looked back just in time to see the back of Cal's hand coming at me from my left. The impact stunned me, pain exploding in my face as my ears rang and black fog seeped into my consciousness. Salty copper flooded my mouth and hands grabbed at me before I fell, digging painfully into my arms. "No," he growled. "No passing out, I haven't had my fun yet."

Whimpering with pain and panic, I twisted my body, trying to get free of his grasp. Fun? Fun? Something in me snapped, and I started screaming. It came from deep inside, pulled from my very fingertips and the tips of my toes.

I screamed not for help. Just the desperate sound of my tired soul. I was done here. Done in this world.

I was vaguely aware of Cal trying to get his disgusting-smelling hand over my mouth, and it made me laugh in the middle of screaming. Because no one could fucking hear me.

His fist found my other side, and as more pain exploded in my skull, my screaming stopped.

I laughed again, despite the pain. "Let me scream," I said, through gasps. "No one can hear me." I screamed and laughed, tears soaking my face, my ears ringing from the blows. "*You* can hear me, Abby. Take me home. Take me where you are."

"Shut the fuck up," I heard Cal yell. "Who the fuck is Abby?"

"Do it. Rape me and kill me. I don't fucking care!"

Suddenly there was an almighty yowl, and a white and brown streak of fur launched from above me and landed on Cal's face, its claws digging in to hang on.

I had a split second. I took it and ran to the door, slamming it open.

Cal shouted in surprise and pain behind me. Please don't hurt the kitten, I thought, but I kept running, taking the chance the gorgeous little beast had given me.

He'd expect me to run down the road toward Mama's,

so I veered away, tripping and scraping through the vegetation, hoping to intersect with the path that led to the beach. My foot caught something hard and I crashed down, breaking the fall with my elbow. Pain radiated up to my shoulder blade and neck, making my teeth clench tight as I tried not to cry out, but I had no time to stop. I grabbed in front of me, my hand closing on a crude stone grave marker. I'd stumbled into an overgrown slave cemetery. At least that meant I was close to the sea. I lurched awkwardly to my feet.

The sound of breaking glass reached me, and as I imagined what he'd thrown through the window, a sob wrenched from my chest. The tears didn't stop, but still I ran, finally merging with the path. My legs were cut to shreds, my breath pounding out of me until I crashed out of the trees and through the dunes to the beach.

Oh God. My dream.

I stopped dead, chest heaving. Minutes ago, I'd asked Abby to take me home. Home to her. Was this what she meant when she'd been on the beach in my dream? That I could choose to die?

CHAPTER THIRTY-FOUR

$\mathcal{I}$ looked left, then right. Nothing but wide-open windswept emptiness. The rough waves, still agitated from the storm, crashed and rolled up the shore. Thick gray clouds oozed overhead.

He was coming.

Did I want to end at his hand, or did I want to choose how I died?

There was no contest. I started running toward the water just as I heard his laugh over the waves.

My feet hit the cold, frigid surf, and it flowed in over my shoes. Instantly they were heavy and waterlogged.

"Do you know why they call this Bloody Point?" Cal called. I turned to face him as he strolled toward me. Blood dripped down his cheek over the tattooed cross and on to the sand. "All those stinking Indians were rounded up and marched out to this beach. Men, women and children." He smiled. "The sand ran red with their blood."

I took a few more steps into the water, and he advanced. It began to rain again. Thunder rolled. I hadn't counted on him following me. I shook, instantly familiar with the clawing terror that tried to paralyze my body. It squeezed around my chest, trying to stop my breathing, trying to stop my heart beating.

No.

This was *my* choice. I'd been on the swim team once. Abby's Little Mermaid sister. I could outswim him. I toed my shoes off, then stripped off my shirt so I was just in my bra.

His hateful eyes lit up. "That's it, baby."

I shucked my shorts off too, then turned and headed for the waves.

Cal whistled. "A game, I love games." He laughed with glee.

I kept going. It was so cold. But the rain and the wind on my skin made the waves seem warm by comparison. Inviting. I was up to my waist. A quick glance over my shoulder saw him start running into the surf to reach me. I guess he finally realized he didn't have me cornered. I dived into the wave in front of me and kept going.

My eyes stung, and I couldn't see anything in the churned-up water. I ducked down and pushed forward into a grasping current, swimming as fast and as far as I could. The water got colder, but clearer. Remembering the scratches on my legs, the memory of sharks in these waters sent my heart racing. I embraced it. I wasn't paralyzed with fear. I was terrified, but I was moving, I was working, I was escaping. When my chest screamed, I broke the surface, hauling in lungfuls of sweet air. A look back through sheets of rain saw Cal nowhere in sight. Was he hidden in a swell? Someone was on the beach . . . no, in the water. Abby? I gasped and choked. No. There was no one, I was going crazy from the panic. I kept moving, parallel to the beach now.

My limbs were tiring, and each stroke kept me longer under the surface, fighting a current that seemed to be coming from every side. Turning on to my back to save energy, I floated, squinting through the rain to keep sight of land. Patches of blue sky and sparkling sun fought with the rain.

I don't want to die.

I don't want to go to you yet, Abby.

I'd drifted far along the beach. Was it safe to go back? Could I get back against the rip-tide current? Where was Cal?

In a minute, I would surely gain strength and start swimming again. But lethargy was creeping up on me in my stillness. My body was exhausted from running. First from Mama's, and then from the cottage. The water was cold. Hypothermia? I was cramping.

I'm not ready, Abby. Please. I'm not ready. I want to try again. I'm going back. Will you let me forgive Whit, Abby? Can I have Tom?

A wave covered me, and I found myself looking up through the surface of the water as the rain fell. I spasmed, gagged, and inhaled the burning sting of salt water. I tried to close off my breathing, to stop it. I pumped my legs but couldn't break the surface. My lungs screamed, then betrayed me and gave in to the powerful need to inhale. Pain exploded in my chest.

My last thought as everything faded was that rain on the water looked like stars. It was the infinity and wonder of space. Except the surface was kind of blue from the sky and the ray of sun that broke through the clouds.

I stretched out my arm, but I would never reach it. Was this what Tom saw when he described a deep blue eternity?

TOM

"Look, we always fish in the Wright River, so we have every reason to be there. If we can get him as far as Elba Island Cut in the marsh, there's no way he'll make it back over to the South Carolina side," I said in the cool dawn air.

For once I was thankful that while one could easily see Savannah from Daufuskie Island, it was a complicated trip through channels cut into the marshes to get there, giving us ample opportunity to carry out our plan.

I was pissed at Pete.

I'd relocated all the cargo Tyler had piled on his boat during the night to mine, stuffing it into the cabin, and set off, only to have Pete follow me and catch up ten minutes into my journey. I was halfway along the Fields Cut and he'd actually run up his Jolly Roger flag. I would have laughed my head off if the situation had been any different. "Prepare to be boarded," he'd yelled across the inky water, his navy T-shirt and frayed khaki shorts completely at odds with his demand.

"Go back, Pete," I countered at his figure in the dawn light. "This was my stupid idea. I'll do my best to get back in one piece."

"Shut up and throw me a line. We go in mine. We'll tow yours."

We couldn't have a conversation shouting over the water, so I did as he asked. He pulled a little ahead, and I dropped a buoy to protect the hull and sidled up to his port side. I tossed him the line and hopped on.

"Pete, listen to me. I'm not sure we're going to be able to do this. I don't really give a shit about Tyler's weed. Actually, I do. Dumping it makes me wanna cry. I'd love to smoke a shit ton of it right now; it's been a hell of a night. But if we can't get Cal Richter there, it's all for shit. Tyler outright threatened Olivia last night if we didn't deliver, and part of me is wondering whether I should do just that. Deliver, this one time. But let *me* do it and take the risk, please. Go back, Pete, and ask Marjoe to marry you. Have a grand old Lowcountry wedding with fiddles and roast oysters. And keep an eye on Liv for me. Take the happiness you can get for however long you have it."

"What the hell has gotten into you, kid?"

"Please, Pete. I'm serious. This is a fucking suicide mission for you. Let me do it. I'm dead anyway, literally and figuratively, and I haven't done one damn thing worth anything in the life I was given."

He shook his shaggy gray head and tied the mooring for my boat to a cleat. Then he looked at me. "Tommy. Son." He cleared his throat. "You've been through more at your age than anyone should have to bear in a lifetime." He sat, his legs splayed and his hands holding his knobbly knees. "Anyway, I'm dead too."

"Pete, that's not—"

"The doc's given me eight weeks at the outside."

Shock hit me like a brick to the chest. "What?" Grief

filled me and expanded at full speed. I looked away as my eyes stung, my heart tumbling over. "God, Pete," I choked out. How many poundings would my heart have to take?

He continued. "This is important to me. Let's get it done. Anyway, I let Gator in on it about fifteen minutes ago; it's all lined up."

We were wasting precious time arguing. If Gator was in the know, the cavalry was coming regardless. I gritted my teeth. "Okay, let's do it."

Pete nodded and we set off. Slowly, now that my boat was in the wake. As soon as we got to the prearranged spot, I climbed back aboard my boat. Each bale had been wrapped in plastic, then a black trash bag, and put in a Styrofoam cooler like those used by day fishermen. I slit open the tape on one of the coolers and taped the Ziploc baggie containing the Graham Family Farms label, kindly provided by JJ, on to the bale. Then I resealed the cooler with tape so water wouldn't seep in. We tossed it into the marsh far enough that the grasses would keep it in place despite the current. Then we repeated the process. Soon there were a couple of hundred pounds of weed bobbing amongst the grasses.

"Hold up," Pete said as I opened the last cooler. He drew out his knife and sank it into the bale, dragging it open. The scent, even over the fresh pluff mud, was strong and fragrant. He grabbed a large handful and stuffed it into a leftover baggie. I tossed him the tape to seal his hole and then the box. "Time to make the call?" I asked.

"I'd say so. Are we sure he'll come?"

I shrugged. "It's a lot." I drew out my cell phone and checked my texts first. There was nothing from Liv. Then I dialed Tyler's number.

He answered right away. "Is it done?"

I watched as Pete tossed the last box out. "God, Tyler, I'm sorry. Pete, he freaked out. He couldn't go through with it."

Pete pulled a pack of rolling papers out of his top pocket. The old sod.

"Don't fuck with me, Tommy," Tyler said in a low voice.

"I'm not, Tyler. I'm so sorry. He got cold feet. I really need this money. Shit!" I added a touch of desperation.

Pete finished rolling the joint and pinched the end. He raised his eyebrows, offering me first. I shook my head.

"Oh my God, you better be fucking joking," Tyler howled. "Shit," he added and snapped orders out in the background.

"I don't know what to do," I continued, watching Pete light up. "Can you get out here and pick it up, and I'll take it for you in my boat in the next few days? I will, I swear. You just say when. Shit, I'm sorry. I really needed this. I'll do it for less, I swear—"

"Shut up, Tommy. Where the fuck are you?"

Pete's eyes crinkled up as he drew deeply. As far as I knew, he hadn't inhaled anything since his diagnosis, despite wanting a medical marijuana prescription. "He's tossed everything into the marsh. It's all just bobbing around out there. I tried to get him to turn around, but he's heading to Bull River. Maybe you can bring Cal or someone to help so you can get it done fast. You've gotta be quick. Right now the grasses are keeping it steady, but the tide's up in a few."

"Where is it?" Tyler snapped, his tone panicked.

"Elba Island Cut," I said. "I'll come meet you in my boat and help."

"No. Just stay the hell away. I need to be able to use you again."

"Sure, sure, okay. Shit. I'm so sorry."

Tyler hung up without responding.

"Okay, he's coming." I took the joint Pete offered me and brought it to my mouth. I inhaled, letting its writhing smoke fingers tickle my throat and lungs. Why did it always feel like it was alive? I held it in for a few seconds then released it into the dawn air. The sun would be up in thirty minutes. Tyler could be here in fifteen if he tried. And he would. "Let's go," I said and looked at my phone again.

Liv, please text me when you get to Mama's so I know you're safe.

She never answered. Why would she?

My cell rang again. Tyler. "Yeah?" I asked. Maybe he'd misdialed.

"Just wanted to let you know, in case you were interested, Twitch will be with me. I'm sending Cal to babysit your girlfriend till I get my shit back."

My soul fell out of my body, through the boat, and sank in the waves.

Pete took a step toward me.

I stumbled away, falling on to my ass. The impact radiated up my spine, but the phone stayed at my ear. "Tyler," I threatened. "You better fucking call him off."

"Guess you should have taken care of my stuff, huh?"

I dragged my free hand down my face. Pete was staring at me. "God. Please say you're shittin' me. You saw how he looks at her. Fuck."

"He won't touch her. Calm the hell down. I'm just holding collateral."

My gut twisted, and I grabbed my hair and pulled so hard my eyes watered. "He has a record, you dumb piece of shit! He's been waiting for this. If he even touches her, so help me, Tyler Graham, I will kill you with my bare fucking hands."

"Well, Tommy, I guess you shouldn't have been so careless then." He hung up.

I stared at the phone, my chest heaving with rage and impotent terror. "God." The voice that came from me wasn't mine. "Oh God."

Pete was already on the phone. He turned away from me into the wind, and I couldn't hear what he was saying. I was paralyzed. Why? Why had I been so fucking stupid?

"Because you didn't know he'd do that," Pete answered. I must have spoken aloud. "Marjoe's tellin' Big Jake," he went on, listening to someone on the other end of the line and reporting to me. "JJ's not there. Can Big Jake go? Jake'll go." He hung up and looked at me. "We'll get to her, Tommy."

"But I did know, Pete. It was a real and dangerous variable, a big one, and I chose to ignore it." I covered my face with my hands, trying to regroup. To think.

He nodded. "You jus' leave me here. Go on."

"Pete . . ."

He climbed off my boat on to his, and untied the line.

I was adrift.

The wind was strong.

I undid the sail ties and checked the reefing lines, taking comfort in the routine safety checks. The fastest way back would be to let the boat run with the wind, not the engine, and I needed to get back as fast as possible. She could probably handle two reefs, so I fitted them and unfurled the sail slowly, even though I wanted to yank the line. When it was up, I set the course.

Big Jake was heading to check on Liv, so as long as Cal

didn't get to her first, she'd be okay. She would be fine. She knew to go to Mama's. She'd be okay. Please God, let her be okay.

The boat sliced through the waves, the salt spray showering my face with every dip.

Please.

Please.

OLIVIA

It was cold. So cold. My body rattled the teeth in my skull. I was under something heavy; it was soft, but it smelled like mildew and old iron. A boat tarp?

I could breathe. Air. There was air. But it hurt to breathe. My face throbbed and my lungs burned. My mind frantically cast back through memories and the water. I was drowning. I drowned. There was no one who could have saved me.

Except the only other person in the water with me. Cal.

I gasped, and the breath seared pain through my chest. It was too much . . . My mind went quiet again.

Voices were talking, and then I was carried, close to a warm chest and a heart that pounded with exertion. Resignation had settled deep inside me, and I no longer felt curiosity or a need to see and hear where I was. My thoughts drifted to Tom. He'd done so much; I was sad it had all been for nothing. Abby was right. Love was beautiful and light. All I had to do was think of it, and nothing else mattered. My mind was living in an empty vessel and soon, when they killed me, it would be free. I'd be like one of the daughters of the air from the fairy tale. Dancing on the sea foam and earning my immortal soul.

"Olivia?" A familiar, scratchy female voice. A safe voice. "Livvy? Can you hear me, honey?" *Oh my God, the pain.* I was on something soft. Very soft. So comfortable compared to the fiery burn and breathtaking agony in my neck and chest.

I willed my mouth to move, or my eyes to open, but there was no response. There was something down my throat. I tried to swallow but couldn't. Or my neck couldn't move.

"Honey, I'm not sure if you can hear me, but don't try to talk, okay? You won't be able to. You're in the hospital." There was a long pause. Someone squeezed my hand tight and sniffed. The voice, when it resumed, was wobbly. "You almost drowned, so they have a tube in you. Two, actually, one for your lungs and one for your kidneys."

Tom, my mind screamed. *Where's Tom?* No one answered.

Days went by, I think. The pain came in waves. Perhaps when the drugs they gave me wore off.

The comforting voice was always back eventually. But no others. Thank you, Marjoe, I wanted to say. Thank you for not leaving me here by myself.

Who else would I expect to be here? Not Bethany, of course. Something bad must have happened to Tom and maybe Pete. Oh, poor Marjoe!

Or Tom had left forever, like he said he would.

Every time I was awake, my mind thought about opening my eyes, but the signal never made it. Eventually, though, I knew I could. My mind was no longer as foggy, and I'd got used to the rhythm of the hospital. The rounds, the visits.

The tube was out of my throat, but I had no recollection

of them removing it. Waiting until it was dark behind my lids, I tried opening my eyes, just to know I could. It was dim, and I was in a hospital room like Marjoe had said. Alone.

Completely alone.

I closed my eyes back up and didn't open them again. Even when Marjoe announced on her next visit that "Pete asked me to marry him," I couldn't bear to open them. "About damned time too," she continued. "You better get your ass up soon and bake me a wedding cake. Now, I know you ain't done one before, but Big Jake'll never forgive me if I don't get one of your grandmama's recipes. We're gonna have a shrimp boil and roasted oysters, play some Lowcountry folk music and generally celebrate life. And you have to be there. So just hurry on up."

The knowledge that Pete was okay dangled like a carrot. Had he been with Tom that day? I was starting to think the reason Marge didn't mention Tom was because there was something she didn't want to tell me.

Expecting to hear my parents' voices, and the fact that I didn't, was the most compelling evidence I could think of for Tom being near. Only he would know to keep me safe from my family.

"Tyler got arrested, did I tell you that?" Marjoe informed me. "What a drama that was. His father too, if you can believe it. Beaufort county sheriff came and chained up the farm, but you know Big Jake and JJ still sneak in there and make sure the veggies don't die. Now I'm payin' them direct. They did all the work before anyway." She cackled. "But damn I was mad at Pete for that hare-brained scheme. Can you imagine, dumping all that pot in the marshes and calling the coast guard? He could have been shot. Very nearly was.

Plus, he was high as a kite, having helped himself to a little on the side. And, well . . ." She trailed off. "One of these days I'm going to say something that's gonna get you curious enough to open those eyes. I'm sorry, honey, that I didn't stop you running back home. Big Jake set out to check on you, but by that time you were . . . gone. Thank the sweet Lord JJ was on the beach that mornin'. Anyway, today I have a surprise for you. Ah, there you are. Come on in. There you go. Just put the little fella right on her chest. Shhh, do it quick before the nurse comes round again. Thank you, JJ."

A light weight pressed gently on me, and I felt the soft vibration of a purr settle into my heart. I squeezed my eyes tight, my nostrils flaring to stop the sting of tears, but in the end I lay helplessly as they leaked out from under my eyelids.

The hand that held mine squeezed.

The little vibrating body was removed and Marjoe left, and the night came.

"Come back to me, Liv. Please." A throaty voice sounded in my ear. My lungs ceased their shallow labor and my heart, like a bag of fragmented shards in my chest, shifted painfully toward hope.

Tom.

CHAPTER THIRTY-SEVEN

Tom's head was tilted back on the chair he slept in. It looked small and uncomfortable under his large frame. I turned my head on the scratchy hospital pillow, wincing at the pain in my neck.

The lights were off, and only a dim yellow glow came from a counter light where there was a small sink and cabinet in the corner. It was enough to show that he was wearing his trademark jeans and a white T-shirt. His legs were apart and his strong arms were folded across his chest, hands tucked in flat under his arms. His hair must be tied back, I thought, seeing it scraped back from his temples. His beard had grown out again like when I'd first met him.

His profile was mesmerizing, nose straight, forehead long. Why had I denied who he was for so long? I'd only seen him once, I think, but . . . I imagined his beard shaved off.

No, wait, I really wanted to do this right. I mentally got up and stood over him. Over his tilted face. I lathered him in shaving cream, smoothing it all over, and ran a razor gently down his cheek in one smooth motion. His eyelids would open, but he wouldn't move. I'd continue running the razor, revealing his chiseled face bit by bit. Revealing his beautiful lips. Until his face was bare and he couldn't hide any flicker of emotion from me. Then I'd dampen his hair and run my fingers through its length, combing it back from his smooth forehead. His eyes would watch my every move, silently, intently, like a jungle cat.

In my mind, I carefully took his hair chunk by chunk and clipped it short, letting the heavy, soft handfuls of it dust the floor. I revealed the perfect round tops of his ears, and his lobes, and the line of sinew and muscle that arced down the side of his neck. I'd see the tic of a nerve in his temple like I always did, but this time I'd also see it in the flex of his smooth cheek. I lowered to kiss it, and his face turned, his lips finding mine.

My heart pounded, my breath was shallow. I'd carried around an unrealized hatred for this person for years, and now he was in front of me, and I kept waiting for the anger and the hatred to come and it just . . . wouldn't. Even the sting of betrayal from his lie was gone. All I could feel was the distance between us, with him sitting five feet away and me lying helplessly in a hospital bed. And I felt his waiting. Waiting for me to be fine, so he could leave with a clear conscience.

I woke curled on my side. A small, warm body vibrated against my belly. It was light beyond my closed eyelids.

"Mornin', honey," Marjoe said, somehow knowing I was awake now. "So, Bethany's been asking to come see you. It would make her so happy. She's been feeling awful since that day. We are all so happy you're okay. And, well, the Beaufort county sheriff's office have a ton of questions for you. Although I may as well tell you—maybe it will help— Cal Richter's body was washed up near Port Royal. What was left of him, anyway. Thank the good Lord. Turns out we won't be the only ones sleeping better at night now he's gone." She sniffed, and her voice wobbled. "It's a miracle you're with us. But now, young lady, you need to get the heck up. I need you, okay. We all need you. And your little furball—I refuse to call him the f-word—needs you."

"Eric," I whispered.

"What? Oh my stars, you spoke. What did you say?" I felt her come close and smelled her unique perfume of lilac and kitchen grease.

"Prince Eric," I whispered again. "The cat." Way better than Fuckhead. He saved me from Cal Richter; it was only fair he should carry the name of the Mermaid's prince. And in the Disney version, they lived happily ever after. Way less depressing.

"I can't believe I'm helping you get ready for a wedding in the hospital," Bethany groused. I was sitting on a rolling stool, a bed sheet around my shoulders, my hair wet, and Bethany's skilled hands were chopping off huge hunks to leave only my natural color.

"A wedding was the only thing that could get me out of here, I guess." I laughed, my voice still grating and tender from having a tube down my throat so long. "I'm so happy for her."

"Aren't we all? Marjoe better not touch her hair and makeup before I get back. I'll only have time to touch up."

"She won't risk your wrath, trust me. Thank you so much for doing this."

She exhaled. "You're welcome."

I swallowed, my tender throat making me cringe. "Why are you being so nice to me? After what I did?"

"Well . . ." Bethany pulled back to look at me, "I feel bad for the way we left things, and you almost dying kinda puts it all in perspective. In a way, it was my fault you ran back to the cottage."

I shook my head, but she gave me a look.

"Okay, I think I'm almost done." Her fingers combed through my shorn locks this way and that, styling it. "I told you it would be stunning short, and it is. Wow."

She handed me the small hand mirror. My face was pale and thin, my eyes a stranger's, especially with the unexpectedly short pixie hair. There was a small white dressing on my neck. I handed the mirror back. "I wouldn't go that far."

"Whatever. Let me do my stuff." She hauled out her makeup bag.

"Bethany?"

Her forehead scrunched as she mixed some foundation in the palm of her hand. "Yeah?"

"I hope you and Tom are happy together. I'm sorry I got in the middle of you two." My heart pounded and squeezed tight.

Bethany stopped and looked at me. "Hasn't he been here? I thought he was pretty much prowling the halls every day after practically carrying you here himself."

Not sure how to answer, I waited. He'd been here that one night when I saw him asleep, but that was it.

"We're not together, Liv. We haven't been since before . . . well, you know. And . . . You know he's leaving, right?"

Of course he was. Like before, only it was delayed because of Marjoe and Pete's wedding. Nodding, I pressed my lips together until they were smashed white to avoid my face betraying me.

"When I saw his face that day, when he thought . . ." Bethany's eyes filled before she blinked rapidly.

I bit my lip. "What? That I drowned?"

"Or that Cal got to you first. Well, it was easy to forgive you. Both. You should tell him how you feel," she said and went back to blending in her palm.

"He knows," I whispered, watching her pull a new makeup sponge out of a bag so she could paint my face.

She stopped what she was doing for a second, then she sighed and gave me a tight smile before reaching forward. "Tilt your head and close your eyes."

She worked quickly. "Okay, so I only had two dresses I thought would fit you. I'm sorry if you hate them both . . ."

"Thank you. I'll love either one of them."

She laughed. "Wait until you see them."

"Oh," I managed a few minutes later when I caught sight of the pink fabric. *Bright*. "Is that . . . is that . . ."

"Fuchsia? Why yes, yes it is. Such a happy color."

"Okay, what else?" I grumbled.

She unzipped a bag to reveal a lilac sateen dress with ruffled sleeves. "My prom dress. What do you think?"

I stared at it, speechless.

"Pink it is then. And thank heavens, because I had the worst luck in that dress. Chip Saunders dumped me to have sex with Reagan Sauls. That slut."

"I'm not surprised now I've seen the dress," I joked.

Bethany swung around, shock on her face.

"Too soon to joke?" I asked, cringing.

Her mouth dropped open and she laughed. "It is pretty bad. And I sweated like a pig in it all night."

"Don't you own anything black?" I asked.

"Of course I do. But for you? Nope. This is it, I'm afraid. And it's cotton, lucky you."

It wasn't all bad. It was short and strapless, and after Bethany pulled it in and pinned the back, it looked like it was made for me.

"Let's go," she said. "Pete's waiting for us at Palmetto Bay Marina."

We swung by the administrator's office. Marjoe had already given them the address at Mama's to send the bills to, so I signed my name one hundred times promising to be responsible for the astronomical balance, and we set out. I'd spend the rest of my life paying that off, but I couldn't dwell on it right now.

Nerves at seeing Tom soon made me feel light-headed as we took a cab from the hospital. I was still a bit weak, having lain flat on my back doing nothing for eight days.

The sun sparkled on the waters of Broad Creek. The sky was crayon-box blue, and the marsh grasses were fresh and bright, stirring in the breeze. I breathed the salty air as deeply as I could with my chest still bruised inside and out. I'd endured long bouts of resuscitation efforts, and my ribs still felt it.

Pete was wearing pressed khaki pants and a striped button-down stretched over his belly. And his trademark cap, though he would surely take it off for the wedding.

"Don't you clean up nice?" I said by way of greeting as I climbed aboard his boat.

He wrapped me up in a salty bear hug, almost crushing me.

"Easy," I gasped.

He released me and wiped a fist under his left eye. "Sorry. I'm just so glad to see you."

"Me too, me too." I laughed and went in for another hug. "And I'm so happy for you and Marge. Congratulations."

"Any time next week you want to come and make your statement to the sheriff's office, you just let me know. I'll be glad to take you, okay?"

I nodded. "Thank you."

Swallowing my nerves, I sat down. As we reached the open water of the Calibogue Sound, my heart rate tripled. I glanced at the surface of the water for a brief moment, then scrunched my eyes shut. I'd received a prescription for anti-anxiety medication at the hospital. I fervently hoped I wouldn't have to start taking them again. Bethany's hand found mine and squeezed. Grateful, I squeezed back and began counting.

"All right," Pete said, picking up speed. "Let's get this thing moving so I'm not late for my own damned wedding. 'Sides, there's someone else who's been waitin' for you to come back to us too."

TOM

$\mathcal{I}$ paced down the jetty for the twentieth time, squinting across the water. Fuck it, *I* should have been the one to go get her. Was she okay being on the water? Was she scared?

Big Jake strolled toward me. "They're comin'. 'Bout twenty minutes till they dock, I reckon."

"How do you know?"

He shrugged his large shoulders. "Jus' do."

I shook my head and stuffed my hands back in my pockets. With Pete not allowed to see Marjoe before the ceremony, and her needing all hands on deck here to get the place ready, it was only reasonable that he would be the one to go get Liv.

The music was already warming up, a bluegrass trio who called themselves Low Country Boil, led by a guy who played the fiddle like the devil would take his fingers if he stopped. And the devil probably would now that I'd heard some of their hilarious and risqué lyrics. Typical Marjoe.

"Well I don't care how you and JJ know the things you do, I'm just grateful. Has JJ managed to communicate anything about what happened on the beach that morning? How he found Liv? What happened to Cal?"

Big Jake shook his head and looked out to the water. "Nope."

A thought occurred to me. "But *you* know, don't you?"

Big Jake shrugged. "I weren't there. But wit' currents like that . . ." He winked and gave me a pat on the back with his large hand.

I stepped forward with the impact, smiling and shaking my head.

"Anyhows," he went on, "seems like that boo hag done gone left de island."

The boat appeared in the distance, and my insides decided to go to the county fair. It was the longest twenty minutes of my life. Actually, scratch that. Not knowing if she was going to live had been worse.

The boat finally neared the jetty. Pete looked up expectantly, mooring line in hand. Bethany was gathering her stuff and hefting a black bag over her shoulder. But my feet were rooted to the spot. Jake stepped forward to help.

My eyes were pinned to the pale waif with the pixie hair, who I could barely see in contrast with the short swathe of bright pink wrapped around her. I'd been in her hospital room every day she'd been there, willing her to be okay, watching her bruises fade to yellow and wishing I could have those pale blue eyes looking at me again.

Now they were.

Did hearts stop beating? Mine did.

Big Jake offered her a hand, and she looked away from me to take it and greet him with a smile. Bethany was walking toward me.

"Beth," I managed and cleared my throat.

She slowed. "Hey, Tommy."

"I, uh." I nodded back toward the boat. "Thank you."

She nodded, a sigh on her lips. "You're welcome. I'm still mad at you. But . . ." She looked to the sky, then back at me. "But nothing. I'm still mad at you. I did it for her."

"That's why I'm thanking you." I smiled and took her arm, pulling her in for a hug. "And I'm sorry." She was stiff for a moment, then gave me a quick squeeze and stepped away, heading up to the restaurant.

Pete and Jake walked up, and Pete stopped to shake my hand. "You ready to be my best man?"

I nodded. "Still a misguided honor. Just give me a few, yeah?"

"Ten minutes and we gotta be standing up front like good little soldiers."

"Ten minutes. Got it."

And then it was just Liv and me. Her pale, slender body—made more so by days of no eating—only added an other-worldly element to her ethereal beauty as she stood in front of me.

Her eyes had a small crease between them. "You shaved," she said, her normally melodious voice scratchy and thin. Her hollow cheeks filled with a splotch of color on each side.

I brought my hand up to my face like a reflex and smoothed over my jaw. It still felt weird.

"You cut your hair," I said. "It looks really . . . pretty." *Gorgeous? Sexy? Stunning?*

"I'm glad you didn't cut yours. I like it longer."

"And my shaved face? Like it or hate it?"

She swallowed, her cheeks getting pinker. "You look different," she evaded.

"Good different?" I pressed, enjoying her discomfort.

"Uh, yeah, it's, um . . ." Her eyes strayed from mine and

ran down my nose to my mouth, then along my cheekbone and up over my forehead and back to my mouth.

"It's um?" I asked, reminding her. Of what exactly? And in truth, I would have been hard pressed to say anything with more substance.

"Uh, it's . . . you look . . . good." Her eyes dropped, and her toes turned in. "Are you okay? Did it all go according to plan? I heard Tyler was arrested."

"No, Liv. It didn't go according to plan. If it had, you wouldn't have been in the hospital. I can't seem to stop adding to the long list of things I need to apologize for."

She shook her head.

"It's true," I said. "I don't seem to be very good for you. I wish I was," I admitted on a whim. She didn't seem to notice, thank goodness. "I'm sorry, Liv. I'm so fucking sorry."

She kept shaking her head and her eyes welled. "You're wrong. I survived because of you."

"You survived because of *you*." And divine intervention of some kind.

"I guess we'll agree to disagree then."

"Don't we always?" I turned, indicating our path up toward the festivities, careful not to touch her instead of gathering her against my chest as I wanted to. "Let's get up there."

"What happened with Tyler's arrest? I wanted to ask Pete, but . . ." She took my arm, her words trailing off as if she seemed surprised by her own action.

The feel of her small hand around my bicep made me close my eyes for a second. "Coast guard arrived before Tyler even got there, and Pete was smoking his head off." I looked at her askance.

"Smoking the pot?" Liv asked, her expression disbelieving.

I laughed. "Yeah. First they arrested *him*. But then Gator, the harbormaster at Bull River Marina, showed up and set them straight." Liv's eyes were wide, staring at me as we walked up the jetty.

"Although apparently Pete got belligerent and almost got himself shot by a rookie who was slow on the uptake." I smirked. "Anyway, Tyler saw the coast guard, and turned his boat around. But we'd planted Graham Family Farms stickers inside all the packages, so they picked him up later that afternoon."

Her brow furrowed. "You're telling me as if you weren't there."

"I was coming back. To the cottage." I stopped and turned to her, taking a deep breath and wincing before I delivered the coming blow. "Tyler told me he sent Cal after you."

Her breath exhaled in a rush, her pale face going whiter as she withdrew her arm from me. She swallowed and looked away quickly, but not before I saw her eyes glassing over with tears of surprise and betrayal.

My hands and body itched and ached to draw her against me, and my throat was tight with the urge to say something to mitigate the pain my words had caused. But there was no way to sugar-coat that. Tyler had known what he was doing. Instead, I stood still as stone watching her cycle through the emotions of knowing that someone she knew had deliberately set out to hurt her. Worse than hurt her. Someone she had trusted at one time. Someone she had allowed herself to spend time with. To . . . I swallowed a surge of acidic jealousy . . . kiss.

God, it was a miracle she trusted *anyone*.

Maybe she didn't. How could she? She hadn't chosen her family and what her uncle had done to her. But she had chosen to spend time with Tyler and put herself in that situation. I could see the self-blame fighting for a foothold.

"It's not your fault," I whispered. "I'm sorry I didn't get there faster."

"Well, it's hardly *your* fault," she choked out.

"But I did know what Cal Richter was capable of," I admitted painfully. "I should never have left you."

There were people milling around under the trees, some sitting on a loose arrangement of chairs adorned with large white bows under one of the big live oaks dripping in Spanish moss. The ceremony would be starting soon. The breeze bore the scent of steaming oysters and cornbread.

Liv turned back to face me. Her eyes were deep and endless as they looked into mine. "I'm happy he's dead. I hope he got ripped apart by sharks in the dark, cold depths of the ocean." Her body shuddered.

I waited as she seemed to be struggling to find more words. "I . . . just don't understand why . . ." *Why me?* she seemed to be asking. *Why do these monsters find me?*

My hand reached forward of its own volition.

Liv shrank back, a tiny movement, and I let my hand drop before reaching her.

Clearing my throat over the hurt her small movement caused inside my ribs, I nodded toward the restaurant. "Marjoe is in her office, I think. Why don't you go and say hi, and I'll find my spot next to Pete."

She nodded and turned toward the restaurant.

I watched her go, taking a moment to compose myself, and wondered how I would ever be able to say goodbye.

CHAPTER THIRTY-NINE

$\mathcal{T}$he ceremony took place as the sun sank in the sky, casting a golden blessing across the assembled guests. Big Jake walked Marjoe down the aisle. She was dressed in a simple long white sundress and her hair was tied up with fresh daisies.

"Marge," Pete began, when it was time for his vows.

I gritted my teeth until they were almost ground to dust as I watched Pete look into Marge's eyes and prepare to pledge his lasting days to her, knowing how few those days were.

"Today we are married in front of all who are dear to us in this beautiful ceremony. But I've been married to you since the moment I met you. You have owned me body and soul, and I wouldn't trade a second of that time with you to gain more." Pete paused and Marge gave him a tearful smile, and a small nod.

He swallowed. "It was the gift I was given, and I accept it gladly and with a full heart. I never thought I was deservin'. But the good Lord thought different. To know such love, even for a short time, is more than any man could ever hope for."

My eyes strayed to the left and found Liv with tears streaming down her face and making no attempt to wipe them away. As if she could sense me looking at her, her eyes found mine, and I held them.

Finally the vows were done and the preacher told Marjoe and Pete they could kiss. And kiss they did. Hard. Everyone whooped and cheered despite their tears.

Marjoe turned around. "Y'all stop cryin' before you float away. Let's celebrate!"

The band started up. I shook Pete's hand.

"I hope you got my message," he said. "Life's too short, you know?"

I clapped him on the shoulder and took a moment to get my words out. "You get your happy ending," I said, voice rough. "There's no one I know who deserves it more."

Feeling a subtle energy on my left side, I turned to find Liv close. "Congratulations, Pete," she murmured.

"Thank you, Olivia." Pete looked at her, and then at me. "Sometimes God strikes us with darkness in order to show us the light." He slapped a hand on my shoulder. "I know you don't want to hear this from an old man, but don't squander your chance for happiness." He looked from one to the other of us. "Now, go dance and eat cake."

"Yes, sir," I said and backed away, reaching for Olivia's hand without thinking. It was warm and soft, delicate and small in mine. It made me want more. I immediately let go and offered her my arm again. Safer.

"I'm so sad I didn't get to make the wedding cake," she commented as she slid her small hand into the crook, her body four aching inches from my side. "Marjoe did ask. I feel selfish for being in the hospital so long. I probably could have come back sooner."

"Could you?" I asked.

She cast her eyes up to me. "I was awake a lot," she admitted. "But I had a lot to process."

We moved away from the crowd and the frantic, jolly folk music. Lights that had been strung in the trees twinkled in the fading light across the water.

So she must have seen me there at the hospital. I'd definitely fallen asleep a few times when I hadn't meant to.

"Why did you never speak to me?" she asked. "Marjoe talked all the time. For a while, I thought something had happened to you." She stopped walking and squeezed my arm, her warmth seeping through my sleeve as she seemed to struggle with her words. "Thinking you weren't there made me want to wake up even less."

"I was there." My insides were totally messed up. Swirling and diving. "Liv . . ." I stopped. *Why are you still putting so much faith in me?*

"What, Tom?"

Whit, I expected her to say *Whit*. "Uh, I fixed the window at the cottage. And Big Jake and I finally painted the shutters. Oh, and the phone, I fixed the phone. Or had it fixed, anyway." Her cheeks had paled as everything I said equated to terrifying memories. *Shit*. "But if you don't want to—" I cut myself off as her shaking hand came up to her chest. I took it and pressed it against my ribs. "I'm sorry."

She looked up at me and flattened her palm on my shirt.

My heart pounded under it.

"It's okay. I'm okay. The cottage . . . it seems different now."

"I understand."

"It's just I realized it was never home to me." Her hand pressed harder against my chest. "*You* were. Are."

Unable to articulate a response, I looked down at her. Her pale blue eyes were luminous with the last rays of the setting sun, her cropped golden hair like a halo. She really was an angel. So damn beautiful, she was almost hard to look at. The angel I wrote about. The girl who couldn't get into heaven because of some stupid oversight. The girl who'd been made to believe in all her flaws. And was I the guy who would let her believe all the shit, so he could keep her for himself? Or would I help her see all the good stuff? When she finally realized how incredible she was, there would be no room for me. I didn't want to be around when that happened.

She swallowed nervously. "I know you're leaving. But you really needed to know that. Come on, let's dance."

I mostly watched and chatted with the other guests and downed a few beers. One eye was always on Olivia as she learned to do a "something" and a two-step and then a shag. But that wasn't easily taught, apparently. "Hey, I need a partner." She came over and grabbed my hand. "Can we shag?"

I laughed and she immediately turned pink.

She leaned in close. "You know, don't you?"

"Know what?" I asked innocently.

"Shagging means fucking in some countries, doesn't it?" she whispered. "Pete was telling everyone earlier."

"Means *what*?" I asked again, because *good God* I had to hear her say that again. Not that I hadn't heard her curse before. But saying it in reference to the act was downright carnal. Blood may have relocated a tiny amount into a lower part of my body.

"What?" she asked.

"Shagging means *what*?"

She narrowed her eyes at me. I grinned and took another sip of beer. It was loosening me up. I wasn't sure if that was good or bad. Bad, definitely bad.

She didn't take the bait and let me off the hook for dancing.

The evening grew late, and I could tell it was getting to her. Her face became drawn and tired.

"Where were you going to sleep tonight?" I asked.

"I was supposed to stay with Bethany, but it looks like she's having too much fun to leave anytime soon. I . . . I don't know."

Shit. "I'm happy to go to the cottage with you . . ."

"No." Her voice wobbled. "I mean, I don't want to stay there on my own, I'm not even sure I'm ready to see it. Not at night anyway. I'll just wait until Bethany's ready to go. I'm fine, really. You don't need to worry about me."

My chest ached with her words. I wanted to worry about her. I wanted her to want me to. "I wasn't going to let you stay there alone, Liv."

I thought back to that first day at the hospital when I'd screamed at one of the intensive care intake nurses, asking if Liv had been touched, if Cal Richter had raped her. She'd asked me who I was.

Brother-in-law, I'd said after a moment's hesitation, and it sounded so wrong. So . . . off-base from the way I felt. *I'm her only family*, I'd added lamely.

All my hard-won decisions over the last few days to remain aloof seemed to be crumbling. The truth was a tough thing to face. I didn't think I would be able to let her go. I wanted to crawl kicking and screaming back through time and get back to the co-existence we'd had. "I have my boat docked nearby. I was going to sleep on it. You can too." The words were out of my mouth before I could think them through.

She looked up at me, and I could see the indecision and confusion warring with the tiredness.

"Let's just go and sleep, Liv. We'll visit the cottage together tomorrow." *Please say yes.*

"Okay." She nodded.

Relief flooded my system.

Liv tilted her face up. "Wow, look at the stars!" Without the lights from Mama's around us, the sky was powdered with galaxies.

I climbed aboard and held out my hand, waiting. The boat rocked gently, the breeze soft and cool. "To quote Pete," I murmured, looking up, "we'd never see the stars if there was no darkness."

She slid her small hand into mine. "So this is her, huh? Your boat, your pride and joy? Where you slept when you left the cottage?"

"Yeah, I guess so." I shrugged as Liv climbed on, her light frame hardly rocking the boat. I showed her down into the tiny cabin. Now that I was sleeping on the boat every night, the berth was permanently made up. I didn't feel like stowing bedding every day.

We had to sit as it was impossible to stand. With her so close, the space was immediately intimate. I fumbled with the small cabin light and flicked it on.

"Do you, um, have a shirt or something I could borrow?" she asked.

"Do you mind wearing the one I have on? I don't have any clean stuff with me at the moment. Marge let me do a load of laundry earlier today, and I forgot to go get it."

She nodded, her bottom lip sliding between her teeth. Her eyes watched me as I pulled the shirt off and handed it to her. Then she presented me with her back. "This dress had to be pinned to make it fit. Would you mind undoing it?"

My pulse spiked, and my throat grew tight. "Sure." My fingers touched her above the dress line and I swallowed as I felt her still.

I got hard. I'd been halfway there all evening. *Shit*. I lifted my hand away. And then my good sense completely deserted me, and I found my finger returning to the spot at the back of her neck, under her hairline, the top of her spine, and running down her smooth skin. A soft sigh escaped her, and her head dropped forward. I reached the top of the dress and remembered what I'd been asked to do. My hands were fucking shaking. What was wrong with me? What was I doing?

Fumbling with the pins that were folding the dress over itself, I managed to get them loose and not prick her or myself. The dress gaped, and I could see inside, the bumps down her spine. I wanted to pull the fabric away and keep running my fingers down her back until I reached the swell of her hips. Then slide my hands around her waist.

My blood pounded so hard, it roared in my ears. I was surprised there was enough of it left in my upper body since most of it had coalesced between my legs. Throbbing.

"Tom," she whispered.

I jerked out of my fantasy and clumsily put the pins into a cup holder built into the wood veneer. "I'll just, uh, wait outside," I said and burst out of the cabin into the night air, breathing hard.

This was not what tonight was about. What any time with her would ever be about. She'd just been attacked and almost died, for Christ's sake. She still had to hate me for lying to her and taking advantage of her feelings for me.

I stood on the deck, hands stuffed into the pockets of my black dress pants, the breeze bringing much-needed cool air to my bare chest. The water was dark and peaceful, although the strains of a fiddle could still be heard as the reveling continued. I needed to start thinking about where I would go after I left here. After Pete. I'd stay as long as *he* needed me, of course. I couldn't think about Liv. I needed to move on. Let her live her life without me and the memories I brought back to her, weighing her down. She thought she loved me, but it was based on shit.

"Tom?"

I turned.

Her small blonde head poked out of the cabin door and her eyes traveled over me. "Are you coming back?"

God, did she think I'd leave her here by herself? But that's what I was busy planning, wasn't it? Not tonight, but soon. "I'm not going anywhere. Go ahead and sleep. I'll be there in a while." But she didn't go back down, she just watched me. I was confused and conflicted and it was doing my fucking head in. And I still wanted her. I wanted to run my hands all over her delicate body and show her how incredible every single part of her was. How her body was an instrument of love, not shame. Joy and not pain. Love. I loved her.

I loved her in a way that swelled so hard in my chest, it felt like my ribs might crack. How long had I felt this way and shoved it aside?

"Why are you looking at me like that?" she whispered.

I squeezed my eyes closed and swallowed the emotion down.

"Because . . ." My eyes opened and found her. "Because I'm at war with myself. Over you."

Her brows creased together.

My hands fisted inside my pockets. "I represent too many painful memories for you. It's not fair of me to remind you of them just by existing. I wish I could take them all away. But I can only take myself away."

She seemed to ponder my words. "You asked me to come back to you," she said.

She'd heard that?

"And I did. Now come inside."

CHAPTER FORTY

Liv was lying curled up on her side when I stepped down into the cabin. The boat rocked gently. Her blinks were slow, and I knew she was moments away from sleep. But she watched me from under lowered lashes.

I toed off my shoes and socks and pulled my pants down over my boxers, knowing that it meant she'd see how aroused I still was. Wishing I could turn it off was useless. It just was. I didn't look back at her to check if she'd seen. Turning off the lamp, I climbed under the covers and lay on my back, hands resting under my head.

After a few moments, she shifted, her head nestling into my shoulder, her body down my side and her arm snuck over my waist. Another wave of lust rolled through me, and I focused on keeping my breathing steady. Could you die from over-arousal?

"Is this okay?" she asked.

I nodded and brought an arm down to wrap around her shoulders. "Yeah." I breathed into her hair. It smelled different, but *she* was still there underneath it. Cinnamon? Was that what she smelled like? I could never pin down the undercurrent.

Her hand came up to my face, running gently over my shaved skin, over the planes and the bones. Her finger traced my lips. Her leg snuck across mine, and I tensed.

"This?" she whispered.

Forcing myself to relax and not feel that she was now fully pressed against me, I tried to think of something else. Pete? Yeah, that was sad. Devastating. But I was still hard as a rock. I couldn't get a handle on this. Was she trying to drive me insane? It was working, I was going fucking insane. I thought I'd been turned on before, but with my head and my heart in on the game, it was . . . it was . . . I couldn't . . .

"Can I touch you here?" she whispered and her hand travelled south. My arm tightened around her.

. . . I was fucked.

Her small, soft hand drifted over my boxers and closed around my hard length.

My breath stuttered out of my chest in a mangled groan. "Liv," I rasped, and my other hand grabbed the sheets, tearing them loose from my side of the berth.

"Please let me." Her voice was soft. "You're aroused by me."

I nodded. I think.

"Yet you don't use it, or make me do anything."

Her hand stroked up and then down.

I heard my own breaths and grimaced that she could hear how little control I had right now.

"Don't you want to be aroused by me?"

How the hell did I answer that? My hand joined hers and squeezed, to still her but also pressing down to relieve part of the ache. "Liv," I managed. "I want you to touch me. I want to touch you. I just . . . I just . . ." *I want so much more.*

"Then let me."

I let her go.

Her hand slid under my shorts, closing around my cock. My chest imploded as the air left.

Her strokes were tentative at first, but it was so incredible to have her hand on me that all I could do was squeeze her shoulder where I hugged her, my hand kneading her arm.

Her strokes became more sure. And I tried not to lose my mind.

My free hand came to rest on her head, brushing through her hair. I needed to kiss her. I tilted her face up even as my lower body moved to urge her, thrusting up into her hand. I wasn't sure I was breathing until I heard my own gasps. My lips found hers. God, this was so fucked up. I hadn't *ever* simply kissed her. Just kissed. For the sake of kissing. Tasting her. I would remedy that sometime. But right now, I wanted to thrust my tongue between her lips, to have some part of me inside her.

As if she could sense what I needed, she opened, and sucked my tongue into her sweet, hot mouth. *Holy hell.* My hips bucked. Her fist got tight. "Liv," I gasped into her mouth. But I couldn't hold the tide back; it roared in, filling my whole body. My spine stiffened. "Oh God," I moaned helplessly, and sensation exploded through me, erupting into her hand. I rode it out, not able to stop, her hand milking me dry until I was shuddering and completely destroyed.

Remorse oozed into the emptiness that remained.

"Thank you," Liv whispered.

"What? How can you possibly be thanking me?" I sounded as disgusted as I felt. With myself. I sat up, shrugging her off me so I could reach the light, and fumbled it on. There was a hand towel near the small sink. I reached over and grabbed it, cleaning myself up. I turned to offer it to her and stopped dead at her eyes spilling over with tears.

"Thank you for letting me do that. Because I've never done that simply out of love for someone." She turned to curl up on to her side again, away from me.

Shame slammed into me. I dropped the towel I was holding. My mouth opened and closed. *Oh my fucking God.*

"Liv." I went toward her, drawing her small frame into my arms and curling myself around her back. "Livvy."

Her body shook with sobs. I rocked her, hating myself all over again. Was there any right way for us? For me? Or were we completely damned?

"Livvy," I whispered in her ear. "You've done nothing but give or have it taken from you. I don't know where I fit into that. I don't know how to be with you. Please," I said brokenly, "I'm trying to never hurt you again, but I don't know what I'm doing."

After a while her arms found mine and held me in place around her.

I wanted to touch her. To give her pleasure. To show her that no matter what had happened to her, no matter what she'd done in the past, I wanted to erase it. Replace it. But I was paralyzed with fear of hurting her. Or reminding her. So I simply held her.

"I'll go by myself, if you don't mind." We'd pulled to a stop under a massive live oak, swagging Spanish moss out of our way with the roof of the cart. I acquiesced with a silent nod.

Liv climbed out of the cart, and I could already feel the swarm of no-see-ums and a few mosquitos from our post-April shower heat descend and start biting.

She hurried over to JJ's door, all pale bare skin apart from the small piece of fuchsia that passed for a dress. I couldn't keep my eyes off her.

She knocked, and when JJ opened up, there were a few moments of nothing before Liv launched herself at him, wrapping her arms around him. I had an odd moment where I was stunned and uncomfortable. Jealous? It was no secret that JJ had somehow been there that day, when I wasn't. But no one knew, and JJ couldn't say, how he'd gotten her out of the water. Or even known she was there. I pursed my lips and got out of the cart.

By the time I joined them, Liv was holding her kitten, with her nose pressed into his fur and her eyes leaking those goddam tears again.

JJ looked over my right shoulder.

"Thank you, JJ," I said.

For saving her kitten, for helping me with Tyler, for saving Liv. Period. "I've decided JJ sounds like a superhero name. What do you think, Liv?" I glanced at her.

JJ tilted his head toward her. A tiny movement, but for him, he may as well have looked right at her.

"Yes. JJ *is* a superhero," Liv agreed.

I raised my eyebrows and looked at JJ. "Guess it's true, then." I shrugged.

He gave a small smile and shook his head.

"No big deal," I said. "I know."

He gave a nod, shuffled back into the dim recesses of his home, and closed the door.

"Some people may say he's autistic," I said.

"Others may say he's an angel," Liv said.

I nodded. "That too."

The sun was bright as we pulled up in front of the cottage. It was strange to be so familiar with a place and have it be so alien all at once. Livvy, Prince Eric (What. The fuck. Ever), and I sat in the cart for a few minutes just staring.

I took her hand. "Come on," I said and climbed out. She slid out behind me, not letting go of my hand, the cat sitting like a baby on her hip under her other arm. We walked across the front yard, already thick with spring weeds in just the few days since I'd come out here to get stuff fixed.

"It looks good," she said when she saw the shutters.

"No more boo hags for you." I smiled.

She let go of my hand and tucked her short hair behind her ear like she'd forgotten she cut it.

I'd had the whole place cleaned too. Seeing the aftermath of their brief struggle had made me physically sick.

We stepped inside and Livvy paused, her eyes resting on certain parts of the main living space. Eric—I refused to use Prince—meowed and jumped from her arms, searching out his familiar spots.

"Well, the living room window with the broken lock was replaced," I said, nervously trying to fill the silence. *Because a kitten was thrown through it.* The fact that the cat hadn't died on impact was a miracle. There were a lot of miracles that day.

She nodded, reminding me I'd shared that information already. "We have a lot of memories here," she said quietly. "In such a short space of time."

I hoped she was remembering all the good ones.

"It's yours too, isn't it? Because you were married. That's why you're here."

"The cottage? Yeah. When Abby died, her half went to me. To be honest, I would have come here anyway. I had nowhere else to go."

"Why did you two marry?"

"Liv, I would have done anything for your sister. But more than that, I just needed to give her something real. Something good. So she'd know I accepted her no matter what. And to be honest, I thought it would give me a way to protect her from her family."

Liv went to the couch and sat down. "Were you drunk the night Abby died?" she asked.

My heart thudded to a painful halt. "Wow. How is it you always totally curve-ball me?"

Her eyes dropped. "Sorry."

I almost went and sat in the chair, but the echo of the night I left, the night before she was attacked, was too loud. "No." I slid my hands into my pants pockets, in a display of calmness I would never feel over this topic. "No. I wasn't drunk. Nor had I had anything that would put my results over the legal limit in a toxicology report. But since you were told I was, why the hell are you asking the question?"

"Because now I know you, I don't believe that to be the truth. And your reasons for marrying Abby don't make it sound like the act of an immature wastrel, which is what everyone claimed you were."

I laughed without the joy that should accompany it. "Well, Liv, I hate to disappoint you, but for most of the year prior to that event, you'd have been wrong. I drank, smoked, swallowed, or snorted anything I could possibly lay my hands on. So in the grand scheme of things, I was bound to be involved in a fatal event sooner or later."

"There was a toxicology report from that night."

"Yes, there was," I agreed.

Liv's mouth twisted to the side, and she bit her lip. "But it wasn't public knowledge. I dug that out. So why would there be a *secret* report saying you were drunk if you weren't? If something was faked, wouldn't there be a report saying you weren't when you actually *were*? Especially because of who your father was?"

"You'd think," I agreed. Her face told me she wasn't going to let this go. "Remember I told you we went to the bar to try and meet Mike Williams?"

"Yeah. I just don't understand why, if he could have faked your toxicology report to make sure it seemed like a random drunk-driving teen accident, which happens all the damn time, why did you then have to . . ." She turned her toes in and sat on her hands. "Why did you have to fake your death?"

"Mike Williams had manufactured proof that I was drunk, so it would, and should, have been an open-and-shut case. And really, it should have been a routine DUI. Jail, probation, whatever. Not a fatal accident. Mike Williams discredits me, and all goes back to normal, right?"

"But your father was a senator?"

"Yes. The choice was go public and have Mike Williams, and his colleagues who all saw us in a bar, discredit the case with his false report and bring my father's entire campaign down at the same time . . . or leave. Disappear.

"It seems so stupid, so trivial now, but when you're young and nineteen and sequestered in a hospital room with campaign staff and crisis management people and they warn you that making claims against Mike Williams will expose your own father and his involvement with the Atlanta PD and open the door to a corruption scandal involving not only the police, but the highest levels of office, and your mother is crying and begging you to just pretend you don't know anything . . ." I paused, drawing in a shuddering breath.

"You do the only thing you can do. They gave me an out. I took it. They gave me the option to not have the toxicology report revealed and go away, or stay and be the drunk senator's son who killed your sister. But the 'go away' option was permanent. It didn't matter how many times I told them Mike Williams had faked the report; credible witnesses had seen us in the bar. I wasn't in a fit emotional state to make the decision, but I did it. And it wasn't even a decision. Not really. They'd basically told me it was easier for me to be 'dead' than deal with my mess. I did the only thing I could think of when I'd already lost everything that ever meant anything to me. I agreed."

Liv's eyes were filled with tears. "They disowned you. They abandoned you. God, it just seems so extreme."

"Yes."

"What happened that night, Tom?"

I closed my eyes.

CHAPTER FORTY-ONE

Before

"Something's not right, Whit." In the dark interior of the car, Abby was shaking. We were back in the car after walking into that freaking bar to try and confront Mike Williams.

"I know." I dragged my hands forward over my cropped hair and then slammed a palm on the steering wheel. "But I don't know what else to do."

"We need to go. Right now. Let's start driving back to the cottage *right now*. We can take the money your parents offered. He won't find us there, he doesn't know I even know about it. Please. We can go back and figure out a better plan than this."

"I'm not taking their fucking money," I yelled, raw with rage at what had happened earlier. They'd utterly turned their back on me, their own son.

"I shouldn't have seen him," she whispered, shaking her head. "I shouldn't have seen him."

"Well, we did."

"I shouldn't have seen him."

"Stop it, Abby." I started the car. She continued to whisper over and over. "Please, Abby," I snapped, as I pulled out of the parking lot and headed for the ramp to the highway. Without a better option, we may as well head back south. It wasn't like I had anywhere to go now either. The shock and anger of my parents' betrayal was nothing compared to the pain and hurt now setting in. My mother's face looking at me with disappointment, and her hands clenching and unclenching her pearls over and over. *Don't you know how hard your father has worked for this? We don't even know if Abigail Baines is telling the truth. We just can't risk that kind of scandal touching us right now.*

"I shouldn't have seen him."

"Please stop fucking saying that," I yelled. I was losing my mind. I checked the rear-view mirror. The highway was fairly empty, but a car's headlights in the distance gave me a weird feeling. I checked the next sign: Northside Drive. Perhaps we should just go back to my parents' house, sleep in the pool house or whatever, and figure it all out in the morning. At least we'd have security. A literal security team. Taking the exit at the last minute, I saw the car behind us speed up and do the same. *Oh shit.*

"I shouldn't have seen him."

"Abby," I roared at her and took a left turn through a red light on the empty road, trying to get away from the car behind us. The car did the same, and my stomach plunged. Northside was a heavily wooded residential street. There was no lighted gas station to pull into, no way to find out who the fuck was following us. Suddenly the headlights loomed, pulling in close. I stepped on the gas out of instinct to avoid the car hitting the back of us. "Abby, please, snap out of it. We're in trouble." *We're going to die.* I had no idea where the thought came from, and I tried to shake it off. But hell, if we did, maybe my parents, and hers, would wake the fuck up.

Abby stopped her repetitive chanting and looked at me. "I love you, Whit," she said. I glanced at her as she gave me a small smile and reached for my hand.

But she didn't take my hand, she took the wheel and pulled.

CHAPTER FORTY-TWO

"What are you saying?" Liv gasped.

I was so caught up in my memory, I wasn't quite sure what had made it out of my mouth. I looked at her pale eyes, filled with shock and, let's face it, horror.

"I don't know," I lied, not wanting to admit the truth even as it came out. "Not really. It may have been a mistake. We were going so damn fast. That's what I tried to tell myself, but . . ."

Liv's face was pale. "Abby killed herself," she whispered.

I looked at her, waiting for the fallout.

"And she tried to kill you too."

"I don't know, Liv. I have to believe she was caught up in some panicked state and just took the easy way out. Made a split-second choice out of desperation. I have to believe she wasn't trying to kill me too." I found a chair from the kitchen table and swung it around. I needed to not be standing right now. Sinking down, I rested my elbows on my knees. "The truth is, I'm not sure she was thinking about me at all. I was just there. She was done, Liv. At that stage, she couldn't think about anything else. Not me . . . and not even you." I grimaced as I spoke, amazed I was finally saying these words out loud, hoping she could take it. Maybe I was waiting to see if *I* could take it.

Liv sat, her light blue eyes staring out of her pale face, lips parted.

I held her gaze. God, that clock was fucking loud.

"I've been angry at her for a long time too," I whispered.

She stood up and came toward me, not stopping until she stood between my knees, and I was forced to sit back. I looked up as her small hands landed on my shoulders, sliding over them and up my neck and into my hair, leaving my skin prickling with sensation in her wake. Then she pulled my head against her. My cheek pressed into her body, and I closed my eyes and wrapped my arms around her hips. My chest was tight as I finally let myself feel the memory. The fear, the panic, the betrayal and confusion. The grief. The anger. I held Liv tighter. She responded in kind. Was she comforting me? Should I be comforting *her*? I simply held on as I let all the crazy emotions tumble through me.

"Tom," she whispered and held on too. The simple utterance of my name, the name she'd said a thousand times, washed over me. It slid over my skin and curled through my body. I wasn't Whit to Liv. I would never be Whit again, and Liv knew it too. Abby Baines had broken me, changed me, and left me melted into a lump of tin in the smoldering remains of her nightmare.

Liv had found me there, and she was dragging us out of the ashes if it killed her. And it almost had. "Livvy," I answered her, saying her name into her body so maybe her heart would hear it first.

We stayed like that for a long time. Holding each other.

"Come here," I whispered finally against her, then looked up.

Her eyes twitched together, questioning.

"Down here." I loosened my arms and tugged on her hips. I just wanted her closer, where I could be closer to her mouth. I wanted to kiss her. Properly. Had she ever simply been kissed?

Chewing her bottom lip, she let me nudge her legs apart and guide her on to my lap. Her hands balanced on my shoulders for a moment before she self-consciously pushed down her dress, which had ridden up her thighs.

My gut clenched and the hot burn of arousal pooled as I realized her dress was definitely not designed to be modest in this position. I simply wanted to kiss her, and now I'd wrapped her entire body around me.

Doing my best to ignore her warm scent, I slid my hands up to hold her face. "Look at me, Liv."

Her eyes flickered and focused on mine as she repeatedly pulled her lower lip nervously into her mouth.

I let myself look, really look at her. She was so beautiful. Every line of her face, from her small nose and full lips to her pale eyes and smooth forehead, came together in perfection. Up close, there was a smattering of tiny freckles on her nose and along the tops of her cheekbones. My thumb smoothed over them. Her bottom lip was being completely mauled by her teeth, so I let my thumb slide to her mouth and rescue it.

I lingered on her lips so there was no doubt in her mind that I wanted to kiss her. And when I couldn't stand not to for one second more, I gently brought her face toward me.

Liv's eyes fluttered closed.

I touched my mouth to hers, brushing over her softness. She inhaled, and I did it again.

Her hands slid back up to my shoulders, her fingers reaching the skin of my neck.

My skin tingled.

Finally, I fitted my lips firmly over hers. Our mouths moved slowly together.

No rushing.

No urgency.

I let everything inside my heart pour out of my mouth with every tiny movement, every slide, every pull and every nip. I tasted her. I worshiped her.

The burn rose between us.

It was stoked higher with every sigh, and every minuscule movement of our bodies, but I refused to give in to the pulsing insistence.

Her mouth was warm, sweet, addictive.

I finally forced myself to pull away and opened my eyes. Liv's cheeks were flushed, lips parted and glistening, chest rising and falling in shallow breaths, her pulse fluttering wildly beneath my hand on her neck. I almost lost my good intentions.

Her eyes opened, pupils dark and dilated.

"Wow," she whispered, and I was suddenly standing on a bloody battlefield, broadsword in hand and dragon slain under my booted foot.

I grinned, unable to help it. "I agree."

Getting up off my lap, she smoothed down her dress and then held out her hand. I took it and let her pull me up.

"What?" I asked.

She dropped her hand, and her cheeks flushed. "I, uh, need help unpinning this dress again, so I can change." She turned and went into her bedroom.

I followed.

She stopped in front of the perfectly smooth bed.

Presented with her back again, I stepped forward to undo the pins, my mind studiously blank.

I slowly took each one out, careful to avoid touching her skin. Then, turning to place them on the dresser, I made the mistake of glancing at her reflection in the mirror. Eyes closed, mouth slightly parted. The blood plummeted to my groin.

"Tom?" she whispered.

I closed my eyes.

"Will you touch me like you did last night? On my back?"

Swallowing, and led by a force stronger than me, I walked back to where I'd been moments ago and placed my finger on the back of her neck. I dragged it down slowly and her breathing jumped at the contact, her skin rising with goose bumps. The strapless dress gaped like before, held only to her front with her arms crossed over her chest. "Don't stop." Her whisper was so quiet, but may as well have been roared with the impact it had on me. My body tightened to brace against the lust that erupted in my gut. My fingers continued down her bra-less spine, pulling the dress as I went.

Unfolding her arms and letting them drop to her sides, she let the dress go, her breath choppy and erratic.

My hand dragged down to the base of her spine, and my other hand joined it. I slid both palms on to her hips, her skin hot under my touch, and down the curve until the dress lost its purchase and fell to the ground.

A small whimper escaped her.

My heart pounded, laboring from pumping absent blood, and filling my body with nothing but crazy, clawing want. My face dropped to press my mouth to the smooth skin of her shoulder. I breathed her skin into me, wanting to open my mouth and devour her.

My hands couldn't stop. I stepped in close, sliding them around the soft curve of her belly, fitting my front to her backside, squeezing my eyes shut at the feel of her.

Gasping sounds filled the air, like she was trying to catch her breath and couldn't. "Is this okay?" I whispered into her ear before I traced the shell of her ear with my tongue on a whim. I was echoing her words from last night but desperately needed to know. The frantic nod of her head spiked my arousal further.

Her hands fumbled on mine and then took over, taking the lead. She ran them up her front, her head falling back, her body arching, giving me a clear view of her beautiful breasts before my large hands, directed by hers, covered them.

"You're so beautiful," I think I was able to say. We both lost our air at the contact. She gasped, but I felt like my lungs exploded. My hand closed over her flesh, kneading her, and my mouth closed around the skin on the side of her neck, sucking at it desperately. She arched. "Tom." She twisted to face me, and I was forced to let go.

Her eyes were wild, but focused on me, as if she saw somebody deep inside me, beyond the man who stood in front of her. Her lips were parted, and her tongue darted out to wet her lips. I brought my hands up to cup her face. Her cheekbones. I felt like a giant holding a sparrow. I'd either crush her, or let go and she would fly away forever.

Her hands took my wrists and her eyes fluttered closed. Lowering my face, I kissed each eyelid before descending to her mouth. I fitted my mouth perfectly over hers, gently grasping her lips with mine. My tongue was desperate to get inside, and my hands slid around her head and back, drawing her as close against my body as I could while I tasted her.

She slid her hands under my shirt, across my sides, along my lower back and then between us to my tensed stomach.

We were nothing but labored breathing and restraint. At least, I was. I needed to know how far she wanted to go, but I couldn't ask. I wanted to devour her, but I needed her to know this was her call.

Her hands pushed my shirt up and I took her lead, forgoing buttons and simply pulling it off. As soon as it was gone, Liv plastered herself to my bare chest, and I groaned at the feel of her. Skin to skin.

"Jesus," I rasped. "You feel incredible." And I realized this moment had been inevitable from the first second she'd arrived and blown my reclusive existence apart. I'd lived it in my subconscious with every minute we'd spent in each other's company, every look, every avoided interaction, and every moment I'd spent next to her the nights she was sick. The knowledge was shocking in its . . . rightness.

"Tom," she whispered, pulling my mouth back to hers. "Please stop holding back on me."

"I'm not."

"You are."

"I'm scared, Liv," I admitted. Everything I'd said to her last night about not knowing what I was doing was true, and so much more. I was terrified something I did or said might remind her of another situation, something dirty, something horrible, something painful. I just didn't fucking know.

"Scared to touch me?" she asked.

"Scared to hurt you."

She shook her head. "You won't."

"Scared to remind you of monsters."

She pulled back and took my hand. Placing it on her chest, right below her throat, she looked up at me, her light blue eyes brimming with emotion. "Tom, you don't get it. There are no monsters when you're with me. I want . . ." Her eyes dropped.

"What?"

"I want . . . the you who took me in the rain. The one who couldn't stand not to hold me, kiss me, be inside me, for one second longer."

I winced at the memory of how crazed I was. How ashamed I was afterward. "But Liv, I acted like an animal then."

"No, you didn't. It's not horrible to want like that, to need like that. To need me like that. And it's not horrible for me to be needed like that. Because I feel the same way, Tom. With you there is no ugliness, or perverted want; there's only you and me and the way you make me understand that desire like this is real and true and the most amazing and beautiful thing I've ever felt. And just letting these words out of my mouth is the scariest part about it."

I didn't know what to say. I wasn't ready to let go with Liv; I'd always be afraid of hurting her. Not reading her signals, her clues, messing things up. But I realized suddenly that in my line of thinking I was using the word always. I wasn't leaving her. I was never going to say goodbye. For as long as she needed me, I'd stay right by her side. Always.

"Don't ever be scared to tell me what's in your head, Liv. I'm always going to need to know, no matter what."

Nodding, she blinked and swallowed. "I used to get high just from the feeling of power when I made guys weak and do things they might normally not do," she admitted, making my gut clench with nausea. "That was all I got out of it."

I tried to block out the images her words conjured by narrowing my focus on the sound of her voice.

"Please," she pleaded. "You have it now. You have the power over what I'm feeling, I'm giving it to you. Please take it. Make me lose my mind over what you make me feel. You tell me I'm beautiful, but I've never felt that way until you. There is nothing, no one apart from you in my head. Nothing we could do together that would feel wrong to me. I can't feel anything apart from you. Please don't be scared, just . . ."

I stared at her hard, trying to get to the bottom of what she was saying, what she was pleading for.

"Do what you want to do," she whispered. "Don't make me ask."

Was this a trap? Was this where I added myself to the list of guys who'd fucked her over? Literally and figuratively. Or was she so afraid of enjoying sex after what had happened to her that she didn't want to make the choice for herself?

My mind warred, trying to figure it out. Did she want me to be rough with her? Was that what turned her on? No, she'd enjoyed the way I'd kissed her earlier, so it wasn't that.

No, today she wanted me to make love to her, not fuck her, but she wanted me to stop holding back like she was going to fall apart every single second. She wanted me to stop forcing her to make all the first moves.

I stepped forward and ran my hand up her back till I could reach her hair and gently tug her head back. Her breath caught, and she looked at my lips through half-lowered lids.

"Okay," I said. "For now, for you," I emphasized, "I'm going to do what I want. But asking me what I want to do is completely tied to what you want."

She breathed out a long breath.

"And I'm going to say what I want to do. So you have a chance to say no. And I'm going to ask you things. Uncomfortable things. Because I never, ever want to hurt you. Do you understand that, Liv? Can you answer me honestly, no matter what?"

She bit her lip, so I kissed her and delved my tongue between her lips before pulling back. I knew some of her answers would shred me inside out. She was nervous. So was I. It was a simplistic thing I was doing, but I didn't know how else to tackle it. "I just want to know what I need to erase. Or try to."

She closed her eyes a moment. Then nodded.

I released a pent-up breath and decided to go for it. "I want to lay you down on that bed, I want to spread your legs." Her eyes flickered, and her breath got shallow. "Wide," I added, and she moaned.

My insides went into free fall.

Now that I'd started and could see how much it was turning her on, I couldn't stop. I reached out and ran a finger from her throat all the way down to her belly button and the edge of her white underwear. "And taste every single part of you until you can't do anything but feel me in every one of your senses. Until there is only me. And no one else. Until everything in the rest of the world fades. So that any time you need to, for the rest of your life, the memory of me will be so strong that you can feel me loving you just by closing your eyes."

Her breath stuttered out in a gasp and I kissed her. Hard. "I don't care how long it takes to get there."

We had a long way to go and so many obstacles still to face, but today I needed to show us both the perfect truth between us. I would show her my heart with my touch and my words and take it moment by moment to make sure she stayed with me no matter how far we chose to go.

I moved her back until her legs hit the bed.

OLIVIA

CHAPTER FORTY-THREE

$\mathcal{I}$ couldn't stop staring at Tom's face. I'd imagined him under that beard of course and had a general feeling he was attractive. I mean, when he clipped his beard close I'd seen his completely lickable lips. And after spending weeks dying to feel them on me, I'd become pretty freaking obsessed. But nothing, *nothing*, could have prepared me for how heartbreakingly gorgeous he was.

The whole way through the wedding, I'd been so conscious of staring at him that I mostly tried to look away at others as he spoke to me. It was only in the dark of his boat last night that I'd let my fingers learn his features. His angles, his cheekbones, his squarish chin. He was different from the Whitfield Cavanaugh I thought I remembered, his face harsher, thinner, more angled, stronger, infinitely more devastating than the all-American boy next door.

He was a man.

I tried to reconcile the Tom I'd spent months falling in love with with this man. The most attractive man I'd ever laid eyes on. He didn't seem aware of it either. I guess because he hadn't shaved clean in so long.

Now that man had me flat on my back. He was kneeling on the bed, his large hands running up my hips to my chest and back down, where they hooked on to my panties.

I tried to keep my breathing steady but it was no use. He was staring at me and asking me a question. "I'm taking these off, okay?" he whispered.

I nodded and lifted my hips for him to slowly peel them down my legs. My breathing, Jesus, my breathing. My heart was pounding. It was reminiscent of a panic attack. But I wanted this one. Tom was my . . . safety. My haven. My sanctuary.

Whatever he did, and whatever he asked me, I knew he was terrified of reminding me of something horrible. But he didn't realize that I already had all those things in my head anyway, every sick grasp, every silkily whispered perversity, every hurt, every associated emotion.

But this, this with Tom, was louder. This was more. This overrode everything.

His hand ran up my inner thigh, and I shifted, spreading my legs wider, making him inhale sharply. "Are you wet for me, Liv?"

I squeezed my eyes closed, tensing, as a similar memory fired.

Tom's voice. I snapped my eyes open to keep them on him. This was him asking. This was Tom.

Doubt stole over his features as he realized.

"Yes," I managed hastily. "Don't stop talking the way you want to. Be you, Tom. I want *you.* I'm wet for *you.*"

"*Christ.*" His mouth came down on my mine, licking into my soul. I grabbed his head to hold him to me. His tongue in my mouth as his fingers glided up my leg, closer and closer, then slicked over my flesh. God. I arched up on a gasp that tore my mouth from his.

"Stay with me, Livvy," he rasped into my ear, sending shivers down my skin. His fingers slid over me, and my legs widened even further, inviting him in. My body literally wept for him, I couldn't control it.

I panted desperately. His breathing was just as harsh. "More," I managed.

Hot, wet kisses trailed down my throat to my breasts, and I arched into his mouth. His lips closed around my nipple, his teeth scraping the flesh, at the same moment that he slid a finger into me.

I let out a guttural moan and shuddered. "Tom," I rasped.

He brought his face up, a lock of hair falling across it. His cheeks were flushed. He breathed hard, his beautiful eyes dark. "Okay?"

"God, yes, more than okay."

"You like this?" he whispered, dragging his finger slowly out of me and then sliding it back in.

I let out a choked sound, and he did it again. His thumb pressed down on my clit and began rhythmic circles.

Unable to catch my breath to answer, I nodded rapidly. Desperately. Which caused an answering quirk of Tom's mouth.

His eyes never missed a beat, watching me closely.

I was on fire. My skin prickled. Every single cell of my body was wired to a fuse that was lit and burning up the inches at a rapid rate. I undulated my hips up as he worked me, played me. I grasped at him, his strong shoulders, his muscled arms, then at the bed sheets. My legs opened further, beyond my control.

"Just let go, baby." Tom's husky voice permeated my senses.

I was caught in the crossfire between my body and my

mind, and he seemed to know it. "Keep talking," I gasped. "I need your voice. I need to hear you."

His breathing matched mine. "You feel so good, Liv. You're so beautiful." His finger slid deep into me again, and his mouth came back to my ear. "I want to taste you. I want my tongue where my hand is. I want to be inside you," he confessed, and my body reacted like an incendiary device.

My head arched back on the pillow, my eyes squeezing closed. I lost my mind, my hips literally riding his hand, crying out as the orgasm crashed through me. It scorched everything in its path, good and bad, leaving me quaking and utterly decimated.

And then I was in Tom's arms, pressed tightly to his chest, my head to his pounding heart. He drew me on top of him and held me tight, leaving no room for my doubts and my fears to creep into the barren wasteland that was left inside me.

His skin was damp, and I pressed my lips to the salty tang of his skin, taking a small taste. His length was rock hard in his boxers against my belly.

His hand drew my face up to his. The look in his eyes—wonder, dark desire, hesitation—made the temporary vacuum inside me fill with fresh and deep longing. I lowered my mouth back to his chest and kissed his skin.

"Liv," he said, his voice strained. "We can stop. We don't need to rush this. We shouldn't rush this."

I reached up a finger and laid it across his sculpted, delicious lips. God, he was gorgeous. "I . . . I need to get to the other side of our first time."

Obviously, we'd technically had that, but the memory of that night was agonizing, and I wanted to eclipse it with this one. "That sounds wrong. I don't mean it's something I want out of the way. It's just . . . and if you don't want to, it's fine," I added, suddenly realizing it wasn't my choice alone.

"I want to, trust me. You don't want to remember how much I hurt you that night. I get it. I don't either. God, I'm so sorry for that, Liv. But also . . . I don't have any protection."

I instantly thought of the box of condoms. Bethany. I had no right really, but my heart dropped. My nakedness, my vulnerability hit hard. I gulped. "Did you—"

"No." Tom shifted, sitting up, moving me to the side and then sliding his hand into my hair. "They're just on the boat. Liv, there's only you. There's been only you for weeks. Months."

"But you . . . Bethany, she—"

"I was utterly unfair to her. I'm not proud of it. I was an ass, but I didn't realize what I was doing. I was too busy fighting my feelings for you, trying to switch them off. Trying to pretend everything was the same. But I haven't slept with her in months."

"It's okay, you don't have to explain. It's not like I have any right—"

"Jesus, Liv. You have every right." His other hand took my cheek until he was cradling my face and staring so intently into my eyes I felt like I should turn away, but I couldn't. "You have every right. I will never, ever hurt you like that. Hurt you period. Do you understand what I'm saying?"

I stayed mute. Not answering. His eyes dropped to my lips and he captured them in a deep, scorching kiss, as if he was trying to communicate with me. God, I loved his mouth. His taste.

He pulled away finally, and dropped a kiss on my nose, before pushing me back to the pillows so he could settle his weight on me. My legs opened to accommodate him, and his erection, still long and thick, pressed against my center.

I moaned at the sensation, and Tom let out a small growl that smacked of frustration. "I'm torturing myself now," he said and rocked against me as he nipped at my lips.

"And me," I said and boldly slid my hands down his muscled back until I could grab his firm behind.

He dropped his face to my neck.

"You know," I said into his ear, "you don't have to come inside me, and I think I'm at a fairly safe part of my cycle . . ."

Tom groaned. "I think you just gave voice to every teenage boy's fantasy." He came up with a smirk across his gorgeous face. "It's never safe. You know that, right?"

I nodded and pursed my lips.

"And sliding into you is going to feel so fucking good, it will be a herculean effort to last, let alone pull out?"

My belly fizzed with arousal. "You asking me?" I quirked an eyebrow at his tone.

"No, I guess I'm telling you. Apologizing."

He leaned up on one elbow and his other hand drifted over my chest, kneading a breast, and tweaking my nipple gently between two fingers as he watched, seemingly entranced by the fact he was touching me.

I let out a tiny, breathy laugh. "Apologizing for what?"

His hand continued down my belly and I had to bite my lower lip and inhale deeply to control the swirling heat inside me.

"That it's not a good enough reason not to at least feel you for a second," he said, and leaned up slightly to pull his boxers down. "I'm a masochist, I guess."

The sight of him ready between my legs sent a red-hot

spike of lust through me. In one smooth motion I instantly spread my legs and wrapped them around his waist as he guided himself toward me. The tip of him slid against my opening. My earlier release welcomed him, and within nano-seconds he'd pressed his thickness all the way inside me.

He hissed a short, sharp breath. The crease of his forehead told me he was fighting for control. But suddenly I was too. And not in a good way.

Images and memories of pain from the past pressed in. Crowding me. My mind began its bloody battle again as I fought to stay in the moment, but I gasped, already tense, and tight with panic. The green of a shirt, the weight, the hot, pungent breath, the grunting, the sharp, tearing pain.

"Liv, Liv," Tom's voice urged. He was utterly still inside me. Not moving.

I squeezed my eyes tighter, trying desperately to get back to the good stuff, the warmth, the heat that made my insides gooey and melty, not stiff and rigid. Why? Why now? It hadn't happened before in the rain storm.

"Livvy, look at me."

I shook my head.

"Yes, Liv. Open your eyes. Please." The last word, a small, broken plea.

His face, beautiful and strained with worry, came into focus. "I'm going to pull out now, okay."

"No. Wait." I clamped my teeth tight, waiting for the memories to fade from the beauty we had in this moment. From the beauty of Tom. Of us.

"It's okay, Liv. We shouldn't have rushed. It's okay, I promise." His hips flexed to move away. I grabbed his back and squeezed my legs tighter around him.

I closed my eyes. "Please. Just stay like this. I'm sorry."

"Don't apologize," he said with force, making me want to apologize again. I nodded instead.

He kissed my nose, and then each eyelid. His lips skated over mine softly and I returned the kiss. Our mouths moved together, every lick and every pull melting me slowly. His tongue slipped between my lips to tangle with mine and I moaned, instinctively moving my body against him. It caused his length to rock within me, and I felt the answering shudder go through him. God, I loved this man. I wanted so much to give him pleasure. To show him how I felt about him.

Even when I was panicked, I never felt threatened. I was always safe with him.

He had endured so much too. So much fear and pain and abandonment. And he was so focused on being there for me, it was hard to remember he also needed someone to be there for him. Me. I wanted to prioritize Tom. His needs. His wants. The knowledge seemed to release the final knot within me, and as it uncoiled, I felt my insides liquefying, heating up, and boiling over.

Sensing the shift in me, he lifted his head, his eyes searching mine. I smoothed a hand across his cheekbone, my thumb across his lips, rocking my hips against his. I let him see in my face the deep pleasure and arousal the feel of him within me caused and the love I hoped was pouring out of my eyes. He answered my movement and captured my thumb between his lips, sucking it against his tongue.

We moved gently, silently, with quick breaths and straining bodies. If our eyes weren't locked, our lips were. His hands cradled my head and mine alternated between grasping tufts of his soft hair and running desperately down his back. His movements became more urgent and erratic.

I tried to match him.

Suddenly he pulled out and slid down my body. Before I could even react, his hands were holding my legs apart and his mouth was on me, his hot tongue working me with urgent rhythmic swipes.

Crying out in surprise, I grabbed his head.

Oh my God.

There was no time to let my mind catch up before my body was coiled tight and my back bowed off the bed. I opened my mouth in a silent scream and my body convulsed, every feeling centered where his tongue set off the charge that detonated throughout me.

Then he was filling my aching core again, his body heavy on mine. I was tight and grasping around him as he stroked in and out. "Tom," I begged. "So . . . good."

"God, Liv, I—" He broke off with a groan and pulled out of me, taking himself in hand and pumping his fist. My eyes were riveted to his movements as he worked himself.

"Oh my God," I managed, just as he erupted over my belly. "That's, like, the hottest thing I've ever seen."

"Christ." He let out a guttural breath.

"And messy," I added, and a giggle burst out of me. He smiled, his beautiful face elevating to devastingly gorgeous.

We were both breathing heavily, and then both laughing out loud. He leaned down and kissed me, our smiling mouths causing our teeth to bump. "Livvy Baines," he said breathlessly.

"Tom Cavanaugh," I echoed, trying his name out.

We locked eyes, our laughter dying out.

TOM

CHAPTER FORTY-FOUR

"Something's bothering you." Liv's voice was small. "Do you regret it?"

"What? God, no. It was incredible. You're incredible." I swallowed. Understatement of the fucking year. My entire universe just shifted.

We were lying facing each other. Liv had moved away, after we cleaned up, to cool our bodies from the damp, humid heat we'd generated. My skin felt the loss of her but welcomed the cool air. She'd captured my hand, though, and had it tucked between hers against her chest.

She smiled. "I believe you. So what is it?"

"You won't like it. But I think we need to do it so we can move on."

Her body tensed.

"Liv, I need you to tell me what's in the box."

Her jaw tightened. Annoyed. "I don't know what's in it."

"I'm asking you to open it. It's not Pandora's box. It's not going to destroy the world. We just need a small piece of closure."

Liv tried to pull away, but I held tight.

"Wait, this is for me too. I need to know if there's anything that can help explain what was going on in Abby's head. More importantly, Mike Williams is still out there, Liv."

She shuddered, swallowing hard.

We hadn't ever addressed the fact that she'd run away and he was still out there. She would never truly heal while he was. And while I had no idea what to do to help her with that—because the last time I tried hadn't worked out so well—she would have to face up to it eventually.

She pulled away again, her eyes refusing to meet mine, and this time I let her go. She flopped on to her back with a huff. After a few moments, she sat up and reached down to grab my discarded white shirt, shrugged it on and stood.

I got out of bed wearing my boxers and followed until we stood in front of the dresser where the locked wooden box sat like a viper.

"We could always use the ax to break it apart," she said quietly as we both stared at it.

A thought occurred to me. "Is that what you were looking for when you searched this place head to toe? The key?"

"Not really, no, but it did cross my mind that maybe it was here somewhere."

My eyes flicked up to the picture of her and Abby as girls on the swing. Liv glanced up and saw where I was looking. Suddenly she reached forward and plucked the frame off the wall, turning it over in her hands.

"You've gotta be shitting me," I said as we saw the small iron key taped to the back. Her hands shook as she frantically tore it loose, dropping the picture with a clatter. Then we both stood, breathing hard. Her heart had to be beating as fast as mine was. She offered the key to me. I shook my head.

Leaning forward, she pulled the box closer and slid the key inside. She turned it and there was a soft click.

My hand shot out and slapped down hard on the top of the box. "Wait."

"What?"

"There could be nothing that will change anything in there, and we could also learn something that will change everything forever."

"I know, Tom." The small crease appeared between her brows again.

"I'm not trying to give the box more power than it has, trust me. It may have nothing to do with me at all. But whatever it is will affect *you*. It affected Abby, so I can only believe it will affect you too."

Liv let go of the box and faced me.

I took that as an invitation to keep going. "You keep telling me I saved you, but you saved *me*. My heart was barely beating before you arrived, and now . . ." God, I sounded so lame, but I didn't care. "Now, every breath I take has you in it." I winced. "Livvy, you deserve so much better than me. I'll do whatever I can to help get you free of your past, but I'm a big part of it, so at some point you'll want—no, need—to let me go." Her head started shaking side to side. "No, listen. I will be here as long as you need me. I'm just telling you it's okay. I need you to be *free* of me more than I need you to be with me. I know that may not make sense to you now—"

"You love me," she said, calmly. "It makes perfect sense."

"What does?"

"You love me. Love me so much you think you don't deserve me. Blah, blah, blah. Set me free, blah, blah, blah. You are talking complete crap," she snapped.

"It's not crap," I managed, finally. "Not the 'I love you' part anyway."

She smiled.

I blew out a breath. "Anyway, I also know that whatever is in there will hurt you, and I hate seeing you hurt. Maybe I needed a moment to get myself together," I hedged. "I'm fine now, go ahead."

She turned to the box and opened it, drawing out a stack of what looked like photographs. I couldn't look at them, I needed to look at her. I watched closely, keeping my eyes on her for the first hint of panic, or fear, or God knows what else. Her forehead creased in confusion at first, before her flushed skin paled to melted wax. Her hands shook as she went through the pictures one by one, picking up speed, then seeming to come to a stop suddenly. She laid them down and her hand came to her mouth. Her body jerked as she retched, and then she pushed past me and slammed out the room toward the bathroom. I was torn for a split second between looking at the pictures and going to her.

I needed to see. Picking up the stack, I wasn't sure I was at the beginning. The first picture, dated from the look of the print quality and the hairstyles, was of a party, it seemed, outside. I tried to identify the people, but I didn't recognize anyone; her dad maybe, but he was young. A teenager.

Then I looked past the assembled group to an open sliding door in the brick house behind, the curtains billowing out. Two people were wrapped around each other; the guy, in a green Hawaiian shirt, his khaki shorts lowered, stood between a girl's tanned legs. She was young. Her light blue dress was shoved up to her waist. An insanely intimate moment between two people caught on camera, by accident. They were clearly in the middle of having sex. He was dark-headed, she was blonde. Not really understanding, I flipped to the next photo. It was a blowup of the previous picture, and I stilled. The hair, the tilt of her head. Her half-smile. It was Abby.

Except it wasn't.

Oh my God.

Bile rose in my gut.

This was Liv and Abby's *mother*, and the man having sex with her was her own brother. Mike Williams. I dropped the pictures, thinking to get to Olivia, who was deadly quiet. Then, past the many blowups of the same photo, I saw another picture. Abby, posed, sitting demurely on the edge of a chair, staring at someone past the lens of the camera with vacant eyes, wearing a light blue dress. *The same* light blue dress. A picture taken at another time. Was it a re-enactment? *Christ.* Nausea rolled. Had he made Livvy dress up too?

I picked up the pictures and stuffed them back in the box, then jogged to the bathroom. Livvy wasn't there.

"Liv?" I called, and looked around the empty cottage.

Prince Eric was perched on the back of the sofa. "Liv," I shouted.

No wonder their grandmother never spoke to her daughter. She must have found out; perhaps she was the one who'd taken the picture. Jesus, did Livvy's dad know? He couldn't. There was no way Mike Williams would have been that involved in their lives if he did, surely. Was what happened to Abby a result of Mike's obsession with a young Susan Williams? And when he couldn't have Abby . . .

"Livvy!"

I burst out of the front door and headed to the porch stairs.

"Here." Her small voice came from my right, where she was curled up on the wicker love seat.

I exhaled in relief. I went to her and picked her up, pulling her into my lap as I sat down.

She burrowed into my neck. Her body was curled up tight, and I cradled her in my arms.

"You smell so good," she said, inhaling against my skin. "You always smell so good. Everything is better when I can smell you."

"God, Liv, are you okay?"

She nodded. A minuscule movement against me.

I thought about Abby's refusals to tell her parents. "It always confused me when Abby said it wasn't about *her*. I guess I get it now," I said. Although, no. Not really. How could anyone ever "get" something so heinous. "My God, all the times he told you that you reminded him of *her*. He meant your mother, not Abby."

"I just . . . My mother, God." Her body quaked, her tone one of horror.

"How much older is Mike?"

She swallowed. "Six or seven years, I'm really not sure."

"So he's a sick, perverted fuck who had sex with his little sister and was clearly obsessed with her at that age, which is why he went for Abby." *And then you.* I didn't add the obvious. How would anyone ever get the logic of such a twisted mind?

"Do you think my mom knew he did that to us?" she asked achingly, and my heart shattered in my chest.

"I don't know, Livvy." Because, truthfully, I didn't. The idea was abhorrent and devastating.

And not entirely impossible.

She broke apart then, shuddering and sobbing into me as

I held her, trying to keep her body together while my head and my heart screamed in silent agony and fury.

We stayed like that, with Liv curled against my chest, for a long time. The sun moved across the sky, and the shadows lengthened across the ground. A breeze picked up and stirred the moss that hung from the trees and danced on the swing beneath the oak.

"I have to go back, don't I?" she said finally. "I need to go back."

Smoothing my hand down her back, I knew she was already sure what she had to do.

"I need to go beg my school counselor to let me take the state test and graduate, or get a GED. And I need to confront my mother and break my father's heart."

I winced, though she couldn't see me. If I could take that burden for her, I would.

"And you can't come with me, can you?" she asked.

"I could." I would, for Liv.

"Do you want to see your parents again? I mean, could you now?"

I exhaled. "My mother has tried to contact me. Sent a few letters through a lawyer in Savannah. I sent them back."

"What did she say?"

"I never opened them." I shrugged in a display of fake nonchalance.

"Aren't you curious?"

I was tense. My instinct was to shut this conversation down, but I owed Livvy an answer. "The hurt I feel over what they did will never go away. I used to dream about going back, that it was all a big mistake. But now I don't think I care if I never see them again. Maybe that makes me mentally unhealthy, but sometimes you realize that people's priorities will always be weighed against you, and to try and change them is emotional suicide."

Liv swallowed heavily, and I knew she understood the concept. I hoped it didn't apply to her when she went back.

"I didn't touch a cent of the money they gave me for years. Until I realized that it would be stupid not to use it to give myself a chance at a normal life in spite of them. That's why I enrolled in college."

"And bought a boat."

I smirked. "Yeah. And bought a boat. But I used my own hard-earned cash for that."

What I didn't mention was that I'd also taken care of Liv's hospital bills. I figured my parents owed her. Not knowing what she'd say about that, especially because of where the money came from, I knew I should wait on that bombshell. Not for long, though. From now on, there would always be truth between us. But we'd had enough for one day.

She shifted in my arms, resting her celestine eyes on me. "You could have become bitter and twisted after what they did. But you haven't."

"So could you."

"I was. Don't you remember me when I first got here?"

"You weren't bitter. You were broken. You were hurting. There's a difference. Your heart was always beautiful, Liv. And my parents let you down too. You and Abby."

"They're fools," Liv said huskily. "If I'm ever lucky enough to have a son one day, I want him to be just like you."

I buried my face in the top of her head and closed my eyes.

The day was fading as we sat on the porch in the embrace of the cottage. The place where we'd both found sanctuary.

The place where we had begun to heal, even though that was by no means done. For either of us. The place where we'd found each other.

I finally understood why life had happened to me the way it had, with all its twists and turns, and all its pain. Even why I'd known Abby.

So I could be here.

So I could love Livvy.

She was my deep blue eternity.

She was young, but her heart was a thousand years old. Mine was too. And a thousand years from now, she'd still be in it.

Dearest sweet Livvy,

You are sunshine. My sunshine. I never tell you that, but you are! I know I've been the worst and grumpiest big sister lately, and you think I don't like you anymore, or I think you're boring. I don't.

There's been some crazy stuff going on that I can't tell you about. But I need to get away. Whit's going to help me. He's so wonderful, Liv. He's amazing. I know Mom and Dad don't like him because they think he's a party boy and isn't taking his future seriously. But he's different than everyone sees him, and he loves me. We're running away together! Doesn't that sound romantic and exciting? You've been wondering where I've been the last few weeks, right? Well, I'm going to the cottage on Daufuskie Island. That's where I'll probably be when you read this.

I'm planning to call you and tell you about this letter after I've been gone a few weeks, hopefully then you won't feel like you need to show Mom and Dad.

You won't be reading it right after I've left when everyone is all surprised and in shock and you'll want to help. And I know you'll want to help because you're a good girl like that, Livvy.

But this time, I need you to help me. Can you do that? Are you reading this right now and thinking you should show it to Mom and Dad? Please don't. I wish I could tell you everything, and I will, but I can't right now, okay?

Some yucky, horrid things happened, and I was a part of them. Whit says we should just go away for a while, somewhere safe, and see if we can work out a way to sort it out.

I know when we get to the cottage I won't want to come back. My hope is you can come too when you're ready. Remember how much fun we had with Gran every summer, catching fireflies, digging for crabs, being muddy and tired every night so she had to spray us down outside with the hose. Weren't those the best times? Do you even remember them? I'll let you in on a secret. The cottage is ours! Gran left it to you and me. Just us. Can you imagine? We can have it to go to whenever we want. Mom and Dad hid it from us, though. I think they wanted to sell it. I found all the papers in Mom's room. You'll be able to come whenever you want to. You're a bit young now to come by yourself, and maybe that will be the thing that makes me come back. Maybe I'll just come back to get you once I know what it's going to be like there without Gran. I'll make you grilled cheese sandwiches with extra butter whenever you like! Won't it be fun?

Anyway, there's something else that's really important. Remember the horrid, yucky things I talked about that I can't tell you? Well, they have to do with Uncle Mike. I don't know how to explain it so you would understand. Well anyway, I found something else when I found out about the cottage, and I need to keep it somewhere super-safe.

Do you remember how you dug up that Indian Head penny in the woods near Bloody Point that one summer, and both Gran and I kept trying to convince you to put it in a jar so you wouldn't lose it? You didn't listen to us, did you? But you never lost it. It's hanging on that leather string on the edge of your mirror right now, isn't it? See? You are so careful!

My sweet Livvy, I'm trusting you with this box. It's locked, and I have the key so you can't open it. Not that you would if I asked you not to, would you, Livvy?

I'll get it back from you when I come back, okay? Just keep it safe, and hide it from Mom and Dad. You must! They won't think to look in your room. It's really important that you don't open it because unless I'm there to explain, you may not understand what you're seeing, or you will and that could be way worse.

I haven't even told Whit. Please don't open it. Please. Please. Please. If I can't be there with you to explain, I just can't even imagine. It hurts my heart. Please don't, okay?

Okay?

I love you, my sweet little mermaid sister with eyes as light as air. Where did those eyes come from? Do you remember Gran's answer? They must have caught the edge of a wisp of cloud as you sailed down from heaven.

Forever, your sister,

Abby

P.S. Love is a wonderful thing. It's not painful like we read about in those fairy stories. It's beautiful and light. I hope you find your own Whit one day who will show you love and save you when you need saving.

Dearest Abby,

I know I'm writing a letter you can never read and perhaps in some way you already know what's in my heart.

In the midst of so much despair and anger, I managed to find something so beautiful, so transcendent that there's no reason to try and put it into words. It would be impossible. Look into my heart, then you'll see. Can you see it? The light that's burning so brightly in there, it threatens, some days, to swallow me whole.

It's love, Abby. That glowing part of me that reaches so high nothing seems impossible and runs so deep that it's woven into the very fabric of my being.

He's my soul and I am his.

Do you know where I am writing this from? Where I always wanted to visit, ever since I was a little girl? Of course you do. Copenhagen. To see the famous sculpture of Hans Christian Andersen's Little Mermaid carved by Edvard Eriksen. She is so small, but so beautiful. I am writing this as I wait for Tom to come back with our coffees, and then we will walk down the Langelinie promenade toward the small statue in the main harbor, where I will set this letter to sail. He's going to propose to me, Abby. And, of course, I will say yes.

We have been dealing with a lot the last few years. The fallout of what was done to you and me. We are almost through it, I think. We've gotten some kind of justice, but nothing will ever be just.

Dad never knew, but I bet you understand that now from where your eyes can see. But Mom did. About you, anyway. No wonder it was too hard for you to stay. I blamed you for leaving me with him. And after I learned what you did, how you tried to take Tom with you, I was even angrier. How could you? I thought.

But I was so tired of being angry.

And then I thought about something. I thought about all the times I've felt you close by, and I know now you were trying to make it right and give me something good, to lead Tom and me to each other. How we never would have found each other if I hadn't needed to run. I understood that too. And I knew it was time to forgive you.

I forgive you, Abby. And more than forgiving, I must thank you.

All I can promise you, in return, is that I will never be parted from him again, and that you will never have to be kept from the peace your soul so richly deserves.

I love you, Abby.

Livvy

Special thanks to the University of Southern Denmark, www.adersen.sdu.dk, for permission to liberally use Jean Hersholt's translations of Hans Christian Andersen's works.

NOTE FROM THE AUTHOR

$\mathcal{F}$orty-four percent of rape victims are under the age of 18. Sixty percent of rapes are never reported to the police, and in two thirds of cases, the assault is committed by a person known to the victim. In the case of juvenile sexual assault victims, a U.S. Bureau of Justice statistics report showed that 34.2 percent of attackers were family members. And in a Commonwealth Fund report of 1998, 12 percent (that is over one out of every ten girls in the study) of girls between grades 9 and 12 (ages roughly 15 to 18) said they had been sexually abused.

For help or more information, please visit RAINN, the Rape, Abuse & Incest National Network, https://www.rainn.org.

Acknowledgements

There are a few people to thank for allowing me to make this journey with Tom & Liv. It was hard to do something new. Something different. And without your support I wouldn't have been able to do it.

Thank you to the residents of the island of Daufuskie Island, SC. You were all so aware of your good fortune at living in such a unique place, the joy and sense of community just radiated from you. Thank you for allowing me my liberties. Any mistakes in representation of the island are my own.

Thank you to my agent, Elaine, for bringing out my best in this book, even when I didn't want to hear it. Al Chaput and Dave McDonald, my critique partners, who always exact excellence from me and will not let me get away with anything (no matter how hard I fight them on it).

Judy Roth: my editor, I hope I never *ever* have to write a book without you.

Adrian, thank you again for your cover.

I had some lovely beta readers who put up with my poking and prodding trying to pull out any tiny thing that was bothering them to see if I could fix it. I particularly enjoyed your messages while you were reading it! I couldn't believe the response. It was hard to believe you adored this story as much as I did. Thank you for your patience and for making it better Rachel, Tugce, Lisa, Julie, Stephen, my mom, RL Griffin, Karina. Karen Lawson for her proofreading and advice, and Kate Byrne, my editor at Eternal.

Thank you, Julie and Lisa, for managing my street team and being the best admins and friends a girl could ask for. Julie, thank you for being an amazing assistant and keeping me on task, as well as for your amazing talent in creating banners, teasers and all the things I could never hope to do myself.

Thank you to Kate and the amazing team at Headline UK for first of all asking me to do something different, and also for their amazing support. It has been a wonderful process.

Thank you to my husband, Stephen, and my two boys. You will never truly understand what your support, encouragement and pride in my accomplishments does for me. I hope I continue to make you proud. I know the sacrifices aren't easy sometimes, but I love that we are all in this together.

To my readers: You humble me. It's an amazing thing to connect with you and see you at signings and interact with you online, and sometimes share your hopes, dreams, struggles and successes. Sometimes you share your secrets and your pain, sometimes you are out there fighting for your very lives, whether it be illness or circumstance. Your bravery astounds me, and I thank you for letting me provide a way for you to escape into another world for a little while.

Finally, to my friends who have had to live with the secret of abuse. You are not casting yourself in the role of the victim by speaking out. You are assuming the role of warrior. The survivor. By speaking out you are potentially saving someone else. Sometimes the journey of the warrior is lonely, but it never means you are alone.

A small-town, southern girl.
A Hollywood A-list megastar.
A chance encounter and an epic, life-changing love affair.

Don't miss Natasha Boyd's

eversea

and

forever, jack

Passionate. Devastating. Explosive. Unforgettable.

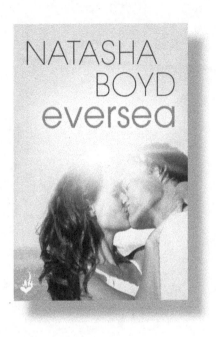

NATASHA
BOYD
eversea

'I don't want to tell you no.' My admission
hung in the air.

His green eyes turned dark as he lowered
his head . . .

'So tell me yes,' he whispered.

headline
ETERNAL

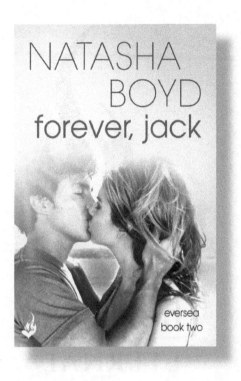

NATASHA
BOYD
forever, jack

eversea
book two

*Jack stared. I couldn't look away.
And then he moved. His arm was round my
body lifting me against his chest, crushing the
air out of me. I breathed Jack in, just as his
mouth crashed on to mine.*

headline
ETERNAL

headline
ETERNAL

FIND YOUR HEART'S DESIRE...